THE
FRAUD
SQUAD

THE
FRAUD
SQUAD

Kyla Zhao

BERKLEY

New York

BERKLEY
An imprint of Penguin Random House LLC
penguinrandomhouse.com

Copyright © 2023 by Jiayi Zhao
Readers Guide copyright © 2023 by Jiayi Zhao

Library of Congress Cataloging-in-Publication Data

Names: Zhao, Kyla, author.
Title: The fraud squad / Kyla Zhao.
Description: First edition. | New York : Berkley, 2023.
Identifiers: LCCN 2022010998 (print) | LCCN 2022010999 (ebook) |
ISBN 9780593546130 (trade paperback) | ISBN 9780593546147 (ebook)
Subjects: LCGFT: Novels.
Classification: LCC PS3626.H38 F73 2023 (print) | LCC PS3626.H38 (ebook) |
DDC 813/.6—dc23/eng/20220318
LC record available at https://lccn.loc.gov/2022010998
LC ebook record available at https://lccn.loc.gov/2022010999

First Edition: January 2023

Printed in the United States of America
1st Printing

Book design by Ashley Tucker

To my grandparents and parents, who sowed
the seed of my enduring love for stories.

THE
FRAUD
SQUAD

Samantha shrugged off her leather jacket and flung it on her desk, breathing a small sigh of pleasure at the blast of air-conditioning against her clammy skin. June in Singapore was much too hot for any kind of outerwear, but she simply *had* to wear the cropped biker's jacket both *S* and *Vogue* had labeled "the season's must-have."

Even if hers came from Taobao and not Tom Ford.

She collapsed into her office chair with enough force to send it swiveling into position in front of her workplace computer. Her reflection looked back from the darkened screen, sporting a halo of messy waves that emphasized the sharp chin of her heart-shaped face. On good days, her hair fell down her back in a curtain of sleek curls. But on hot days like this—and Singapore had plenty of those—her naturally curly hair frizzed up in a way no hairbrush could wrangle into submission.

"Sam, there you are!"

Heads turned as Anya strutted the short distance from her desk to Samantha's like it was her personal catwalk, wearing a denim minidress belted with a brightly patterned Dior scarf that violated Arrow Public Relations' corporate dress code in half a dozen ways and made Samantha wish she had kept her leather jacket on despite how it stuck to her skin. At least it would make her outfit seem a little less plain compared to her friend's.

But only Anya could get away with an outfit that, on anyone else, would have meant being hauled in for a "talk" with Human Resources. The higher-ups turned a blind eye to her misdeeds as long as they weren't *too* out of line, since it was an open secret Anya's father was tight with Arrow's leadership. Even during a recession when people were getting laid off left, right, and center, a spot at Arrow had magically opened up for Anya, even though she lacked the university degree that the job listing had asked for—and in the most prestigious financial products group, no less.

"Hey, what's up?" Samantha asked as Anya nudged the leather jacket out of the way and hitched herself onto Samantha's desk. Her feet—clad in lace-up combat boots with the distinctive Gucci stripes—dangled slightly off the ground.

"I heard Heather kept the entire food and beverage team back for a meeting yesterday," Anya said, adjusting her headband so that two front strands of hair fell out and framed her face perfectly. "What was that all about?"

Samantha laughed, her hands instinctively flying up to pat down her curls as she took in Anya's full blowout. "Don't tell me you're so starved of gossip you're actually interested in a work meeting."

"It's been a slow week, but at least it's Friday now." Anya smirked. "Anyway, dish."

Samantha leaned back in her chair and sighed. "She wanted us to brainstorm ways to attract new F and B clients. We haven't been doing too well these last few months."

"Neither has the financial products team," Anya admitted, not sounding bothered at all. "You would *think* finance is an evergreen industry, but nope. A recession hits and boom—the first thing they slashed was their public relations budget."

Samantha shrugged. "I guess they know that no one's looking for a fancy investment fund during a recession. But yeah, the meeting didn't go well, and Heather looked like she was ready to tear her hair out toward the end. *I* was ready to tear my hair out too." She gave a small shake of her head. "But enough about my work woes. How was your evening?"

Anya heaved an exaggerated sigh. "After a long day at work, I was really looking forward to a nice home-cooked meal. But when I arrived home, there was nothing on the dining table! My mom forgot she had given our maid the day off."

"Don't you have two maids? Why couldn't the other one cook?"

Anya pouted. "Only Siti is a good cook, while Meri's better with taking care of our pets and garden. In the end, my mom and I decided to pop over to Burnt Ends for dinner. They require reservations, but they let us walk right in since we're regulars."

"I was just reading about Burnt Ends in this month's issue of *S* over breakfast!" Samantha groped in her bag but came away empty-handed. "Damn, I must have left it at home." Then again, what was the point of showing Anya the article anyway when she had already seen Burnt Ends' crisp white tablecloths and monochrome paintings in person? The other woman could simply waltz into one of Singapore's top restaurants for a casual Thursday dinner.

"Although the food was delish as always, I'm trying to lose five kilos before my birthday in two months," Anya said, her pout deepening. "I should be healthy like you and stop eating so much restaurant food, but I'm going out again with a friend tonight."

Samantha's eyes darted to the lunch box in her work tote,

filled with leftovers from the dinner Ma cooked last night—her standard work lunch. Anya might think she always ate home-cooked food for health purposes, but if she had Anya's money, she would be ordering in the tuna Niçoise salad her friend got for lunch every day.

A glint appeared in Anya's eyes. "Say, Sam," she began, her tone sugary sweet, "would you like to join my friend and me for dinner?"

Samantha eyed her warily. "I don't want to crash your hangout with *your* friend."

"You won't be crashing! Timothy's going through some relationship troubles and wants to drink his sorrows away—it's always the more the merrier for that! Besides, you straight people always have the wackiest relationship problems that I can't relate to."

"Why would he tell me anything when he doesn't even know me?"

"It's *precisely* because he doesn't know you that he might be more willing to tell you stuff! Timothy's social circle is pretty . . . insular, so he and his girlfriend share a lot of mutual friends. I think he's pretty frustrated to have no one to vent to."

"He has you, no?"

Anya scrunched up her face. "He knows I'm not her biggest fan, so he's learned not to ask me for relationship advice." Her voice perked up. "But you're perfect! You're not part of his world, so he can get a more objective opinion from you."

Now it was Samantha's turn to pull a face. Whoever this Timothy was, he sounded like he had a much too complicated background. "I don't want to spend Friday night playing Dr. Phil . . ."

"But you'll be doing a heartbroken man a favor! And also, me—your work wife. If I've to listen to straight-people relationship drama for an entire night, I need support." When Samantha still looked unconvinced, Anya leaned closer. "You've heard of Enzo, right?"

Samantha snorted. "Do I live under a rock?" *Prestige* had called the newly opened bar-cum-restaurant "*the* place to be seen on a Friday night," and the accompanying photos of Enzo's official launch featured the crème de la crème of Singapore society.

"Well, Tim's treating dinner at Enzo tonight. Eileen—that's his mom, by the way—knows the owner, so we get to skip the ridiculous wait list." She nudged Samantha's leg with her foot. "Come on, how can you say no to Enzo? People would sell their kidney to eat there."

The sharp studs on Anya's Gucci boots dug into Samantha's flesh, but she barely noticed. Eileen . . . surely Timothy's mother couldn't be Eileen *Kingston*? The *Prestige* article had included a photo of Eileen Kingston beaming next to Enzo's owner, while carrying a limited-edition Chanel minaudière and wearing her trademark vintage Patek Philippe watch, her jet-black perm setting off her alabaster skin.

Gnawing on her bottom lip, Samantha mentally sifted through everything she'd ever read about Eileen Kingston. A Hong Konger who had come over to Singapore over two decades ago. Invited to every party that counted. The wife of the chairman of Kingston Management Group—she herself ran Kingston Foundation, the company's philanthropic arm. Had one son in his mid-twenties, whom Eileen referred to simply as "T" in an interview last November with *Highsnobiety*.

A chance to experience—even for just one night—how Singapore's elites lived? Samantha smoothed back her curls and smiled up at Anya. "You know what? I'd love to get dinner with you two."

SAMANTHA DARTED A quick look at her watch and cursed beneath her breath as she pushed open the door to her flat. She'd rushed home the moment her lunch hour started, but thanks to peak-hour traffic, it was now thirty-five minutes into her break. It looked like lunch would have to be an al desko affair today.

Still, this detour home for a change of clothes was a necessity. There was no way her simple linen sheath would cut it at a place like Enzo.

The door whined a protest as it swung open on its rusty hinges. Samantha took only a few steps into the flat before she stopped cold. Her mother was slumped on the couch, her eyes squeezed shut and a sharp grimace etched deep into every line of her face as she massaged her left wrist. She was still wearing her nail salon uniform—a stiff white button-down tucked into plain black pants—and her nondescript work flats. More than anything else, the last observation was what sent alarm bells blaring in Samantha's head—her mother was usually fastidious about not wearing outdoor shoes into the house.

"Ma, what's wrong? Is it the pain again?" Samantha dashed up to her mother, her words tumbling out in a panicked rush. Ever since her father had passed away from a heart attack at the age of thirty-nine, she had been on high alert about her mother's health. She was the one who had pushed her mother to finally visit the doctor last April after years of hearing the older woman grumble about the sharp pain that sometimes shot through her wrists, especially her left one. And it was then that Ma had officially been diagnosed with carpal tunnel syndrome, which the doctor suspected was due to her many years of working as a nail technician.

Her mother's eyes fluttered open as she grunted out an affirmation. "It's acting up again. My hands were shaking so badly I spilled gel polish all over a client's shoes. I got sent home early by the boss, and he said he's docking my commissions this month. *And* I've to pay for the woman's Prada heels—I bet they aren't even real."

Samantha couldn't muster up the laugh her mother was look-ing for. Ma wouldn't be trying to make light of the situation if it weren't so awful to begin with. Her hands balled into fists. "But that's so unfair! Your carpal tunnel's getting worse *because* he's making you work overtime so much."

The groove between Ma's brows deepened. "The next time he asks me to work extra hours, I'm going to tell him where to stick it. The pathetic pay's not worth all the health issues this job's given me."

"That's right, you tell him." Samantha nodded furiously, but her words rang hollow to her own ears. How many times had they had this conversation before? And how many times had Ma slunk back to the nail salon where she had been working for the past decade like a dog with its tail tucked in between its legs?

Ma would wash people's feet and buff their calluses, accept their complaints with a smile, and readily obey all of her asshole boss's demands. All because she had no other choice. The work was demanding and her pay was paltry, but it was still an income their family couldn't afford to give up, not with debt hanging over their heads like a guillotine blade.

"Have you been to the doctor yet?" Samantha asked, desperate to focus her attention on something practical they could do. "Were you able to claim any medical subsidies?"

Her mother sighed. "Aiya, the doctor will just tell me to rest, but how can I take any time off? The boss will threaten to dock my commissions again. And even with the subsidies, it will still cost quite a bit. Not worth the money." She waved her good hand around in an airy gesture that made Samantha's heart squeeze. "The best way to deal with pain is to push through it—that's life."

A lump swelled up in Samantha's throat. When she was younger, all she wanted was to grow up faster so she could start working and help Ma out. But being older just meant she understood better that life was about playing the hand you were dealt. If only there was more she could do besides collecting the financial aid forms from the community center every four months. If only she could offer more than the meager pay of her entry-level public relations job.

She had been lucky enough to even find a job during this recession, but career advancement opportunities had been scarce, and one year on, she still didn't have much to show for it. Ma had been ecstatic when Samantha graduated from university and found an office job—two things the older woman had never achieved—but that pride was now a distant memory.

Before Samantha could say anything, her mother fixed her with a piercing stare. "Why are *you* home?"

Samantha tore her eyes away from her mother's swollen left wrist, tonight's plans swiftly coming back to her. "I'm getting dinner with Anya and her friend tonight and the place is pretty atas, so I came back to change into something slightly fancier. But I'm not going anymore."

A look of incredulity crossed her mother's face. "Why not? A posh dinner sounds fun."

"Ma, what about *your* dinner? You can't cook with your hand like that. Of course I'm going to stay in and take care of you."

The corners of Ma's mouth quirked up into a faint smile. "That's very sweet, Sammy. But you don't have to do that. You're young—you should go out and have fun!" She paused, then lightly asked, "Is Anya treating?"

Samantha understood her mother's unspoken concern. "Her friend's treating. Don't worry, Ma—I know better than to eat at restaurants like that otherwise."

Her mother relaxed back into the couch, still flexing her wrists methodically. "Good, good. And who's this friend? Guy or girl?"

"It's a guy," Samantha said, rolling her eyes. "Do you want to know his shoe size and horoscope too?" Despite her snark, her heart lightened. Her mother's face was still pale, but at least she had recovered her usual Asian-mom nosiness.

Her mother clucked her tongue. "Don't be cheeky, Sam. If he's someone who can pay for three people at an atas restaurant, then he must be very rich like Anya. Nothing wrong with being on your best behavior around him."

"Ma! I don't know this guy, and I'm not interested in dating someone for their bank account. Don't try to pimp me out to him."

"This isn't pimping you out," her mother huffed. "This is creating opportunities for yourself." With a small groan, she slowly pushed herself off the couch with her right hand, wobbling a little before she steadied herself. "Come, let's see what we can find in your closet. Even if you aren't interested in him, there's no reason why you shouldn't look your prettiest tonight. You shouldn't waste the good looks I gave to you."

Samantha could only muster a small laugh as she followed her mother. When she was younger, all the neighborhood shopkeepers would jokingly ask if the two of them were sisters—a blatant attempt at flattery that used to annoy Samantha as much as it pleased her mother. But no one would ever make that kind of comment now. Everything that had transpired in the past decade made Ma look at least a dozen years older than her actual age, streaking white through her curls and carving lines into her once smooth skin.

As they walked past the dining table, the copy of *S* she had been reading over breakfast that morning caught Samantha's eye. Lucia Yen, heiress to the Yen-Heng Corporation and an aspiring event host, smiled winningly back at her from the cover in a sleek gold Olivier Theyskens gown, her teeth as white as pearls. Splashed beneath her studded leather stilettoes was the subtitle:

LUCIA YEN ON BEING A GEN-Z SOCIETY STARLET: "THE WORLD'S MY OYSTER AND I DON'T WANT TO WASTE IT"

Samantha's throat tightened and she looked away. Lucia Yen was only a year older than her but seemed like she inhabited another world altogether. What Samantha wouldn't give to step into the other woman's Balenciaga boots and leave all her worries behind for even one day.

Samantha forced that thought out of her head. Noon was still too early for any fanciful, implausible dreams.

SAMANTHA AND ANYA followed Enzo's maître d', jealous stares from those waiting in line burning into their backs. Timothy was running late, but a casual mention of his name had immediately gotten them ushered past the queue that snaked through the busiest street of Clarke Quay, the epicenter of Singapore's night scene.

Her white maxidress might not be as fancy as Anya's outfit, but the delicate embroidery made it look a lot more expensive than its price tag. For makeup, Samantha had brought out the big guns tonight—the designer samples that sometimes came with the magazines she subscribed to. She could never bear to use those for work, but a swab of Armani blush and Charlotte Tilbury eye shadow tonight would give her a much-needed dose of confidence. It wasn't every day she got to dine at a five-star restaurant like Enzo with a Singapore blue blood.

As they passed tables of happily buzzed guests mingling over pricey cocktails, Samantha tried hard to not look like she was gawking. From the pink terrazzo marble floor to the lush velvet banquettes, every inch of Enzo screamed opulence. The lounge was fully packed on a Friday night, but every table was spaced far apart enough from the others that you could be sure you wouldn't be overheard. It created an illusion of privacy, intimacy. Exclusivity.

And here she was, being taken to the best spot in the lounge: a curved booth in the back, set against a picture window offering an arresting view of the Singapore River. In the day, the river was a murky green, but right now, it looked like a strip of smooth ebony velvet; lights from the establishments lining its banks reflected in the water like twinkling stars.

"I can't believe Tim's late for a dinner he proposed," Anya grumbled as they settled into their seats. "He's the one who wanted to drink his sorrows away tonight."

Samantha carefully draped a napkin over her lap, even though any drink or dish she might spill on herself most likely cost more than her dress did. "Maybe he got held up by traffic?"

"Nah. This is just classic Tim—he'd be late to his own funeral."

"Oh," Samantha said, frowning slightly. Whenever Ma was sent by the salon to do house calls, she came back grumbling about how the clients would keep her waiting around—sometimes for almost an hour. Teenage Samantha had once innocently asked, "But don't you get overtime pay? So, isn't their tardiness a good thing since you make more money?" To which her mother had snapped, "That's exactly what those people think too. They think they don't have to feel guilty as long as they throw money at me. What they don't think about is whether I might have clients after them—I'll be forced to cancel *those* appointments and get screamed at by the pissy ones."

Samantha looked up as the maître d's voice floated over the lounge's chatter, drifting closer to their booth by the second. The stiff-backed man was practically bouncing on his toes, looking like he'd had one too many cups of coffee. In contrast, the man beside him sauntered leisurely, his loose-limbed gait making it clear he was not used to operating on anyone's schedule but his own.

For someone who was supposedly going through a heartbreak, he sure looked good.

Anya leapt up as the two men approached. "Tim, you ass! You're late again."

As Timothy reached over to embrace Anya, Samantha gave him a speedy once-over. He towered over five-foot-four Anya even in her high-heeled combat boots, which meant he was at least six foot three. Timothy's olive skin glowed with a natural tan, and beneath that was a rippling of muscles his Oxford shirt could not quite cover up. However, his scruffy hair and big eyes gave his face an unexpected boyishness. His button-down and chinos fit Enzo's dress code to a tee, but there was a hint of irreverence in his five-o'clock shadow, unbuttoned cuffs, and loosely looped Hermès belt.

Samantha quickly straightened up as Timothy slid into the seat across from hers and nodded at her. "Hi, I'm Tim." There was the slight trace of a British accent in his voice.

Samantha smoothed her hair. "Hey, I'm Samantha, but you can call me Sam."

"Sam," he repeated, a hint of a smile around his mouth. Samantha's cheeks warmed—why did those three letters sound so different coming from him? "And how do you know Anya?"

Timothy's eyes appeared dark brown initially, but now that he was directly under the light, Samantha could see they faded into a lighter amber around the rims. Whiskey brown—that was the best word for his eye color. "I—uh—" Samantha's mouth dried, a layer of heat creeping up her face. She had been so busy studying him, she couldn't remember his question.

Thankfully, Anya took over. "Sam's my work wife," she said, bumping Samantha on the shoulder. "She started almost a year before I did and is on another team, but we started talking one day 'cause she recognized my Khaite bag and told me she saw it in *L'Officiel*. She's the only other person at Arrow who keeps up with society news and knows the hippest luxe brands beyond Chanel and Dior. Everyone else is so stuffy and middle-aged."

Timothy raised an eyebrow. "Work isn't for sitting around and talking about bags."

"Says the person who is unemployed," Anya retorted.

A shadow passed over Timothy's face. "Funemployed," he corrected. "And not exactly. I'm still working on—"

A suited waiter swooped down on their table. "Compliments of the manager," he announced, setting three glasses on the table and deftly filling them from a garnet bottle. "This is one of our finest wines, a 1975 Chateau Lafite Rothschild. I hope it is to your taste. And please do not hesitate to call me over if you need anything else, Mr. Kingston."

"Brilliant. Thank Marcus for me."

"Of course," the waiter said smoothly, placing the half-empty bottle down before sliding away.

Timothy raised his glass. "Cheers, everyone! Bottoms up."

"Cheers!" Samantha and Anya echoed, before bringing their drinks to their mouths in unison.

The flavor exploded in Samantha's mouth like a burst of fireworks. She held the rich liquid on her tongue, letting the luscious blackberry undertones marinate in a heady fizz. When had she ever gotten to enjoy such an expensive drink? The food tastings she organized at work came nowhere close to this standard.

Across from her, Timothy drained his entire glass in one impressive swig, then promptly refilled it. He apparently had no need to savor what he could so easily get for free.

"Anya, seriously, though, how's work going?" Timothy asked once Anya had set her drink down. "I've been meaning to check in with you."

Anya groaned. "God, you nag at me even more than my mom does. It's only been two months so it's still too early to judge, but so far, so good. Happy now? You can report that to your dad so he can tell mine."

Samantha looked between the pair, feeling like she had missed a beat somewhere. "Your parents know each other?"

Timothy grinned. "We actually met through our parents. Anya and I have been close mates since childhood, and I'm basically like her naggy older brother. Her dad, Fo Tian, worked at my father's company for almost twenty years before he moved to China."

Samantha's eyes widened. "Anya, *your* dad is Fo Tian Chen? The *Fo-rtune Maker*?"

A broad beam spread across her friend's face. "You've heard of him?"

"Yeah! I've read an interview of him in *MillionaireAsia* before, and hasn't he been on the cover of *The Peak* a couple of times?" Looked like the office gossip about Anya being a nepotistic hire was true. Her mysterious hotshot father was one of Singapore's leading hedge fund managers. Or at least he was before he migrated to China . . . after divorcing Anya's mother.

A few years ago, the society magazines and tabloids had been dominated by Fo Tian's acrimonious split from his socialite wife,

Janice, and the latter's demand of a six-figure monthly alimony. Fo Tian eventually acquiesced, but Janice's victory was bittersweet. The media gleefully reported that many of Janice's society friends ended up taking her ex-husband's side due to her mercenary tactics. Her premarriage career as a yacht girl only cemented her gold-digger reputation.

"Yup, my dad is good friends with Tim's dad," Anya confirmed. "In fact, Mr. Kingston was the one who got me my job in Arrow's financial products division even though I know nuts about anything finance related."

"My father probably thought he was doing you a favor. Just because he thinks finance is the greatest thing, he assumes everyone else wants to do it too. Because who doesn't want to be Albert Kingston, right?" Timothy deadpanned but drained his glass of wine too quickly to match his nonchalant tone.

"Hey, I'm not complaining!" Anya immediately said. "I'm grateful your dad helped me get a job that I'm totally not qualified for." She turned to Samantha. "After I flunked out of university, my dad told me I had to get my shit together, so he reached out to Albert and voilà! I've been having the time of my life at Arrow ever since, being the responsible working adult my dad wants me to be."

Any other time, Anya's sarcastic drawl would have made Samantha laugh. But now, her jaw dropped as she turned to Timothy. "*Your* parents own Arrow Public Relations?"

He shifted in his seat. "They don't own Arrow. The Kingston Management Group just has a stake in Arrow's parent company, that's all."

"A *majority* stake," Anya cut in. "So potato, potahto—for all intents and purposes, they own Arrow."

Samantha's heart quickened. She leaned forward and asked, "Which means they also own *S*, right?"

Timothy blinked. "How did you know that?"

"Aren't Arrow and *S* both under Merlion Media?"

"But most people wouldn't know that," Timothy said, narrowing his eyes. "They would have heard of *S*, and there's a small chance they might have heard of Arrow. But no one really pays attention to the parent company, much less knows its name."

Samantha's cheeks reddened beneath Timothy's intent gaze. "I mean, I work at Arrow . . ."

"So do I, and I didn't even know this," Anya piped up. "Most people don't even think of *S* and Arrow in the same bracket. *S* is all glitz and glamour, while Arrow is more community club than country club. Our clients are mostly small brands and businesses."

Confronted by both Anya's and Timothy's questioning looks, Samantha had no choice but to come clean. "To be honest, I never wanted to go into PR," she mumbled. Great. Her first time meeting Timothy Kingston and she was rehashing the details of her failed job search. "I've always dreamed of writing for a magazine like *S*—I studied communications at uni and even interned at *Tatler* my last year. But competition for full-time roles was so fierce that I just kept getting rejections, so in the end, I decided to accept an offer from Arrow. PR was a good way to use my comms degree, and I figured it could help me pivot to *S* someday since they're both under Merlion Media."

Anya's eyes widened. "Whoa, Sam, you've never mentioned this before. Why do you want to write for *S* anyway?"

Samantha's breath lodged in her throat. The bright jabber of surrounding diners melted away, and suddenly, in a bustling restaurant full of Singapore's most affluent people, she was fifteen again. Watching as scarlet bank statements and past-due notices piled up on the dining table; Ba's shoulders stooping as though the mounting stack were a physical weight on his body; Ma screaming at him to do something, *anything*, to fix their problems.

One day, desperate to escape her feuding parents and the loan sharks who always came knocking, she fled to the neighborhood bookstore and—with nothing better to do—picked up a random copy of *S*. Immediately, Samantha found herself drawn into the pages of jet-setters and highfliers, of elaborate parties and designer brands. From that day on, her troubles at home became a little easier to bear; she could escape into *S* and lose herself in a picture-perfect world where the word "debt" didn't exist.

"Sam?"

Anya's voice drew Samantha back to Enzo. Her fingers clenched around the stem of her wineglass. "I've always thought of *S* as kind of a gateway," she finally said. "The photos, the articles—all those reminded me so many possibilities exist beyond my life."

"Right? *S* is basically my shopping list!" Anya squealed. "So are you hoping to be Argus 2.0?"

Samantha straightened up, a flicker of excitement sparking within her. Any Singaporean worth their salt would have heard of Argus, the anonymous socialite behind *S*'s infamous society column, As Seen by Argus. Launched eight months ago, her monthly articles had immediately gripped Singaporeans with their witty observations of the vanities and foibles of her fellow elites.

"Having my own column in *S* would be a dream come true," Samantha admitted. "But it's so hard to get an editorial position these days if you don't have connections or the right background. Argus got her column *because* she's a socialite and *S* knew people would be interested in what she has to say about high society. But I don't have that, or anything else that would convince *S* I'm the right person out of hundreds of applicants to write about leading a luxe lifestyle."

Timothy winced. "Damn, I didn't realize magazine publishing was so competitive. Still, I think it's cool you're interested in a creative pursuit like writing." His voice turned wistful. "I wish I had the chance to try something like that, but my parents would probably disown me."

He laughed quietly and downed his second glass. Anya widened her eyes at Samantha as if to say, *What should we do?*

Samantha stared right back. *He's* your *friend; you say something.*

Their silent exchange went unnoticed by Timothy, who was more focused on refilling his glass.

Finally, having lost the eye battle, Anya ventured, "Tim, is everything okay?"

Timothy's lips twisted into a wry smile as he looked up from his drink—his third in less than twenty minutes and almost empty again. "If by 'okay,' you mean my parents have threatened for the dozenth time to cut me off if I don't rejoin the Kingston Management Group and I fought with my girlfriend again because she sided with them, then yes, everything is just groovy."

His slightly bloodshot eyes met Samantha's. "Sorry, I know you weren't expecting dinner at Enzo to come with a side of bitter man." He glanced down at the table, blinking as though seeing it for the first time. "Huh, we haven't even ordered yet. What do you two feel like getting?"

Timothy's words were starting to slur, his British accent coming out stronger. This time, Samantha acquiesced to Anya's wide-eyed plea for help. She pushed the complimentary bread basket and dish of fig tapenade in front of him. "Eat this. You need something to soak up all the alcohol in you." Somehow, she doubted any of them were in the mood to discuss what tapas to get, and the last thing Timothy needed was a chance to see the drinks menu.

"I'm not drunk," Timothy muttered, but obediently stuffed a chunk of sourdough into his mouth. The next moment, he let out a groan that sounded so indecent it made Samantha's stomach swoop. "Damn, this is some good bread. I haven't eaten anything all day."

Anya rolled her eyes. "That explains it. I knew your tolerance wasn't this bad."

"I'm not buzzed," Timothy retorted through a mouthful of bread. "I'm *pissed*. Not buzzed pissed, but pissed-at-my-parents pissed. You'd understand if you knew what happened last night." He gulped down his sourdough and exclaimed, "Ah, you know what, fuck it! I'm just gonna tell you guys. My parents try so hard to pretend we're the perfect family in public when that's nowhere close to reality. They're always warning me not to air our dirty laundry because they care more about what others think of us than what their son thinks."

Samantha winced as heads turned in their direction, including that of the frowning maître d', but his expression immediately smoothed once he identified the source of the vehement declaration. Enzo wasn't a place that would stand for raised voices, but nobody wanted to be the one to tell off the heir to the Kingston fortune.

Still, Timothy probably should quiet down for his own sake. For all they knew, Argus could be in this lounge at this exact moment, silently noting down what the Kingston scion said for her next column.

And yet, Samantha couldn't deny a part of her longed to hear what Timothy had to say. Albert and Eileen Kingston always looked so glamorous together in the society pages of magazines, but what sorts of family secrets did they keep behind closed doors?

"I should have known something was up when my parents asked to get dinner," Timothy continued, his words coming out faster now. "I can't remember the last time we all sat down for a meal together, but I stupidly thought things would be okay since they asked my girlfriend to come along. Joke's on me, because even before aperitifs were brought out, my father had already launched into his spiel about how I need to quit playing around and go back to the family business. I've heard his little speech so many times I could basically recite it back to him."

Anya frowned. "How can they say you're playing around? You've already done your time at KMG and they *agreed* to let you take a one-year sabbatical! Why are they mad about it now?"

"Done your time?" Samantha cut in. "Why do you make working at Asia's biggest hedge fund sound like a prison sentence? Almost everyone I know would kill to work there." And couldn't because their dad wasn't the KMG chairman.

For the first time all conversation, Timothy looked slightly embarrassed. "That's what I tried convincing myself of too," he said quietly. "I joined KMG right after graduating from Durham University, and I knew I was lucky—most fresh grads with a classics degree don't get hired at hedge funds, much less during a recession."

Samantha blinked. Classics? That hardly sounded like something Asian parents would approve of, especially parents as demanding as Timothy's.

"But helping the rich get richer just isn't something I feel for. While growing up, I was always more interested in listening to my mother talk about the artworks she was collecting than to my father go on about KMG's latest investment."

"So . . . you want to be an artist?" Samantha asked, hoping the doubt she felt wasn't leaking into her voice. She tried to imagine Timothy as a starving artist, but the label seemed antithetical to the man sitting across the table from her, clad in a pristine white shirt that probably cost more than her monthly salary.

"Not exactly. I love art, but I also love music and film and writing." Timothy paused, pursing his lips as he tried to come up with the right words. Finally, he said, "I think I just really want to do something creative—ideating and owning something that's completely mine. I grew up with everyone telling me I would be the chairman of KMG someday, and I know that's a job many would kill for, but hearing that over and over again just makes me feel like a cog in the machine—the latest in a long line of Kingston men expected to keep the family business running. But I want to do something that would get people to recognize me as Timothy, not as a Kingston."

Timothy breathed out a laugh so soft it might as well have been a sigh. "Sorry, I know this is really dumb," he said quietly, the way a person would when they were trying to tell a joke but could tell no one was listening.

As Samantha took in his hunched shoulders and downcast eyes, her heart clenched. She could imagine a younger Timothy saying the same thing with full earnestness to his parents, only to have them laugh it off, never taking it seriously, and steadily making him feel more and more ashamed of his dream.

"This isn't dumb at all," Samantha said. "It makes a lot of sense."

She waited until he met her eyes before giving him a small, encouraging smile. That seemed to unlock something in Timothy, for he drained what remained in his glass and exhaled deeply. "I swear, it feels like our lives revolve around KMG. My mother even gave up her career in Hong Kong after marriage to take care of KMG's philanthropic activities." His tone softened. "She'll never say a word against my father, but sometimes . . . I get the feeling this isn't really what she wants to be doing with her life."

Samantha tried to mask her surprise. KMG's corporate charity events were so exclusive that even people willing to fork out thousands of dollars for a ticket were regularly turned away. In the magazine coverage of those parties, Eileen always sported a Colgate-commercial-worthy smile, looking like there was nothing in the world she loved doing more than throwing fundraising dinners. But here was her son revealing what those magazines were never privy to; Argus would have a field day if she was a fly on the wall at this dinner.

"Well, at least your parents let you take time off when they found out you weren't happy," Samantha offered, even as a tinge of bitterness welled up in her. At least he (and Anya) had parents who were able to secure them jobs.

At this, both Timothy and Anya scoffed. "Look, Tim's dad is great in many ways," Anya said, "but the only happiness he knows is measured in commas."

"Commas?"

"The number of commas in a dollar amount. Then again, only someone like that can run one of the world's most successful hedge funds," Anya added, as though realizing she shouldn't be criticizing the man who had gotten her her job.

"Yeah, whenever I mentioned wanting to work in the creative field, my father would shut me down immediately and give me a long-ass lecture about how that's too soft and unbecoming of someone from my background—whatever that's supposed to mean. He would say, *All my friends' sons do finance. Generations of Kingston men have done finance. What will people think if my only son turns his back on the family business?*" Timothy imitated in a British-accented voice that was much gruffer than his own.

Samantha bit her lip, overtaken by a peculiar feeling that took her a few moments to place. *Pity*. Something she didn't expect she would ever feel for the heir to a multibillion-dollar fortune. Wasn't having money supposed to lead to more freedom and options in life, not fewer?

"How did you even get him to agree to your sabbatical?" she asked.

"I spoke to my mother and she intervened," Timothy admitted. "She made the case for me that I wouldn't be able to do my job well when my heart wasn't even in it. Finally, my father relented. He allowed me to take a sabbatical on the condition that whatever I do in this one year must make a splash. If it isn't successful, I must return to KMG and never say a word against it again. And I was so grateful; I really thought my father was finally coming around, and I was determined to not waste this opportunity to accomplish something on my own."

From the way Timothy's expression hardened, Samantha sensed a "but" was coming. And sure enough: "But then they summoned me to dinner last night, and that was when I found out they had all been waiting for me to fail this entire time."

"Damn. Your parents actually said that?"

Timothy barked out a harsh laugh. "Pretty much. My father told me that the only reason he agreed to the sabbatical was because he wanted me to realize for myself that I wouldn't get anywhere without my Kingston background. He expected me to learn the hard way that I couldn't support myself doing *airy-fairy creative bullshit* and would go crawling back to KMG within four months tops. So, when I didn't, he got mad. Called me to dinner and demanded to know when I planned to stop playing around and get back to doing real work."

"But here you are coming onto nine months!" Anya chirped, sounding determined to overshadow Timothy's moodiness with her own exuberant cheer. "They totally underestimated you."

Samantha made a toasting motion toward Timothy with her glass. "Props to you—that's basically a pregnancy."

That drew a small chuckle from Timothy. "Yeah, with a baby that will be rejected by its grandparents once they find out about it." His smile faded. "When my mother told me about dinner, I thought they were actually interested in learning how I was doing. Honestly, it's kind of embarrassing in hindsight how excited I was to tell them what I've been working on, but not anymore; they wouldn't consider it real work anyway."

Samantha bit back the urge to ask Timothy about his work—clearly a touchy subject with this man she had just met. Besides, he was already going on. "At this point, they are just waiting for the one year we agreed on to end. Unless I really do something big in the next three months that will make them sit up, I'm going to end up working for my father again in no time."

His expression taut, he reached for a bacon breadstick, sinking his teeth into it as though the dough had personally wronged him. At a loss for what to say, Samantha did the same, opting for a chunk of sourdough bread. She saw Anya's eyes follow the movement of her hand toward the bread basket, but the other woman looked resolutely away from the carb pile and at Timothy instead. "You said your girlfriend was there? How did she react?"

A muscle worked in Timothy's jaw. "Elle immediately took my parents' side despite knowing I'm not remotely interested in KMG. She *always* takes their side—I bet they invited her to dinner as additional ammo." A bitter note crept into his voice. "I just wish Elle could be as supportive of me as I am of her. Whenever she came complaining to me because her parents gave her shit for her career ambitions and said stuff like *Ladies should be seen and not heard*, I always sided with her. So why can't she do the same for me?"

Elle? Samantha racked her brain, but no socialite with that name came to mind. Was it maybe short for Ellen or Eleanor?

"I already knew she wasn't happy with me when she found out I was giving up my hedge fund salary for at least a year, possibly even longer," Timothy continued, his earlier anger fading into resignation. "It was goodbye Maldives and hello Malaysia for our monthiversaries."

Samantha took another bite of her sourdough bread so she wouldn't blurt out anything she regretted. What sort of couple just casually flew to a different country for a monthiversary? She would be lucky if she could go to Malaysia for her honeymoon.

"I can't provide the lifestyle she's used to anymore, and I need some time and space to figure my stuff out, so I told Elle this morning we should take a break." Timothy let out a long, weary exhale. "At least we kept our relationship low profile the last few years while I was studying overseas, so no one will be badgering me about this."

Anya slapped the table. "Good for you, Tim! You know I don't like to say anything against her"—Timothy's snort said otherwise—"but I don't see how you can be with someone who has such different values from you."

Timothy hummed noncommittally, but Samantha noticed the way he shifted in his seat. He might be going through a rough patch with Elle now, but it still couldn't be easy for him to hear his girlfriend being criticized by his good friend. Samantha came to his rescue: "Your girlfriend will come around. Maybe some time apart will help her see things from your perspective."

Timothy's eyes darted to the bottle, his brows knitting together once he realized there were only a few drops left. He sighed and leaned back in his seat, his forehead creased in thought. "I need my parents to come around to my perspective too," he mused, picking up another breadstick and playing with it absently. "While I do my own stuff, I also have to use the time left of my sabbatical to soften them up, make them more receptive to the idea that there's more than one path in life for me, that—"

"The background you're born into doesn't define who you can be," Samantha said quietly. Her breath hitched as Timothy's eyes locked with hers.

Timothy's face brightened, and he pointed his breadstick at her. "Precisely! You took the words out of my mouth."

Samantha pressed her lips together to hide a smile. It was nice to feel like she could contribute to the conversation in some way, despite her outsider status in this trio. Who would have ever thought she would have something in common with a Kingston?

"That's because I can totally relate to that. I probably know as much about high society as Argus does and I'm confident I write well, but without the right background . . ." She shrugged. "The government always says that we're a meritocracy, but at the end of the day, some people are just luckier than others by virtue of birth."

Timothy stuffed the breadstick in his mouth and raised his hands with a self-mocking smirk. "Guilty as charged."

Samantha's face reddened. "Oh, I wasn't trying to imply anything."

Timothy's smirk softened into a smile. "I know, but you aren't wrong. If I weren't a Kingston, my father would have never hired me when I'm probably the least qualified person to work at a hedge fund. And it's also really unfair that only people of a certain status can write for a magazine like *S*."

Samantha laughed. "If only there was a way I could become a socialite. Too bad it's not going to happen in this lifetime—" She broke off, a thought striking her like a thunderbolt.

Samantha's heart started hammering. The idea was audacious; Timothy and Anya might laugh her out of Enzo . . . but what did she have to lose? At the rate things were going, she was headed down the same path as Ma: stuck in a job she wasn't passionate about to make ends meet; going through the hamster wheel of life but never truly *living*; forever trapped in the drabber side of society and dreaming about what could have been if only Lady Luck were kinder.

Maybe it was time she created her own luck.

Samantha cleared her throat. "Tim, I think there might be a way we can help each other out," she said in a voice steadier than she felt.

Timothy arched an eyebrow. "Oh? Pray tell."

"Well . . . what if you turn me into a socialite?"

3

Silence stretched across their table, made all the more conspicuous by the swell of conversation drifting in from the other corners of Enzo. Over Timothy's shoulders, Samantha caught sight of the waiter from earlier striding over, another wine bottle in one hand and three leather-bound menus in the other. His steps faltered as he registered the stillness hanging over their booth. To his credit—or to the credit of Enzo's undoubtedly exemplary staff training—he looked bemused for only a moment before doing a smooth U-turn.

Anya's jaw dropped. Timothy blinked forcefully a few times, as though hoping that would snap him out of his alcohol haze and convince him he hadn't just drunk hallucinated Samantha's question.

Samantha wanted nothing more than to join the retreating waiter as he slinked away. What had she been thinking, making such a ridiculous proposal? She couldn't even blame her neural short circuit on alcohol since Timothy had polished off most of the bottle.

But before she could pretend she was simply joking, Timothy spoke up. "What do you mean?" he asked, suddenly sounding completely sober. His eyes—the brightest and most alert they'd been all evening—were fixed on Samantha's face, and she had to force herself to hold his gaze.

"You want a way to convince your parents that what you do shouldn't be determined by the background you were born into, right?"

The moment he nodded, Samantha rushed on, afraid she would lose her nerve if she didn't get her words out immediately. "Listen, I'm the furthest thing from a socialite—I live in a small flat in Serangoon with my single mom, I shop at Cotton On and only when there's a good sale, and I have an unglamorous PR job that looks like it's headed nowhere in this recession. In short, I'm the exact opposite of someone like your girlfriend or your mom."

If she'd thought admitting her job-search failure earlier was embarrassing, it was nothing compared to how Samantha felt now. But she steeled herself and pressed on. "However, if I can somehow transform into an 'It girl,' it would prove that the background we're born into doesn't have to determine where we end up in life."

There was a sharp intake of breath from Anya, but Samantha continued like she hadn't heard. "If I can succeed in high society despite not having the right last name or background, then your parents and girlfriend will have to admit those shouldn't be limiting factors in life. It will help your case that you should be free to do what you want instead of being pigeonholed by your identity as the Kingston heir. And, uh, there's that," she finished weakly while Timothy and Anya stared at her agog.

Trying to look nonchalant, she reached across the table for the bread basket, her long, curly hair falling across her face and hiding her burning cheeks from view. She must have sounded like a used-car salesperson. It was only when she bit into a slice of rye that Samantha realized how parched her mouth was. Damn Timothy for polishing off the wine, and damn the waiter for not appearing again when she needed him most.

Just as she was praying fervently that a fire would break out in Enzo and save her from this mortifying situation, Timothy let out a low whistle. "That's quite a proposal."

Samantha's head shot up, a flicker of cautious optimism lighting within her. Timothy sounded vaguely amused, but at least he wasn't laughing in her face. She attempted a casual shrug despite her pounding heart. "Well, you were the one who said you wanted a way to nudge your parents around to your perspective. And it's not like you have much time left—didn't you say your sabbatical's almost up? Last night's dinner didn't seem like a good sign."

She held her breath as Timothy's jaw clenched, wondering if she had taken it too far. But he merely nodded. "You're right about that." His gaze drifted into the distance before abruptly snapping back to Samantha's face, a new glint in his eyes. "You know what? This plan might be just what I need. You'd be a case study . . . evidence of the point I'm trying to make."

His words unhinged Anya's mouth. "Sam, are you crazy? High society isn't some Mickey Mouse clubhouse anyone can join if they feel like it. Those socialites will chew you up and spit you back out." Her voice quietened as she added, "I would know."

Timothy grimaced. "Anya has a point. High society can be incredibly vicious."

Samantha rolled back her shoulders. "I know what I'm getting myself into," she said, pressing her voice low to make it firmer. "I must have read hundreds of society magazines over the years and interacted with dozens of socialites during my *Tatler* internship. Anya, you just said I'm up-to-date on society news and high fashion, and it's true—I can gabble about Isabel Marant and discuss if Aspen or Saint Moritz offers better skiing conditions with the best of them. Not even Argus will be able to find fault with me."

A small grin flickered across Timothy's face. "For the record, it's Saint Moritz, hands down." He leaned forward and steepled his hands. "Okay, even if you're up for the task, what will *you* get out of it?"

The million-dollar question. Samantha took a deep breath. "I'm hoping that if you bring me along to your society events and introduce me to the people in your circle, I can get my name out there and have one foot in at magazines like *S*. Lots of well-known magazine writers got their jobs because they are socialites, like Argus, *Vogue*'s Lauren Santo Domingo, *Hong Kong Tatler*'s Olivia Buckingham, or Tatiana Santo Domingo for *Vanity Fair*. People are obsessed with what they think and do and want to hear everything straight from them."

Timothy raised an eyebrow. "Damn, you really know your socialites."

Samantha smiled, feeling settled for the first time in the conversation. "Like I said, I know what I'm talking about."

He drummed his fingers against the table. "Even if we do this, it can be only for three months until my sabbatical ends. By then, I will know for sure if I have to go back to KMG."

Samantha's mind immediately flashed to what she had read in *S* that morning. "The S Gala is in three months!" she exclaimed, unable to control her excitement. "That can be our last event together."

At this, Anya burst into laughter. "Trying to break into high society is already a tall order, but the S Gala? Every socialite I know would kill for an invitation, but the closest most of us will get to the gala is reading about it on *S*'s website the next day. This is the grandest event organized by Singapore's snobbiest magazine—"

"Which is precisely why it'd be the perfect closure to our plan," Samantha countered. "I won't be able to keep up this socialite facade on my own after our three months end. But like you said, an invitation to the S Gala will be the surest sign I'm somebody who matters—who's good enough to write about high society for *S*."

Catching how fast her words were spilling out, Samantha forced herself to slow down. "At first, I'll have to work for my name, but if I make it to the gala, my name can start working for me. I won't need to rely on Tim's help or connections anymore, and that would help him prove *his* point." She looked straight at Timothy. "Feel free to present me to your parents as evidence, case study—whatever."

Anya shook her head. "Tim can invite you to all those other events, but the S Gala is so freaking exclusive that only family members are allowed as plus-ones. If not for that rule and his girlfriend, I would have made Tim bring me as his plus-one long ago. I've dreamed about attending the gala for ages, but even though my mom has donated plenty of money to *S* over the years, I've never seen a whiff of an invitation."

"Oh." Samantha deflated in her seat. "I guess we can figure out something else."

"Actually, there might be a way," Timothy cut in, rubbing one hand over his stubbled chin.

Samantha perked up. "What is it?"

"Think of it as a two-pronged approach," he said, raising one finger. "You should definitely build up your socialite reputation bit by bit. Attend events and be photographed. Network with people and charm them. Put yourself on the gala committee's radar."

Anya scoffed. "Everyone knows the only person who matters is Missy. She's the one with final say over the guest list."

Samantha nodded furiously. Missy, the woman so cool she didn't even need a last name. Everyone, *everyone*, in Singapore knew *S*'s editor in chief, who had come up with the stroke of genius that was the As Seen by Argus column and turned *S* from just another luxury magazine into one that even old uncles at kopi-tiams would discuss. Everyone said the magazine industry was slowly dying, but *S*'s improved circulation numbers over the past few months stood in sharp defiance.

"Exactly. Which brings me to the second prong of this plan." Timothy held up another finger. "Missy comes over quite a bit because she's good friends with my mother, and I sometimes overhear what they discuss. A couple of weeks ago, Missy was saying that she felt like her magazine keeps featuring the same people over and over again. And that for *S* to remain on top, it has to be the one to uncover the next It girl instead of just profiling her like all the other magazines do. And of course, my mother asked, *But if she doesn't have the right family and upbringing, how can you be sure she's S material?*" He rolled his eyes. "Typical. But my point is: Missy is on the lookout for new blood, and that can be you if you play your cards right."

Samantha sat up straighter, her eyes trained on Timothy's face. "And how do I do that?"

"You'll run into Missy at some point over the next couple of months, so just impress her and you might score an invitation."

Timothy said it so casually that Samantha was tempted to let herself get swept up by his confidence, but she hesitated. A man like Timothy Kingston never had to bother impressing anyone, so how could he understand the unique challenge of doing so, especially with someone as discerning as Missy?

For a moment, Samantha considered asking Timothy to just put in a good word for her with Missy, but swiftly dispelled that notion. She and Timothy had only known each other for an hour, and Missy wasn't the kind of woman who could be persuaded so easily; Samantha would have to win over *S*'s editor by her own merit.

"How do I make sure I appear on Missy's radar?" Samantha asked instead.

Timothy thought for a moment. "My mother is invited to lots of parties and brand events, but only attends those organized by her good friends. I can pass you her invites if she's not going."

Samantha's eyes widened. Unfettered access to A-list events—this time as a guest and not because she was dispatched to cover it for *Tatler*? "That would be great," she said as calmly as she could, knowing it might be the biggest understatement she had ever uttered.

"But I can't accompany you to them," Timothy added apologetically. "I'm avoiding those public events in case I run into my girlfriend there since we're on a break now."

"Can't you just come to the first few with me?" Samantha prayed her nerves weren't leaking into her voice. "I'll be okay on my own after a while, but I don't know anyone now." Attending a society party Missy might be at—awesome. Attending a society party where she didn't know anyone yet and having Missy see what a loner she was—less awesome.

"I'll organize smaller gatherings so you can meet some of my friends," Timothy began, but Anya interjected.

"Why don't I go with Sam? Don't these invites usually come with plus-ones?"

Timothy smacked his head. "Right, duh. I should have thought of that."

Samantha relaxed back into her seat. Anya might not be as well-connected as Timothy, but she had also grown up among Singapore's most affluent families and would have a natural understanding of high society to share.

If anything, Anya looked even more delighted than Samantha was. "Great!" she exclaimed, rubbing her hands together. "I almost never get to go to such events. Sam, I'll show you the ropes and give you all the clothes, accessories, and makeup you need to pull this ruse off."

A chance to play dress-up in Anya's designer closet? Samantha beamed. "That would be incredible."

"And I'll pay for whatever else we need—the meals, the drinks, anything," Timothy chimed in.

"Good, we need fuel for strategizing," Anya said. "And it'll be ironic using your parents' money to fund our plan to pull one over on them."

Timothy scoffed. "Give me some credit. KMG does pay very well, so I have quite a bit saved up from my one year there. And now that Elle and I are on a break, there are no dates or gifts I have to pay for."

His mouth quirked up. "You know, Elle's always prided herself on being invited to the S Gala every year. I can't wait to see her reaction when she finds out an ordinary woman will be a guest just like her." He sat up straight suddenly. "We should spring the grand reveal of your real identity on her and my parents at the gala. That will really drive home the point I'm trying to make to them."

His words brought Samantha sharply back down to earth. "But what if they tell others about my real background before I've won over Missy? I'll be ostracized by high society, and no magazine will want me to write for them anymore."

"The first thing you should know about high society is how pretentious and image obsessed everyone is," Timothy said calmly. "There's no way my parents will let anyone know they've been fooled by their own son. They do such a great job of keeping up our perfect-family facade that even their close friends like Missy have no idea we've been fighting about my career. And my girlfriend will sooner die than have people find out we aren't a perfect couple. Your secret—*our* secret—is absolutely safe." A smirk danced on his lips. "It's the Fraud Squad against the Snob Mob."

Anya did a little air clap. "Snob Mob's the right term—I'm sick of how uppity those socialites are toward my mom and me. It will feel so good to get the better of them for once."

Samantha held her empty glass aloft. "In that case, I propose a toast: to the Fraud Squad!"

Timothy arched an eyebrow. "You know, it's bad luck to toast with an empty glass."

"It wouldn't be empty if someone hadn't finished all the wine," she shot back, then promptly wanted to kick herself. For Christ's sake, this was the Kingston heir she was being snarky to.

To her relief, Timothy grinned. "Guilty as charged," he said, raising his own glass as Anya did the same.

Three empty glasses met in the air. "To the Fraud Squad!"

4

Samantha brushed her fringe off her face, but it was stuck to her skin with sweat. She could almost hear her curls frizzing up from the humidity. Despite the soaring temperatures, the kopitiam was so packed that strangers had to squeeze shoulder to shoulder at the same table. Thankfully, she and Raina had gotten there early enough to score a table for two at the back of the cramped coffee shop, right beneath the lone ceiling fan, which turned so slowly and wheezed so loudly that it was probably more useful as a white noise machine.

Having heard plenty of tales of friends growing apart after entering the workforce, the two women started a weekly Sunday brunch tradition upon their university graduation. The kopitiam just a stone's throw from their old secondary school was an obvious choice. It had been around for so long that its white-haired owner, Madam Pang, was basically a neighborhood institution. A chalkboard behind the counter broadcast a short menu that never once changed in all the years Samantha and Raina had been going there.

Samantha took a generous bite of her kaya toast, her teeth crunching through the crisp white bread. Her eyes fluttered shut as she swirled the sweet coconut jam around her mouth, some of it oozing down her lips.

"You're making your big-O face again. How long has it been since your last man?" Raina joked, looking irritatingly unbothered by the heat in her trademark denim jacket, bedazzled with feminist pins she had collected over the years. At least once a month, she would have a new acquisition to show off. Sometimes, Samantha had trouble reconciling this Raina—the one she had known for almost half her life—with Raina Chandra, one of Singapore's best up-and-coming young female lawyers who owned the same Calvin Klein skirt suit in four different colors.

"I swear, there's something about this kaya. I've asked Madam Pang for her recipe so many times, but she's not budging." Samantha jammed another piece of bread into her mouth. "Anyway, what were you saying about your job? Something about an art collection?"

Raina sighed and laid down her pork floss toast. "It's a divorce case I've been working on since forever. And it's going to drag on for at least a few more months since the couple can't agree on how much their art collection is worth and how to split it. My client's art appraiser valued it at eight hundred ninety million dollars, but the guy her husband hired said it's seven hundred eighty-five million at most."

Samantha sputtered, sending crumbs flying everywhere. "Their art collection is worth almost *a billion*?"

Raina shot her a half-amused, half-exasperated look. "Sam, you're missing the point here. Because they can't agree on the value, *I* have to work overtime until this case is settled." She shook her head. "Sometimes, I don't even know why I'm doing this."

"At least your job's never dull," Samantha said soothingly. "Besides, you've always wanted to be a divorce lawyer. You can't just quit!"

"Because I thought I would be helping low-income women or

spousal abuse victims achieve emancipation! Instead, I'm working with some rich woman whose biggest priority in life is selling her rare Rothko painting so that her husband can't get it."

Samantha couldn't help but grin at Raina's *woe is me* voice. Whenever Raina considered switching careers—a monthly occurrence—it fell on Samantha to remind her best friend that her no-nonsense attitude and unwavering moral compass made her perfect for the legal field. That had been obvious even back in secondary school, when Raina leapt to Samantha's defense against a bully's teasing about her shoddy backpack. The string of profanities Rai reeled off had gotten her sent to the discipline master's office, but it also sparked the two girls' friendship—one that had lasted ever since.

"I'm sorry, Rai. But with legal fees for contested divorces usually running over six figures, it's no wonder most of your clients are of the Rothko variety."

Sighing, Raina bit into her toast. "I guess so. Any news in your life?"

Samantha perked up. "Actually, yes! It all started when Anya introduced me to—"

Raina wrinkled her nose. "The girl from your office?"

"Yup. I think you met her at Arrow's Lunar New Year party a few months ago."

"Oh. Right," Raina said, her face blank. A little *too* blank.

Samantha narrowed her eyes. "What's up?"

"Nothing," Raina quickly said. "Anyway, who did Anya introduce you to?"

"For a lawyer, you have a lousy poker face. Rai, come on." Samantha prodded her shoe against Raina's. "No secrets between best friends."

"It's just . . . Anya's kind of braggy, isn't she?"

Samantha's brows shot up. "Braggy? What do you mean?"

"When I met her, she couldn't stop name-dropping designer brands or the famous people she's hung out with. I just didn't say anything because it was clear you liked listening to her stories."

"Anya isn't trying to show off," Samantha protested. If it was true that she enjoyed Anya's name-dropping, what did that make *her*? "Her family's very wealthy and that's just the life she's used to. Those designer brands are to her what Taobao deals are to us, you know?"

"If they're so normal to her, then why would she even think to boast about them? She's either really braggy or really insecure—" Raina broke off and shook her head. "Sorry, I didn't mean to go off on her like that. I might not like her, but she's still your good friend." She pasted a smile on her face. "Anyway, who did she introduce you to?"

Sunday brunch was too precious to be spent discussing any unpleasant topics, so Samantha gladly went along with the subject change. "Her friend, Timothy, who's even more well-connected—"

"Ooh!" Raina leaned forward. "Is he cute?"

"He's pretty attractive," Samantha offered, her heartbeat picking up as an image of Timothy's piercing eyes and sharp cheekbones popped into her head. "But don't get any ideas because he has a girlfriend," she added firmly when Raina's eyes gleamed, though she wasn't sure if Raina was the only person she meant that disclaimer for.

"The lady doth protest too much," Raina sang, her smile broadening as Samantha scowled. "Fine, fine. I'll shut up. What's this about how well-connected he is?"

"It's kind of a long story . . ." Samantha's voice trailed off as, for the first time, it dawned upon her just how outrageous the Fraud Squad scheme was.

Raina picked up her cup of kopi o with an exaggerated flourish. "Time for a CCC."

Grinning, Samantha took a sip of her own kopi. Candid Coffee Confessional was something they had invented in secondary school, requiring only two things: coffee (or any drink, really) and a willingness to unload anything on their minds. "Basically, Tim and Anya are going to help me break into high society so that I can impress Missy, the editor of *S*—you know, the magazine I've always wanted to write for. No big deal or anything."

Her joke fell flat as Raina narrowed her eyes. "What do you mean by 'break' into high society? Why does it sound like you're gonna commit a crime?"

Samantha set her cup back down. "Funny you should say that, because the three of us are calling ourselves the Fraud Squad."

"*Fraud*?" Raina screeched, her voice thankfully drowned out by the kopitiam's morning babble and the creaking fan overhead.

"It's nothing illegal! Maybe a little shady, but"—Samantha pinched her fingers together—"just a little. They're going to help pass me off as a socialite, because who better to write about high society than someone from that world, right?"

Raina pursed her lips. "Tell me you're kidding."

Samantha took a deep breath. "I know you're going to say this won't work, but I've thought it through. You know how hard it is to get a magazine writing job. You've seen the dozens of applications I sent out and the dozens of rejections I got. Having a perfect GPA and being editor in chief of two school magazines got me nowhere. And after six months of working my ass off at *Tatler*, they couldn't give me a return offer because of budget cuts. Since relying on merit got me nowhere, don't you see how I *have* to change tacks and score my dream job in a more . . . unconventional manner?"

"By pretending to be someone you're not," Raina said shortly.

A flicker of annoyance shot through Samantha. "Don't put it like that."

"But that's what you're doing! What happens if—what's the name of that woman? The magazine editor you just mentioned?"

"Missy," Samantha supplied. Not for the first time, she wondered how two such different people ever became best friends. She couldn't even remember a time when she didn't know of *S*'s editor in chief.

"What happens if Missy finds out you aren't actually qualified to write about high society and luxury lifestyles and all that jazz?"

"But I am qualified! I know so much about designers and where socialites go on vacation and which hotels offer the best high tea sets."

"So does probably everyone else applying to write for *S*," Raina countered. "You're hoping Missy will hire you based on your new socialite persona and make you the next—who's that columnist you like reading?"

"Argus. She writes As Seen by Argus."

Raina perked up. "Ooh, Argus as in the Greek giant Argus Panoptes? Argus is supposed to be all-seeing and all-knowing because he has a hundred eyes. Fun fact: The concept of panopticon came from his last name—I read that in a legal journal about surveillance theories."

It wasn't until Samantha burst into laughter that she realized how tense the mood at their table had been. Still, it was nice to enjoy a chuckle with her best friend about how different they were: While Raina's fun facts came from obscure legal literature, the tidbits Samantha liked to share usually hailed from her favorite magazines, especially the As Seen by Argus column ("Did you know some socialite turned fashion designer with the initials E. A. supposedly steals designs from small businesses?").

Samantha tapped a finger against her chin. "All-seeing and all-knowing? Jeez, I wonder which magazine columnist that reminds me of. Anyway, what's wrong with wanting to be like Argus?"

"There's nothing *wrong* with that, but unlike Argus, you aren't actually a socialite."

Samantha knew it was just Raina being her usual rational self, but the words still stung. She tipped her chin up. "It's about faking it till I make it, and that's what I'll be doing for the next three months with Tim and Anya's help. By the time the S Gala rolls around, I'll be more than ready. And if I'm invited, it means I've been recognized by *S* as one of Singapore's top socialites, so I won't even have to pretend anymore."

Raina pinched the bridge of her nose. "And what if Missy finds out before the gala you aren't actually some great heiress? Your lies could easily blow up in your face."

"I'm not gonna tell any lies! At least not outright ones," Samantha amended as Raina shot her a look. "If there's one thing I've learned from PR, it's that a story's not about representation, but *re*-presentation. I don't have to lie about being some great heiress—I just have to make people think I'm one."

As Raina's frown deepened, Samantha reached across the table to grip her friend's hand. "Rai, I love you and really appreciate you always looking out for me, but I know what I'm getting myself into."

She couldn't help but smile as Raina bit her lip. Between the two of them, Rai had always been the mother hen. The one who yelled at those who laughed at Samantha's yellowing and frayed uniforms. Who threatened to beat up those who spread rumors about Samantha's homelife. Who actually pummeled a boy when he sneered that the only reason Samantha had beaten him out for the Distinguished Student Award was that the school board felt sorry for the girl on school meal subsidies and with the dead dad.

Finally, Raina sighed. "Okay, you do you. How's this *fraud* going to work exactly?"

Samantha pretended not to notice the clipped note in Raina's voice. At least her best friend seemed to have accepted the idea, even if she wasn't completely on board with it.

"We're gonna start things off slow," Samantha said brightly, as though the perkier she made her voice, the easier it would be to dispel Rai's suspicions about the Fraud Squad. "Tim and I are getting dinner with a couple of his friends tomorrow night, so I can meet more people from Singapore's rich crowd in a more low-stakes scenario. Then we're going to turn up the heat a little with a public event. And then, three weeks from now is our first big test: a dinner party hosted by Tim's parents at their house."

"A dinner party at home sounds like a step-down after a public event, no?"

"Nope. Because according to Tim, his parents are inviting some of Singapore's biggest names, including Missy."

Raina pursed her lips. "I'm gonna say one final thing and then I'll shut up. Just be careful, yeah? If your little Fraud Squad gets exposed, Timothy and Anya have their family wealth as a safety net, but you're on your own."

Samantha held up her hand like she was swearing in court. "I'll be very careful. No one's gonna find out."

Raina snorted and picked up her kopi o again. "Famous last words."

5

As the elevator crawled up to Cé La Vi, the rooftop restaurant on the fifty-seventh story of Marina Bay Sands hotel, Samantha examined her reflection in its mirrored walls. Thanks to the three massive boxes of clothes and accessories Anya had couriered over to her flat yesterday, she was at least dressed perfectly for the part she was about to play.

However, even the sight of how well her off-shoulder Sandro dress flattered her body did nothing to quell Samantha's agitated heart rate. This was Day One of the Fraud Squad's scheme, and it *had* to get off to a good start.

Next to her, Timothy popped up the collar of his black dress shirt. "Do I look like a frilled lizard?"

A surprised laugh bubbled out of Samantha's mouth as she turned to him. "A *what*?"

"You know, a lizard with—"

"I know what it is." Samantha rolled her eyes but smiled. "It was just such a random question."

Timothy smoothed down his collar and adjusted it. "Good, a smile at last. You looked so tense."

So Timothy had been watching her . . . watch herself. Great, now he knew she was nervous, and probably thought she was a narcissist to boot. "Besides you and Anya, I've never interacted with high-society folks in a personal setting before," Samantha admitted. "What if I say something wrong that makes it obvious I'm not a real socialite?"

Timothy reached out to cup Samantha's shoulders, waiting until she met his gaze before saying, "What happened to the confident woman I met at Enzo? You look the part, you know the right lingo from all the magazines you read, and Anya made sure you erased any incriminating information from your online profiles, right?"

The smile in his voice wrapped around Samantha like a comforting hug. She nodded, her eyes tracing the amber rims in Timothy's.

"Then you're all set!" Timothy grinned. "And don't worry about my mates—they don't bite."

Samantha forced herself to smile back at him. If only she shared his confidence. Based on the little Timothy had shared about the Liem brothers, she wasn't sure she had anything in common with them. Clement, the older sibling, held some lofty title at Goldman Sachs, while Keith flew around the world "doing research for his documentaries."

Timothy drew back as the elevator rolled to a stop and its doors slid open. Samantha hugged her arms to her body, her bare shoulders instantly feeling colder without Timothy's touch.

Or maybe it was from the breeze whipping around Cé La Vi's open-air pavilion. Samantha let out a small gasp as she emerged from the elevator. She'd once written about Cé La Vi as part of a *Tatler* dining guide, but looking up photos on Google was nothing compared to being here in person. Bathed in a red glow, the restaurant looked more like a nightclub. The perimeter was encircled by a five-foot glass partition—the only thing protecting diners from a sharp plunge down into the ocean. The spectacular city skyline blended seamlessly into the horizon. This high up, even the other skyscrapers in the vicinity looked like mere Lego pieces.

The sun was just beginning to set, streaking the darkening sky with bold ribbons of red and orange like one of Ma's abstract manicure designs. "*Stunning*," Samantha breathed, not making a move to brush back the curls whipping into her eyes. "There's something about this view that's so . . . indulgent."

"Indulgent?" There was a teasing note in Timothy's voice. "But watching a sunset is free."

"Yeah, but you have to be truly at peace in the moment and not worrying about other crap in order to appreciate the beauty. And an open space like this with no skyscrapers blocking the view is perfect for that." A pang rocked her heart as she recalled that one evening years ago when her parents had brought her to Jumbo Seafood restaurant at East Coast Park. They had arrived at the beachside restaurant just as the sun was setting, and Ba's business was still doing well enough then that they didn't have to think twice before ordering two Alaskan crabs that each cost more than a hundred dollars. Ba had cracked the claws and served them to Samantha and Ma first before having any himself. Even today, Samantha could still picture the scene perfectly in her mind: Ba's face red from both Heineken beer and physical exertion, the sweetness of the crab meat on her tongue, and how Ma's face—much younger and smoother then—had glowed in the golden rays of the sunset.

Samantha forced that memory out of her mind as Timothy said, "That's how Cé La Vi gets all their great reviews—it's hard to find fault with the food when you're eating with such an amazing view." His eyes caught on something over her shoulder. "Oh, there they are!"

Samantha stifled a giggle as they approached the Liem brothers. So this was what Timothy meant when he said, "Clem looks just like a banker—you'll see." Clement wore a starched white shirt and the same deep stress lines around his eyes shared by many of Anya's clients in Arrow's financial products division. His well-coiffed hair didn't budge in the wind, and his mustache was so tidy it looked like he'd trimmed it with a ruler against his cheeks.

Keith, with his oversized tortoiseshell glasses and jaunty beret, seemed slightly more approachable, so Samantha turned to him first. But he was looking straight at Timothy, a smirk playing about his lips. "You rascal, hasn't it only been a few days?" he asked, slanting his eyes pointedly toward Samantha.

It took Samantha a few moments to register his words. When she finally did, she felt like she'd been doused in cold water. She quickly stepped away from Tim. How was she supposed to win their respect if they just thought she was trying to make a move on him?

But Timothy didn't miss a beat. "Shut up, you prat," he said good-naturedly. "This is Samantha, a friend of Anya's, who's now also a friend of mine."

Despite her embarrassment, Samantha felt her insides warm at his words. They might not even have stayed in touch after Enzo had they not come up with the Fraud Squad scheme, but now, they were on the same team.

"Sam, this git is Keith, and that's Clement."

Hitching on her brightest smile, Samantha stepped forward to press her cheeks against Keith's.

But she never got there. He had taken a quick step back, his hands held up in front of him. "Whoa, lady. We don't do that here."

Samantha's smile froze, her body shrinking away from Keith and instinctively nestling closer to Timothy. His body heat felt like a comforting anchor amid the swirl of embarrassment that threatened to swallow her alive. Wasn't an air-kiss supposed to be the society set's salutation of choice? How could she have gotten it so wrong? This was the same mortification she felt back at her *Tatler* internship when she'd once grabbed the wrong dress for a stylist who had instructed her to "pack the off-white dress for the shoot," not realizing he was referring to the brand, not the color. The photo shoot had been held up for an hour while she dashed back to the office to get the right dress, and the icing on top was that the pricey two-way cab trip came out of her own pockets.

Timothy whacked Keith on the shoulder. "Ignore this prat," he told Samantha. "Keith could never be arsed about manners."

"Only people like our moms would do something so pretentious like an air-kiss."

Timothy scoffed. "You used to go into fits of ecstasy whenever Kate Low gave you an air-kiss, and she's older than both our mothers."

Keith clapped a hand to his chest, looking mightily offended. "That's a low blow! Kate Low might be fiftysomething now, but she's still smoking. She's basically the Asian JLo."

"Maybe we should all sit?" Clement cut in sniffily.

Clement might look like the place fun went to die, but in that moment, Samantha could have kissed him (maybe not—given her humiliating air-kiss faux pas). She slid into the seat closest to the glass partition, the cool breeze against her heated cheeks and the sight of the soaring sunset easing the weight in her chest.

All around the sinking sun, the sky stretched off into the horizon like a seemingly endless expanse. The way her future could be, if she tried hard enough. Dinner might not have gotten off to the best start, but the night was still young.

After they placed their orders and their menus were whipped away, Keith leaned forward and dropped a car key ceremoniously in the center of the table. "Tim, check this out."

Timothy's eyes widened. "Mate, no way! How did you get this?"

Samantha furrowed her brows. The car key was emblazoned with the distinctive Ferrari logo, but what was so impressive about that? Surely Timothy and his friends could afford all the luxury supercars their hearts desired.

As though sensing her confusion, Timothy turned to her. "This is the key to a LaFerrari Aperta. There are only two hundred of them in the world."

Cars—the one thing in magazines her eyes had always glazed over. Still, Samantha mustered her most enthusiastic voice. "Wow! Keith, good for you—"

"It's not good," Clement bit out. "The last thing my brother needs is another outrageous car, especially after he wrecked his Bugatti not long ago. Our parents were not at all pleased to learn about this new purchase."

Keith smirked. "He can't say anything about it because I technically didn't buy it. Tim, you remember Evan, right? The son of that Macau casino owner who kept bragging about how he joined the Ferrari Owners Club before we did? We were clubbing at Altimate the other night and he made a bet with me about who could take more vodka shots in a row—"

Timothy grinned. "I see where this is going."

"That poor sucker had the worst Asian flush I ever saw. He had to cough up the keys to his darling car after only seven shots."

"Bloody hell, mate."

"Can you believe that guy thought he could outdrink me?" Keith shook his head. "Rookie mistake."

Samantha's cheeks were starting to hurt from smiling so brightly. All she could do now was sip her aperitif, nod along, and try to look like she knew what they were talking about. If she didn't find a way to speak up soon, Clement and Keith would surely think of her as an airhead with heels higher than her IQ.

Clement groaned. "Can you two stop talking about cars for one second and focus on something more important?"

Keith rolled his eyes. "Sorry we're too childish for you, bro. What important world news would you like us to talk about?"

Clement ignored the sarcasm in his brother's voice. "We could discuss the new tax policy being debated in Parliament these days," he said as he straightened his already very straight tie.

Samantha cleared her throat, resisting the urge to look down as all three men turned to her. Clement raised an eyebrow, which she pretended not to see. She might not know anything about the LaFerrari, but she knew plenty about the tax policy he was referring to, having read up on it extensively to figure out how the proposed tax hikes might affect her mother's salon commissions.

"Well, I think this policy is awful," she began, hoping no one else could pick up on the shakiness in her voice. Beneath the table, her hands bunched around the hem of her dress. "It claims to reduce income inequality, but the only people it would benefit are the top one percent of—"

"Excuse me," Clement cut in, ice dripping from every syllable. "The minister who proposed this is my uncle. And since he's the minister of finance, I reckon he knows a thing or two about what he's saying."

A deafening silence roared across the table, and the temperature seemed to drop by ten degrees in seconds. From the corner of her eye, Samantha saw Timothy lower his head, as though to distance himself from the social carnage. She longed to do the same, if only to avoid looking at the triumphant glint in Clement's eyes. She was suddenly aware of how high above the ground her bar stool was and how her feet dangled in the air, making her feel like a child sitting in a high chair who was desperate to join in the "adults'" conversation.

"As vice president at Goldman Sachs, I've also been thoroughly analyzing the effects of this policy," Clement continued. "The principles behind it are rooted in Keynesian economics, which I wrote my undergraduate thesis on at Harvard and also my master of finance dissertation on at Cambridge. And based on what I know"—he gave a little cough, as though to emphasize just how much he knew—"I can tell you this policy is extremely well-thought-out. Why would the government push it through if it's not? All the pushback comes from Singaporeans who have nothing better to do than complain. They've been so spoiled by our government that they don't know how well we have it compared to other countries. If they don't like it, they should just move somewhere else."

Have nothing better to do than complain? Spoiled? Don't know how well they have it? Samantha clenched her jaw. Clement might be a hotshot banker with an abundance of posh degrees and the minister of finance as his uncle, but how could someone living in an ivory tower really understand how a policy affects people on the ground?

"We have a good government, but that doesn't mean they always get things right," Samantha said, making every effort to keep her voice pleasant but firm as she looked Clement in the eye. "Your uncle has always done a great job of championing the interests of the masses, which is why I'm surprised by this policy—"

"This policy is designed to help the masses by reinvigorating the economy after the downturn in the last six months," Clement interrupted, "following Keynesian theory that tax hikes are a less recessionary move to stimulate growth than spending cuts."

Timothy finally looked up and pulled a face. "Mate, come on. There's no need to get pissy about—"

Clement raised his voice even higher. "Samantha, surely you're not saying John Keynes didn't understand how the economy works?"

She volleyed back, "Of course not. But this fiscal policy would disproportionately stunt small businesses that don't have the reserves to tide them through the tax hikes. I believe an expenditure-based austerity response is more appropriate in this case to kick-start private consumption again."

Another silence fell upon their group. Blinking, Clement opened his mouth, then closed it again. Samantha's fingers dug into her palms. Why had she spoken up? What had she achieved except to piss off Timothy's friend, another member of the billionaire heir club?

Then Timothy snickered. "She got you, mate! Don't look so surprised you aren't the only one who knows Keynes."

For a second, it looked like Clement was gearing up for a fiery retort, but he seemed to think better of it in the end. With a tight-lipped smile, he said primly, "Samantha, you sure seem to know your economic concepts. Did you study finance too? Which school did you go to?"

Samantha sent a telepathic message of thanks to the *Business Times* journalist whose last Thursday's op-ed she had just lifted extensively from. To Clement, she simply said, "I just like to educate myself on the latest finance policies."

Keith's face broke into a grin. "It's nice you're doing that and not relying on your family accountant. Not to sound sexist, but I think the only thing my female friends know about taxes is tax-free shopping in Europe."

THE REST OF the meal passed much quicker once the food was brought out. Even Clement stopped his finance-bro shtick for longer than five minutes to dig into the platters of Fine de Claire oysters and Hokkaido scallop ceviche. Before Samantha knew it, she and Timothy were at the parking lot, bidding farewell to the Liem brothers as they slid into their cars—Keith into his splashy orange LaFerrari ("It used to be black, but I got Ferrari to repaint it in a custom color after I won it. Gotta put my own stamp on it, you know?"), and Clement into a much more understated Tesla.

Once both cars pulled away, Timothy glanced down at his phone. "My driver's arriving soon, but I'll wait with you until your ride comes."

"Oh, I'm just going to take the bus home."

"The bus?" Timothy repeated as though he had never heard of one before.

"There's a bus stop not too far from here, so I'll take 97, then switch over to 174."

Frowning, Timothy raked a hand through his hair. "That sounds like an awfully long trip. I can give you a ride back."

Samantha's mouth twitched. Timothy's hair was endearingly windswept after hours sitting in the rooftop restaurant—very unlike Clement's curated look or Keith's deliberately hipster aesthetic. "It's okay. I took the bus here."

Timothy held up his hands. "I'm not trying to imply you can't take care of yourself; I know you can—just look at how you put Clem in his place earlier. But it's not safe for a woman to be out alone so late at night, and I'm sure your feet are hurting in those crazy high heels. My girlfriend complains about wearing heels all the time."

It was only then that Samantha became aware of a dull ache in the balls of her feet. She had been in Anya's Christian Louboutins for so long her toes were almost numb. The lengthy journey home suddenly seemed a lot more daunting than it had moments ago, so she relented with a smile. "Thank you. That's very nice of you."

Timothy grinned back. "It's the least I could do. So . . . how do you think dinner went?"

Samantha shrugged. "The food was good. Amazing, actually."

"Come on, you know I wasn't asking about the food. What did you think of Clem and Keith?"

"They seem like . . . interesting people. I guess I shouldn't have been surprised they're so well-connected, seeing as they're friends of yours, but how was I supposed to know the freaking minister of finance is their uncle? And when Keith casually said he was glad I don't depend on my family accountant, I was so tempted to tell him I didn't have one just to see his reaction. Does everyone you know have a family accountant?"

Timothy's smile dropped. "I'm sorry about letting Clement have a go at you for so long. I should have stepped in earlier, but I didn't want you to feel like I thought you couldn't handle it yourself." He scuffed his shoe against the ground. "Our families also have business dealings together, so I can't really, you know . . ."

"Doesn't it get tiring always having to watch what you say? I can't imagine being so on guard with Rai, my best friend."

"It's not ideal, but that's just how it is. Many of the families in our circle are connected in some way or another." Timothy hesitated. "To be honest, I'm always a bit uneasy around Clem. Not because of anything he did, but because my father always compared me to him. Clem's the finance-guru son he wished I could be. And whenever I point out Keith gets to jet around making documentaries, he retorts that my situation is different because I'm an only son."

His matter-of-fact tone made Samantha's heart clench. How many snide comparisons must he have heard from his father to be able to recount this so calmly? "I for one am glad you aren't like him," she said firmly. "Clement couldn't stop humblebragging all throughout dinner. At some point, I started taking a sip every time he mentioned his Cambridge degree, his Harvard degree, or his—"

"Goldman Sachs title," Timothy finished with a laugh. "I was wondering why you started drinking so much." His voice softened. "Hey, thank you."

"For what? You're the one who just treated me to dinner at one of Singapore's most famous restaurants."

"For making this dinner way more fun than I expected it to be."

Samantha's stomach fluttered. Turned out she wasn't the only one who had reservations about tonight. "Thanks for having my back at my first socialite outing." She raised her hand for a high five. "We made it out alive!"

Instead of slapping her hand, Timothy gripped it and pulled her in for a hug. "It was all you," he said into her hair. "You were a natural."

Samantha wondered if he could feel how loud her heart was pounding against his chest, then wondered why it felt like her heartbeat was playing at triple speed. Timothy drew back, meeting her wide-eyed look with a conspiratorial grin. "But brace yourself—everything's only going to ramp up from here."

6

Three days later, Samantha's phone buzzed with a message from Timothy—an invite for a VIP preview of Christian Dada's latest collection. Wanna go to this?

Sam: You had me at VIP. ☺ Should we meet up directly there?

Tim: My girlfriend might be there and it'll be weird appearing with you in front of her, so I'm gonna sit this out.

Samantha's stomach curdled. The meal with Clement and Keith had been intimidating enough, but at least it had been a private get-together. Timothy did say at Enzo he would give the social events a miss, but how was she supposed to get through her public debut without him by her side?

She looked down as her phone buzzed again.

Tim: But don't worry, Anya will be going as your plus-one. And if the door gift is good, snag one for me please.

SAMANTHA HAD PASSED by the Christian Dada flagship store on Orchard Road many times, but she had never dared to go in. Through the floor-to-ceiling windows, she could always see that there were more staff than customers—the group of people who didn't mind shelling out hundreds of dollars for a T-shirt was clearly a small one.

But tonight, she finally got to be on the other side of the door, and it was the busiest she had ever seen the store. Staffers carrying important-looking clipboards rushed around the display cases and benches made of matte-black perforated sheet metal. Statuesque models with razor-sharp jawlines posed in the center of the room, decked out in designs from the collection and seeming thoroughly unbothered by the harsh white fluorescents overhead.

And milling around with champagne flutes in hand and examining the gleaming silver clothes rails were the VIPs.

Samantha raised her head a little higher and smoothed the sides of her wrap dress, the material crackling beneath her fingers. The outfit was khaki green and nylon—a combination she never thought would go together but was the main aesthetic for Christian Dada's latest line. At least it helped her fit right in; all the invited guests were wearing Christian Dada creations, some even odder than hers.

A salesman with slicked-back hair sidled up to her and proffered a tray. "Some champagne for you, miss? Or maybe you would like to try some of the hors d'oeuvres while I tell you all about our latest collection? There's a minidress that I think will look so good with your long legs."

Although Samantha knew it was the salesman's job to flatter customers, her heart leapt nonetheless. While she had entered plenty of luxury stores before, it was always to pick up items that *Tatler* was borrowing for a photo shoot. Once the salespeople found out she was only a magazine intern, their smiles had dropped and they would watch stonily by the side as Samantha struggled to lug out half a dozen bags full of clothes on her own. She had certainly never received *this* kind of reception before.

"Ooh, I think I'll try this stuffed mushroom—"

"No, you won't," Anya said, coming up to them and gripping Samantha's elbow. She had wandered off earlier toward a rack of jackets that had caught her eye. "No food grease on your mouth until we have our photos taken. We should have done that the moment we arrived when our makeup was at its freshest. Were we really here if we aren't in any of the photos?"

Samantha cast a longing look at the appetizers, but she followed Anya as her friend marched purposefully toward the official photo area. A black carpet was rolled out across one end of the room, backdropped by a blown-up canvas of the Christian Dada logo. As the two women neared, Samantha's steps faltered at the sight of the photographers flanking the carpet, but Anya's hand on her arm was a persistent force propelling her forward.

"Stand really close to me so our bodies are squished together and we look skinnier," Anya hissed as she steered Samantha toward one end of the black carpet while simultaneously tightening the belt in her satin cargo pants. "Jut your chin out. Don't smile— you want to look bored and over it. There's a trick my mom likes: If you pucker your lips and mouth the word 'prune' when you're being photographed, your mouth will appear perfectly pouted."

"Jesus, you're an absolute pro," Samantha whispered back, her mind racing to commit those tips to memory.

Anya gave her a small wink. "Aren't you glad I'm here to guide you along? Now let's put those tips into practice!"

As Anya strode onto the black carpet, Samantha concentrated on planting one foot in front of the other, praying she wouldn't trip in her towering platforms. She could feel her legs trembling like a newborn fawn's as she made her way in front of the panoply of cameras that glowered from all sides like a firing squad. Sweat wormed down the back of her neck despite the air-conditioning, plastering the collar of her nylon dress to her skin. By now, the jitters in her legs had spread to the rest of her body.

Someone off to the side must have given a signal, because without warning, camera lights began to blaze.

Chin out. Brightest smile on—wait, no smiles. Lips pouted. Shoulders back. Samantha's eyes gradually adjusted to the bright flashes. She could now make out the photographers manning the equipment, each person completely indistinguishable from the one next to them. Their mouths opened and closed in quick succession. *Look here! No, here! Turn left. Look straight! Can we have a side profile?*

Samantha's body felt like a conglomeration of different parts Frankensteined together, each moving independently of the others to mimic Anya's poses. Beads of sweat rolled down her face as the cameras flashed relentlessly. She wanted to wipe them away but couldn't remember if she had put on waterproof bronzer, and the fear of smudging her makeup kept her hands down by her sides. If anyone published a photo of her with bronze streaks down her face, Argus might pounce upon that in her next column. That would spell the end of Samantha's socialite journey before it had even truly begun.

"Done. Next!"

"That's it?" Samantha croaked as she let Anya pull her off the black carpet. Already, another group of ladies was click-clacking their way into the cameras' path.

Anya grinned at her. "Why, you haven't had enough? But I get it—being the center of attention is so addictive."

"It's not that. The ending just felt so . . . unceremonious."

"That's 'cause neither of us are well-known yet, so the photographers don't really care about us. Speaking of which, there's still one more thing to do."

Before Samantha could answer, Anya was walking up to a

woman standing by the side of the black carpet. She wore a head-set curved around her face and carried an iPad in her hand.

"Hi, I'm Anya Chen, and this is Samantha Song. We just got our photos taken."

The woman nodded and jotted down something on her iPad. "Got it, thanks."

As they walked away from the woman, Samantha whispered to Anya, "What was that all about?"

"Making sure she got our names so she can give them to the press people, in case any media wants to use our photos and caption them." Anya cocked her head to one side. "Wouldn't you know this from working at *Tatler*?"

"It was always my editor who liaised with the photographer and selected the graphics," Samantha mumbled, her stomach sinking. To think she assumed reading magazines and having a six-month editorial internship would teach her everything she needed to know about high society. In hindsight, her display of bravado at Enzo seemed downright laughable.

Anya wrapped an arm around Samantha's shoulders. "Thank God you have me around to guide you then! You can't call yourself a real socialite if you've never appeared in a leading magazine's *Society Scenes* segment! Those features put the 'social' in 'socialite.' Now, come on, let's go check out the clothes."

Samantha wriggled out from under Anya's arm. "You go ahead. I'm going to walk around a bit, maybe get some food." It would be no fun following Anya and watching her swipe her credit card as briskly as people swiped on Tinder, when Samantha herself couldn't afford anything here even with the discount given to all guests.

Anya shrugged. "Suit yourself. See ya!" she called over her shoulder as she made a beeline for the racks.

Samantha glanced up at the faceless mannequin standing

next to her. "It's just you and me, buddy." With a small sigh, she turned away from the mannequin and found herself face-to-face with a bespectacled man.

At first glance, the man looked to be in his thirties, but the deliberately sloppy man bun beneath his Burberry tartan fedora gave him a more youthful vibe. His eyes bulged out slightly behind his fashionably thick Prada glasses. A male socialite was Samantha's first guess, until her eyes caught on his press tag. Someone else might have been surprised a journalist would be wearing eyewear and headwear that cost a combined four figures, but she wasn't.

When you spent forty hours a week writing about designer products and the people who could easily afford them, it was hard not to get sucked into the mindset that you deserved them too. She ought to know, going by the number of hours she spent scouring designer consignment sites. Meanwhile, her boss at *Tatler* would skip lunch every day to save up for the high-fashion sample sales that magazine staff regularly got invited to.

Samantha relaxed slightly when it appeared the man hadn't overheard her talking to an inanimate object. She smiled and held out her hand. "Hi, I'm Samantha."

"Nice to meet you," he replied, shaking her hand with an unexpectedly strong grip for his reedy frame. "I'm Winston, a fashion writer at *Elle*."

Samantha perked up. "Winston Baey? I've read your articles before! Your 'Belle of the Ball' feature last month about the basketball Paralympian was genius. I especially liked the photo of her doing a slam dunk in that massive Giambattista Valli tulle gown—it created this wonderful juxtaposition."

Beaming, Winston adjusted his Prada glasses. "Thank you! For so long, we've only put celebs and society ladies in our magazine, but we really want to branch out and feature regular folks with interesting stories and backgrounds. Amid this recession, I think our readers would really welcome more tales of resilience and grit."

"I think that's a great idea. It's awesome *Elle*'s always coming up with such fresh takes."

Winston's smile broadened. "Say, would you like to give me a quote on what you think about Christian Dada?"

Samantha blinked. "Me?"

"Mm-hmm. I want to get a roundup of what Singapore's top socialites think about this new collection."

Samantha's mouth dried. "Right now?"

"No time like the present!" Winston clicked a pen against his notepad. "Whenever you're ready."

Samantha wet her lips. "Right. Well, uh, I think this collection perfectly captures the spirit of the Dada art movement." She cleared her throat to remove the last trace of shakiness, her voice growing stronger as she continued, "The designs are delightfully irreverent, which really highlights—"

"There you are!" Anya exclaimed, popping up beside Samantha so unexpectedly that she startled. "This collection really isn't—" Her eyes dropped to Winston's press lanyard. The next moment, she was standing up straighter and smoothing the pleats of her cargo pants.

"Hello! Nice to meet you—"

"This is Winston," Samantha chimed in. "He's a writer from *Elle*."

"Pleased to meet you, Winston! I'm Anya Chen. You might have seen my dad, Fo Tian, around before."

Recognition flashed in Winston's eyes, but his expression and voice were both mild as he replied, "I can't say I have, but it's nice to meet you too."

Anya gave him a dazzling smile. "I suppose you're looking to get some thoughts on this new collection? Well, I've plenty to say about it. Ask Sam—she'll tell you I'm Christian Dada's biggest fan."

Winston pushed his glasses up his nose. "Uh, I was actually in the middle of interviewing Samantha. She was saying something about Dadaism, which is fantastic because not many people actually know that's where the name Dada came from. But I'd love to hear from you as well," he quickly added as Anya's smile tightened. "Just as soon as I'm done with Samantha."

"Sure," Anya said easily, her expression relaxing. She threw her arm around Samantha's shoulders. "I'm sure we will give you some fantastic sound bites for your article."

Samantha nodded, her heart lifting. At least Anya was by her side again, and they could get through this together.

And who do we have here? ☺

Timothy's text in the Fraud Squad group chat the next day came with a link that directed Samantha to *Elle Singapore*'s website. When she opened it, a high-quality image of Anya and her posing side by side, eyes smoldering and arms around each other's waists, filled her phone screen.

ANYA CHEN AND SAMANTHA SONG, the caption declared, heralding her official entry into the world of Singapore socialites.

Holding her breath, Samantha clicked to enlarge the image. A smile unfurled across her face as she ran her eyes over every detail with laser-sharp focus. She looked okay. More than okay, actually. She had felt so stupid during the photo taking, but by some miracle, her picture had come out amazing. She still wasn't a fan of Christian Dada's aesthetic, but she could now appreciate how perfectly the wrap dress nipped in at her waist and draped her hips. Even the khaki-green color miraculously ended up looking just right on camera.

Sam: Oh my God. This is wild.

Tim: They even quoted you in it.

Samantha quickly opened the link again. This time, she clicked out of the gallery and scrolled down to the article. She didn't have to look for long. There it was, making up the entire second paragraph:

> The line will be officially released to the public on 20 June, but the clothes have already won praise from Singapore's most fashionable women. Socialite Samantha Song calls the designs "delightfully irreverent." Her favorite piece from this new collection is a deconstructed ivory pullover. "The seemingly random rips and slashes are actually a clever tribute to the provocative Dada art movement that inspired Masanori [Morikawa, the brand's founder and designer]," she said.

Samantha scanned through the article's remaining three paragraphs—two about Winston's rather tame thoughts on the collection, and the final one telling the readers where to purchase it once it was released to the public. She scrolled back up the second paragraph again, this time letting her eyes linger longer on each and every word.

Socialite Samantha Song. The alliteration sounded delightfully snappish, as if her name had been created to specifically complement the socialite prefix. These were only the words of one man, but surely it meant something when said man was a writer at one of Singapore's top luxury publications.

Hands shaking slightly, Samantha texted back:

Sam: Reading my own words feels kind of bizarre, but also pretty damn cool.

Tim: It's very cool, Miss Socialite. Hey, let's go out for celebratory drinks. My friend just opened a new bar in Haji Lane called the Apothecary.

Samantha hesitated. She was definitely in a celebratory mood, but it was Sunday night. The only thing worse than the Monday blues were the Monday blues with a hangover thrown in.

As though he could sense her reluctance through the screen, Timothy sent a new message.

Tim: Stop thinking and Nike.

Nike? Oh. *Just do it.* Samantha laughed under her breath. Only someone like the Kingston heir could "just do" things.

Then she paused, the three words blossoming into something bigger in her mind. Why *couldn't* she do it? Why couldn't she, just for one night, pretend she was someone like Timothy, someone who could get away with living life on the edge and never having to look over her shoulder? She wanted to be like the person Winston imagined she was—a woman who could be out having fun whenever she wanted without worrying about how a hangover might affect banalities like a nine-to-six job.

Her lips curving up, Samantha's fingers flew across her phone.

Sam: Okay, see you two there in 30.

HOWEVER, WHEN SAMANTHA arrived at the Apothecary half an hour later, she found only Timothy at the entrance along with a few stragglers. Everyone's heads were bent over their phones, except his.

He was leaning against a pillar, hands shoved in his jean pockets and eyes trained on the night sky. Samantha followed his gaze, but there didn't appear to be anything interesting. Thanks to Singapore's horrible light pollution, the sky was a boringly smooth expanse of black. But Timothy looked so peaceful standing there, lost in thought, that she couldn't bear to disturb him.

However, as though he could sense her gaze, Timothy glanced over, his eyes immediately finding hers. His somber expression melted into a smile that lit up his face. "Sam! You made it."

Praying he hadn't caught her staring, Samantha hurried up to him. "Hey, where's Anya?"

"You didn't see her text?"

"No, she must have sent it after I left my house." She hesitated. "I, uh, don't have mobile data." Timothy didn't seem like a snob, but years of being teased in school over all the things she could not afford had left its mark.

"Well, she said she can't come out tonight because she's busy with work."

Samantha snorted. "Anya doesn't care about work. Unless by work, she means scouring Shopbop for some retail therapy. Most likely, she just wanted to stay in with her dogs."

Grinning, Timothy shrugged. "Looks like it's just you and me tonight. After you then, milady," he said, brandishing his arm toward the Apothecary's entrance with a courtly bow that made Samantha giggle.

Unsurprisingly for a Sunday night, the pub was almost empty. Glass skulls leered from the walls, lit up by lanterns that sent eerie shadows dancing across the floor. Vials and flasks of brightly hued drinks lined the open bar. A stuffed owl trained its large, unblinking eyes on Samantha and Timothy from a perch behind the counter as they made their way toward a table at the very back.

Once they were seated, Samantha picked up a laminated menu, but Timothy whipped it out of her hands before she had read past the fourth line. "Don't bother with that. There's a secret menu only friends of the owner know about."

Samantha smiled. *Ah, to be an insider for once.* "You pick for us then."

It didn't take long for Timothy to place their drink orders at the bar and come back holding two cauldron-shaped flasks. Samantha squinted doubtfully at the neon-red drink he set in front of her. "This looks poisonous."

Timothy's mouth curved into a wicked grin as he clinked his glass against hers. "Only one way to find out."

Samantha hesitated, but Timothy was already tossing back his drink, so she gritted her teeth and did the same. The burn hit her throat like a truck. "Jesus," she sputtered, her eyes watering. "Did they add chili to this?"

"Bingo." He coughed. "A pinch of very powerful chili padi in this aptly named Chili Cauldron cocktail."

Samantha wiped away her tears with a finger and pushed her drink toward him. "Please finish this. My liver begs you."

Timothy pushed it back. "*My* liver regretfully declines your request."

"Uh-uh, you have to. Think of it as punishment for shirking your Fraud Squad duties and not coming to the Christian Dada event."

"Now you're just playing dirty."

Samantha quickly took a sip of her cocktail, the spicy drink a welcome—if slightly painful—distraction from the heat that had pooled in her stomach. Somehow, the word "dirty" sounded oddly seductive when curled up in Timothy's faint British accent.

"Besides, you can't blame me for not wanting to go," he continued, wrinkling his nose. "Don't tell Anya this, but I seriously can't be arsed about Christian Dada's designs. They're plain bizarre."

"Oh my God. Absolutely. I thought I was just not posh enough to appreciate them."

Timothy shot her a smirk. "What happened to them being 'delightfully irreverent'?"

Samantha tried not to be charmed by how he actually fashioned his fingers into air quotes. "It's not like I could say they were bad, and the *Elle* reporter would have never published anything less than complimentary. The pullover I said was my favorite piece? I can't imagine why anyone would pay so much for something so tattered it looked like it came from a trash can."

Timothy chuckled. "That's what boomers say about ripped jeans. But seriously, though, I think that's just people's way of making a statement. Like, *I've so much money I can spend it on something I know deep down isn't worth the price at all.*"

Samantha arched a brow. "Like your Alexander Shorokhoff watch?"

"Hey! What's wrong with my watch?" Timothy asked, sounding more amused than anything else.

"Nothing. Unless you actually want to read the time." With a boldness that surprised herself, she grabbed Timothy's left arm and tilted it so that the watch face was clearly displayed.

"Okay, it *is* incredibly beautiful," Samantha conceded. The mother-of-pearl hour ring was inscribed with the twelve Western zodiac signs and backdropped against a stunning engraving of swirling constellations. Its beautifully hued hands shimmered even in the dim pub. "But there are so many details that it must take you thirty seconds just to spot where the hand is pointing to, and another thirty seconds to figure out the number each zodiac sign corresponds to. Are plain old numbers too basic?"

Timothy inclined his head. "Fair enough. I only wear this watch out of habit because it was an old birthday present from my girlfriend." With a small sigh, he dropped his hand back into his lap, the watch disappearing beneath the table.

Samantha's expression faltered. Oh God, she had just inadvertently criticized his girlfriend, the mysterious Elle. "A watch? That's so cool!" she exclaimed, making her voice extra perky to make up for her mistake. "Is it supposed to symbolize you coming of age?"

Timothy's mouth crooked into a smile. "Nothing like that. It's an inside joke, actually. When I was younger, I used to write my name as Tim E. because my father always included his middle initial in his signature. So my group of childhood friends, including Elle, used to make fun of me and call me 'Time.' They would even shout 'Time out!' to annoy me. Hence this watch."

Something twisted in the bottom of Samantha's gut, and she quickly took a sip of her cocktail. It still burned as it slid down her throat, but somehow tasted more palatable the second time round. For all of Tim's grousing about his girlfriend, it was clear there was history between them—years of fondness and love that could not be erased by just one fight.

It was less clear to Samantha why she was so bothered by that.

Setting her glass back down on the table, she tried for a smile. "What does the *E* stand for?"

The sheen of nostalgia lifted from Timothy's eyes as a shadow flashed across his face. "Everest. My father's choice. To represent his high hopes for me."

The mood at their table instantly dulled. Samantha shifted in her seat, grasping for a way to change the subject. "Oh! Um, speaking of gifts, that reminds me: I got you a door gift from the Christian Dada event like you asked. It's a leather luggage tag with the brand's logo on it, which is Dada—obviously. You can hang it on your suitcase or—"

"Sam." Timothy cut off her rambling gently. "I was kidding when I asked for a door gift."

Samantha tried for a laugh. "Of course," she said like she had been in on the joke all along. After all, why would Tim even need a luggage tag when his suitcases were probably Louis Vuitton ones with his initials monogrammed on them?

Timothy smiled. "You can keep it for yourself, but it's very thoughtful of you."

Samantha simply nodded, not revealing that she had already grabbed two luggage tags for herself and her mother even though they hadn't taken a trip in years. She could always sell Tim's luggage tag on Carousell for some spare cash.

"How did the rest of the event go?"

Samantha shook her head slightly to clear her thoughts, which were still stuck on the origins of Timothy's watch. "Well, Anya and I had a great time exchanging stories about you since you weren't there." She smirked. "Shall we discuss your fanboy adoration for Bon Jovi?"

Timothy's face blanched. "Hey, every bloke I know went through a Bon Jovi phase. One of my Durham mates even got a tramp stamp of Bon Jovi after getting really pissed during a pub crawl." He caught her fighting a smile. "What?"

"Nothing. It's just . . . funny hearing you say stuff like 'bloke' and 'mate.' We get it—you're half-British," she said, then grinned to show she was joking.

Timothy grinned back to show he didn't mind. "I guess that's one thing I picked up from my father. He's been in Singapore for over two decades, but he definitely retained a lot of his British slang. When I was young, I wanted to be just like him, so I went around imitating all his mannerisms. At least it helped lessen the culture shock when I was studying in Durham."

"What was it like in Durham?"

Timothy's face lit up. "It was brilliant. For once, people didn't know me as the Kingston heir, so I was free to do whatever," he said, suddenly sounding much more animated. "Attend quiz nights at the pub, cure the resulting hangover with cappuccino from this café called Leonard's, hike the hills, and visit the local castles on weekends."

"Wow, that sounds amazing," Samantha said softly. She had longed to do a study abroad program at university, but her scholarship didn't cover that. She could only watch through Instagram as all her friends flew off to different corners of the world; even

Raina spent three months in Mexico, where she sent weekly post-cards and, once, a shirt with the image of a taco above the words **taco to me about intersectional feminism**.

"Honestly, it was the best three years of my life, and I'm not just talking about the stuff I got up to outside of school. The coursework was tough, but in the best way possible."

"I've been meaning to ask—why did you study classics? Based on what you said about your parents, I'm surprised they approved."

Timothy's lips twisted into a wry smile. "They didn't. They wanted me to study—surprise, surprise—economics. But to be honest, my IB results weren't good enough for a top econs program. My parents were totally ready to donate a library wing to Wharton, my father's alma mater, but I didn't want to be accepted by a school because of what *they* did. So I researched all the programs my grades qualified for, and classics at Durham was the best I could find and as unlike econs as possible."

"Did you end up liking it?"

"Liked it? I loved it! Ancient Greek and Roman cultures are bloody fascinating. Literally—there was a lot of blood involved in many of the myths." He laughed, but soon, the light in his eyes faded and his voice dulled.

"However, my parents only agreed to let me attend Durham if I promised to join the Kingston Management Group after graduation. At that time, I was so desperate to get away I would have agreed to anything, but I regret it now. I could tell people at KMG didn't even respect me—it's not like most classics majors get hired at Asia's top hedge fund right out of school."

Samantha wrinkled her nose. "If anyone at KMG looked down on you because of your classics degree, it just means they're intellectual snobs."

"I meant they didn't respect me because it was obvious I only got in thanks to who my father is," Timothy said, a hint of red now on his cheeks. "And to be honest, I don't blame them. It just sucks to always be living in Albert Kingston's shadow. That's why I want a chance to establish myself apart from my family."

"I respect that." Samantha tipped her glass toward him. "One problem though. Regardless of whether you work at KMG or anywhere else, how can you ever shuck off your Kingston identity? It's not like Chinese surnames, which are so common. I mean, I never once guessed Fo Tian Chen is Anya's dad, because of how popular Chen is."

"Yeah, Anya told me Chen's the Chinese equivalent of Smith in the UK."

"Exactly. And the reason why I can even get away with this socialite ruse is because if anyone tries googling Song, they'd probably find a dozen millionaires out there with my surname. But Kingston? Only someone living under a rock wouldn't immediately deduce you're from the Kingston Management Group family. You're always going to be treated differently."

Timothy pulled a face. "Yeah. That's also why my parents don't take my creative desires seriously—they think I wouldn't dare pursue a field with such little job security if I didn't already have the Kingston name to pave the way. So I want to figure out some way of making a name for myself without actually involving my last name."

He took a sip of his cocktail, grimaced, and put it down. "Bloody hell, I had forgotten how disgusting this was. Anyway"—he steepled his hands—"enough about my parents. Tell me about your mother."

Samantha's heart did a little flip. She'd made only the briefest mention at Enzo of being from a single-parent household, but Timothy had remembered, saving her from having to give an awkward reminder of her fatherless status as she had needed to do so many times before with other people.

"There's not much to say . . . Ma works really long hours, and after work, she's usually too tired to do anything besides scarf down a quick dinner and sleep." Samantha shrugged, rifling her fingers through the dish of salted peanuts on the table. "I don't feel like I know her that well."

It was only when Timothy said softly, "We don't have to talk about her if you don't want to," that Samantha caught the stiffness in her voice. Years of school bullying had trained her to keep mum about her family situation except with a few close friends like Raina and Anya.

But the gentleness in Timothy's gaze and voice loosened Samantha's throat. "It's okay," she heard herself saying. "I don't get to talk to Ma much because she's so busy, so it will be nice to talk *about* her with someone."

To her relief, Timothy simply nodded, not trying to make the moment a bigger deal than it had to be. "What does she do?"

"Ma used to be a housewife, but after my dad's business went belly-up and he fell sick, she became the only breadwinner. She didn't have many options, though, since her highest qualification was only an O-level cert. So she borrowed money from a relative to do a nail technician course, started working at a salon near our flat a decade ago, and she's been there ever since. I used to follow her to work and study in the salon's back room, but her boss got annoyed, so I switched to hanging out at the neighborhood bookshop instead."

"Why did you follow her to work? Weren't you old enough to be left home alone?"

Samantha cast her eyes down. "Loan sharks would come to our flat to look for my dad," she admitted quietly, bracing herself for the sympathetic frown and *"I'm so sorry"* that she'd heard countless times from school counselors and town council members over the years.

Timothy was silent for a few moments before he said, "Your mother sounds like a very strong woman. It couldn't have been easy entering the workforce when she was, what, already in her thirties?"

Suddenly, Samantha's eyes felt too hot. As she stared at her hands, an image of Ma's hands crashed into her mind. The only thing of beauty to Ma's hands was the fancy manicure the salon owner insisted all his employees get—the cost of which came out of their own pockets. But even the smooth gel polish and sparkly rhinestones could not distract from the angry red calluses on Ma's palms or the tremor of her hand whenever her carpal tunnel acted up.

"Yeah, Ma was in her late thirties then. And you're right—it wasn't easy for her." Samantha swallowed, the bitter aftertaste of the cocktail coating her throat. "We were always scrambling to meet loan deadlines, wondering every month if this would be the month we fell behind on our payments. I want us to—for once—be able to live in the moment, not have to worry about anything, and just *enjoy* life." To her horror, she heard her voice break at the end.

Timothy must have heard it, too, but thankfully showed no reaction. Instead, he simply asked, "Like those socialites that always appear in *S*?"

Samantha eyed him, but his tone was curious, not judgmental, so she nodded. "I know some people think reading about haute couture and yacht parties is frivolous. But honestly, my life could do with some frivolity," she said, trying for a breezy laugh that died the moment she heard how flat it sounded.

"I don't think that's frivolous," Timothy said, eyes locked on hers. "Sometimes, we read things because we see ourselves in them, but other times, it's because they give us a temporary escape from our own lives."

Samantha's breath hitched. She pulled her cardigan tighter around her. In the dimness of the pub, Timothy's eyes were so dark they appeared black, so intent that it felt like he was peering into the depths of her, all her hopes and desires laid bare on the table.

Samantha shook her head. "Not just an escape, no." Her fingers clenched around her sleeves. "They provide something to aspire toward."

8

This was it—the big one. Dinner with the Liem brothers and the Christian Dada event had been challenging, but Samantha knew they were merely a rehearsal for the first true test of the Fraud Squad's scheme: a dinner party hosted by the Kingstons.

A few days in advance, Timothy sent his house address to the Fraud Squad group chat, though Samantha knew it was for her benefit only—Anya had been a steadfast visitor for years. She had been with Raina when his text came, and immediately, they plugged the address into Google Maps, scouring the satellite images for a hint of what to expect.

From the aerial perspective, all they could see of Timothy's exclusive neighborhood were little pockets of blue set among green plots—pools and expansive backyards, both rarities in land-scarce Singapore. The street view revealed even less: just the barest glimpse of slate-white walls tucked behind an allée of cypress trees in the prime position on a cul-de-sac.

Raina's expression had soured when she saw the trees. "Did you know Vincent van Gogh had a thing for cypresses?" she asked darkly. "Well, neither did I until I had to sit through *two* meetings where my client and her husband squabbled about who gets to keep their Van Gogh collection."

Cypress trees aside, Timothy's house—a mansion, really—was even more awe-inspiring in real life: a rambling estate with carved columns, more windows than anyone could count, and a sprawling garden that looked like something straight out of Versailles. As Samantha traipsed toward the house, her ears pricked up at the faint babble coming through the open door.

She quickened her steps as much as her delicate Fendi pumps would allow, cursing herself for not factoring the long trek up the winding driveway into her time calculations. It would have been much easier if she were wearing flip-flops, but finally, panting and praying the gravel hadn't ruined her heels (on loan from Anya), Samantha reached the colonnaded entryway. She barely had time to slick back the curls sticking to her face before a maid ushered her into the foyer.

Samantha had never stayed in a five-star hotel before, but she imagined the lobby of one must look something like this. One entire wall was a patchwork of hanging ferns and massive blooms, with a man-made waterfall winding lazily through this vertical garden. In the center of the room was a sunken pit filled with smooth white pebbles. A massive cluster of bamboo stalks rose from them, soaring toward the high ceiling and glittering oddly beneath the chandelier. It took Samantha a moment to realize the "bamboo" was made of jade.

On second thought, it was a good thing she wasn't actually wearing flip-flops—the flimsy rubber soles would squeak so offensively against the gleaming marble floor. And thank God she hadn't trusted Tim's assurance of "It's just a simple dinner!" and instead heeded Anya's advice to dress up—all the men here were in starchy shirts and the women in elaborate dresses, some cocktail length and some floor-sweeping.

Samantha looked around the room, her eyes landing almost

immediately on Albert Kingston, who stood at least a head above everyone else. His face was more lined and his full head of hair had more silver streaks, but otherwise, he looked just like his cover photo in *Robb Report* two years ago. He was holding court in one corner with a group of men all wearing slight variations of the same dress-shirt-and-slacks combo. Timothy, however, was conspicuously absent from this all-male huddle.

Samantha wandered around the foyer, eyes peeled for a sign of either of the only two people she knew. Here and there, she spotted faces familiar to her from society magazines, and it was all she could do to keep from gawking. All those characters—no, not characters, *people*—suddenly seemed larger than life now that they were right in front of her.

And suddenly, there *she* was.

Samantha had seen countless photos of Missy before, and even once from afar at a Loewe event both *S* and *Tatler* had covered during her internship. But seeing the editor up close was disconcerting, like a little kid running into her teacher at the grocery store and realizing they had a life outside of work.

Missy was almost six feet tall, but her spine was ramrod straight and her head held aloft like a ballerina with her trademark asymmetric bob—a haircut that would have looked like a disaster on anyone else but somehow fit her perfectly. The only woman here not wearing a dress, she cut a striking figure in a crisp men's shirt tucked into a pair of wide-leg sailor pants. A dark red handkerchief in her shirt pocket added a dash of color to her otherwise monochrome outfit.

A sharp squeal of her name made Samantha look up. "You look amazing!" Anya exclaimed, flouncing over in a leather blazer dress Samantha had last seen on a mannequin at the Christian Dada event. Anya's brows furrowed as she drew near. "Wait, why are you sweating so much?"

"Damn, is it obvious?" Samantha turned her phone on selfie mode and pushed her face close to the camera so she could study her makeup even through the cracked phone screen. "Walking up that driveway was a real workout."

"You didn't take a car here?"

"Nope, I took the bus." Staring at her phone, Samantha dabbed at the corner of her eye to remove a mascara clump. "The walk from the bus stop to here was even worse than the driveway."

"I could have given you a ride! This neighborhood isn't very accessible by public transport—there're probably more cars than people here."

Satisfied she had done all she could to fix her makeup, Samantha put her phone away. "That would explain the odd look Tim's security guard gave me. Guess he isn't used to anyone arriving on foot. Anyway, I'm trying to figure out how to approach Missy." She gestured surreptitiously toward the editor. "If I can make a good impression on her tonight, that would really fast-track our Fraud Squad plan."

Anya pursed her lips. "You aren't going to ask her about writing for *S*, are you? Because I can tell you the people here won't like to talk about business in social situations. That's a major faux pas."

"I know that," Samantha said defensively, feeling like a schoolkid being lectured. She pulled Anya toward a corner of the foyer that was out of earshot of everyone else, but lowered her voice anyway just to be safe. "I'm going to play the long game—make sure I register on Missy's radar, show her I belong in this world, as if I've been going to parties like this since forever. Then, after she's seen me around long enough in high society, I'm going to very, *very* gently mention to her I've always loved magazines and writing."

"Real subtle." Anya grinned. "Looks like you've got it all thought out."

Samantha let out a small sigh. "Only because I've been think-ing about it for years."

Anya's smile turned sympathetic. "Well, tonight's your chance. For your info, the Kingstons' dining table is one of those long ones where you can only talk to the people sitting close to you. Since Missy is so important, she's probably going to be sitting with Tim's parents and not near you. Now's the best time for you to approach her."

"I wish I could. I've been watching her, hoping for a chance to introduce myself, but she's always in a conversation with someone else."

"That's to be expected—people are always trying to suck up to Missy. The woman talking to her right now is Trina Leung, the—"

"Heiress to Leung Jewelers. I've read about her before."

"She used to be friends with my mom, before . . . my parents got divorced." Anya cleared her throat. "Anyway, my mom says Trina has always been gunning to appear in S. According to the grapevine, she even offered Leung Jewelers as the S Gala's official jewelry sponsor just to win Missy's favor, but I heard Missy de-cided to go with Van Cleef and Arpels in the end."

Samantha's eyes widened. One of the great things about being friends with Anya was hearing all the high-society gossip that never made it into magazines. "Isn't Missy worried she might of-fend the Leung family?"

Anya snorted. "Missy's so powerful people are usually worried about offending *her*, so it's not going to be easy for you—"

"Hello, ladies," came a smooth voice from behind them. "Why are you two standing in a corner?"

Samantha whirled around. The moment her eyes landed on Eileen Kingston, her back instantly snapped straighter. Almost by instinct, her hands flew up to smooth her hair. She winced as they made contact with the copious amounts of mousse she had sprayed on to tame her curls.

"Hi, Eileen!" Anya chirped, her face now wearing a bright smile. "I've been looking around for you so I could say hi."

Eileen Kingston smiled, her immaculate—if slightly overpowdered—skin stretching over the set of aristocratically high cheekbones her son had inherited. Oddly, she looked better in real life despite being one of Singapore's most photographed women. With her shiny hair, shiny skin, and even shinier teeth, pictures sometimes made her appear more like a marble statue brought to life.

"Anya, dear, it's always wonderful seeing you. And how's your father? Albert managed to see him last month when he flew to China for business, but I wasn't able to join him on that trip."

"He's good. I'm hoping he can make it back for my birthday next month."

"I'm sure he will. And have you said hi to Albert yet? But I warn you: He will go on and on about how none of his golfing buddies are as skilled as Fo Tian is!"

Anya laughed. "I'm going to let my dad know—maybe it will convince him to come visit Singapore more often. I'll go say hi to Albert now."

Samantha's heart plunged as her friend trotted away. She resisted the urge to squirm as Eileen Kingston turned the full force of her scrutiny toward her. "And I don't think I've met you before, dear."

Samantha braided her fingers together so she wouldn't fuss with her hair. "Hello, Mrs. Kingston—"

The older woman waved it off. "Call me Eileen. Being called Mrs. Kingston makes me feel old."

"Oh, I'm sorry . . . Eileen." It was strange, being on first-name basis with a woman she had been reading about for years. "I'm Samantha."

"Lovely to meet you, Samantha. And I'm guessing you're one of my son's friends?"

"That's right. We met through Anya."

"How wonderful. I always love meeting the people in Timothy's life. Most of the time, I don't even know whom he's running around with. That boy barely tells his father and me anything." Eileen chuckled like she was joking, but Samantha caught a barely perceptible trace of hurt in the other woman's voice that sounded just like Ma's whenever she tried to downplay her workplace or health troubles.

"I think every parent has the same gripe about their kids," Samantha offered. "I'm sure my mom will say the same if you ask her."

"Is that so?"

"Yeah," Samantha lied. She usually told her mother everything she was up to so Ma wouldn't have more cause to worry.

Eileen peered down at her. "And do I know your mother?"

Samantha's mouth dried. Why didn't the Fraud Squad prepare for a situation like this? How was she supposed to tell Eileen that the only way she and Ma might have crossed paths was if the billionaire's wife had, for whatever reason, decided to visit a nail salon that used nail polish from Sally Hansen and not Chanel?

"No, I don't think so," Samantha finally said. "She doesn't come out much."

Eileen arched one perfectly sculpted brow. "Oh? That's too bad." She was still smiling, but her eyes flitted absently around the room, her interest in Samantha gone now that she couldn't establish the younger woman's family standing.

Samantha racked her brain, pulling forth everything she had ever read about what Eileen liked. Anything that could keep this one-on-one exchange going. Winning over Missy was the ultimate goal, but impressing Eileen Kingston could help her get one step closer—she was not only one of Singapore's most celebrated socialites, but also Missy's close friend.

Samantha's eyes caught on a painting hanging on the wall behind Eileen. Something tugged at her mind. Didn't Eileen once tell *Harper's Bazaar* her favorite thing to do on vacation was visit art museums?

"I love your art," she blurted.

Eileen's eyes snapped back to her. "Pardon?"

Samantha cleared her throat. "Uh, that painting"—she gestured toward the artwork—"it's very . . . vibrant." In truth, the massive riot of paint splatters looked like something a kindergartener might have created.

Eileen looked to see where she was pointing. "Ah, yes. A Larry Poons painting I got at a Sotheby's auction two years ago." She eyed Samantha. "Do you like Poons as well?"

Samantha immediately nodded. "Of course! He's a genius."

"Why do you say that?"

"Why do I think he's a genius?" Samantha repeated to buy herself more time as her mind raced. Larry Poons—she had come across that name once, when writing about *The Price of Everything* for *Tatler*'s monthly "must-see" entertainment roundup. Although she never got around to watching the art documentary Larry Poons had starred in, she did read half a dozen film reviews as part of her research.

However, Samantha knew what really mattered here was what Eileen liked about Poons. But what *were* Eileen's tastes? "I don't get the fuss over monogram street wear," she'd told *S* in an interview last year. "Everyone and their grandmother are wearing it these days. But I prefer unique, one-of-a kind couture creations to flash-in-a-pan trends." After reading that, Samantha had gone to her Pinterest wish list and deleted every pinned image of the monogrammed pieces from the LV Squared collection.

Inspiration struck like lightning. Samantha met Eileen's expectant gaze and smiled. "I admire how Poons always sticks to his style instead of trying to pander to the market, even when he wasn't doing that well in the nineties. He creates art for art's sake, as opposed to someone like Jeff Koons," she said smoothly, referencing the man who had been set up as Poons's antithesis in *The Price of Everything*. "Koons seems to care more about monetizing art by producing stuff that's trendy and kitsch. But when something becomes so commonplace, I just don't think it's that valuable anymore," she finished, praying with her whole heart that the Kingstons didn't own one of Koons's works.

Eileen's face lit up. "Samantha, you took the words right out of my mouth! Jeff Koons's works are so passé these days, so commercialized. And as for his handbag collaboration with Louis Vuitton?" Her wrinkled nose made her feelings clear.

"Exactly! Larry Poons is definitely more of an original artist. I find it bizarre Jeff Koons has an entire studio of people working to produce his ideas like a machine line. So many people have one of his balloon dog sculptures! Makes me wonder if they genuinely appreciate the quality, or if it's because they just want to own something with his name on it."

Eileen's smile broadened. "I like the way you think, Samantha. You should come see my gallery sometime."

"You run a gallery?"

An indecipherable expression flickered across Eileen's face. "Not an official one," she said with a slightly stilted laugh. "The Kingston Foundation keeps me too busy for that. It's just a small gallery at home of all the artworks I've collected over the years—"

"Mother"—Timothy squeezed the word out through gritted teeth as he walked over—"what in the world made you think it was okay to—" His eyes widened as they landed on Samantha. "Hey, I was looking for you earlier."

Aware of Eileen's eyes on her, Samantha offered him a small grin that she hoped conveyed platonic friendship and nothing else. "Hey, you. I just arrived not too long ago." So, *this* was Timothy Kingston. Hair combed back, dress shirt beneath a tailored black blazer, pressed black pants, and gleaming leather shoes. The only sign of Tim-ness was the crooked Windsor knot of his tie that she itched to fix.

"Timothy," Eileen cut in with a tight-lipped smile. "Whatever it is, we can talk about it later. I was just having a wonderful conversation with your friend."

A strained silence descended upon the trio for a few agonizing moments. Samantha forced herself to speak up once it became clear Timothy didn't plan to. "Uh, yes, as I was saying, I'm a huge fan of what Poons stands for. He's such a free spirit, and that really comes through in his art style."

Timothy's tight expression gave way to a knowing smirk. "Sam, I didn't know you were so into art."

"Timothy, don't make fun of your friend," Eileen said before Samantha could respond. "Most of your generation only cares about Instagram memes these days, so I think it's wonderful there are young people who can still appreciate classic art."

It was disconcerting hearing Eileen Kingston utter "memes" in her posh accent, but Samantha didn't have much time to linger on that as Timothy retorted, "Funny you should say that, when you and Father have made it clear I'll never be allowed to pursue something in the creative field."

There was now a distinct strain to Eileen's smile, though her voice was as calm as ever as she said, "Timothy, you know I think an understanding of art is a useful conversational tool. After all, it's important to show your business partners you appreciate culture. But where will you even find the time for your creative projects when you have a hedge fund to run?"

Timothy's face went taut again, but before he could say anything, Eileen turned to Samantha. "Dear, don't you agree with me? We ladies can dabble in the arts—why, I used to work in the acquisitions department at Christie's Hong Kong—but a career in that isn't very appropriate for a man like Timothy, mm-hmm?"

"So Larry Poons isn't a man then?" Timothy retorted.

At this point, Eileen's smile looked like it had been carved into her face. "Timothy, you know you aren't just any man. You were born into a certain position that comes with certain expectations."

When Timothy replied, Samantha could tell he was straining to keep his voice even. "But I didn't ask to be born into this position. I just want to work on stuff *I'm* passionate about, but you and Father refuse to entertain anything outside of KMG."

Eileen's eyes darted to Samantha, then back to her son. Samantha shifted from one foot to the other, casting her mind around desperately for something she could say to break the tension or at least an excuse to escape. It was hard to tell who was more mortified here—Eileen or herself.

But then, Eileen sighed softly, loosening the hard set of her mouth. "Oh, Timothy . . . your father always says you're a Kingston man through and through, but deep down, I think you take after me more. All he cares about is business and data and analytics, but you and I—we both love the arts and are able to appreciate the softer beauty in our world."

She paused, lifting her chin and drawing herself erect. "But there are other pursuits in life just as or even more deserving of our attention," Eileen continued, her voice firmer. "As family, we must both do what we can to help your father out with the Kingston Management Group. I take care of the Kingston Foundation, and you're expected to take over the entire company someday." She raised one pale shoulder in an elegant shrug. "C'est la vie."

Samantha's heart clenched. In front of her eyes, Eileen's perfectly made-up face morphed into Ma's, speckled with wrinkles and age spots. Hadn't Ma said something similar not too long ago when her carpal tunnel was acting up? "The best way to deal with pain is to push through it—that's life," she'd uttered, the words slipping out like a sigh.

For a few moments, Timothy simply stared silently at his mother, his clenched jaw throbbing as though to hold back a deluge of words. Then, abruptly, his shoulders deflated. "Yes, Mother. I understand." The snap was gone from his voice, and in its place was a quiet resignation that made Samantha want to wrap him in a tight, comforting embrace.

After a moment, Eileen reached out to adjust her son's tie. "There, all good now," she said, a semblance of a smile on her face. She swept a hand over Timothy's lapels. "Be on your best behavior for me tonight . . . please?"

Wordlessly, Timothy nodded. Samantha looked down at the ground. It somehow felt even more intrusive witnessing this unexpectedly tender moment between mother and son than their earlier argument.

A gong sounded. Eileen raised her head and rolled her shoulders back. "Ah, time for dinner! Timothy, bring Samantha to the dining room, won't you? I'll go and take care of the other guests," she said, the consummate host once again.

CHAPTER

9

The dining table was as long as Anya had described, stretching along one entire end of the massive dining room and punctuated at even intervals with ornate *look, don't touch* glass candelabras. Bone-white china glistened against the dark red tablecloth, every utensil arranged at precisely the same angle as the next, as though the placements had been measured out with rulers and protractors.

It was a table meant for entertaining—a far cry from the one Samantha had at home. That dining table was so small that back when Ba was still around, family meals meant everyone's elbows often bumped into one another's. But its circular top and snug size made it seem more welcoming than this sculptural behemoth with its elaborate place settings.

Samantha bit back a groan when she finally located her place card. Not only had she been seated far apart from Timothy and Anya, she was also all the way at the opposite end of the table from Missy, who was with Timothy's parents as Anya had predicted. Even worse, she was stuck in the undesirable end seat, which put her close to only two other guests.

One of them was a gray-haired man who had been in Albert Kingston's conversation huddle earlier. He was now blowing his nose noisily into a napkin, the wisp of mole hair on his chin quivering from the robust movements of his jowls.

Her only other option was the woman on her right, who appeared to be in her early twenties as well. Samantha's eyes widened when she finally got a good look at her neighbor.

This wasn't just *any* twentysomething woman, but Lucia freaking Yen in the flesh, looking just as polished in real life as she had in her *S* cover photo. Her ivory off-shoulder jumpsuit set off her long jet-black hair, alabaster skin, and defined collarbones perfectly.

Lucia turned her head and caught Samantha's eyes before she could pretend she hadn't been staring. Thankfully, Lucia was much too well-mannered to point it out. Instead, her expertly painted bee-stung pout curved into a smile. "Hi, I'm Lucia," she said, her voice tinkling like wind chimes.

Samantha stopped herself from blurting out "I know" just in time. "Hi! I'm Samantha, but you can call me Sam!" She wanted to grimace when she caught the over-the-top chirpiness in her voice.

Lucia arched one brow. "So, *you're* Samantha."

"You've heard of me?"

"Of course. Not much goes unnoticed in this crowd," Lucia said as she flipped her hair behind her, sending a waterfall of ebony silk cascading over one bare shoulder. "I hear you've been making quite a splash on the social circuit lately."

Lucia's words sounded like a compliment, but there was a blandness to her tone that made Samantha think otherwise. Before she could respond, Lucia continued, "Funny thing is, I only heard about you pretty recently. How did I miss you before?"

Samantha ran a hand through her hair. "Uh, I used to be quite a homebody, but I'm trying to get out more these days. That's why I took up Tim's offer for this party tonight."

Lucia tilted her head to one side. "How do you know Tim?"

"Through our mutual friend, Anya."

"I see. I used to know Anya quite well." Lucia picked up her wine and took a delicate sip, keeping her eyes trained on Samantha. "Tim's family has always been pretty private, so you two *must* be close if he invited you to this party."

Samantha shifted in her seat. What had started out as simple small talk now felt more like an interrogation. "You sound like you know Tim's family very well, so you must also be good friends with him," she tossed back.

Lucia put her glass down and smiled. "Tim and I go way back. Our families have known each other for ages."

She leaned in, sending a waft of crisp Chanel No. 5 up Samantha's nose. Lucia's eyes gleamed as she added lightly, "We've also been dating for four years."

Samantha stared back, unable to speak. She felt like she had been hit over the head. *Elle—L!* Why didn't Timothy tell her his girlfriend was *the* Lucia Yen? And why didn't he warn her she would be here tonight?

"Tim—I mean, Timothy, never told me about you," Samantha choked out.

Immediately, she could tell she had said the wrong thing, as Lucia's smile dropped. "Well, he's also never bothered mentioning *you*."

"No, no, I didn't mean it like that!" Samantha said, her words tumbling over one another. "I think it's because I only met Timothy after you two went on a break, so obviously he wouldn't be speaking—"

Her voice died as Lucia's face darkened. "He told you about our *break*?"

Samantha gulped. "Yeah?"

Lucia leaned closer, her eyes boring into Samantha's like two unyielding missiles. "Listen, I don't know who you are," she began quietly, but there was a coldness to her voice that made Samantha almost wish Lucia were shouting instead, "but I hear you've been spending way too much time around *my* man. Tim and I already know we're getting back together after our break ends, so don't try to make a move on him." Her narrowed eyes dragged up and down Samantha's body. "You aren't his type anyway."

With that, Lucia leaned back in her chair and smiled prettily again, as if she had simply been discussing the weather.

Samantha's blood ran cold. She felt as though her entire being had just been turned inside out, all her flaws picked up and magnified by Lucia's razor-sharp, kohl-lined eyes. Her hands fisted in her Zimmerman dress, which suddenly seemed much too flimsy, exposing every inch of her to scrutiny.

Samantha tugged at the dress hem, but as her hand moved, the massive Ileana Makri ring on her left index finger snagged around a loose thread in the tablecloth, jerking it slightly. As though in slow motion, she saw her wineglass catch in a fold on the cloth. Time stood impossibly still as the glass teetered precariously on its edge, the dark red wine sloshing around within.

Then it fell over to its side. Wine poured out, darkening the tablecloth in its wake as it streamed straight over the table's edge and onto Lucia's ivory jumpsuit.

For a moment, both Samantha and Lucia could only gape as a scarlet stain blossomed across the latter's chest like blood from a gunshot. The next moment, Lucia's loud gasp pierced the dinner babble, drawing every single eye to their end of the table.

"Are you seriously so desperate to get Tim that you're resorting to cheap tricks like this?" Lucia spat out, her voice so low only Samantha could hear. Her upper lip curled. "Have some pride."

Samantha's face blanched. "What? No! I swear I'm not trying to steal him from you. I'm so sorry, but this really is an accident!" She grabbed her napkin and leaned toward Lucia. "Please, let me help."

Lucia recoiled. "Spare me your lame excuses. You knew it was my first time seeing Tim after our break and you wanted to make me look bad."

Samantha's fingers clenched around the napkin like it was a lifeline. The wine was still dripping steadily onto the rug beneath the table. "I didn't know that! I wasn't trying—"

"What's the matter?" Eileen asked, her heels click-clacking against the marble floor as she hurried over. "Lucia, dear, are you all right?"

Lucia was glaring straight at Samantha, her back toward the rest of the table, so only Samantha saw Lucia wipe the murderous look off her face and plaster on a rather pitiful smile before turning to Eileen. "Aunty Eileen, Samantha accidentally knocked her glass over, but it's no big deal, really! Samantha was just telling me she doesn't get out much, so she's probably feeling really nervous about being at this party. Everyone makes mistakes, right?"

Samantha flushed as a dozen pairs of eyes shot toward her. Great, now all the guests thought she was some socially awkward recluse. One man even pushed himself out of his chair to get a better look, like a tourist in a safari trying to spot some exotic animal. Timothy's face wore a sympathetic frown, Anya's a grimace, and Albert Kingston's was inscrutable.

But the only one Samantha had eyes for was Missy's. Her eyebrows were drawn, her lips were pursed, her expression was stony, and she looked like she was already thinking of the damage Samantha might wreak on the tablecloths at *her* parties.

Samantha's heart plummeted. She had just ruined her chances with Missy—and S—for good.

A MAID PROMPTLY cleaned up the mess while Timothy led Lucia away to get cleaned up. She returned to the table wearing one of Eileen's Chanel shawls over her ruined jumpsuit, but the wine stain peeked out from underneath—a constant, mocking reminder to Samantha of how her clumsiness had sent the Fraud Squad's progress down the drain.

Samantha fled the party at the first possible moment it was polite to do so, pulling Anya with her and only stopping briefly on her way out to thank Timothy's parents. They graciously made no reference to her earlier gaffe, but she still found it hard to meet their eyes. Timothy was caught up in a tête-à-tête with one of his father's business partners but managed to mouth, "I'll text you guys," when they hurried past him.

Samantha rubbed her exposed arms as she stepped out of Timothy's house, the nighttime chill piercing through the thin gossamer of her dress. A long trek awaited her—down the Kingstons' driveway, then up the cul-de-sac, then a right turn onto the main street—followed by an even longer bus ride.

Anya laid a gentle hand on Samantha's shoulder. "Do you want a ride home? My car's right over there." She nodded at a blue Camaro sandwiched between a sleek limousine and an Audi with a diplomatic license plate. A chauffeur leaning against the limousine glanced over at them before taking another drag of his cigarette.

A lump welled up in Samantha's throat. The entire dinner, Lucia had monopolized the mole-hair man's attention, smoothly cutting in every time Samantha tried to speak to him. Frozen out of the conversation, Samantha had spent the meal playing with the food on her plate, the laughter among the other guests making her feel even more alone. After the night she'd had, Anya's kindness was enough to send tears prickling her eyes.

Samantha blinked them away and slid her arm through Anya's. "I'd really like that. Thank you."

Anya squeezed her hand. "Don't thank me. What are friends for?"

10

Only two days passed before Samantha found herself returning to Timothy's house. If not for Anya's insistence that the Fraud Squad meet up somewhere private to conduct a postmortem of the dinner party, there was no way she would have returned so soon to the site of her latest social fiasco.

At least she came prepared this time in a pair of Salvatore Ferragamo flats more suitable for the long driveway—much needed since she was also carrying a massive box of Anya's clothes to return to her. She had run through the garments more quickly than expected after a whirlwind of events and parties over the past few weeks, and God forbid she wore any outfit more than once—a strict no-no for any self-respecting socialite.

By the time Samantha met Timothy at the door, her arms were aching from carrying the box for over forty minutes on a crowded bus. It would be much easier if she could use a courier service like Anya had or simply take a cab, but alas. She was about to ask Timothy if she could just set it down in a corner in the foyer but hesitated. The last thing she needed was for Albert and Eileen Kingston to come back home and stumble upon an unsightly cardboard box on their sleek marble floor. After the dinner party, she needed to reduce chances of any further faux pas.

Thankfully, Timothy solved her conundrum by immediately offering to carry the box for her. He rolled up his sleeves, the vein running down his right forearm throbbing as he heaved it up. A corner of the box rubbed against his shirt, pulling it up slightly to flash a strip of tanned stomach.

Samantha quickly looked down in case he caught her staring. In a loose Henley shirt and black Vetements sweatpants, Timothy was the most dressed down she had ever seen him. Vetements was known for oversized clothing, but his sweatpants must have shrunk in the wash because they hugged his lower body like a glove—

Samantha tore her eyes away from Timothy's legs, heat pooling in her stomach. *What's wrong with me?* She was supposed to be angry with him for not warning her about Lucia, not admiring his sweatpants-clad legs. Or his abs. Or his arms.

There was a small hole in the left shoulder of his Henley that seemed safe enough, so Samantha fixed her eyes on it and cleared her throat. "Is Anya arriving soon?"

Timothy grinned at her over the top of the box. "Why? Scared of being alone with me?"

Samantha tried for a scoff but it came out strangled. "Of course not," she said with all the dignity she could muster. "I just thought she'd be on time since she was the one who called this meeting."

"Well, since she isn't here yet, you get to pick our meeting spot."

"What are the options?"

"Do you feel like drinking tea, coffee, or"—he waggled his brows—"something a little stronger?"

Samantha shot him a severe stare that was probably undermined by her twitching mouth. "It's ten in the morning."

"So? Normalize day drinking! Our wine cellar has two thousand bottles. My father won't miss one."

Getting buzzed with Timothy while he was in *those* sweatpants was a dangerous combination. "Red wine *is* my favorite . . . but let's do tea instead." Some nice herbal tea might be just what she needed to settle herself.

"The tea room it is then!"

On the night of the dinner party, Samantha had been so nervous she barely noticed her surroundings as a maid led her to the foyer. But now, when it was just her and Timothy walking through the house, there was more time to slow down and catch the details she'd missed previously. Lining the walls were framed photos of the three Kingstons, sometimes joined by other people. Everyone looked so perfectly put together—their poses like those of an *S* model, their mouths curved to just the right degree—that the photos looked more like the stock images that came with store-bought frames. In these, the resemblance between Timothy and his father was much more obvious, though Albert Kingston's narrower eye shape gave him a harder look.

Samantha and Timothy soon arrived in front of a frosted glass door with a keypad lock. Timothy tightened his left arm around the box, hoisted it onto his hip, and wrestled with the keypad buttons with his now freed-up right hand, chewing on his lower lip in concentration. He caught Samantha turning her face to the side as he keyed in the code. "It's okay," he said with a laugh. "I don't mind if you see it."

The first thing Samantha saw when the door opened was a snow-white carpet that covered the entire floor. She breathed a sigh of relief, thankful that she was wearing a pair of flats she'd borrowed from Anya, so new the tags were still on when she picked them up. She could only imagine the marks her own sneakers might leave on the pristine carpet.

In the center of the room was a handsome redwood table, with dragon engravings all around the side. Ink-wash paintings, calligraphy scrolls, and Chinese opera masks hung on three of the walls, while dark panels ran down the back wall. A ledge encircled the room's perimeter, holding teapots of all shapes and sizes, some so ornate they looked like they ought to be in glass cases in museums.

But something was conspicuously absent. "Where's the tea?"

Timothy put the clothes box down and swept his arm out toward the far wall. "You're looking at it."

Samantha walked toward the wall. What she had initially mistaken for wood panels were actually a grid of niches packed tightly together, each hole filled with a dark block. "That's tea?" she asked in disbelief.

"Yup, tea bricks. Finely ground tea leaves packed into molds and compressed into blocks."

Samantha leaned forward to take a closer look, her nose tickled by a faintly earthy aroma. "I didn't know tea came in this form."

"Art and tea—my mother's greatest loves. Though if you ask her, she'd tell you tea can be art too. Like this one." Timothy eased out one of the tea bricks from its cubby and placed it in Samantha's hands; on it was an engraving of rolling hills and twin pagodas. "My father gave this to her for her forty-eighth birthday."

Samantha thought of the room's keypad. "Must be pretty valuable."

"Yup. It was one point two million."

One point two million dollars? Samantha gaped down at the unassuming lump. Good lord, she was basically holding an entire house in her hands. A fine sheen of sweat gathered in her palms, and she quickly pressed the tea brick back into Timothy's hands, her shoulders untensing only when his fingers closed around it.

"Wow, that's quite a gift," Samantha said, watching Timothy slide the block back into place. She hugged her arms close to her body as her voice drifted back in a faint echo. This room was much too big.

Timothy furrowed his brows. "Are you cold? Sorry, my mother keeps the temperature low in this room for the tea bricks. I'll run and get you a cover-up."

"It's okay. I'm sure some hot tea will do the trick," Samantha quickly said. The only thing more nerve-racking than being alone with the man Lucia Yen had staked a claim on was being alone in a house so massive it probably came with its own zip code.

Timothy looked like he was about to insist further, but an intercom nestled by the door crackled to life. "Yo, I'm here. Let me in," came Anya's voice.

"Sam, make yourself comfortable. Be right back." And before Samantha could offer to go with him, Timothy was striding out of the tea room.

Samantha slid into a hard-backed chair at the table, averting her eyes from the sinister-looking opera masks leering down from the wall. Thankfully, the door soon opened, and Anya bounded in with Timothy right behind.

"Hey, sorry I'm late," Anya said, plonking herself down on the chair next to Samantha while Timothy took the one across from them. "I had to bring Mochi and Peanut to the vet. It's nothing big," she added when she noticed Samantha's eyes widen, "I think Siti didn't cook their steak well last night so they had an upset stomach."

Samantha nodded sympathetically, but her mind was busy trying to remember when the last time was that *she* had eaten steak.

"They are okay now, but my vet wants to keep them overnight

just to be safe," Anya went on mournfully. "It was so hard saying bye to them. I don't know if Mochi can sleep without her white noise machine."

"I'm glad they're okay. By the way, I brought your clothes." Samantha jerked her head toward the box. "Thank you so much for them."

"No biggie. After we're done here, why don't you follow me to my house to pick up the next batch of clothes? It's easier if you come in person so you can choose what you want and try them on first."

Samantha grinned. "I'd love to."

"Speaking of clothes," Timothy cut in, "Sam, catch." He tossed a wad of cloth across the table. "In case the tea doesn't warm you up."

"Thanks," Samantha said in surprise, her hands automatically closing around the cloth. Her fingers tightened when she registered the design: this was the exact same Chanel shawl Lucia had worn to cover up her wine-stained jumpsuit. However, there was nothing Samantha could do now but drape it gingerly around her, feeling the humiliating memory press down on her shoulders like a dull and heavy weight that even the soft cashmere could not alleviate.

"All right, folks. What are we having? There's black tea, green tea, oolong, pu-erh, tieguanyin," Timothy said, ticking the items off his fingers. "And also some wackier options like panda dung tea."

Samantha couldn't help but smile. "Panda dung? I kinda want to try that."

"Never mind that," Anya interrupted. She leaned forward and propped her chin on her hands. "I'm here for the *real* tea—what happened at the dinner party. I figured you needed some space after the party so didn't want to ask you then, but we should talk about it."

Samantha raised a brow. "You want the tea? Let's see. Not only did I make a mess, I also made an enemy out of Lucia and a fool of myself in front of Missy. Is that enough tea for you?"

"I'm sorry. I didn't mean it like that," Anya said, looking chastised.

Samantha's shoulders slumped and she sighed. "No, *I'm* sorry. I'm just upset I embarrassed myself so badly. But seriously, why did Lucia have to make such a big deal out of it? Missy might not even have noticed if Lucia hadn't gasped like—"

"Sam," Anya cut in, a warning in her voice.

Samantha could have kicked herself. Wincing, she turned to Timothy. "I'm sorry. I shouldn't have said that. It was my fault for—"

Timothy held up a hand, his expression indecipherable. "It's okay," he said gruffly. "Let's not talk about it anymore."

Anya eyed him. "What's the deal with you and Lucia anyway? Isn't the point of a break to not see each other?"

Samantha wondered if she had imagined Timothy glancing over at her when Anya asked about Lucia, but the next moment, he was saying defensively, "It's not like I knew she would be there. My parents probably invited her hoping we would patch things up. At least they had more sense than to seat us together. Except that meant she got put next to Sam, and we all know what happened . . ."

Despite herself, Samantha's heart lifted. Tim wasn't the one who had invited Lucia after all; he hadn't been trying to keep her in the dark on purpose.

"And did you guys make up?" Anya asked, still looking beadily at Timothy.

Suddenly, Samantha's heartbeat quickened again. She stared at Timothy, longing to hear his response but scared of what it might be. She didn't even know what she wanted him to say.

Timothy shrugged. "We chatted for a bit."

Anya snorted. "Please, it's so obvious you still have a soft spot for Lucia. We all saw how you led her away afterward so she could clean herself up."

An odd hollowness entered Samantha's chest. Timothy and Lucia alone in a bathroom; Lucia's soaking wet bodice clinging to her torso; Timothy reaching out a hand to gently dab at the stain . . .

"What else was I supposed to do? She's still a guest. Anyway, I thought you wanted us to meet to talk about Sam, not Lucia."

Samantha's cheeks turned pink as both Anya and Timothy turned to look at her, clearly having decided her social disaster was even more pressing than their Lucia squabble. "Tim, I just want to say I'm really sorry about the wine spill. Um, did your parents manage to get the stains out?"

"Oh." Timothy scratched his jaw. "Uh . . ."

Samantha's shoulders slumped; Timothy's hesitation was all the answer she needed.

Timothy leaned forward. "Sam, it's all right. My parents know it was a genuine mistake and they won't hold it against you at all."

Samantha sighed. "Maybe they won't, but Missy will," she said glumly, trailing her fingers around a dragon engraving on the table's rim. "She'll think I'm too much of a liability to invite to her parties. And being socially sidelined by Missy means I can kiss my magazine column dream goodbye. Who's going to take my reporting on high society seriously if I'm not an A-lister?"

"The gala is seven weeks away, so there's still time for you to impress Missy," Timothy said encouragingly.

Anya shot him an incredulous look. "Not to be a buzzkill, but that's a tall order. Missy only goes to the most selective events, so who knows if Sam will even get to meet her again? And let's face it—the wine fiasco really didn't do Sam any favors. I just don't think we should set her up for failure."

Samantha bit her lip. Anya's words were harsh, but the truth behind them was undeniable. Even Timothy was quiet, as though he couldn't think of a way to rebut that.

Anya's expression softened. "I don't mean to be a Debbie Downer. Sam, *Vogue* hosts a luncheon at the Singapore Repertory Theatre the second Sunday of every month, so how about we hit it up this week? Even if Missy's not there, it's still a good social opportunity."

"I'd love to! Oh, wait." Samantha's voice dulled. "I can't. I'm getting brunch with Raina then."

Anya frowned. "Can't you hang out with her another time?"

"But Sunday brunch is our tradition."

"And a *Vogue* event is prime socialite time," Anya fired back. "So many society events are held on Sundays. Don't you think you should put your nonsocialite life on the back burner for a bit? After what happened at Tim's party, we have to *really* get serious about our Fraud Squad plan."

Samantha straightened up in her seat. "I was never half-assing it! I've attended as many social events as I could in the past month. After that one dinner with Clement and Keith, I even went online and read everything I could about the LaFerrari in case another person ever brings it up. I probably know enough to join the Ferrari Owners Club now."

Anya raised her hands in a placating gesture. "I'm not saying you weren't taking things seriously, but giving up a Sunday brunch isn't asking for much, is it? Besides, don't you think you should distance yourself from your old life? Missy's like a shark, so you should minimize any chance she might discover your real identity."

Timothy rolled his eyes. "Anya, chill. Missy's actually a lot nicer than people think she is."

"To *you*. Because you're her good friend's son and a Kingston to boot. Missy has never extended the same niceties to me and my mom."

"Even if Missy doesn't find out, Argus very well might," Samantha interjected before her friends could start bickering again. "That woman has eyes and ears *everywhere*. For all we know, she might be writing about my wine fiasco at this exact moment." Just the thought made her swallow roughly. "She's already done a scary number of exposés in less than a year. Remember that time she revealed the 'N sisters' never buy any of the clothes they take OOTDs in at designer stores?"

Anya smiled smugly. "Exactly, I always knew Ruby and Pearl Naik were trying to appear richer than they actually are. And what about Argus's February article where she disclosed F. L. champions animal conservation causes but owns snakeskin and ostrich-leather Birkins? My mom immediately guessed that was about Frances Lee. And even Tim was one of Argus's victims a few issues back!"

Wide-eyed, Samantha turned to Timothy, but he simply said, "You guys are overreacting. I'm sure Argus has better things to do than go around digging up Sam's dirt."

"Yeah, but why risk it?" Samantha shot back. "Argus is always calling out pretentious socialites, and our Fraud Squad scheme is literally the epitome of pretense. All it takes is one slipup for my background to be exposed, and if that happens—" She gave an exaggerated shudder, her theatrics belying the genuine fear coursing through her.

Grinning, Anya pretended to stroke a long beard. "Very good, my young Padawan, you're catching on quickly. As I was saying, you should shove your nonsocialite life to the side for the next couple of months—maybe cut back on the time you spend with people like Raina."

"I don't want to ditch my best friend because she isn't a socialite," Samantha protested, but her voice now sounded slightly weaker to her ears. "I don't want to be *that* kind of social climber."

"Sa-am," Anya huffed, drawing her name out. "I literally just praised you for being a quick learner. Look, our Fraud Squad scheme is all about faking it till you make it, right?"

Samantha nodded, her face flushing at Anya's reproachful tone.

"How can you fake it if you're still clinging so tightly to your old life? Not only is it eating into time we could spend making progress on our Fraud Squad scheme, but you're also making things harder for yourself by juggling two *very* different social circles. If you try to have the best of both worlds, you will slip up at some point."

Next to Anya, Timothy grimaced in a *shit, she might have a point* way.

Samantha gnawed on the inside of her cheek. Since they met eight years ago, she and her best friend had never gone more than two days without speaking to each other. Rai, who'd accompanied her on her all-nighters when she was studying for her scholarship exams. Who'd offered to read through not just Samantha's but also Ma's work contracts with her lawyerly eye and pointed out where they could negotiate better terms. Who was the first person she shared all her news with—good or bad.

"I'll think about what you said," Samantha finally said, unable to meet Anya's eyes.

But when Anya spoke, her tone was gentle. "I just want the best for you, Sam. High society is an all-or-nothing world, where the people on the inside will do anything to keep you out—I know this better than anyone else." Samantha looked up to see Anya lean back in her chair, her eyes fixed on Samantha's face. "You can think more about it if you want, but I won't guide you wrong."

11

The dinner party postmortem wrapped up not long after. Once Timothy brought out the panda dung tea, it became much easier for Samantha to squash down her unease as the Fraud Squad turned their focus to the steaming teacups in front of them. Panda dung tea might have unfortunate origins but turned out to carry an unexpectedly delicious nutty flavor that drove them to finish every last drop.

Samantha and Anya decided to leave ten minutes before Albert and Eileen Kingston were due to arrive home. Although Tim said his parents weren't upset about her faux pas, Samantha didn't plan on sticking around to find out. He helped carry the clothes box to Anya's Camaro, then waved farewell from his doorstep as they sped off toward Anya's bungalow along Nassim Road.

"Just come say hi to my mom, then we can pop up to my room," Anya said as they got out of the car. "My dogs are still at the vet, so you can try on my clothes in peace."

But when they walked into the bungalow, two separate voices

drifted from the sitting room. Anya poked her head in, then pulled a face. "It's my mom with her friend, Cassandra Ow."

"I think I've run into her at an event before. Is her husband the one who owns that rubber oil refinery business?"

"Yeah, Royal Rubbers." Anya sniggered. "Tim and I used to call them the Condom Couple. Anyway, she's super chatty, so let's try to sneak past. Their backs are turned toward the staircase."

Samantha nodded. Both women tiptoed through the sitting room, making a beeline for the staircase leading up to Anya's room. But despite Samantha's best efforts to be careful, the box of clothes in her hands slid as she moved. She froze as a thud echoed through the sitting room. *Damn, that must be the heavy Givenchy leather boots.*

Anya's mother and Cassandra immediately whirled around. The former wore a bright floral Dolce & Gabbana dress, while Cassandra's whippet-thin figure was clad in a Chanel tweed jumpsuit and matching jacket, her hair pulled back in a severe bun that emphasized her square forehead.

Cassandra's face brightened. "Anya, I haven't seen you in a while. Bring your friend and come sit with us," she instructed as if she were the lady of the house. Beside her, Anya's mother puckered her mouth like she had sucked on a lemon.

"Cassandra, it's so nice seeing you again," Anya said as she approached the guest. "This is my friend—"

"Samantha Song!" Cassandra beamed. "I knew I recognized you from the Gucci event at Straits Clan last week."

Suddenly aware that she was still carrying the bulky box and probably looked like the help, Samantha quickly set it down and hitched on a bright smile of her own. "Cassandra! I didn't get a chance to tell you at Straits Clan, but I thought your dress was so elegant. Gave me total Grace Kelly vibes."

"It's funny you should mention Grace Kelly, because wasn't she known for her charity work? Well, style isn't the only thing she and I have in common," Cassandra said coyly. "I was just telling Janice here that I've quite an interesting nonprofit project on my hands and I'm hoping to pick your brains for a bit. I'm sure you young people will have much more interesting ideas than us two old ladies!"

"Oh, please, Cassandra, you are so not old," Anya said automatically. "I was actually going to ask you for your skin-care routine. I don't even think Instagram filters can make my skin look as dewy as yours."

Samantha kept quiet. Cassandra was probably around Ma's age, but the socialite's undoubtedly expensive upkeep, not to mention being free from financial worries and a manual job surrounded by noxious chemicals, meant she looked at least ten years younger than Ma.

A preening Cassandra opened her mouth, but Anya quickly continued, "Anyway, what's your project about?"

Cassandra straightened up. "Drumroll please!" She waited a moment, but the other three women simply stared back at her.

Undeterred, Cassandra smoothed back her already slick bun and announced, "Ladies, I'm going to be a published author soon." She nodded firmly as though she could hear surprised gasps all around her. "That's right, I'm releasing a cookbook—*Deluxe Eats for the Discerning Diner.*"

Samantha blinked. "For sale?" Cassandra Ow and Anya's mother, Janice Chen, belonged more to the faction termed politely as "professional socialites"—women famous more for how they spent their husbands' (or ex-husbands') fortunes than for doing any actual work.

"For charity!" Cassandra beamed. "You see, I'm part of the Singapore Women's Committee for the Advancement of Disadvantaged Youths, and a board position recently opened up." She clapped a hand on Anya's mother's arm. "Janice, I'm sure you know how prestigious being part of the committee board is."

Without waiting for a response, Cassandra turned back to Samantha and Anya. "Writing checks and organizing fundraising parties are all very admirable, of course, but anyone with money can do that. To really impress the board, I have to get creative, and that's when my idea struck me!" Her eyes widened theatrically. "I'm going to write a cookbook and donate the proceeds to The Hunger Project—I've already got a publishing deal lined up with Paradise Books. Brilliant, no?"

"Very brilliant," Anya agreed so easily that Samantha had to take a sip of water so she wouldn't laugh. Anyone who knew Anya well knew better than to fall for this simpering sweetness. "It looks like you've got it all figured out, Cassandra. I don't see how we can help."

"The thing is, I'm not impressed with Paradise's marketing plan so far. They are a rather small establishment," Cassandra said delicately, "so I don't think they have much experience handling grand projects like mine. Do you girls have any ideas of what I can do to promote my book?"

"What about TropicalChef?" Anya suggested. "He's a food blogger with twenty thousand Instagram followers. Maybe you can get him to host a cooking demo on Instagram Live?"

Samantha glanced at Anya. How did her friend, who only dined at the most high-end restaurants, even know of Tropical-Chef? The middle-aged man was famous for his advice on how to meal prep on a budget.

"And social media's definitely important, but I think roping in the mainstream media will help too," Anya continued. "What about sending your cookbook to foodie magazines like *Cook and Crate*? I remember seeing a copy of that in my gyne's office."

"*Cook and Crate*," Cassandra repeated beneath her breath as she jotted it down on her phone.

This time, Samantha threw Anya a longer look, but her friend either didn't notice or didn't understand. *Cook and Crate?* Whose main draw was the roll of produce coupons at the back of every issue? At this rate, Cassandra's cookbook promotion was headed nowhere, and what if she blamed Anya afterward?

Samantha couldn't hold herself back anymore. "Cassandra, correct me if I'm wrong, but I don't think your main goal is to make a splash on the culinary scene."

"That's right," Cassandra said cheerfully, patting her chignon. "I just need people to hear about how passionate I am about philanthropy."

"Yes, but you want to make sure it's the right people—the women who run the committee board. Anya definitely has the right ideas and she knows social media inside and out," Samantha said carefully. "But I've helped out on a few cookery projects at work before, so I might be a bit more familiar with the players in the local culinary landscape."

Cassandra tilted her head. "Go on."

"Well, I just don't think TropicalChef and *Cook and Crate* are aligned with the image you're trying to portray. When I think of them, I think of cozy recipes and cheap cai fan, not deluxe or discerning. They aren't the best fit for your status, or the status of the committee you're trying to join."

Cassandra knit her brows. "Oh, I wasn't aware that's their image. To be honest, I've actually never heard of them, but I just figured they might be something only you hip young people know about. Oh dear, what should I do? My book's coming out in a few weeks, and if it doesn't arrive with a splash, I'll look so pathetic."

Samantha's mind kicked into overdrive. Hadn't Heather, her manager at Arrow, been complaining lately their F&B team was too stagnant and needed to attract new business? Here was Cassandra, someone much more country club than community club, to borrow Anya's descriptor—in other words, very unlike Arrow's typical clientele. But if she took on Cassandra's project, this might carve out a more high-end profile not only for Arrow, but also for herself—*this* was the kind of upscale project that might catch S's eye.

Samantha cleared her throat. "As you might know, Anya and I both work at Arrow Public Relations, and it just so happens I'm on the food and beverage team. I think we'd be a perfect fit for what you're trying to do."

She kept her eyes on Cassandra, ignoring the incredulity she could sense rolling off Anya in waves. Cassandra squinted. "What kind of projects has your team handled in the past? Anything similar to mine?"

"Arrow is a very selective boutique agency," Samantha said smoothly. No need to admit the cookbook launches her team had handled previously bore titles like *Hawker Dishes for the Singapore Soul* and *Mom's Home Cooking Made Easy*. "We deliberately keep our list small to give each client the attention and time they deserve."

Cassandra crossed one leg over the other. "What are you thinking for my project?"

Samantha leaned forward. For years, she had been reading about high-society parties, and over time, those profiles and descriptions had sunk into her mind almost by osmosis. Finally, there was a way to put her knowledge to good use.

"For starters, we're going to engage the country's top influencers and celebrities to hype up your book; I've already got a list in mind. And those culinary magazines aren't enough—I'm going to get you featured in all the top society magazines, and I've the connections to make that happen. And on the day your book comes out, let's go big with an exciting launch party. We'll hire a top chef to whip up your recipes for the party guests—perhaps Julien from Odette?"

Cassandra tapped a finger against her chin. The diamond rosary bracelet on her wrist caught the overhead light, sending a bright flash into Samantha's eyes that made her blink. "Judging from how well you were mingling at the Gucci event, I don't doubt you know all the right people. And your ideas do sound fantastic. But can you actually deliver what you're promising?"

Samantha met Cassandra's beady gaze and nodded. "Absolutely."

Cassandra clapped her hands together. "That's exactly what I want to hear! I can already imagine photos of the table settings from my launch party appearing in *S*." She turned to Anya's mother. "Janice, isn't it such a stroke of luck I ran into Samantha today? With her help, the committee's board members will be lining up to attend my party."

Anya's mother was smiling the way Ma did whenever she received a difficult customer at the nail salon. "That would be lovely," she said, then coughed lightly. "You know, I've been thinking about joining a charity board. Now that Anya's working, I've more time on my hands, and some philanthropic work is just what I need to fill my schedule."

Cassandra tutted. "Philanthropy isn't meant to be a schedule filler. You should only do it if you are genuinely passionate about helping people."

It took a considerable amount of effort for Samantha to not roll her eyes. This coming from the woman who was more worried about seeming pathetic if her book failed than the hungry kids she was supposedly eager to help.

Janice Chen's smile turned slightly strained. "Of course. I just meant that I'm glad I can now give more of my time and attention to helping others."

Cassandra patted her friend's hand. "Once I'm on the board, maybe I can nominate you for the membership vacancy I freed up. And even if it's not the Singapore Women's Committee, I'm sure I can refer you to some others I'm a part of."

Samantha felt Anya stiffen next to her. But before she could think more about it, Cassandra's eyes were on her again. "Samantha, you can get my contact details from Anya. I'm very excited about your plans for my project. Have your company send me a quote, but really, that's just a formality—I'll spare no expense to make my book launch a success!"

A FURTHER FIFTEEN minutes ensued of Cassandra gushing about her committee and her cookbook before Anya said, "Sam, don't you have to leave soon?"

Samantha immediately caught on. "Yeah, thanks for reminding me. Let's drop off my stuff in your room now."

They bade farewell to Janice and Cassandra before heading up to Anya's room. The moment the door shut, Anya burst out, "I can't stand her!" She tossed a throw pillow off a burgundy armchair and plopped down, splaying her legs over one arm.

The vehemence in her friend's voice made Samantha's brows shoot up. "Cassandra? Yeah, she's kinda phony. But her charm offensive strategy is similar to what we're doing as the Fraud Squad, no?" she asked, dumping the box of clothes on the floor and sinking into the armchair opposite Anya's.

There was an identical throw pillow taking up half of the chair. Samantha was about to toss it off like Anya did, but the pillow's Hermès insignia gave her pause. Nothing costing three figures should ever be flung so irreverently on the floor, so she dragged it onto her lap and held it gingerly by the corners.

"I don't give a damn about her dumb charity project. In fact, I was giving her the most ridiculous suggestions so her book promotion would tank."

Samantha's eyes widened. "I thought something seemed off with you, so I tried stepping in to help you out. But why would you want to sabotage your mom's friend? You heard Cassandra—if she's elected to the board, she might be able to make your mom a committee member."

"Friend?" Anya scoffed. "Did you not hear the way Cassandra talks to my mom—talks *down* to my mom? The whole time, she was trying to rub it in my mom's face that they're on different levels—Cassandra's on her way to joining the board while my mom isn't even a regular member."

Samantha stared at her friend, slightly sickened. First Tim and Clement; now Janice and Cassandra. Besides Tim and Anya, did anyone in high society genuinely like each other? "Why would your mom even put up with that? Or invite Cassandra over?"

Anya sighed, her eyes fixed on a rubber bone toy on the floor. "She can't exactly afford to be picky about her friends, not if we want to remain in the mix and still get invited to parties."

"But you were invited to the Kingstons' dinner party. That's gotta mean something—Tim's mom basically rules high society."

Anya's expression went pinched. "But notice how they didn't invite my mom? Albert and Eileen are nice to me because I'm Tim's good friend. But more importantly, Albert was my dad's business partner before my parents even met. Most people in high society couldn't care less about my mom once she was no longer Mrs. Fo Tian Chen." Each syllable of the name came out flinty sharp. "And because she's the one who got custody of me, everyone associates me with her, which has done no favors for *my* reputation."

The undisguised bitterness in Anya's voice made Samantha wince. "I'm sorry."

"Don't be." Anya chuckled humorlessly. "It's not like any of this was your fault."

"I'm sorry for offering to work with Cassandra. I didn't realize—"

Anya waved her hand. "It's cool. You wouldn't have known about her deal with my mom anyway." Suddenly, her face broke into a grin. "A highly selective boutique agency? Where the hell did you get that from?"

Anya's voice was a little too bright, but she was smiling so determinedly Samantha had to go along with the abrupt subject change. "The same place Cassandra got her 'small publisher' cover-up from. How much do you want to bet that she's paying them to publish her book?"

"You couldn't pay me to work with her. Cassandra is super demanding, and with all your Fraud Squad commitments, do you even have time to take on such a big project? We're going out every night next week."

"It's precisely *because* of our Fraud Squad plan that I'm doing this. Cassandra might be a hard-ass, but she's a really high-profile hard-ass. If I pull off her project, it could totally put me on Missy's radar. After that dinner party fiasco, I need to do everything I can to change her impression of me, especially with the gala less than two months away."

"Why, you sneaky little—" A smirk crossed Anya's face. "I like this," she declared. "I'm all for you using Cassandra for your own agenda. Serves her right for being so passive-aggressive toward my mom."

Anya leapt up from her armchair. "Since you'll be seeing so much of Cassandra, you should start dressing the part even at work," she called over her shoulder as she strode toward her walk-in closet and flung the door open. A moment later, she turned around, holding up a blush-pink sheath. "Wear this Carolina Herrera dress to your next meeting. My mom told me that's Cassandra's favorite brand."

Samantha jumped to her feet, her heart swelling. She carefully deposited the Hermès cushion and hurried over to Anya. Most relationships in high society might be two-faced, but with true friends like Anya and Tim by her side, she could handle anyone.

CHAPTER

12

After hours of trying on clothes and eating a gluten-free dinner (thankfully without Cassandra), Anya drove Samantha home. When she entered the flat, Samantha did a double take. It was past ten, but Ma, who was usually so exhausted from work she would head to bed right after dinner, was still at the dining table. She was squinting at a sheaf of papers, her head propped up on her good hand. But at the sound of the door opening, she looked up, her tired eyes brightening slightly. "Sam! Come here for a sec, I need your help."

Samantha put down her new box of clothes and went up to the dining table. Her mother pushed the pile of documents toward her, jabbing at strings of numbers and words that quickly blurred into an indistinguishable jumble. "What do these all mean? Can you translate the terms for me? And which financial subsidies do we qualify for?"

The questions pounded in Samantha's head like a jackhammer. "Hang on, don't you know these already? We've been applying to these subsidies for years."

"Aiya, the government changes their policies every other day. How's anyone supposed to keep up?"

Samantha plopped down on the only other folding chair and flipped through the pages. In their mix were the financial aid forms she would collect from the community center every six months. "I guess you'll get the usual debt relief subsidies—"

"I know that," her mother cut in. "I'm asking about the tax breaks for widows. Your father's death anniversary is coming up soon and I want to make sure those benefits haven't expired."

Samantha's hands tightened around the forms. "Wow, yeah. It's been almost a full decade since he left us," she said softly. She looked around the dining table, remembering the days when it held a complete family. So much time had passed since then that she had to strain to remember the sound of her father's guffaw, the scent of his slightly pungent cologne that he always spritzed on excessively, how he used to always make her drink a spoonful of cod-liver oil before she left for school, claiming the omega-3 would make her smarter. He hadn't lived long enough to see her graduate from university—the first in their family to do so.

"Horrible, isn't it?" her mother said absently as she scanned the forms. "The amount of widow benefits I get drops drastically after ten years."

Samantha's eyes snapped to her mother. "Don't speak about Ba like that," she said in a low, tight voice. "As though he only matters in terms of how much he can help us save."

Her mother looked up and raised one brow. "Excuse me, missy? Those tax deductions were the one good thing that came out of that man's death, so excuse me for trying to work with the little we have. Do you think I'm spending those benefits on myself? All of that money goes toward repaying the debt that *he* stuck us in!"

She had been speaking levelly at first, but by the end, her voice had risen to a crescendo. Samantha stared wide-eyed at her mother, wondering if she had ever seen the older woman so emotional before. "Ma, I'm sorry," she said, her voice softened by shame.

"I didn't mean to criticize you, but it hurts me when you always call Ba 'that man' as though he didn't mean anything. Remember the stories you used to tell me of your relationship? How he proposed to you? You two loved—"

"Samantha, you're being too sentimental. I'm not saying that's a bad thing," Ma said in a voice that indicated it was a bad thing. "But I don't have room to indulge in sentiment when I'm already doing all I can just to keep our heads above the water."

"I know, but—"

"You're just like your father," Ma continued, her voice back to its usual steadiness, but the five words alone were enough to make Samantha shrink back in her seat, a sense of foreboding building within her. "I only agreed he could use our savings on his business venture because he swore up and down it would make us millions. But instead of sourcing from the best suppliers, that sentimental fool decided to work with his childhood friend who he said was like a brother to him. *A trustworthy worker is harder to find than a skilled one*, he told me. Which was all fine and well right up until the moment that supposedly trustworthy friend gambled away all our money."

At that, Ma's voice cracked. She turned quickly away, but not before Samantha saw the wetness in her eyes. Guilt seared her like a fiery wave, instantly drowning out her previous anger. After all these years, the events that led to their present situation was still a fresh wound for her mother, and she hated herself for being the one to rip the stitches wide open. "Ma, I am so sorry" was all Samantha could say.

When Ma looked back at her, her eyes were dry but ringed with red. "It's okay. I know you're a good girl, but your heart is too soft. You think the loan sharks who hounded him day and night cared that he had a wife and a young daughter? Of course not. They didn't care that he became so stressed he suffered a heart attack before he even turned forty, leaving us behind with his debt."

The older woman's throat throbbed as she swallowed, and her

eyes dropped to her bare ring finger. "And just because we loved him doesn't change the reality that I can't even bear to spend money on a doctor for myself because I'm still trying to pay off his hospital bills. The world doesn't operate by sentiment but by money."

"Ma, I get where you're coming from," Samantha said in her gentlest voice. She grasped her mother's hands, marveling as she always did at the contrast between her fancy manicure and the age spots on her hands. "I know how hard you've worked for this family and how much you've sacrificed over the years. And I want to do everything I can to make your life better."

Her mother smiled, but it was a fragile and tired attempt that only emphasized the crow's-feet around her eyes. "Sammy . . ." she sighed. "You're a good girl. But I've accepted this is the life I'm meant to lead." She squeezed Samantha's hands before letting go. "However, it's still not too late for you—you can still meet a better man than I did, a man who can provide for you all the things you never had while growing up."

Samantha lowered her eyes, scalded by the resignation written all over her mother's face. "I don't need a man to provide for me. I can support myself."

"Even if you can, I don't want you to have to," her mother said softly. "It breaks my heart you never got to enjoy a carefree childhood like your friends did, and you still have to handle responsibilities no young woman should face. And yes, I'm glad you have a university degree and a better job than me, but are you truly satisfied with our life? Don't you hope for something more?"

Samantha looked up as Ma gestured around their flat, her eyes catching on the Windex stains on their scratched dining tabletop, the tears in their worn faux-leather couch, and the jumble of foam slippers piled around the doorway, their soles caked with grime. Had she worn those to Timothy's house today, she would have definitely left a scuff on the tea room's perfectly white rug.

"Look at all those ladies I do nails for—many of them never had to work a day in their lives because they married well. And look at your friend Anya. Her parents are divorced, but you told me her mother received so many stocks and assets as part of her settlement, and she's still getting half a million every month from her ex-husband. Meanwhile, I get half a million in debt. Really, *Xué dé hǎo bùrú jià dé hǎo*'—'It's better to marry well than to study well.'"

In that moment, Samantha had a strong urge to confide in her mother about the Fraud Squad's scheme. She imagined the deep furrow between her mother's brows smoothing out as she painted a picture of the lavish establishments she had stepped foot in over the past month, the whirlwind of extravagant parties, and the people so fantastically wealthy and powerful they seemed to come from another planet altogether.

But Samantha stopped herself from blurting it out. Ba's business had looked like it was going well . . . until it wasn't. She might be living the high life now, but it was only thanks to Tim's connections and Anya's clothes. She wouldn't tell her mother anything until she had achieved her own success, until she had an S Gala invitation in the bag—the surest confirmation her life was finally on the right track.

Samantha pulled the benefits forms toward her. "What did you want my help with again?"

Instead of responding, her mother just looked at her for a long moment. Samantha chuckled nervously and rubbed a hand over her mouth. "What? Is there food stuck in my teeth?" Anya's mother had served cauliflower "steak" for dinner, and those pesky florets were sometimes hard to dislodge.

A smile flickered on Ma's face. It was just the barest curl of the corners of her lips, but she suddenly looked a lot more like the woman Samantha remembered from her childhood, before stress had etched deep crevices into her face. "No, I'm just thinking that no matter how angry I am with him, I could never regret meeting your father. Without him, there wouldn't be you."

The older woman reached out to smooth back her daughter's hair. Samantha closed her eyes, savoring this rare moment of tenderness from her mother. Ma always said she didn't want to touch Samantha with the same hands she used to clean people's feet for sixty hours a week.

Ma withdrew her hand. "Go to sleep. You must have had a long week at work."

Samantha's eyes flew open. "No, let me help you with the forms."

"It's okay. These aren't for you to worry about."

"But—"

"Sammy, you use your brain at work the whole day, so I bet you can't even think straight now. Me—I just use my hands at work, so I can handle these." Ma swatted Samantha on the arm with a roll of paper. "Now, shoo! Off you go to bed."

Samantha stared at her mother for a moment longer. Was it her imagination, or did Ma seem to have even more white hair than last week? In an alternate universe, one where she didn't have to work her fingers to the bone to support her family, would Ma look more like Eileen Kingston and Cassandra Ow—skin unblemished, eyes untouched by dark circles, and without the permanent groove between her brows that came from furrowing them too much?

"Good night, Ma. You sleep early too," she finally said.

Her mother nodded absently, already rifling through the financial forms once more. Samantha picked up her bag and headed to her room, unable to get the image of Ma working at the dining table out of her head.

She lay in bed for what felt like hours, tossing and turning, her eyes caught on the crack beneath her door where a sliver of light shone through from the living room. It was a long time before she finally drifted off to sleep. And even then, the living room lights were still on.

CHAPTER

13

Samantha took a deep breath and brushed her clammy palms against her pencil skirt before rapping smartly on her manager's office door. Even though she was the one who had asked Heather for this meeting to discuss Cassandra Ow's book, the prospect of a one-on-one was still terrifying, especially since this was her first time pitching a project.

"Come in!" Heather called out, her voice muffled by the thick wooden door.

The moment Samantha sat down, Heather began, "I've a busy day, so let's cut right to it. I've taken a look at the proposal you sent me, and I'm confused about why you would think this cookbook is a good fit for us."

Samantha's hands started sweating again. "Well, uh, we've done some cookbook launches before, so I figured—"

"Bill Gates and I both breathe, but I wouldn't presume we lead the same lives." Heather put on her reading glasses and peered at her computer. "I skimmed the e-book you sent me. At least half the recipes include langoustine, foie gras, king crab, or bird's nest as an ingredient. We could play a drinking game with the number of times the words 'organic,' 'holistic,' 'gourmet,' and 'artisan' appeared. And on page one hundred eighteen, for a recipe for caviar and crème fraîche blini"—she cleared her throat—"*Caviar should never be served on stainless steel or silver. Every good hostess knows to use a mother-of-pearl, bone, or gold-plated caviar spoon.*"

Beneath the table, Samantha's fingers curled into her palms as she tried to quell her rising panic. Arrow associates were not allowed to take on new projects without their manager's permission, and she should have cleared it with Heather before signing Cassandra as a client. But if she hadn't acted immediately, Cassandra might have very well taken her ideas to another PR agency, and she would have lost this chance altogether. However, it meant there was now a very real possibility she would have to slink back to Cassandra, shamefaced, and admit she couldn't take on this project after all.

"Samantha, you did the calculations. With the cookbook priced at fifty-nine ninety-nine, this Cassandra Ow woman would need to sell at least a thousand copies just to break even. This is a country where food courts reign supreme and people come to blows over where to find the most affordable chicken rice. Tell me—how are you going to find a thousand people who even give a damn about special caviar spoons?"

Samantha mustered a shaky smile. "The good news is, the client doesn't care about profits. She's just . . . a very enthusiastic food lover who wants to do whatever it takes to share her favorite recipes with the world." Actually, Cassandra's own, much less diplomatic words were "my husband and I will be more than happy to cover the donation to the Hunger Project. I don't care how many copies the public buys as long as all the right people hear about my book."

Heather wrinkled her nose. "Seriously? That's so eccentric."

If only Heather knew even half the eccentric antics those socialites got up to—that was, if "eccentric" were simply a euphemism for "devious." Samantha cleared her throat. "Also, as I mentioned in my proposal, the client is setting aside a massive five-figure marketing budget, so we're well covered on that front."

"That does make things easier," Heather conceded, but her voice was still laced with doubt. "However, I also have an issue with your proposed guest list and media partners. Many of them are huge names who can't even be paid to attend an event they're not interested in. I hope you aren't making any false promises to the client."

Samantha straightened up. "Absolutely no false promises. I've already discussed those with Cassandra, and she's fully confident I have the connections to make those happen."

Heather raised an eyebrow. "And where exactly are your . . . *connections* from?"

"Uh, just from my personal life." Even if the Fraud Squad plan didn't succeed, at least all the networking and socializing she had done for it was being put to some use.

Heather's face took on a weird expression Samantha had never seen before from her demanding manager. It took her a few moments to decipher it: Heather was *impressed*. Samantha almost wanted to laugh. After all the late nights she had pulled and the extensive research she had done for the *Deluxe Eats* proposal, the one thing that had finally impressed Heather was her personal connections.

But the next moment, Heather's brow sank back into its usual frown. "Your plan is well-thought-out, but I'm just not sure this project is aligned with Arrow's ethos."

Samantha wanted to scream in frustration. Instead, she smoothed the sleeves of her Veronica Beard jumpsuit and leaned forward. "Heather, you were the one who said we're stagnating and need to branch out more. We've lost quite a few clients because of the recession, so this project is exactly what we need."

"I meant we need to get new clients, not posher ones."

"But why shouldn't we aim higher? We don't have to become the *S* of PR agencies, but we could carve out a luxury niche for ourselves and offer different tiers of service for different levels of clients. Cassandra Ow's a big name in Singapore society. and if her project goes well, it could catapult us"—*and me*—"into a whole new stratosphere."

"Samantha, as you said, we're in a recession," Heather said flatly. "Cassandra might be eccentric enough to not care about profits, but most clients would. If we take on more high-end clients, how can we guarantee them the reception they want? People aren't interested in buying luxe products now when the economy is shit."

Channeling her inner Missy, Samantha clasped her hands on the desk and looked Heather in the eye. The project's success—the project happening—depended entirely on the outcome of this meeting. "The economy isn't doing great now, but my Goldman Sachs vice president friend said there are encouraging signs domestic consumption is on the upswing." Thank God for all the mansplaining Clement did at Cé La Vi.

"And as the economy recovers, we need to be ahead of the curve. In a recession, it's our current clients who must cut back more, but high-end clients can still afford significant marketing budgets. So diversifying our client base beyond the low-to-mid-budget market can actually help cushion us if the economy takes another downturn."

Heather removed her glasses and gazed up at the ceiling, tapping her fingers against her desk. Her long nails made a steady click-clacking sound that fanned the flames of Samantha's nerves. After an unbearably prolonged silence, her eyes snapped back to Samantha. "Fine."

Samantha held her breath. "Fine, as in . . . I can do this project?" This entire conversation felt like playing Whac-a-Mole with Heather's never-ending questions.

"Yes. But I can't spare anyone else to help you on something so risky, so you'll be working on this alone."

"No problem," Samantha said, her body finally untensing. This was the first project she had ever initiated—the first time she would ever get to apply her vision from start to finish; it hadn't even kicked off yet, and she already felt a fierce ownership over it.

"You know, Samantha, I was actually getting quite concerned about your work performance," Heather continued, putting on her glasses again and peering at her over the half-moon lenses. "For the past few weeks, you've been booking it out of the office at six on the dot every day."

Samantha's cheeks reddened. This past fortnight, the number of society invitations she had received had rocketed—great for the Fraud Squad's scheme, but not so great for her job performance.

"So I'm pleasantly surprised you took the initiative to source for this client and prepare this proposal. I still have my reservations about how this could turn out, but you make a strong case for it. And if everything goes like you said, this might very well launch Arrow into the big leagues," Heather said, a grin spreading across her face.

Samantha felt her own mouth tug up into a smile. Forget Arrow. If Cassandra Ow's project went well, this could launch *her* into the big leagues.

14

Samantha squinted at her laptop screen. Four neat columns stared back at her: **MUST-HAVE GUESTS**, **MUST-HAVE MEDIA**, **SECONDARY GUESTS**, and **SECONDARY MEDIA**. It was nearly midnight, but official invitations for the *Deluxe Eats* launch party would be sent out tomorrow, and it was her job to make sure all the details were right and that the bespoke Benneton Graveur stationery was ready and stamped with Cassandra's monogram. So far, everything was right on track.

Unless people don't want to come . . .

Samantha whipped her curls into a bun, trying to squash the anxiety thrumming through her like a live wire. The socialite-influencers would probably attend since they were always looking for a reason to be out and about, but it was the luxury magazines who were the true movers and shakers of high-society opinion. And their RSVPs were far from guaranteed. Back at *Tatler*, even the interns received a dozen press releases and PR invitations every day, which meant making snap decisions about the ones not worth going for.

In hindsight, she probably could have been more sympathetic about how hard the PR staffers had it.

Samantha's ringing phone pierced the still night air. It came from an unfamiliar number, but she answered it anyway. Partly so it wouldn't wake Ma up, but mostly because anything would be a welcome distraction from the self-doubt swirling around her mind.

"Hi, Samantha! This is Winston. I don't know if you remember me, but I asked for your number at the Christian Dada event in case I needed to follow up with you about your quote."

Winston . . . from Elle? "Of course I remember you." Samantha's voice perked up as a thought struck her. "In fact, you're just the person I want to talk to."

A laugh drifted down the line. "Funny, that's what I was going to say to you. But ladies first."

For a moment, Samantha smiled as she imagined Raina's reaction toward such an "unfeminist" statement, but quickly snapped to attention. "So, I do PR at a communications firm under Merlion Media, and we have a huge project coming up."

"Merlion Media? That's the company S is under, right?"

"That's right," Samantha said casually, as though that wasn't the main reason she had name-dropped Merlion Media in the first place. Winston might not have heard of Arrow Public Relations, but any association with S—however tangential—was sure to pique his interest. If there was one thing she knew, it was how competitive the magazine publishing industry was. "Do you know Cassandra Ow? Yes, her husband is the chairman of Royal Rubbers. Well, Cassandra has written a cookbook that I know will be a great fit for your readership. I'm organizing her launch party, and I'd love to have you there."

"When's this party?"

"Friday three weeks from now."

Samantha held her breath. Securing Winston's attendance would make it much easier to reach out to the other media outlets with a casual mention they'd be in the company of renowned publications like *Elle*.

"I won't be able to make it—"

Samantha swallowed her disappointment. "No worries. I—"

"But I can send another writer along."

Samantha's hand clenched around her phone. "Great," she said, her calm tone belying her excitement. "If you can give me their email, I'll send them an official invite and press kit ASAP."

"Wonderful. I can't wait to see what you come up with. In my experience, socialites always throw the best parties because they themselves have been to so many good ones." Winston cleared his throat. "Anyway, I do have an ulterior motive—I'm hoping you'll now say yes to *my* request. *Elle*'s been engaged to do an advertorial for Bulgari's latest fine jewelry collection coming out in mid-August. Since that coincides with the Qixi Festival, the Chinese Valentine's Day, my idea is to make love the theme of this campaign. It will totally win over the Chinese market."

"That's brilliant!"

"Right?" Winston sounded pleased. "I'm glad you think so because I'm looking for three of *Elle*'s young society friends to front this advertorial. I'm sure you know where I'm going with this . . ."

Samantha pressed the phone closer to her ear to make sure she hadn't misheard. "Me? You want to feature *me*?"

Winston chuckled. "That's right. You were so well-spoken at the Christian Dada event that I thought of you immediately."

In the reflection of her computer screen, Samantha saw her wide eyes and parted mouth. *Is this seriously happening?* A feature in *Elle* would be a surefire booster for her socialite profile.

"Winston, I'd love to do this," she said evenly, as though interview requests fell into her lap all the time. No one listening in would have guessed she was shrieking on the inside in the most undignified manner.

"Perfect. You'll model a piece from the Bulgari collection in a photo shoot. And then there's going to be an interview where you'll share a personal story about love."

"Uh, I'm not dating anyone right now."

"It can also be from a past relationship. It doesn't even have to be about you—it could be about your parents, for instance. Just as long as it's something that has left an impression on you."

Samantha swallowed. "Right. I'll think of something."

"I can't wait to hear it, especially after you set the bar so high with your great response at the Christian Dada event. And I've no doubt your photos will come out beautifully."

By the time she and Winston finished discussing the photo shoot details, there was no way Samantha could bring herself to keep working on *Deluxe Eats*. Scoring the coup of *Elle*'s presence at the launch party entitled her to a well-deserved break. So once Winston hung up, Samantha snapped her laptop shut and automatically hit one on her speed dial. If she didn't share this amazing news with Raina, she might just combust from pure excitement.

But before the call could connect, Samantha hung up. After a moment, she clicked two on her speed dial instead. The celebrating could wait; what she *really* needed was advice for the biggest step she'd taken so far in the Fraud Squad plan.

After a few rings, Anya picked up. "Hi, sorry if I sound weird," she said, her voice lapsing in and out. "I'm in my closet right now and the connection is pretty bad."

"Hey! That's totally fine. Do you remember Winston, the *Elle* writer who spoke to us at the Christian Dada event? Guess what? He just called and said he wants me to appear in *Elle*!"

"Whoa. Is this some follow-up to the Christian Dada thing?"

"No, it's going to be so much bigger than that!" Samantha leapt up and began pacing around the dining table, needing to channel her exhilaration into some physical activity. "I'll be fronting a campaign for Bulgari's latest jewelry collection. This could really take my high-society profile to a whole new level!" A fresh wave of excitement surged in her with every word. "There's going to be a photo shoot and an interview, but I've never done something like this before. How should I prepare myself?"

For a long moment, there was nothing but crackling static. "Anya? Can you hear me?"

"Yes. Why are you so nervous when it's obvious Winston thinks very highly of you?"

Samantha paused. Anya's voice sounded oddly flat, but maybe that was just because of the poor connection in her massive walk-in closet. "It's way easier talking about a brand than about myself. And it's not just the interview I'm nervous about; there's also the photo shoot."

A hollow feeling crept into Samantha's stomach. Why did she think she could do this? She had always been the one admiring the pretty magazine photos, not starring in them. Winston would probably regret ever asking her to participate once he saw how stiff her poses were, her inexperience obvious next to the other two socialites.

Samantha held back a groan as a new thought struck her. In her excitement and panic, she had forgotten to ask Winston who else was participating in the campaign.

Anya sighed. "Sam, listen, it's all going to be fine. It's really no big deal. Since you're so nervous about it, maybe you should take a rain check on this. Anyway, I have to go now. I'm in the middle of trying on my recent Balmain haul to see if any of the dresses are good enough for my birthday party."

"Isn't that still over a month away?"

"Damn. You're right—the trends would have totally changed by then."

Samantha laughed. "Anya! I meant isn't now still too early to decide your party outfit?"

Anya made a *pfft* sound. "Of course not. I'm inviting lots of important people and media representatives to my party, so I *have* to look my best. Anyway, let me know what you decide to do about this *Elle* thing, okay? You shouldn't do it if it stresses you out so much. Love ya!"

Samantha sank back into her chair as the line went dead. The call had done nothing to dispel her nerves, only exacerbate them. But there was still one person who could help; she had never seen Tim in a magazine before, but he might have picked up some tips from his mother, a regular in Asia's society publications.

Timothy answered her call almost immediately. "Sam! What's up?"

"Hey, you. Remember the *Elle* article I was quoted in a few weeks ago? Well, the writer just asked me to participate in an advertorial for Bulgari. I'll be doing an interview, photo shoot, the whole shebang."

Timothy let out such a loud whoop that Samantha's eyes automatically darted to her mother's room even though it was completely impossible for the sound to have traveled so far. "Look at you, taking high society by storm! This is better than anything I could have expected for our scheme."

The obvious sincerity in his voice swaddled Samantha like a cozy blanket, warming her from the inside out. Tim was right: This was taking *Socialite Samantha Song* to a whole new level—an opportunity she couldn't possibly turn down regardless of how nerve-racking it might be.

"Tell me all the details of this advertorial."

Samantha leaned back in her chair and stretched her legs out. "It's based on Qixi—"

"What's that?"

"The Chinese Valentine's Day, happening in mid-August. I'm gonna have to come up with some romantic anecdote to share in my interview."

"Well, I'm sure you have plenty of options to choose from."

Samantha furrowed her brows. What was it with her two friends today? First Anya and now Tim also had a weird edge to his voice. "What's that supposed to mean?"

There was a pause before Timothy replied, "Just, you know, I bet you are pretty popular with the guys."

"What, you think I'm some sort of loose woman?" Samantha joked, but the sting of Timothy's words hit her more than she expected.

"Of course not! You can date whoever you want. It doesn't matter to me how many people you've been with." He was saying all the right things, but it sounded to Samantha like her dating past *did* matter to him.

She fired back, "And how many ex-girlfriends have *you* had?"

His reply was swift: "None, if Lucia and I get back together after our break."

So, Lucia wasn't just Timothy's girlfriend but also his first love. His first everything. "Wow. Lucia's really 'the one' for you, huh?" she asked softly, surprised by the heaviness that had suddenly filled her chest.

A pause, then: "I feel like I'm still too young to really know who's 'the one.' Lucia and I've known each other our whole lives, and it's easy dating someone from the same world who understands how crazy things can get."

From the same world. Samantha's heart clenched. *You aren't his type,* taunted Lucia in her head. "Yeah, you two are a good match," she managed.

Timothy sighed. "Not anymore. Lucia and I used to laugh about our parents' crazy demands together, but now, she's completely gone over to their side. I guess people change."

"I'm sure the Lucia you know is still there, somewhere," Samantha forced out over the rancid taste in her mouth. "If our scheme goes according to plan, she will come around to your perspective and you two will patch things up in no time. And isn't this *Elle* feature great news for our plan? Speaking of which, do you have any tips for how I can prepare for that?"

Samantha knew she was rambling, but didn't care. Their Fraud Squad plan was what they should have stuck to talking about, instead of digressing to unrelated topics like their respective relationship histories.

"You don't need tips. You probably know more than me about what makes a good interviewee since you've interviewed plenty of socialites for *Tatler* before."

Samantha's eyes fell on the tower of magazines stacked on the coffee table—the piles of *S*, *Elle*, and their contemporaries she had accumulated over the years, puffing up from the hundreds of dog-ears in between their pages. Whenever Ma threatened to sell the magazines to the karang guni man, Samantha would retort they served more use covering the table cracks than whatever pitiful amount the rag-and-bone man would pay for them.

At the top of the stack was a rather creased *Tatler* issue, the first that she'd ever had a byline in. The legs of the Barbie-like cover model—a local socialite even younger than she was—seemed to stretch on forever.

"Maybe . . . but what about the photo shoot? I've absolutely no clue how to pose," Samantha whispered, her eyes tracing the socialite's legs. "I'll look really stupid."

"Sam, I don't think it's possible for you to ever look bad," Timothy said, surely and steadily.

Despite herself, a blush blossomed across Samantha's cheeks.

15

There was a slight whiff of mildew hanging over the studio's walls, mixed in with a faint fragrance that screamed *luxury*. A man built like a tank stood by the doorway, wearing a polo shirt with the word **Security** on the back. He glanced up at the sound of Samantha's footsteps and checked her face against a piece of paper in his hands before waving her through and returning his attention to the padlocked case on the table beside him.

The Bulgari logo stood out in sharp relief against the white lid. Samantha eyed it, wishing she had X-ray vision. A couple of days ago, Winston had sent her a photo of the necklace she would be modeling, but nothing could compare to seeing it in person.

One entire end of the studio was taken up by a massive white screen. On set, the burly photographer fiddled with his camera while his assistant adjusted the lights. Matthieu, whom *Elle* had recently poached from *Her World* to be their new fashion director, prowled around them, gesticulating dramatically. A black-and-gold Versace bandanna cinched his shoulder-length platinum-blond hair into a ponytail, while a goatee in the same shade scruffed his pointy chin.

To one side, a willowy woman wearing a hijab was hunched over a rack that held a dozen floor-sweeping dresses. She stuck her tongue out slightly as she ran a handheld steamer carefully over every garment. At her feet lay two large duffel bags, each spilling forth a tangle of accessories—braided belts and veiled fascinators and feathery boas.

A sharp wave of nostalgia hit Samantha. Had it really been just two years ago when she was in that young woman's shoes at *Tatler*? She could feel the phantom weight of the photo shoot materials digging into her fingers as she lugged them into the studio, the heat of the clothes steamer scalding her hands, and the ever-constant fear she might ruin a five-figure couture piece if she brought the steamer too close.

And now, she would be the one modeling the couture.

"Thank God you're here!" a breathless voice cried out. Winston rushed up, his glasses askew on his nose and man bun sliding out of his hair band.

Samantha frowned at the note of panic in Winston's voice. "I'm not late, am I?" she asked, perfectly aware she wasn't. She had woken up at 5:35 a.m. in a fit of nerves and busied herself with the *Deluxe Eats* project until it was finally an acceptable hour to get ready for her 9:00 a.m. call time.

"No, but the other two ladies are! I've only booked the hair and makeup people till noon, and Matthieu and our photographer have to rush off to another assignment at one," Winston bleated, his hands flailing around his face, and nearly knocking his glasses off. "If they don't show up soon, we'll need to give the crew overtime pay and everyone's schedules will be messed up and—" He broke off as though just realizing he shouldn't be bad-mouthing any socialites.

Winston cleared his throat and continued more calmly. "Samantha, why don't you head off to hair and makeup first? It's over there." He nodded toward a small room tucked off in one corner of the studio before dashing away, leaving a stream of muttered curses in his wake.

With a small chuckle, Samantha walked over to the hair and makeup room. But her footsteps screeched to a halt when she caught sight of the call sheet taped to the door. "You've got to be kidding me." Beneath *Samantha Song*, the other two names read *Lucia Yen* and *Daisy Taija*.

Lucia standing by the side making snide remarks about my photo shoot poses. Lucia in the background rolling her eyes at my interview responses. Samantha's skin crawled. She had a sudden urge to turn around and flee out of the studio, but before she could do anything, an ebullient voice was exclaiming, "Darling, welcome!"

A bald man who made up for his lack of hair with an impressively bushy beard bustled up. "My name's Da Ming, but I'll kill anyone who calls me that," he said cheerfully as he dragged Samantha into the room and sat her down in front of a wall of mirrors. "I feel more like a Kim on the inside, ya feel me? Oh, forgot to mention—I'm your hairstylist. And before you say it, yes, I know how ironic it is that the man with no hair is in charge of yours."

Kim narrowed his eyes as he ran his fingers through Samantha's waves, before pronouncing, "Darling, your hair is sublime, absolutely sublime! I so very rarely work with natural curls with my Chinese clients. You're wearing this stunning art deco necklace and off-shoulder dress, so I'm going to put your hair up to show off your Parmigianino neck. Sounds good?"

The what neck? Without waiting for a response, Kim started rummaging through his caddy of hair products and tools. Samantha hid her smile. The hairstylist would probably stick with his vision even if she dared disagree.

Kim did enough talking for both him and the makeup artist,

whom he helpfully introduced as Cheryl, "the woman who can contour a nose on Voldemort." Cheryl didn't say a word as she whipped out a selection of brushes and palettes from her portable vanity, except to bark, "Hold still," once when Samantha sneezed from a ticklish brush.

But even Cheryl's brusqueness couldn't dampen Samantha's excitement. She leaned back in her chair and closed her eyes. When was the last time she had been pampered like this? Was this how Ma's salon customers felt, receiving top-notch attention from the nail technicians while getting their hands and feet beautified?

Crash! Samantha jumped in her seat as the door slammed open. The eyeliner's tip zigzagged crudely down one side of her face, but she ignored Cheryl's hiss of displeasure and craned her neck to investigate the intrusion, her heart thudding wildly—

Samantha sank back in her chair with a small sigh of relief. It wasn't Lucia but Daisy Taija in the doorway, escorted by a panting Winston.

Born and raised in Indonesia, Daisy had been appearing in Singapore more often in recent months, which tabloids attributed to an imminent separation between her Singaporean mother and Indonesian father. Her pastel-pink Valentino dress perfectly complemented her doll-like features: large round eyes, apple cheeks, and a snub button nose above a rosebud mouth.

"Hi, everyone, I'm so, so sorry I'm late," Daisy huffed out, a tangle of friendship bracelets sliding down her arm as she wrung her hands. "I went to pick up doughnuts for everyone, but I forgot Donut Delights opens only after noon and the peak-hour traffic was sooo bad."

Samantha gave a tiny wave from her chair. "Hi, I'm Sam! I adore Donut Delights too."

Daisy clapped her hands together. "What's your favorite flavor? Mine's the Biscoff Caramel Delight."

Winston coughed. "Uh, Daisy, since Sam's getting hair and makeup done now, why don't we get started on your interview first? Let's go to the back of the room, where it's quieter."

The two of them made their way to the other end of the room. Samantha closed her eyes again, savoring the faint lavender scent of the hair mousse and the rustle of brush bristles against her face. Everything was so calming, almost like a lullaby—

Crash!

Samantha jerked upright in her chair, her stomach twisting into knots. This time, there was only one person it could be.

"Sorry I'm late, everyone," Lucia said as she sauntered in, not sounding sorry at all. "Where should I sit?" She was dressed in a red silk slip dress that Samantha immediately recognized was from the Row's latest collection. Despite herself, Samantha couldn't help but admire the slinky outfit—Lucia could probably make even low-rise jeans look good.

The intern rushed into the glam room behind Lucia, a measuring tape dangling around her neck. "Uh, Lucia, Samantha's getting hair and makeup done now. But Winston will interview you next when Daisy's done."

"Not possible," came Lucia's swift reply. "I'm due for lunch at the Singapore Island Country Club, which means I have to leave here at eleven thirty."

"But it's already ten twenty—that's not enough time to do the photo shoot and the interview."

"Why don't I do the photo shoot first?" Lucia suggested silkily. "And Winston can call me another time to do the interview over phone." Her eyes still trained on the intern, she raised her voice. "I already have the perfect story to share with him about this incredibly romantic surprise my boyfriend planned for our last anniversary. I can't believe we will be celebrating half a decade together in just a few months!"

Samantha's hands bunched into fists at her sides, but she kept her face blank just in case Lucia could see it through the mirrors. She wasn't about to give Lucia the satisfaction she sought.

Tapping her heel against the ground, Lucia shot a pointed stare at Samantha's glam station. "I'm going to need hair and makeup now if we want to finish the shoot in time."

The intern cast a panicked look over at Winston, but he was caught up in his interview with Daisy, completely oblivious to the tension brewing at the other end of the room.

"But Samantha is doing the photo shoot next," the intern stammered, hands bunched around the bottom of her hijab. "If she waits too long, her makeup and hairstyle won't be fresh anymore . . ." Her voice trailed off as Lucia's smile dropped.

"I'm lunching with my grandfather and his co-founder of Yen-Heng Corporation. Surely you don't expect me to keep *them* waiting, do you? I'm not going to be late for my lunch because you didn't arrange things well. I've appeared in *Elle* many times and this has never happened before." Lucia paused. "You know, I think your editor and I are both attending Narval Networks' anniversary dinner next week . . ."

"No! Please don't tell Beatrice." The intern's voice warbled. "I'm doing this for school credit, and if I get fired, I'll lose my scholarship."

As the rims of the intern's eyes turned red, Samantha's hands tightened around the arms of her chair. She had been a scholarship student too—all throughout junior college and university.

"Hey, it's nothing personal. I get asked by Beatrice to work with *Elle* a lot, so I just want to make sure this doesn't happen again," Lucia said, smiling prettily again. "But if you can fix this right now, Beatrice never has to know about it."

Something in Samantha snapped. At *Tatler*, she'd met plenty of socialites who didn't hesitate to flaunt their power and wealth to get their way. But her mother had it even worse at her nail salon. Almost every night, Ma came back home grumbling about the rude demands and unreasonable complaints she put up with at work because "the customer was always right."

Samantha pushed herself out of her chair and whirled around to look Lucia straight in the eye. "Lucia, you can do hair and makeup first, okay?" she said, her voice shaking with barely controlled anger. "But it's not because you have the right. I'm only letting you go first because I can't wait for you to get out of here."

Lucia took a step forward, her face darkening. "*What* did you just say to me?"

"You heard what I said," Samantha retorted. But a sliver of fear began to lap at the edges of her anger. What was she thinking—going up against the Yen-Heng Corporation heiress? And would Timothy be upset with her if he heard about how she criticized his girlfriend in public?

Samantha's fight-or-flight response ticked toward the latter. Shoving her hands into her jeans pockets so no one would see them shaking, she flicked a pointed look up at the clock and said, "I guess you'd better get started now if you want to make it to your lunch on time, huh? I'm out of here. Someone call me back once it's my turn."

Without waiting for a response, Samantha turned sharply on her heel. She shouldered past Cheryl, whose poker face hadn't budged at all, and a comically slack-jawed Kim, making a beeline for the door and hoping she appeared far more composed than she felt.

"Samantha, you ready?" Winston called through the door to the glam room. "We're running behind schedule here."

"Just one second," Samantha shouted back, trying to keep her voice pleasant while she struggled with the dress. Why did its corset come with so many laces? And it wasn't *her* fault the shoot was behind schedule. At least the whole mess had produced one silver lining: Lucia, now on her way to the Singapore Island Country Club, wouldn't be around to judge her photo shoot or interview.

Samantha yelped as the door flew open, her hands instinctively coming up to cover her exposed chest with half the dress still pooled around her waist. In the doorway, the intern flinched as though she were the one who got walked in on half-naked.

"I'm so sorry. Winston sent me to help you, and I knocked but I guess you didn't hear . . ." She gestured meekly toward the humidifier puffing away loudly near the clothing rack.

"Oh, that's my bad." Samantha smiled to put the other woman at ease. "Yeah, I could really use some help with this corset."

The intern stepped forward and quietly began braiding the corset ties together in deft, quick movements. She kept her eyes down on the dress the whole time, and after a while, Samantha's self-consciousness began to fade. But in such tight quarters, the silence between them seemed all the more deafening.

When it finally became too awkward for Samantha to handle, she gave a small cough. "So, uh, I'm Samantha. What's your name?"

The intern looked around the room, then back at Samantha. "Are you asking me?"

Samantha chuckled. "Yes, you. Unless there's a third person in this room I don't know about, in which case I will be very concerned."

She immediately regretted her joke as the intern's face reddened. "Sorry. It's just . . . I've worked on a lot of shoots but none of the talent has ever asked me for my name before. They usually don't notice me."

Now it was Samantha's turn to feel embarrassed. Hadn't she been calling the other woman "the intern" in her head the whole time?

"I'm Munah. Munah Amin."

Samantha smiled. "Hi, Munah. And you said this internship is for school?"

Munah went back to fastening the corset, cinching every hook carefully to avoid pinching Samantha's skin. "Yup. I'm a final-year comms student at NUS, but fashion is my passion. Hey, did you study at NUS too?"

Samantha stiffened as alarms began blaring in her head. She willed herself to calm down; this was surely just an innocuous stab in the dark. After all, in a country as small as Singapore, there were only a handful of universities, and the National University of Singapore was the most well-known among them.

"Yeah," she said in her most nonchalant voice. "I studied comms too."

But the alarms intensified as Munah snapped her fingers. "I knew it! I thought you seemed familiar. You were three years above me, but I remember seeing you at a scholarship reception when I was just a freshman and you were a senior."

"Scholarship reception?" Samantha echoed, only dimly registering Munah pulling the dress up over her chest.

"The one FASS holds at the start of the year for all scholarship recipients. I was there for the Dean's Merit Scholarship."

Her heart racing, Samantha allowed the other woman to lift her limp arms and tug the sleeves into place like she was a mere doll. NUS Faculty of Arts and Social Sciences gave out plenty of financial awards every year; maybe she could get away with telling Munah that hers was a merit-based scholarship too—

"I was really inspired by the speech you gave that night," Munah continued, smoothing out the creases in the dress bodice. Her head was so close to Samantha's torso that Samantha wondered if the intern could hear her pounding heart. "You spoke about how it wasn't easy for you to study when you also had to work part-time to help your family, but that the Student Advancement Bursary would allow you to focus more on school."

Samantha watched as her face in the mirror turned pale. She still remembered how relieved she had been to get the bursary after finding out *Tatler* was unable to give her a full-time offer. With that financial aid, she could afford to devote more time to job hunting in her final year instead of spending all her nonclass hours working at the Starbucks kiosk on campus.

Bursary. For needy students.

That meant Munah knew she was a fraud—as far from a wealthy socialite as one could be. The amount awarded by the bursary couldn't even pay for this dress she was currently wearing.

Munah's eyes rose to meet Samantha's in the mirror. Before

Samantha could say anything, Munah opened the door and shouted toward the photo shoot set: "She's ready!"

AS SHE FOLLOWED Munah out of the glam room, Samantha felt like her body was moving on autopilot. Behind her calm facade, her mind was a roiling mess as she grappled for some plausible explanation for how she went from bursaries to Bulgari. What had she been wearing at the scholarship reception? Her outfit must have been decent since it was such an important occasion, but that wasn't saying much when most of her pre–Fraud Squad wardrobe was made up of thrifted finds and items from Cotton On's sales rack.

However, she could have been wearing Chanel and it still wouldn't change the fact that Munah knew the only way Samantha had afforded her university education was through a combination of part-time work and school bursaries. Winston had said he remembered her for her eloquence, and the article would focus on her romantic anecdote and not her background. But her inclusion in this feature—that she even got on Winston's radar in the first place—was undeniably in part due to his presumption of her as an affluent heiress. One she had never explicitly endorsed but also never corrected.

A facade that would go up in smoke if Munah let slip what she knew of Samantha's past.

"Oh my word!" An exclamation from Winston sliced through Samantha's churning thoughts. "Samantha, you look stunning!"

Matthieu, the fashion director, sidled up. "My vision for her outfit is genius, no?" he purred, twirling his goatee. "And wait till you see her with the necklace on. Come, Samantha. It's time for the star of the show."

Samantha couldn't help but smile. "Oh, I wouldn't call myself that."

Matthieu threw his head back in laughter. "Ma chérie, you're simply adorable. I wasn't talking about you, although you are, of course, magnifique! I was talking about your necklace," he said, sweeping his arm out dramatically to the padlocked Bulgari case.

Under the watchful gaze of the security guard, a woman wearing a Bulgari lanyard snapped on a pair of cashmere gloves, unlocked the case, and flung the lid open ceremoniously.

As Samantha pressed forward for a closer look, the studio's bustle faded into the background as if someone had pressed "Mute." All she could focus on was the trio of pieces nestled in the case's velvety depths, each studded with gemstones so glossy and lustrous they glowed beneath the studio's lights.

However, the necklace in the middle seemed to gleam just a bit more than the other two items. Its rose-gold chain, embellished with pavé diamonds and emeralds, dipped down into a pendant with an emerald so obscenely large it took Samantha's breath away.

But Lucia Yen and Daisy Taija probably wore jewelry like this all the time, so Samantha made sure to keep her expression neutral. She reached for the necklace, then paused and looked at the Bulgari woman. "May I?"

The woman's right eyebrow rose by the tiniest fraction, as though surprised Samantha had bothered to ask for permission. "Of course, but let me help you put it on. It's pretty heavy."

"Pretty heavy" was an understatement. The necklace pressed down on her collarbone as it was draped around her neck, the coldness of its precious metals seeping into her skin. When the Bulgari woman was at last satisfied the pendant was centered perfectly, she stepped back and prodded Samantha toward a mirror.

Samantha glanced up, her breath catching in her throat at her reflection. Her black Chantilly lace gown swooped around her hips and flared out at her knees, a smattering of pearls along the hem. Its understated elegance and bateau neckline provided the perfect backdrop for the scene-stealing Bulgari lavaliere, allowing the vibrance of its jewels to shine.

"It's beautiful," she breathed, her fingers fluttering up to brush against the pendant. "Beautiful" felt inadequate, but Samantha doubted any description could capture the necklace's perfection.

"Ma chérie," Matthieu said gently. "*You* are beautiful."

"Beautiful." The word danced around Samantha's mind as she stared at her reflection. She had never thought of herself as beautiful—nowhere close to Lucia's league. But in the outfit Matthieu had thoughtfully put together for her, with another few tens of thousands of dollars circling her neck, she didn't feel like herself. She stood taller, her eyes appeared brighter, her skin glowing as though lit from within. The couture felt like armor, buffing away her imperfections, drawing out the best in her and transforming her into an apparition of herself.

"Are you ready?" Winston asked, smiling like he already knew her answer.

Samantha rolled back her shoulders and returned his smile. She was ready.

THE PHOTO SHOOT started off even better than Samantha could have hoped for. She swiveled on her heels and jutted out her hip and gave the camera her best moody-supermodel pout as the photographer clicked away. Winston had rushed off to interview Daisy, but Matthieu stood by the side, exclaiming every once in a while, "Magnifique, Samantha! Magnifique!"

And then, from the corner of her eye, Samantha saw Munah standing in a corner of the studio. She was so silent and still she might as well have been a statue—as a good intern should be, there to serve but not to be noticed. Still, Samantha's skin crawled beneath the other woman's unmoving gaze.

Calm down, she told herself. *You're being paranoid.* Munah was just doing her job, on high alert for any stray hair or even the tiniest fingerprint smudge on the necklace that might mar the photo shoot.

But Samantha's mind continued churning. Any moment now, Munah could expose her. Could casually mention Samantha was on financial aid all throughout university, that three days a week, she spent her after-school hours making fancy Frappuccinos for students who could actually afford to buy overpriced coffee.

A loud exhale from the photographer drew Samantha's attention. "Samantha, babe. You gotta turn that frown upside down, yeah? We want the readers to believe Bulgari jewels make them happy. Think sparkly thoughts!"

Red-faced, Samantha gave a tiny shake of her head to dislodge her distracting ruminations. "Right, sorry. Sparkly thoughts, got it."

But try as she might to reclaim her earlier confidence, Samantha couldn't ignore Munah's presence hovering on the periphery—a ticking time bomb. She attempted to pivot her weight from one foot to the other, but her heels now seemed twice as spindly, her enormous gown weighing her down and threatening to pull her into the ground. Now she felt like she did back on the Christian Dada black carpet: a little girl trying way too hard to appear like someone she was not.

The photographer lowered his camera. "Babe, what's wrong? Were you out partying too late last night?" He guffawed at his own joke, but Samantha detected a hint of irritation behind his jovial tone.

Samantha forced a smile. "I'm fine." An idea struck her. "But you know, I could definitely do with some caffeine . . ." She let her voice trail off meaningfully.

"Of course. You!" the photographer barked at Munah, who promptly straightened up. "Go to the kopitiam two blocks away and buy three kopis—actually, make that two kopis and one kopi o kosong." He winked at Samantha. "I know you ladies don't like having sugar in your drinks."

"Great, thank you," Samantha said. Frankly, coffee with no sugar or milk sounded horrible, but it didn't matter what drink Munah got so long as she wasn't in the studio. It was similar to the countless coffee, salad, and even cigarette runs she herself had to do at her *Tatler* internship. Really, a magazine intern was basically a glorified gofer.

"Oh, can you also get me the smoked salmon salad from Sarnies?" Samantha called out to Munah, naming the salad shop that was a twenty-minute walk away. The longer Munah was gone, the better. "You can grab the money from my wallet—"

"Nonsense!" Matthieu interjected. "Of course lunch is on us. It's our fault the photo shoot was delayed."

Samantha thought about protesting but decided against it. A twenty-dollar salad was still a sizable expense for her.

The moment Munah disappeared through the studio doors, Samantha's entire body felt much lighter. The photographer had no more complaints for the rest of the shoot, and when it wrapped half an hour later, Samantha could barely recognize herself in the raw photos, standing tall and proud like some glamazon. The final images published in *Elle* a month later would probably look even more amazing after a round of Photoshop ("Just a teeny-weeny bit," Matthieu said, pinching his fingers together, "to brighten the colors").

As Daisy was led on set for her turn, Winston steered Samantha back into the glam room for her interview. Thankfully, it was empty now since Kim and Cheryl had followed Daisy on set to provide last-minute touch-ups. The fewer people around to witness her interview, the better.

"The necklace you just modeled is probably the most romantic piece in the whole collection," Winston told her, looking down at his phone as he fiddled with the recording app. "It was inspired by a similar one Richard Burton gave to Elizabeth Taylor, and oh boy, wasn't their love story just one for the ages?"

Samantha's stomach clenched. Great, no pressure or anything.

Winston set his phone down on the table. "Have you prepared what you want to say?"

Samantha took a deep breath. "Yeah, I'm good to go."

As Winston's phone recorder whirred into action, she began, her fingers fisted in the folds of her gown, "My mom always said from the moment she met my dad, she knew he was the man she wanted to marry. She was the prettiest girl in her town with many guys chasing after her, some who were perhaps more eye-catching on paper, but the only one she had eyes for was him—" She swallowed, her breath rasping in her throat from over-enunciating every syllable.

Just pretend you're talking to Tim.

Samantha's tongue loosened, her voice coming out smoother. "They married within a few months of knowing each other. Some people might think that's too quick, but my mom always said when you know, you know. At that time, my dad didn't have much. In fact, he proposed with two rings he made himself from copper but promised her he would one day give her a real diamond ring. For years, my dad never spent a single cent on himself, but whatever my mom wanted, he always tried to get it for her. Finally, when I was ten, he had enough savings to start his own electronics business."

Winston nodded absently. He probably thought the business had eventually grown to become the KMG of the electronics industry. In reality, it had only been a small neighborhood shop, one street over from Madam Pang's kopitiam, but it had been Ba's pride and joy, and therefore their whole family's.

That was, before everything had gone belly-up.

"The day his company broke even for the first time, the first thing he did was to fulfill the promise he made to my mom all those years ago. Mom didn't even remember it, but he immediately went out and got her the most beautiful diamond ring. What's more—he held a surprise vow-renewal ceremony." Samantha's eyes crinkled. "He roped me in to help. My job was to throw flower petals all over them, and then vacuum those up later. I remember being embarrassed and looking away when they kissed. But in hindsight, I've never seen my parents look happier than they did on that day."

Samantha's throat tightened, her tongue suddenly as heavy as lead in her mouth. That day now felt like a lifetime ago. So much had happened since then she sometimes couldn't help but wonder if her imagination had conjured it up—a desperate attempt to reassure herself that her parents really did love each other once, that screaming and fighting hadn't always been a part of their marriage.

Was Ma right? Was she too sentimental for her own good?

Winston leaned forward, his Prada glasses catching the overhead fluorescent as he asked, "Is that it?"

No, because Ba's business later went bankrupt, Ma pawned off her diamond ring to pay the loan sharks, and the only reason they didn't divorce was because Ba died first.

The glint of the light on Winston's lenses obscured his eyes, and not being able to see his expression made it easier for Samantha to swallow the lump in her throat and say, "That's it. That's my story."

Winston shook his head. "Samantha." He sighed. "Oh, Samantha."

Samantha's stomach roiled. Had she said something wrong? Perhaps she ought to have left out the part about Ba not having much—

No. She couldn't disrespect her father's memory by twisting his story.

"That was fucking brilliant!"

The churning in Samantha's gut screeched to a halt. "Wait, really?" Catching the disbelief in her own voice, she quickly said, "I mean, right. Thank you."

"Abso-fucking-lutely brilliant! Now I'm stressed-out. I have to make sure my article does your story justice." Chuckling, Winston shook his head again. "Okay, I just have to get some details right. What is it you said your parents do again?"

"Uh, my dad opened an electronics business."

"Right. But what is it exactly? And what does your mom do?"

Shit. Samantha glanced around the room, hoping a way out of this question could be found lurking in the smudges on the white-washed walls. But nothing came. Her heart pounded in her ears. *Think, Samantha, think.* But how was she supposed to tell him Ma worked as a nail technician and Ba's business—and him—was six feet under?

Then a brain wave struck her. During her *Tatler* internship, she had interviewed a hotel heir getting ready to launch his own brewery who insisted his family not be mentioned in the article—"They wouldn't like to be publicly associated with alcohol in any way."

Samantha looked Winston in the eye. "I'm not very comfortable revealing that," she said pleasantly. "My family is very private, and the last thing they would want is to see our business mentioned in the media."

Winston immediately put down his pen. "Of course, of course.

My apologies for putting you in a tough spot. I'll just mention they run a family business, if that's okay?"

"That's perfect." Thank God for Winston's tact, honed through years of dealing with socialites and their eccentricities. "Can you refer to them simply as Mr. and Mrs. Song?"

"Of course I can. Well, that was my last question!" Winston turned off the recorder app on his phone.

Breathing out a small sigh of relief, Samantha registered a dull throb in her palms. She glanced down, blinking at the crescent-shaped marks in her flesh. She hadn't realized she had been clenching her fists, or that her mouth was so parched it felt like she had gone days without water.

Winston gathered his phone and notebook and stood up. "Samantha, that was a wonderful interview. Thank you so much for doing this with *Elle*. I'll leave you to get changed now."

He walked to the door, paused, and turned around again. "Don't tell anyone else yet, but I'm going to make your story the lede for this advertorial. The way your voice throbbed with emotion—why, it almost made me tear up. And everything about your parents' love story perfectly captures the sentiment and romance of Bulgari's brand. I've never felt sadder about being single than in the past half an hour!"

Samantha could only smile weakly in response.

CHAPTER

17

After changing back into her own clothes, Samantha emerged from the glam room, only to run smack into Munah. "Hey, you okay?" Samantha asked, furrowing her brows at the sight of the other woman's wet hair and shirt.

"Yeah, just got caught in the rain," Munah said in between pants. She passed a takeaway coffee cup and salad bowl to Samantha. "Here you go. I'm sorry it took so long. Hopefully the kopi is still hot."

Samantha glanced out the window. It wasn't just raining, it was absolutely *pouring* outside, which must have started while Winston was interviewing her in the glam room. She bit her lip, guilt squeezing her insides like a vise. Because of her request, Munah had ended up getting soaked through.

Munah peered at her anxiously. "What's wrong? Did I get the wrong salad?"

"Oh no. This is the right one," Samantha said, forcing a smile on her face even as her guilt grew. It didn't matter which salad Munah got because Samantha had never planned on eating it; she already had lunch scheduled with Raina, and her request was nothing but a fool's errand to send Munah out of the studio.

The sight of Munah shivering snapped Samantha back into action. "Sit down," she urged, shepherding the intern into the glam room and settling her down in front of the dehumidifier. She pressed the takeaway food into Munah's hands. "Have these. I bet you haven't had lunch, and the coffee will help warm you up."

Munah immediately shook her head. "Thank you, but I can't. It's yours."

"Really, just take it," Samantha insisted. "I'm not hungry." That, at least, was true—guilt had a funny way of erasing her appetite.

Munah hesitated, glancing down at the salad that cost more than her salary for an entire workday. "I really can't," she finally said. "It will look bad if Winston or Matthieu sees me eating the salad that they know you asked for."

Samantha fell silent. She'd forgotten what little power interns had, how they were beholden to those above them. "Maybe you can hide it in your bag and eat it at home," she said at last.

"Munah, where are you?" Winston called from outside. "You're supposed to be packing up the clothes."

"Coming!" Munah shouted, leaping to her feet. But before she could leave the room, Samantha grabbed her arm.

"Munah, uh, about my scholarship—"

The intern's mouth quirked up into a small smile. "I don't know how you did it, but I'm really inspired. You started off in the same school and major as me, but look at you now—"

"That was ages ago," Samantha interrupted. "I'm not, you know, like that anymore."

After a beat of silence, Munah nodded. "Yeah, you're not. And I guess there's no point in rehashing the past."

Samantha ran a hand through her hair. "Precisely. It's way

more important to look ahead. And speaking of the future, if you're ever looking for a job in fashion, hit me up. Maybe I can connect you to a few stylists and designers." *It's not a bribe*, she told herself as Munah's face brightened. *I'm just trying to help someone whose shoes I was once in.*

"Munahhhh! The clothes aren't packing themselves!"

"I can't wait to read your interview when the article comes out," Munah said quickly. "I'm rooting really hard for you." And then she was gone.

Samantha stood still in the empty dressing room, watching her reflection in the mirror as color returned to her face and her heart rate mellowed. For some reason, Munah had decided to keep her secret. Winston and everyone else could still go on thinking of her as *Socialite Samantha Song*, while her past as *Scholarship Student Samantha Song* remained tightly buried beneath her layers of makeup, designer fineries, and priceless jewels.

"There you are!"

Samantha whipped around to find Daisy Taija in the hallway. The Indonesian heiress raised her hands. "Whoa, didn't mean to scare you. Winston told me I could find you here."

"It's okay," Samantha said, feeling suddenly drained as the adrenaline left her. She seemed to have gotten a lot jumpier after the Fraud Squad scheme began, constantly worrying that her facade would be exposed.

Daisy beamed. "I was wondering if you wanted to grab lunch together? I'm starving and can't believe I never got those doughnuts this morning."

Samantha glanced down at her phone's time display. She had to leave now if she wanted to be on time for her food court lunch date with Raina. A catch-up session between them was long overdue, since she had canceled brunch two Sundays ago for the *Vogue*-Singapore Repertory Theatre event as well as brunch last week to attend a charity polo match at the Singapore Turf Club with Anya.

"I don't think I—"

"Come on, Sam. I know this fantastic Thai place nearby," Daisy wheedled. Samantha ran a hand through her hair, slightly stiff from all the hairspray earlier. She had taken the entire day off for this photo shoot, but Raina would be popping out during her lunch break, and forty minutes just wasn't enough time for a proper catch-up. It probably made more sense to just reschedule.

Samantha met Daisy's expectant gaze and smiled. "Thai food sounds amazing."

"Perfect! You're going to absolutely love the curry at this place. It will wreck your tummy, but that's how you know the spice is legit."

Samantha dashed off a quick text to Raina asking to reschedule their lunch, then switched off her phone and dropped it back into her bag before a response came. Hooking her arm through Daisy's, she said, "Lead the way!"

FROM THE PASSENGER seat, Samantha blinked as Daisy's car pulled up next to a small shop on a side street in Bugis. Were it not for the faded and chipped signboard hanging over the entrance that read *Tommy Thai Cuisine*, she wouldn't have thought they were even in the right place. A cluster of round tables, lined with red plastic tablecloths, perched on its small tarp-covered veranda. The rain was beating down so heavily that the tarp looked like it might collapse at any moment.

Catching Samantha's look of surprise, Daisy shrugged. "I know this place might not look like much, but my Thai helper told me this is one of Singapore's hidden gems for authentic Thai cuisine."

"Oh, everyone knows that it's the holes-in-the-wall that are the real deal," Samantha said, and smiled to show she meant her words. *I'm not a snob*, she wanted to tell Daisy. *I was only surprised that a* real *socialite like you would eat here.* "Anyway, some comfort food is exactly what I crave on a rainy day."

Daisy giggled as she pushed open the glass door. "Exactly! I just want something warm and greasy. I can finally pig out now that the photo shoot's over."

The restaurant's interior was as sparsely decorated as its veranda. Six round tables like the ones outside took up most of the space. Their table was slick with oil residue, but Samantha, not wanting to give Daisy more reason to think of her as a snob, propped her arms on it anyway, though she kept them close to her body to avoid getting stains on Anya's Dion Lee blouse.

Their dishes arrived within minutes of their orders—green curry with rice noodles for Samantha, baked spicy chicken wings for Daisy—along with a jug of complimentary tea. Steam rose off the plates in tendrils, wafting along the aroma of a dozen spices.

Daisy closed her eyes and inhaled deeply. "Ahhh. I wish I could bottle this up into a perfume."

"Yeah, this is so much better than the usual sandalwood and eucalyptus nonsense," Samantha said, mentally kicking herself as she studied her own dish. Why did she order noodle soup when there was simply no conceivable way of eating it gracefully in public?

But Daisy was already tearing into a chicken wing with her bare hands, paying no attention to the juices dripping down her fingers and onto her Cartier Love ring. So without further hesitation, Samantha picked up her spoon and started slurping down her tangy broth with gusto. If even the Taija heiress didn't care about pristine table manners, then neither would she.

The muffled crooning of a Thai song over the loudspeaker was broken by Daisy's exclamation: "My helper's right—this is so freaking good! I wish they would serve this at events instead of those bite-sized pieces that look better than they taste." Her nose wrinkled. "If I have to eat one more molecular-gastronomy experiment . . ."

Samantha lifted a piece of chicken from her curry broth. "You know what I wish they would stop serving at events? Sparkling water."

"Exactly!" Daisy exclaimed, raising her hand for a high-five but quickly dropping it. "Oops, my hand's oily. Let's do an elbow five instead." She offered up her right elbow, which a grinning Samantha bumped hers against.

"Sparkling water's *nasty*. What's wrong with plain tap water, huh?" Daisy went on emphatically. "Recently, my mom brought home a bottle of Acqua di Cristallo—I definitely butchered the pronunciation—that cost almost fifty thousand. She got pissed when I didn't want to try it, but there's no way I'm drinking any water with stuff floating inside, even if it's pure gold dust."

"I can't imagine drinking that either," Samantha said. Why would anyone pay the cost of a car for something that would leave your system within a few hours? "I don't even like fruit-infused water, so the whole lemon water trend completely went over my head."

Daisy clapped a hand over her chest. "You're a girl after my own heart, Sam." She paused. "You know, I didn't expect to like you."

Samantha raised a brow. "Thanks, I guess?"

"Oops, that came out wrong," Daisy said with a giggle, before her face turned somber. "It's just . . . I haven't really had a great experience with people in Singapore so far."

"I'm sorry to hear that," Samantha said softly. "But maybe you just haven't met the right people yet."

"People have been nice enough to my face, but I know what they're saying about me behind my back," Daisy mumbled, fingering the fraying ends of her friendship bracelets. "The socialites here look down on me just because Indonesia's less developed than Singapore. They don't want to befriend someone who comes from the same country as their maids."

Daisy's voice grew smaller. "And the tabloids have been *awful*. They're all saying I'm moving here because my parents are getting divorced and I've decided Singapore is better than Indonesia. A couple even asked their readers to weigh in on whether I should be accepted since my mom chose to 'run off with a dark-skinned Indonesian instead of marrying a fellow Singaporean.'"

"Oh, Daisy . . . That's awful. I don't even know what to say except I'm so sorry you have to put up with that." It was one thing to have read the magazine speculations, as she and half a million others had done, but it felt very different when she was actually sitting across from the subject being discussed—*dissected*—in the tabloids. How must Daisy feel, knowing that countless strangers were deriving a voyeuristic—maybe even sadistic—pleasure from unpacking the most intimate details of her life?

Was this what the socialites mentioned in As Seen by Argus felt like?

Daisy raised her head, a mischievous smile playing about her lips. "You know what's funny though? The tabloids have got it all wrong. I'm not moving to Singapore because my parents are getting divorced—quite the opposite, actually."

"Your parents are getting married again . . . ?"

"No, silly, I am!"

Samantha's eyes darted to Daisy's ring finger, which was conspicuously bare.

Daisy followed her gaze and laughed. "If I wore my engagement ring today, Winston would have spotted it and asked a million questions, and it would be so awkward because I already guaranteed *S* exclusive rights to break the story of my engagement and cover my engagement party. The whole time I was doing my interview, I was so afraid of letting something slip because my romantic story was about my fiancé." She heaved a long-suffering sigh. "Juggling all these magazines can be so tricky—you know how it is."

Samantha nodded like she did. "Yeah, that's got to be really awkward. But congratulations! I'm so happy for you."

"Thank you! It was the *most* romantic proposal ever," Daisy trilled, her eyes shining. "Lincoln—that's my fiancé—flew me to his family's island and we had a lovely candlelit dinner by the beach. I kind of guessed he was up to something but the whole meal, I was more worried my caftan was going to catch on fire because it was billowing all over the table from the wind. So I was truly shocked when fireworks exploded in the shape of a daisy, a string quartet started playing, and he kneeled down and asked me to marry him!"

"That sounds absolutely amazing! Your fiancé clearly put a lot of thought into the proposal."

"Right? Lincoln's the absolute best. But his mother though . . ." Daisy pulled a face. "Let's just say Pan Ling has some *very* traditional views. She didn't like me at first because I'm so tanned and two years older than Lincoln, and she's already hinting I should become a stay-at-home wife after the wedding. *And* she made me sign a prenup three hours after Lincoln proposed." She sniffed. "As if my family doesn't have our own money."

Samantha winced. "She sounds like a mother-in-law from hell."

"That's why I put my foot down with Lincoln and told him there's no way I'm moving to China just because she lives there.

He's her only son, so I know Pan Ling's going to find any excuse to drop in on us. She can't stand another woman being more important in Lincoln's life."

"China's really big though," Samantha pointed out. "Won't it be quite easy avoiding her?"

"China's not too big if you have two private jets like she does. So that's out of the question, but I know Pan Ling's going to throw an absolute fit if he moves to Indonesia. Which is why Lincoln and I decided to go for a happy medium and make Singapore our home instead. We told Pan Ling it's because Singapore is a good investment hub and Lincoln can set up his company here, so she can't say anything about that!"

Samantha clapped her hands together. "It's awesome you'll be settling down in Singapore! I can bring you around to my favorite places and introduce you to all my friends, like Raina, Tim, and Anya."

"Yes, please! I haven't been in Singapore for very long, but I'd absolutely love to spend more time with you and meet new people."

Before Samantha could respond, Daisy reached out to grasp her hands. "Hey, you should come to my engagement party!"

Samantha blinked. "Are you sure? I'd love to go, but you've only known me for a few hours. I don't want to intrude—"

Daisy let out a delicate snort. "Don't be so formal with me! Friendship isn't measured by time. I know you're a good person, and that's enough. I saw what you did for that poor girl today."

It took Samantha a moment to realize Daisy was referring to Munah. "You heard that? I thought you were busy with your interview."

"It was hard not to since Lucia was being so loud about it. Even Winston heard—I saw him wincing when Lucia raised her voice."

Samantha frowned. "But he didn't even step in! How can he let his own intern be knocked around like that?"

"I guess he was just looking out for himself? I wouldn't want to get caught up in Lucia's cross fire either. Honestly, she scares the shit out of me."

Samantha couldn't help but grin. "I know, I'm scared of her too. But I just couldn't stand the way Lucia talked to the girl like she was a nobody. I hate it when models look down on the photo shoot staff, who are the real backbone of the whole operation. Interns work really hard, and so do the hairstylist, makeup artist, manicurist—"

Daisy shot her a weird look. "There wasn't a manicurist today. Cheryl did our nails, too, no?"

"Oh, uh, I was just speaking generally. Anyway, my point is that those people deserve so much respect. And since their jobs are already hard enough, we should all try to make things easier for them wherever we can—"

Samantha's voice faltered at the memory of Munah's dripping wet hair and the twenty-dollar salad bowl that never ended up being eaten. She might not have been as outwardly rude to the intern as Lucia had, but hadn't she also taken advantage of her status so Munah would be sent out on a pointless errand?

Daisy dropped her finished chicken wing on the plate and leaned forward. "You know, I think you're the most genuine socialite I've met in Singapore so far. You're nice to everyone: me, the intern—"

"Not Lucia," Samantha joked, even as guilt surged through her. Here was Daisy calling her "genuine" when she was actually the biggest fraud of all.

"To everyone who deserves it then," Daisy amended with a grin. "You're nice, period."

Samantha waved it off. "Oh stop, you're making me blush."

And making me feel horrible because I'm not the person you think I am.

"Say you'll come to my engagement party, then, so I can stop flattering you."

Samantha laughed, relieved the conversation was now back in safer, less guilt-inducing territory. "Of course I'll come. I can't wait to celebrate you and Lincoln. And to see your mother-in-law's devil horns in person."

Daisy did a little jig in her chair. "Goodie! But I've to warn you—the reason why my mom bought that gold-dust water is because we were testing out what drinks to serve at the party. She's calling all the shots, so don't be surprised if the refreshments are weird." Daisy picked up the jug of complimentary barley tea to pour herself another glass. "I, for one, happen to like this free iced tea much more."

"Amen to that," Samantha said, holding out her own glass for Daisy to refill.

18

With just two weeks left until Anya's party, Samantha and Timothy headed to Takashimaya department store to pick up a gift. As they scanned the shelves of perfumes in the fragrance section, the ornamental bottles and pretty boxes began blurring into one another before Samantha's eyes. Pear and rose sounded good, but so did cherry blossom and mandarin orange . . .

Samantha sighed. "Buying a birthday present for Anya is so hard, especially when she already has everything or can buy whatever she doesn't have."

Timothy scoffed as he read the label on a Burberry bottle. "Shopping for women is hard, period." He brandished the perfume beneath her nose. "Does white musk and amber smell good?"

"Don't bother with Burberry—Anya boycotted them once she found out they still do animal testing. And come on, you were with Lucia for four years. Surely you would have picked up a trick or two by now."

Timothy put the Burberry perfume back on the shelf. "Nope. I remember not knowing what to get Anya for her birthday last year either. I think I played it safe and got her flowers in the end."

Samantha picked up a Chloé fragrance. Ambergris and wood . . . What was ambergris even? "Couldn't you have at least asked Lucia for help?"

"Yeah, that would not have gone over well. Lucia doesn't like Anya much."

"Why not?"

Timothy scratched the side of his jaw. "Let's just say Lucia's parents are very strict about the people she associates with."

Samantha whirled around to face him. "Are you kidding me? Lucia doesn't like Anya because she thinks she isn't good enough?"

"No, it's Lucia's *parents* who think that. They think Anya's mother has a reputation, so they don't want Lucia around Janice or Anya."

"Don't you think Lucia's way past the age where you can blame her behaviors on her parents?"

"I'm not saying what she's doing is right, but it's complicated in families like ours." Timothy shrugged. "Like it or not, the people Lucia and I are surrounded with do care a lot about reputation. If Lucia didn't go along with what her parents wanted, they would have punished *her*."

Like ours . . . Lucia and I . . . Samantha dumped the Chloé bottle back on the shelf. "How can you be shopping for Anya's birthday when you won't even stand up for her against your—your girlfriend?" she said, hating the way she stumbled over the last word. She didn't know whom she was more upset with: Lucia for looking down on Anya, Timothy for defending that, or herself for being so bothered that even with the Fraud Squad scheme, she would always be an outsider in the world Tim and Lucia had grown up in together.

Timothy's eyes widened, as though surprised by her vehemence. "It's not that straightforward. I'm lucky my parents never cared much about who I hung out with, but that's because men are judged mainly on their careers and net worth. Which is a big reason why my parents are so insistent on me rejoining KMG. Meanwhile, women are judged on more superficial things like their appearances and their relationships. Why do you think people cut Anya's mother out after her divorce?"

Pinpricks of unease needled Samantha. She had always found Lucia judgmental, but never gave any thought to the even more judgmental environment that might have shaped the other woman.

"Lucia's parents will be furious with her if she's hanging out with 'unreputable' people," Timothy continued. "Do I hate that my girlfriend and best friend don't get along? Definitely. But I also know Lucia's just looking out for herself. Nothing I say will change anything, so all I can do is focus on being a good friend to Anya in other ways. We all have to pick our battles."

"Yeah, let's go back to shopping," Samantha said, suddenly desperate to get off this topic. There were some things Timothy and Lucia had in common that she could never understand, having not grown up in their world. "We're still nowhere close to deciding what to get."

Timothy smoothly picked up the conversation as though they had been discussing *eau de parfum* all along. "What fragrance do you use?"

"Me? I don't put on anything."

"Seriously? But you always smell so—" He broke off, the tips of his ears turning red. "I mean, I figured we could get Anya whatever you use," he finished gruffly.

Samantha heaved an exaggerated sigh. "Oh, Tim. A woman's fragrance is like her signature. And you know Anya likes to stand out—she would never want to use the same thing as someone else." Beneath the snark, the pressure in her chest eased. This banter at least was familiar territory; it was what they should have stuck to from the very beginning, far away from any discussion about Lucia.

Timothy swept an eye over the shelves. "I don't think we're going to find anything here. There are so many options I don't even know where to begin."

Samantha perked up. "But I know something that can help us. Follow me."

TIMOTHY'S BROWS SHOT up as Samantha pulled him toward a magazine rack. Catching the dubious expression on his face, she explained, "Trust me, magazines contain really comprehensive gifting guides for any occasion you can think of. I would know—I must have written dozens of them. I even wrote one about what to give your friend who's getting married for the second time."

That made Timothy crack up. "Send me the link—I have to read that. But surely you know Anya's tastes better than some random gift guide."

"But the gift guides show that those items are the must-haves of the season."

His eyes still crinkled with laughter, Timothy shook his head. "You set too much store by what those magazines say."

Was that simply lighthearted teasing, or was there something more pointed behind his words? "It's not like I take these magazines as gospel. I'm just trying to get inspiration," she said, turning back to the magazine rack before he could respond.

Her eyes landed on *S*'s August issue, placed front and center in the rack. PAINT THE TOWN RED, the cover headline screamed, above a shot of a waifish model swallowed up by a scarlet tulle gown. And in one corner of the cover: AS SEEN BY ARGUS: THE SISYPHEAN PURSUIT OF FAME IN THE AGE OF SOCIAL MEDIA.

Samantha nudged Timothy and jerked her head toward the

issue. "Check out what everyone's favorite columnist is dishing out this month."

There was a moment of silence as Timothy digested the subtitle, then his face broke into a smirk. "*Sisyphean*? Looks like Argus was feeling extra pompous when she wrote this."

Samantha grinned at him. "I'm guessing you aren't her biggest fan. Wait, didn't she single you out once? I remember Anya saying that when we were in your tea room."

Timothy rolled his eyes. "Yeah, it wasn't too hard to guess the T. K. in her column was referring to me. My crime was bidding on a first edition copy of *The Iliad* a few months ago at a charity auction. According to Argus, I was only aiming to appear intellectual, and the fact I didn't try to top the thirty-eight-thousand-dollar winning bid showed I wasn't serious enough about it."

"That was *you*? I remember reading that! God, Argus can be so ridiculous sometimes, picking on people for such dumb things."

Timothy raised an eyebrow. "What happened to wanting to be Argus 2.0?"

Running a finger absently down the magazine spine, Samantha mused out loud, "I used to think I'd be happy to write about anything as long as I had my own column for *S*, but I just . . . don't feel the same way anymore. Daisy, this socialite I met at the *Elle* shoot— she's been having a hard time lately because of the tabloids piling on her and her family. And that's basically what Argus does every month to socialites—including you. I don't want to see the people I care about get hurt by people who don't know the real them."

Her eyes widened as Timothy leaned in. "So what I'm hearing is—you care about me?" His voice carried a teasing lilt, but there was an intensity to his gaze that made Samantha's breath catch in her throat. Since when did Timothy tower over her like that? And had his shoulders always been this broad?

Samantha swallowed, hoping he couldn't see the movement of

her throat, that he wouldn't realize how much his mere presence had flustered her. "That's not the point," she managed, her words coming out more like a squeak. "My point is, I realized I don't want to build a writing career out of making personal attacks. I used to think Argus was cool for calling out other socialites on their pretentious behaviors, but she was wrong about you. For all we know, all her accusations could be way off base. She might think she's like some high-society Deep Throat, but if she has to rely on exploiting her fellow socialites to attract readers, then maybe she's just not a good writer."

Timothy nodded. "I'm with you on this. But I think the blame can't be on Argus alone—it takes two hands to clap, no? If people didn't care so much about the socialites, Argus wouldn't even have a platform like that."

His words sank in, hollowing a pit in Samantha's gut. Wasn't it people like her—those who relished the insights into this exclusive, gilded world—who gave Argus the incentive to publicize her snarky judgments? Who helped turn As Seen by Argus into a cultural phenomenon? If she was going to call Argus ridiculous, then what did that make her?

Hardly able to meet Timothy's eyes, Samantha finally said, "I know I seem like a hypocrite. I guess I thought of socialites differently back when I was only reading about them. They didn't seem like—"

"Real people?"

"Like people who could get hurt," she answered softly. "I thought that when you were that rich and well-known, you wouldn't be bothered by what other people thought of you. But I've come to see that it's because of how superficial the public can be that socialites, especially women like Janice, Daisy, and even Lucia, are judged all the time on such meaningless things. And why they end up judging one another."

"Hey, it's okay." Timothy placed a hand on her shoulder. "I never thought of you as a hypocrite," he said, his voice even gentler than before. "I would never think of you badly."

Her blouse sleeve slipped, and his fingers felt like a flame against her now exposed skin. Samantha quickly took a step back. "Well, if I ever get my own column, you can count on me to write about something less shallow than how much a person's auction bid is," she said, her voice extra loud to mask how unsettled she felt on the inside, how unsettled Timothy had made her.

Timothy crossed his arms and leaned against the magazine rack, looking straight at her. "You're right—Argus *is* shallow. That makes me care less about what she thinks of me, so thank you."

Seeing the smile playing about his lips made Samantha's own mouth quirk up at the corners. Tim was the one passing her invites to society events and footing the bills for the Fraud Squad's endeavor, so being able to give *him* something for once—even if it was just free words of comfort and advice—made her heart lift.

"Exactly. Don't even bother reading her column anymore; I know I won't be," she told him. "Now come on, back to work."

Samantha was halfway through reading a list of animal-print designer housewares when a thought struck her. She snapped the magazine closed, prompting Timothy to look up from the *Esquire* issue he was reading.

"On second thought, *you're* right," Samantha declared. "We don't need a magazine to tell us what to get our friend. Let's go—I think I know just what to give Anya for her birthday."

19

Samantha winced as her ringing phone pierced the quiet of Raina's office, drawing annoyed looks from all directions. Being in proximity to a dozen lawyers was like walking on eggshells, but Samantha supposed no one would be too pleased about having to come into work on a Saturday. At least she was there by choice.

When Raina had suggested working together at her law firm on Saturday, Samantha immediately agreed. She told herself it was because Raina's office offered two things her flat didn't: air-conditioning and Wi-Fi that moved faster than a snail's pace—both of which she needed to finalize the *Deluxe Eats* press kit before Monday's meeting with Cassandra.

Her quick agreement had nothing to do with her guilt over canceling brunch tomorrow to attend *Vogue*'s luncheon at the Singapore Repertory Theater for the second month in a row. Nothing to do with that at all.

"Hey! Took you long enough to pick up," Anya said the moment Samantha answered the call. "Are you in the middle of something?"

Samantha's eyes darted toward Raina, then quickly away as though Anya could somehow sense Raina's presence through the phone. "Just getting some work done," she mumbled, pressing her voice low to cover up any traces of guilt. "What's up?"

"I am absolutely freaking out about what guest favors to give at my party."

It didn't sound like it was going to be a quick call, so Samantha mouthed, "I'll be right back," to Raina and hurried to a quiet corner outside the office.

"I thought we discussed two days ago you'd be giving out personalized Oscar figurines and hundred-dollar gift cards to any Golden Village cinema."

"Yeah, but is an Oscar statue too corny? I was thinking I could offer everyone a 23andMe testing kit, to play off the fact it's my twenty-third birthday? Shit, what if someone finds out they were adopted or their mom cheated on their dad or something—"

It took every ounce of self-control for Samantha to not sigh out loud. When Anya—impressed by all the work Samantha had done for Cassandra's project—enlisted her to help out with party planning, Samantha was so flattered she'd immediately agreed. She'd naively thought there wouldn't even be much for her to do since Anya also hired a professional event planner who charged a five-figure retainer fee. But since then, every lunch break and office pantry conversation the past few weeks had been dedicated to making all sorts of decisions about Anya's upcoming birthday party.

Anya's voice perked up. "Wait, isn't twenty-three known as the Jordan Year or something? What if I put up basketball arcade machines at my party? Do you think—"

The rest of her words were drowned out by a loud chime from Samantha's phone. She pulled it away from her ear for a moment to peer at the screen—another email from Cassandra, the only person who hounded her even more than Anya did these days.

Samantha pressed her phone back against her ear. "But arcade machines would look totally out of place at an Oscars-themed party," she said as patiently as she could.

"What if I change my party theme?"

Samantha sagged against the wall, the enormous leaves from a fake money plant brushing against her face. This was the fourth time this week Anya had considered that. "But 'A Night at the Oscars' is a genius theme. All the gold decor would be a great play on the fact that it's your golden birthday."

"But—"

"No buts," Samantha said firmly. "Your party sounds absolutely amazing, so stop second-guessing yourself."

A heavy sigh floated down the line. "I wish I shared your confidence, but you don't get it," Anya said glumly. "This is supposed to be my grand reentry into high society, and I've invited just about everyone who matters. But people are backing out now because they will be going to Daisy Taija's engagement party instead. How am I not supposed to be stressed-out?"

Samantha straightened up, her mind roiling. "*Daisy*'s party is on the same night as yours?"

"Yeah, *S* just announced it online. Isn't it ridiculous Daisy's holding her engagement party in Singapore when she didn't even grow up here and her fiancé's from China? I guess all those rumors about Daisy's parents divorcing are true."

They're not, Samantha almost blurted before she caught herself just in time. Although she had told Anya every last detail of her *Elle* photo shoot, she had said nothing about her lunch with Daisy or the engagement party invitation—that conversation felt too intimate to be shared.

Samantha blew out a breath, her mind racing to digest this newfound realization. How could she not have realized the two parties fell on the same day? But this meant she would have to miss Daisy's engagement party. After all, Anya was one of her closest friends, and she had RSVP'd to Anya's birthday way before she even knew Daisy.

On the other end of the line, Anya was still in the middle of her lament. "It seriously sucks that out of the entire year, Daisy chooses to have her party on the exact same day as mine. It's going to be so embarrassing when no one shows up to my party and all the journalists snap a photo of an empty ballroom."

Samantha forced herself to push aside her inner turmoil and focus on Anya's words. "Hey, you know I'll be there, so at least that's one person."

"Yes, thank God. But I need some truly well-known socialites to show up. Without their stamp of approval, my party will be a flop."

At this point, Samantha couldn't resist rolling her eyes. Whatever the birthday equivalent of bridezilla was, Anya was it.

"Daisy totally lucked out because her dad runs Indonesia's biggest production company and Lincoln's family owns one of China's largest biotech firms," Anya continued. "Everyone thinks those divorce rumors are true and she's going to make Singapore her home base, so they're going to her party just to get in her good books."

"Come on, Anya, that's not really fair," Samantha said, trying for a lighthearted tone. The last thing she needed was for Anya to get suspicious about why she was coming to Daisy's defense. "Besides, it's not like you're from a no-name family—your dad's one of the world's top venture capitalists, for crying out loud."

Anya let out a small snort. "My dad spends all his time in China these days at his company's Shanghai office, with his new Chinese wife and twin baby boys. Out of sight, out of mind, so everyone just associates me with my mom now. And you know what that's been like . . ." Her voice grew small. "If I want to establish myself, I can't depend on either of my parents. I need this party to be a big success."

Samantha's heart softened. No wonder Anya was so stressed. "I know party planning is tough, but you can do it. And I'm here to help in any way I can."

"You're right—I can do it." A slight rustling sound drifted down the line, and Samantha imagined Anya straightening up. "I can do it," Anya repeated, more loudly this time. "I'm going to call my event planner right this second and hammer out details for the party favors. Thanks for your help, Sam! I'll see you at work on Monday."

"Wait, Anya! I want to ask you about—"

But the line went dead.

Slowly, Samantha plodded back into the office, goose bumps breaking out over her arms from the blast of air-conditioning. Raina's things were still on her desk, though she was nowhere to be found. Samantha sank into her chair and turned to her laptop screen, where Cassandra's email beckoned. Sam, are we good to go on . . . I invited all the board members of my committee . . . Everything needs to be even better than perfect . . . Really need to blow their socks off.

She just spent half an hour listening to Anya fret about her socialite future, and now she had to spend the rest of the day help-ing Cassandra with hers. But what about *her* socialite career? Anya had hung up before she had a chance to discuss their Fraud Squad's progress.

Samantha stared at her laptop without taking anything in. Anya was quite right that Samantha wasn't truly well-known yet. The whole point of the Fraud Squad's scheme was to help her get there, but Timothy shunned society events to avoid a Lucia run-in, and all of Anya's attention was devoted to her party these days.

A steaming coffee mug landed on the table in front of her. "Hey, I figured you could do with some caffeine," Raina said, her hands cupped around her own mug. "You look kinda dazed. Is everything okay?"

"Not really," Samantha admitted, picking up the mug and blowing on it.

Raina slid into her chair. "Tell me about it. We're overdue for a CCC anyway."

Samantha gnawed on the inside of her cheek. Rai was right—when was the last time they had a Candid Coffee Confessional? But could she really be candid about her Fraud Squad conundrum? Anya had said to keep her high-society and normal lives separate.

Screw it—she needed to confide in someone, and Rai was her best friend. Samantha took a tentative sip of her scalding hot coffee before admitting, "Anya invited me to her birthday party on July twenty-third, but I also want to attend Daisy's engagement party on the same night. I think it's going to be impossible, though, unless I can somehow magically teleport."

"Wait, who's Daisy?"

"This socialite I met at an *Elle* interview."

Raina's jaw dropped. "*Elle* as in the fancy-schmancy magazine I see in my firm's lobby?"

Samantha nodded. "I'm sure you've seen me reading it before."

"You read so many magazines that I've stopped taking note of the titles. How did you manage to finesse a freaking interview with them?"

For the first time, it struck Samantha just how much had gone unsaid between her and Rai in the past few weeks. "It's a long story," she mumbled, hoping Raina would just leave it at that.

"But *Elle* is a really big publication, right? Tell me about this interview, which I know nothing about."

Samantha allowed herself to smile. "One of the biggest." Choosing to gloss over Raina's pointed closing remark, she told her best friend everything about the couture and the jewelry, the five-star glam treatment, and the set team made up of the industry's top professionals—all of which Raina took in with wide eyes and a few "no ways" sprinkled in for good measure.

But Samantha also didn't leave out her close brush with Munah. "Thank God I was nice to her," she concluded. "If I had treated her the way Lucia did, she would probably have busted me faster than you could say 'Bulgari.'"

Raina's eyebrows knitted together. "Why do you make it sound so . . . transactional?"

"Make what sound so transactional?"

"Being nice. You make it sound like it was only worth it because she kept your secret."

Samantha stared at Raina, wondering if this was just her friend's usual deadpan humor. But there was no hint of a joke in the other woman's face. "Of course not! It's not like I would have gone Lucia on her if she'd exposed me." She tried for a stab at levity: "I would be too busy saving my own ass to worry about busting hers."

Raina nodded slowly. "Okay . . . but what about how you treated her just like those socialites used to treat you at *Tatler*?"

"I didn't know it was raining! If I did, I would have never asked for the coffee or the salad."

Raina rubbed her eyes and took a big swig of her coffee. "Sorry, I don't know why I said that. You needed food anyway since the photo shoot ran so late and ate into our lunch."

Samantha looked down, afraid her guilt was written all over her face.

"Anyway, you've clearly impressed *Elle*, so maybe they could offer you a writing gig if you mention you're interested."

Samantha exhaled deeply—half in relief that the conversation was finally back on safer ground, and half in dejection that things weren't going as well as Raina assumed. "It's not nearly that easy. Besides, *S* is Singapore's most famous magazine. That's the one I really want to write for."

Raina nodded, but Samantha could tell that, to her friend, all the magazines were pretty much one and the same. "But your *Elle* feature might make you famous enough to catch what's-her-name's eye, no?"

"Missy. And maybe . . ." Samantha tapped a finger against her mug. "But that feature comes out after the S Gala, which I need to be at to cement my socialite status. That means I have to up my game *now*. If only I could see Missy again and actually make a good impression this time—"

In a flash, the answer came to Samantha, so obvious that she wondered how she could have possibly not seen it earlier.

She *had* to go to Daisy's party.

Daisy had said her engagement celebration would be covered by *S*. Not only was that a clear indication of the party's exclusivity, but it also meant a strong possibility Missy would be there. This could be her last chance to impress the editor before the S Gala.

Raina clocked the change in her demeanor. "What is it? You look like you're up to no good."

"I'm not getting up to no good." Samantha grinned. "I just decided I'll be going to Daisy's party after all. If I leave Anya's party around eight thirtyish, I can still catch the last hour of Daisy's party." Although she would be cutting it close, it would have to do. The Fraud Squad might have helped her get one foot in the high-society doorway, but it was time she stopped relying on her friends and start taking more ownership of her own plan.

Raina's brows went up. "What happens if Anya finds out?" But before Samantha could answer, she said, "Actually, who cares what she says? You totally deserve to let your hair down for one night and have fun. You've been spending so much time on this cookbook project that I barely get to see you anymore."

"Yeah, this project is killing me," Samantha said, squashing down sharp twinges of guilt. It was true she'd been working hard, but the never-ending carousel of society events was the true culprit behind all their canceled plans.

With a sigh, Samantha cupped her hands around her eyes and returned her attention to Cassandra's email as Raina turned back to her own laptop. Thinking about work was far easier than thinking about the burgeoning number of secrets she was keeping from her best friend.

20

Samantha could not stop smiling as she surveyed the fruits of her labor. After countless Pinterest boards, seven mock-ups, and a dozen checks that Cassandra approved without batting an eye, the society doyenne's dining room had been dramatically transformed into a rustic-glam landscape inspired by *Deluxe Eats'* focus on organic food.

The black vinyl Kaws figurines that used to flank the entrance had been replaced by dwarf lemon trees in terra-cotta pots. All around the room, wildflowers cascaded out of earthen bud vases and wicker baskets overflowed with impeccable-looking produce, varnished with hairspray for extra shine. Cassandra's dining table had been removed to make space for a dozen cocktail tables, each draped with a hand-appliquéd linen tablecloth and garnished with a Kim Seybert floral table runner. The serving island held a gleaming row of platters from Herend's Blue Garland collection, the vivid blue of the hand-painted cornflowers a stark contrast to the bone-white porcelain.

Everything was in place and exactly as Samantha had envisioned, everything except the pièce de résistance of tonight's party.

Due to a scheduling conflict, Julien Royer, head chef of French restaurant Odette, was unavailable tonight. Thankfully, restaurateur Bertha Ling had been happy to take over the cooking as long as her upcoming food show was plugged in the media coverage. But with Bertha filming right up to just ninety minutes before the party began and all the serving platters still empty, there was plenty of room for things to go wrong.

Samantha picked up her phone and dialed a number she had come to know by heart over the past few weeks. "Hey, Penny, is Bertha gonna get here soon?" she asked the moment the call connected.

"We're wrapping up soon," snapped Bertha's assistant, sounding even more harried than usual.

Samantha willed her tone to remain cordial. "If she doesn't get here soon, the food might not be ready in time."

"I *know*," Penny barked. "Anyway, I have to go now. Unless it's something urgent, don't call. The director doesn't like ringing phones on set." She hung up before Samantha could respond.

The steady ticking of the handsome brass clock on the wall pounded in Samantha's head—a reminder that in under two hours, Singapore's most influential people and news outlets would be descending upon the room she was standing in right now, the room she had painstakingly put together. Even *S* had agreed to send a writer over.

But what if they didn't like what she had put together? What if people didn't fall for Cassandra's "second coming of Mother Teresa" act and Cassandra blamed it on her?

Samantha looked around Cassandra's dining room, hoping the bustle of activity among the service staff would calm her down with a reminder that everything was still on track. But the swarm of people simply made her feel very alone—as the one in charge, she had to put on a confident face at all times and keep her worries to herself. Even though Anya's mother would be attending the party as

Cassandra's "friend," Anya herself was tied up in a cake tasting for her upcoming birthday party. ("I'm so sorry about missing your event, Sam," she'd said apologetically. "But this guy has made cakes for the Japanese royal family and he isn't available again until 2025.") She had already sent over half a dozen texts that afternoon to ask for Samantha's opinion on lychee-rose versus salted caramel.

Meanwhile, Timothy was in Malaysia to attend a family friend's baptism. And Raina—

Guilt surged within Samantha, twisting her stomach into knots. After their joint work session, she had to cancel her next couple of catch-ups with Rai: first because of this month's *Vogue* luncheon, then because of a fashion show at Dover Street Market. She had wanted to invite Raina tonight, but Cassandra had been adamant that her party should be VIPs only.

Samantha whipped out her phone and jotted down a quick reminder to catch up with Raina soon. She would tell her then how tonight's *Deluxe Eats* party had gone and also find out if the art collection divorce case ever got resolved. Just one more month of this hectic high-society life, then the Fraud Squad's scheme would end, and she and Rai could resume their weekly kopitiam brunches.

Samantha slid her phone back in her pocket and took a deep breath. Now was not the time to worry about her personal life, not when her professional life was at stake. She had a kick-ass party to pull off and people to impress.

"THE COQ AU vin? To die for!"

"My favorite is the arancini. The white truffle shavings in them—" The speaker in question gave her fingers a loud kiss.

"I heard Cassandra had the truffles airfreighted all the way from Alba."

"It's obvious she cares a lot about the quality of her food. Why, she even got Bertha Ling to cook her recipes tonight."

Samantha pressed her lips together to stop a smug smile from slipping out. Blessedly, Bertha Ling had arrived on time and whipped up a feast so incredible that even the most body-conscious socialites couldn't resist helping themselves to seconds. White truffle arancini fried a golden brown; popiah stuffed with king crab meat; tender Wagyu strip loin with karashi béarnaise; slivers of the freshest sashimi arranged on platters like art; and petit four bites that glistened like colorful jewels. And those still feeling peckish afterward could help themselves to thyme-and-pepper meringue cups, drizzled with hundred-year-old Giusti Modena balsamic vinegar.

The media representatives ambled around, peering closely at the dishes and the decor and interviewing the gushing guests. Samantha even overheard *S*'s writer saying to her counterpart at *Esquire* that this was the best work assignment she had ever gotten. Hopefully, she would tell Missy the same too.

Darkness engulfed her as a pair of hands slid over her eyes. "Guess who?" someone whispered from behind her.

Samantha's heart leapt. The perpetual grin underlying his voice. The faint British accent that sounded so much stronger when she couldn't see anything. The slightly spicy undertones of his cologne.

Samantha whirled around and found herself face-to-face with a grinning Timothy. "You came!" she exclaimed, and before she could think it through, she was throwing her arms around his neck.

For a moment, as their bodies made contact, her heart seized with a sudden fear that she was doing something very wrong. But almost immediately, Timothy's hands were coming up to pull her even closer toward him. She breathed in his cologne, which smelled even better when laid over the clean, cotton scent of his shirt. It was a heady, intoxicating combination.

Clang! Samantha jerked back, her skin tingling. A waiter had dropped his tray on the ground and was murmuring apologies to everyone in the vicinity. That's right—she was at a work event for crying out loud; she couldn't just go around hugging the guests. And more importantly, the guest in question had a *girlfriend*. Who hated her.

Samantha smoothed her jumpsuit and cleared her throat. "Didn't you say you were in Malaysia tonight?"

He grinned. "I lied. I wanted to surprise you. There's no way I would miss your first big PR event. I brought you flowers by the way, but they're in my car since I figured you can't hold on to them now." He cast his eyes over the profusion of blossoms all around the room. "Anyway, I see you have more than enough here."

"You didn't have to bring anything—"

Timothy's voice was low and even as he said, "I wanted to."

Suddenly, Samantha couldn't remember how to breathe as she looked into Timothy's eyes, dark and liquid like two pools of malt whiskey. "Thank you," she whispered. "I—"

"Why, surely it isn't Timothy Kingston!" exclaimed Cassandra as she rushed up toward them.

Even though they had been standing a respectable distance apart, Samantha immediately sprang away from Timothy, praying their interaction didn't look too suspicious. When she had suggested inviting him before knowing about his "family friend's baptism," Cassandra had responded with a patronizing smile. "You clearly don't know Timothy Kingston very well. He's famously reclusive, and I don't think I've seen him at a single event in recent months. At this rate, I'm not even sure if he will show up to the S Gala. There's no point wasting an invitation on him."

Technically, Timothy shouldn't even have been let into the party without an invitation, but Samantha supposed the Kingston name worked as a universal pass.

"How are you finding my party so far? Is there anything you need?" Cassandra cooed to Timothy in a saccharine-sweet voice that made goose bumps break out all over Samantha's skin.

"Your party is wonderful, and this place looks incredible. Remind me to ask you later where you got your chandelier from; my mother has been on a renovation spree lately, and I know she will love this," Timothy said, flashing Cassandra a bright smile.

Knowing Eileen Kingston, there was no way she would deign to imitate anyone else, but Timothy's charm was clearly working. "Oh gosh, you're much too kind," the host said, her eyes shining.

Somehow, this made Samantha feel slightly more comforted—if Timothy could make a society maven like Cassandra Ow flustered enough to say "oh gosh," then she could cut herself some slack for how unsettled she sometimes felt around him. Maybe he just had this effect on everyone.

"And I'm sure your book will be a huge success," he went on. "Sam did a great job with everything, don't you think?"

Cassandra's brows shot up. "I didn't realize you two knew each other." Her face brightened as she turned to Samantha. "Oh, Samantha, you must have been the one to convince Timothy to come! You really are a PR wonder."

Although Cassandra's gushing was probably a show put on for Timothy's sake, Samantha still had to press her lips together to stop a smile from slipping out. Regardless of what everyone else felt about the party, Cassandra's approval was the most important one.

With a conspiratorial air, Timothy leaned closer to Cassandra as though to tell her a secret. "Well, I just knew I couldn't miss the launch event of the year."

Cassandra's beam got even wider—something Samantha didn't think was possible. "Thank you so much! It's really lovely to have you here. In fact, I was just talking to someone who said she knows you." She looked around. A moment later, her eyes lit up and she waved at someone in the distance. "There she is! Lucia, come here for a minute."

Samantha's chest constricted. *Lucia is at my party?* Instinctively, she turned to Timothy, but his face had gone blank.

Samantha's heart sank as Lucia swanned up, smiling brightly in a body-con cream knit dress and her hair flowing down her back like she was in a Pantene commercial. To wear something skintight *and* pure white to a food party—how could a woman be so unabashedly confident?

"Sam! So wonderful to see you again," Lucia said, swooping down and kissing Samantha on both cheeks.

Samantha stiffened. She had to hand it to Lucia—the other woman was doing a much better job of faking niceties than she was.

Before Samantha could say anything, Lucia turned to Timothy. "And, Tim!" Her voice took on a teasing note that made Samantha's jaw clench. "Aren't you glad to see me?"

There was a moment of silence, then Timothy smiled. "Hi, Lucia. I must say I'm a little surprised to see you here," he said pleasantly.

Lucia tossed her hair back. "But you were the one who told me about this party, remember? Anyway, I'm here with Randall Lai. You remember Randall, don't you? Wasn't he a year above you at UWC? Well, *Forbes* just rated him as one of Asia's top investment bankers. They called him a stock market wizard."

Timothy's smile tautened, his eyes flickering around as though searching for an escape route. Samantha couldn't muster any sympathy for him, not after he'd told Lucia about her party.

"Lucia, you're too modest!" Cassandra exclaimed. "Don't just talk about Randall's achievements. Weren't you just sharing some good news of your own with me? I'm sure Timothy and Samantha would love to hear it too."

Lucia gave the host a playful swat on the arm. "Cassandra! That was supposed to be on the DL"—from Cassandra's blank smile, Samantha guessed she had no idea what "DL" meant—"but yes, I do have some exciting news," she said, staring straight at Timothy. "The news hasn't been announced to the public yet, but you're looking at this year's host of the S Gala!"

For a few moments, no one said anything. Finally, Timothy mumbled, "Congratulations. That's an amazing accomplishment."

Lucia gazed up at him through her long eyelashes. "Oh, Tim, you know better than anyone just how long I've wanted this. You were the first person I told years ago about my dream to host the S Gala someday. Oh, and the National Day Parade."

"Congratulations. You must be so thrilled," Samantha forced out, hoping Cassandra couldn't tell how strained her smile was. Now even if she managed to score an S Gala invitation, the excitement of her high-society debut would be dampened by the knowledge that she'd be staring up at Lucia with her perfect figure and undoubtedly perfect outfit for an entire evening.

Lucia turned her big doe eyes on her. "Thank you so much, babe!" she trilled as though the two of them were best friends. "Well, I should probably go find my date now. Randall said he wanted to introduce me to some folks—I guess being well-connected is part and parcel of being such a big player in Asia's financial scene! See you all around."

Lucia floated away, leaving a cloying cloud of Chanel No. 5 and a heavy silence in her wake.

21

Cassandra's phone buzzed. "Shoot," she muttered, squinting at the screen. "That was a reminder to touch up my makeup before I give my big speech. Please excuse me." She straightened her necklace and marched off purposefully.

The moment Cassandra was out of earshot, Samantha dragged Timothy to a corner and hissed, "You told Lucia about my party?"

He held up his hands. "I swear it's not what you think."

Samantha crossed her arms, her stony stare a strict order for him to start explaining. He let out a sigh. "All right. If you noticed any weirdness between Lucia and me, it's because we broke up last night."

"*What?*" Samantha yelped, then lowered her voice as heads turned toward them. "Why didn't you say anything earlier?"

"I was going to tell you tomorrow. Tonight is your big night, so who cares about me and Lucia?"

"I care!" Samantha's cheeks reddened. "About you, I mean. A breakup is huge and"—she cleared her throat—"as your friend, I want to be here for you." There were a million questions running through her mind, but the only one she had a right to ask, as a *friend*, was "How are you feeling?"

Timothy took his time to form a response. "It feels a bit weird because we were together for quite a while," he said slowly. "But I think the breakup was a long time coming, to be honest. Anyway, Lucia wanted to meet up in person to talk it out, but I told her I wasn't free tonight because I was coming to this party. I'm sorry for letting it slip. I didn't think she was going to snag a plus-one invitation at the last minute."

Samantha shrugged, her heart suddenly much lighter. "I can't say I'm thrilled about her being here, but any party attended by Lucia Yen is automatically seen as a big deal, so this is great for my career."

Timothy's mouth quirked up into a half smile. "Thanks for being a good sport. But honestly, you don't need her attendance to confirm what everyone already knows—this party is bloody brilliant." He swept an arm out toward the room. "Look at you, being an absolute PR badass."

Samantha looked around Cassandra's dining room again, trying to see everything through Timothy's eyes. "I can't believe all my years of reading magazines actually came in handy for this. Not to mention all the parties Anya has brought me to."

"And now you've come full circle. It's going to be *your* party being featured in those magazines and read by thousands of people across the country."

"Technically, this is Cassandra's party, not mine."

"But the articles are going to say something like *Cassandra Ow's book launch party, planned and organized by*"—Timothy spread his hands apart in midair like he was framing a picture—"*Samantha Song of Arrow Public Relations.* You're going to see your name in big, bold print. Don't forget me when people start knocking down your door to be your client."

Laughing, Samantha batted his arm. "Stop teasing me. But I must say, there's something pretty poetic about how I'm not a magazine writer—"

"Yet."

"Fingers crossed. But yeah, it's pretty cool my name is still gonna appear in magazines, even if it's not as a byline."

Timothy grabbed a wineglass off a nearby table and stuck it under Samantha's nose like a microphone. "Tell me, Miss Song, how does your current PR job compare to your childhood dream of being a magazine writer?"

Giggles threatened to erupt from her mouth, but Timothy looked so earnest that Samantha suppressed them. "Well, Mr. Kingston," she said solemnly, "they're quite different indeed. If I'm a writer, I'll still be cut off from the action, you know? I can only admire everything from afar."

"Right. But now, you're the one orchestrating everything."

"Exactly! Now I'm in the thick of the action, helping to create the fantasy and bringing it to life. For once, it's *my* vision."

Timothy grinned. "Miss Song, this is only your debut solo project. What else can we expect from you?"

"I think this will be a good launchpad for attracting a more high-end clientele, so I foresee several upscale projects in the near future. Hey, maybe you can even—"

Samantha broke off. She'd been about to ask Tim to come to her future events, too, but who knew where they would be in a month when the Fraud Squad's scheme ended?

"Maybe I can what?"

"I was going to say, maybe you can come to my next few events too," she said softly, casting her eyes down so she wouldn't have to see his reaction. "But only if you want to, of course. No pressure."

She looked back at Timothy's face as he chuckled—a low baritone sound that rumbled from his chest and wrapped around her.

"Oh, I plan on showing up to all the events you organize," he said, gaze locked on her face. "You won't be able to keep me away."

Something swooped in Samantha's stomach, turning her insides warm and melty like honey. "I'm holding you to that."

For a long moment, it was just them looking at each other. But far from the silence being awkward, it felt more like the two of them were sequestered in their own little bubble, far apart from the other party guests.

Finally, Timothy broke the silence. "Hey, don't make any plans for after the party, all right? I want to take you out for celebratory drinks." He grinned. "A toast to your professional success."

"I'm not sure when this will end—"

"I'll wait as long as it takes."

Samantha tucked a lock of hair behind her ear and smiled back, suddenly feeling rather shy. "Okay. I'd love to."

A shrill pinging sound rang through the dining room, drawing every eye to the center of the room, where Cassandra stood, rapping a spoon against her crystal wine goblet.

When she was at last satisfied that everyone's attention was on her, Cassandra spread her arms wide and beamed around the room. "Dear friends, thank you all for joining me tonight in my humble home. As you probably know, I pride myself on being an epicure, and it's always been a dream of mine to create a book of my most beloved recipes. And finally, my dream has become a reality. My cookbook, *Deluxe Eats for the Discerning Diner*, will hit bookstores tomorrow!" Cheers roared across the room as Cassandra held up a copy of her cookbook, its glossy cover shimmering under the room's bright lights.

Once the applause died down, Cassandra dropped her smile. She furrowed her brows and laid a hand against her chest, her diamond rosary bracelet glinting on her wrist. "But tonight, even as we all feast on the sumptuous dishes from so many different cuisines," she continued, her voice suddenly much lower and heavier, "I'm once again reminded of how so many around the world are less fortunate than we are. There are millions of children who go to bed hungry every day, and nowhere more so than in sub-Saharan Africa, where a shocking twenty-eight million children live in a constant and chronic state of starvation." Her voice cracking, she paused to dab at the corners of her eyes.

Samantha pressed her lips together to hold back a snort. Cassandra was laying it on a tad too thick, but it appeared from all the bobbing heads that everyone bought her words. "And that is why I will be donating all proceeds raised from the sales of my book to the Hunger Project, an organization that's near and dear to my heart. I hope my donation will go a long way toward helping children around the world enjoy good, nutritious food that invigorates their bodies, minds, and souls."

In unison, the guests burst into a thunderous ovation, and that was all it took for Cassandra's sorrowful expression to break, a broad smile blooming in its place.

From her spot at the back of the room, Samantha saw the media representatives' heads bent over their press kits, busy recording down the overwhelmingly positive response shown toward Cassandra Ow's great culinary and charity triumph. She leaned back against the wall and exhaled. The *Deluxe Eats* project was, by all accounts and measures, an indisputable success. Cassandra would be happy, which meant Heather would be happy, and that was all that mattered.

Cassandra held up a hand. "I'll let you all return to your food soon. But first, I must thank my publisher, Paradise Books, for helping me turn my dream into a reality. And of course, our delightful dinner tonight is courtesy of Bertha Ling, chef extraordinaire, and her wonderful assistants. And lastly, I'd like to thank the brilliant Samantha Song from Arrow Public Relations, who orchestrated tonight's party as well as the publicity for my cook-book. If you need PR help with anything, Samantha's your girl!"

What? Samantha jerked upright as the audience, following the direction of Cassandra's gaze, turned toward her. She had drafted the speech and heard Cassandra rehearsing so many times that she could have recited it word for word at this point, but none of those renditions had included Samantha in the acknowledgments. PR staff rarely received public recognition anyway; her job was to show up, make sure everything went smoothly, and then fade into the woodwork while her client basked in adulation and glory.

Timothy gave her a gentle nudge. With all eyes on her, Samantha stepped forward as a new round of applause filled the room.

So, this was what it was like being the center of attention . . . Samantha felt like she was back at Cé La Vi again, literally on top of the world and larger than life as she saw how small the city looked from fifty-seven stories up in the air.

Samantha rolled back her shoulders and put on her brightest smile. If only Argus was around to witness this moment and record her triumph.

22

Walking into Atlas was like a gold-rush assault to Samantha's eyes. From the chandeliers that dripped down like stalactites to the three-story-high cocktail cabinet behind the bar, almost everything in the lounge was decked out in the decadent metallic shade.

Less than forty-eight hours ago, she had been drinking in this exact place with Timothy, right after the *Deluxe Eats* launch party. They had stayed there past midnight, toasting to the event's success and laughing themselves silly as they recalled the other guests' antics.

In the light of the day, the baroque frescoes unfurling across the cathedral ceiling looked even more beautiful. Sunlight flooding the lounge lit up the rows of brightly hued bottles in the cocktail cabinet like a stained-glass window.

"A place of bacchanalian worship," Timothy had called it. She had in turn called his words "pretentious." But indeed, they had worked themselves into a revelry fueled by the most lavish alcohol money could buy, their empty glasses piling up on the bar counter. At some point, as she looked over at Timothy's flushed, animated face, Samantha couldn't even remember what they were laughing about; she only knew she never wanted it to end—the perfect way to cap off an unforgettable day.

Raina was already seated in a booth, her trademark jean jacket the only piece of denim in the whole place. "Hi, hi! So sorry I'm late," Samantha exclaimed as she collapsed onto the leather banquette.

"That's okay," Raina muttered. She was perched on the edge of her seat, back stiff as a board and hands clasped tightly on her knees. "Nice dress."

"Thanks! It's from Badgley Mischka." Samantha peered at Raina's jacket. "Is that a new pin I see? Near the collar?"

Raina fingered the pin—a cartoonish rendition of an ovary with its fallopian tubes wrapped around the word **Cuterus**. "Yeah, I got it as part of a two-for-ten-bucks set from this Etsy store specializing in feminist accessories. The other one says **Overchiever**."

"Where's that one?"

Raina shrugged. "Somewhere on the back."

Samantha waited for her to turn around to show off the other pin, but when Raina didn't budge, she rushed to fill the silence. "Well, those are so on brand for you." Raina's jacket was more pins than denim at this point, and it was a wonder Atlas's notoriously fussy maître d' hadn't carded her for the dress code violation. Perhaps their rules were more relaxed during the day.

Or more likely it was because they had both been put down as guests of Timothy Kingston.

"Thanks. Anyway, the food arrived just before you did." Raina nodded at the three-tier rose-gold tray on the table.

Samantha's eyes lit up as they ran over the medley of sweet bites and savory canapés. "Perfect! This is exactly what I asked for when I made the reservation this morning."

"This morning? But I heard it takes weeks to get a reservation at Atlas."

"Tim's good friends with the owner, so he helped me out with this last-minute reservation. In fact, the afternoon tea set isn't even available on Sundays, but Tim spoke to the owner and ta-da!" Samantha rubbed her hands together. "I can't wait to dig in. The last time I came, it was too late to order this set, but I heard the raspberry financier is—"

"Wait, you've been here before?"

"With Tim two nights ago." Samantha's mouth twitched at the memory. As they sampled Atlas's offerings, Timothy had related—with an endearing excitement—everything he knew about the mythical Atlas from his classics courses at Durham. "I know it might seem like overkill to come here twice in one weekend, but this place is seriously so stunning that I just *had* to bring you here."

"Oh. So that's why you texted me this morning asking if we could change our brunch spot."

"I figured we could switch things up from the kopitiam. It's nice to have brunch without worrying about whether my curls look like crap because it's so humid." Samantha popped a generous chunk of financier into her mouth. "Oh my God. All the online reviews are right—this is absolutely incredible. Rai, you *have* to try it."

Raina made no move to do so. "Isn't this place pretty . . . pricey?" she asked, raising a brow. "Especially since you also offered to cover my share."

Samantha reached for a scone. "Actually, I'm not paying," she said, picking up her spreading knife. "Tim has an open tab at Atlas, so he said he'd cover the bill." She spread a thick layer of clotted cream onto her scone, then dropped a perfect dollop of ruby-pink jam in the middle. *There, the perfect cream-to-jam ratio.*

Putting down her knife, she looked up to find Raina staring hard at her. "What? Is there something on my face?"

"Since when are you so comfortable spending so much money? Money that's not even yours."

There was an unfamiliar edge in Raina's voice that gave Samantha pause. "It's not like I forced Tim to do this. He was the one who suggested I bring you here for a change after I told him about our Sunday tradition." She summoned a bright smile. "And now that the Cassandra Ow project is over, I want to make up for all my previous flakiness by treating you to a gourmet brunch."

Compared to Samantha's perky voice, Raina sounded extra quiet as she said, "The Sam I know wouldn't act like throwing money around is the way to fix things, and she wouldn't have chosen this atas place over the kopitiam we've been going to for years."

Samantha's smile faded. "I just wanted to switch things up for once. How's that a crime?"

Raina continued like she hadn't heard. "And I thought you only wore Anya's designer clothes to those fancy society events, but now you're even wearing them to brunch with me."

"Because Atlas has a strict dress code!"

Raina narrowed her eyes. "Don't think I didn't notice you judging my outfit earlier."

"I wasn't judging! I was just surprised you weren't called out for violating the dress code."

"Atlas's dress code or your dress code featuring designer brands with unpronounceable Italian names?"

"Badgley Mischka is an American brand," Samantha deadpanned, but Raina's face remained stony. "Come on, Rai, I wasn't judging you. You're just imagining things."

"And did I also imagine the part where you've been flaking out on our plans to attend fancy parties, while letting me believe you were at work?"

Samantha froze, her stomach sinking. Something brushed against her hand and she looked down—half her scone had broken off in her tight grip, scattering crumbs and cream all over herself. Dimly, Samantha registered that Anya would be less than pleased to find stains on her new dress, but right now, all she could think of was that she had never seen Raina's eyes so cold before.

"How did you find out?"

A wan smile flitted across Raina's lips. "After you told me about your *Elle* interview, I became curious about what those magazines were like. So I picked up a copy of *L'Officiel* one day from my office's reception to take a look. And lo and behold, who do I see staring back at me from the society pages but my best friend, who said she had to cancel our meetup to work overtime but was actually attending the release party for the *L'Officiel* Luxe List on the same night."

"Rai, I'm so, so sorry—"

Raina scoffed. "Yeah, you looked hard at work all right. Hardly working, that is."

"I'm really sorry," Samantha repeated morosely, wishing she could shrink into herself. She had never felt as small as she did now. "You're right—what I did was completely unfair to you. I've been so preoccupied with my Fraud Squad stuff because there's only a month left to impress the S Gala committee." She leaned forward, her eyes wide and earnest. "But I promise this will all blow over soon and afterward, I'll hopefully be writing for *S* and things can return to normal."

Raina folded her arms, the pins on her jacket jingling with the movement. "Oh, really? Do you want to write about socialites for *S*, or do you want to be one of them?"

Samantha squinted. "What's that supposed to mean? You know I don't have the background to be a socialite."

"But you *want* it," Raina said, looking steadily at Samantha. "That's why you want to write for *S*, because you know that's the closest you can get to that world. You'd rather be on the fringes, wearing designer PR goodies while hanging around socialites and hoping their glamour rubs off on you secondhand, than not be in the mix at all." She shook her head. "This fancy lifestyle of yours isn't temporary anymore—it's become a part of you, and you've made it clear there's no place for people like me in it."

"That's not true!" Samantha exclaimed, then dropped her voice as heads turned in her direction. *Shit, what if Argus is here?* "This is all just a means to an end."

Raina pursed her lips. "Once you get used to something, it's really hard giving it up. It only takes three weeks to form a habit, and by the time the S Gala rolls around, your high-society project would have been ongoing for three *months*. Do you seriously believe you can go from this"—she swept an arm around Atlas—"back to kopitiams with no air-conditioning that make your hair frizz up?"

"Yes, I can," Samantha said stoutly.

"So you won't be upset giving up Anya's designer clothes? No longer being able to go to parties where there are red carpets and waiters serving you champagne?"

Samantha threw her hands up. "What do you want me to say? It's obvious you've made up your mind about me, and nothing I say will change what you think. This isn't a conversation anymore."

Raina was silent for a few moments. "You're right," she finally said. "We've nothing more to talk about. Maybe I'm not being understanding, or maybe I'm right that you're no longer someone I recognize." Raina stood up and pulled her jacket tighter around herself. "Thank you for treating me to brunch, but I have to go now."

Even as her heart ran cold, Samantha kept a smile on her face as she watched Raina walk away—just in case Argus or one of her sources was around. For a moment, she had a strong urge to call after Raina, to drag her back by her pin-covered lapel so she could apologize. But when her best friend disappeared through the doors, the urge passed. Samantha let out a deep exhale and sank back in her seat.

She eyed the trays of uneaten food, the clink of utensils from surrounding tables ringing hollow in her ears. It would be a shame to waste Timothy's generosity, so Samantha reached forward and picked up Raina's discarded financier. She popped it into her mouth and chewed slowly, but the soft and spongy cake weighed down on her tongue like lead.

Even a meal costing three figures could taste unappetizing without the right person to share it with.

Samantha swallowed the last morsel and shrank further into the banquette. Maybe Anya was right all along: Her high-society life and old life just weren't supposed to mix.

23

Samantha paced around her living room, her eyes darting up to the clock for the third time in as many minutes. It was 4:29 p.m. Timothy would be arriving any minute now.

Her phone buzzed as a message popped up on the screen.

Tim: Hey, I'll be at your place soon. #08–13, right?

Yup, Samantha started typing. Getting to Sentosa Island for Anya's party was an absolute hassle by public transport, so she had gladly accepted Tim's offer to give her a ride. To thank him, she had invited him up to her flat for a drink before they set off.

But before Samantha could send the message, a sharp exclamation came from the kitchen. "*Ta ma de!*"

Samantha shook her head wryly; Ma must have stubbed her toes for the dozenth time on the loose tile by the fridge. She'd insisted multiple times they get it fixed, but her mother had been just as insistent their money could be spent on other, more important things.

Samantha froze as a new thought struck her. When she had invited Tim to her flat, she hadn't accounted for her mother being there. Ma was supposed to be at work but had been sent home early because her carpal tunnel flared up again. This meant introducing

Tim to Ma . . . It meant Ma trying to deduce his background and eligibility with a series of unsubtle questions she'd perfected on all of Samantha's ex-boyfriends, her excitement skyrocketing the moment she discovered he was the Kingston Management Group heir. And with her Asian-mom nosiness, uncovering that connection was only a matter of time.

Samantha quickly deleted her draft and composed a new one.

Sam: We're running late, so I'll come down and meet you at the void deck instead.

AS ANYA HAD requested, Samantha and Timothy arrived at the Capella hotel on Sentosa Island a full thirty minutes before the party's official start time. "There's something I want to show you later," Timothy said as they breezed past the doormen flanking the entrance.

Samantha picked up the hem of her long dress with one hand to avoid getting it snagged in her heels. "Ooh, what is it?"

He grinned over at her. "It's a surprise. Nothing big, but I think you'll like it."

Samantha tugged on the sleeve of Timothy's suit to pull him to a stop. "Spill," she said, narrowing her eyes. "If not, I'll be thinking about it the whole evening."

"You're too cute to look intimidating," Timothy said with a laugh. "You'll see soon—we just have to find a time to slip away from Anya's party for a bit."

Just the two of us? Ignoring her suddenly pounding heart, Samantha jutted out her lower lip. "Ugh, you're the absolute worst," she grumbled, but couldn't fight a smile. "Why do I even put up with how secretive you are?"

Placing a hand on the small of her back, Timothy started leading her toward Anya's party venue. "Because of my devilishly good looks and wit," he quipped, shortening his strides to match her in heels. "You know you love me deep down."

Tingles shot through Samantha's body—whether from Timothy's words or his hand on her back, she couldn't tell. "No, it's really because you're my ride here," she informed him loftily. "That's pretty much the only reason why I keep you around."

"Ouch. And there I was thinking we had something special."

Samantha's stomach did a little flip. Timothy's palm against her skin suddenly felt burning hot, but he dropped it as Anya strode down the hallway toward them. Her sleek bob hugged the sides of her face, which was expertly painted with makeup, but it was her outfit that made Samantha's brows shoot up: a knee-length Burberry trench coat, belted at the waist and paired with a pair of fluffy hotel slippers. Still chic, but not exactly fitting for an Oscars-themed party.

"Hey, Sherlock Holmes," Timothy said. "Happy birthday! What's with the outfit?"

"Thank God you guys are here!" Anya cried. "I've been freaking out so much and I need to talk to someone before I go batshit crazy. And don't even get me started on this coat. The corset of my Balmain dress is so tight I can barely breathe, so I'm only gonna change out of the coat and slippers right before guests arrive."

"Well, you look amazing!" Samantha wrapped Anya in a big hug, careful not to get too near to her face in case the makeup smudged. "Happy birthday, girl! I can't wait to see what you've done with the venue."

Anya drew back, gnawing on her lower lip. "I don't know if it's good enough. I keep going online to read about past society parties—I even looked up your *Deluxe Eats* party—and I can't tell if mine's on the same level."

"Sam and I can tell you," Timothy offered. He winced as Samantha gave him a sharp jab in the side.

"What Tim means is that we can tell you all your worries are for nothing because it's going to be obvious to everyone you have incredible taste. Right, Tim?" Samantha shot him a pointed look.

Timothy grinned. "Yes, boss. Exactly what you said."

Anya cleared her throat. "Here goes nothing then." She braced both hands on the double doors behind her, took a deep breath, and then threw them open.

The room was filled with so many service workers rushing around that it took Samantha a few moments to make out what she was seeing. When her eyes finally adjusted, the first thing they landed on were two larger-than-life replicas of the iconic Oscar statue looming over her, one on each side of the entrance. Their gold bodies shimmered beneath the sunshine flooding in from an entire wall of floor-to-ceiling windows. Samantha knew the windows were a key reason why Anya had picked the Capella hotel's Gallery room for her party: She wanted a clear view of the sunset so that the birthday song would be timed right at the beginning of golden hour, which was not just theme fitting but also when Anya looked her best (according to the birthday girl herself).

On the other side of the glass wall was a lush rain forest, and beyond that, a ribbon of the ocean on the horizon, its waters sparkling beneath the late-afternoon sun. The other three walls held a montage of studio shots, each featuring Anya in a different silver screen outfit: in a flouncy white dress as Marilyn Monroe's character in *The Seven Year Itch*; as Holly Golightly in a sleek black Givenchy gown; as Mrs. Smith in a slinky thigh-bearing sheath; and the list went on.

"Anya, are you kidding me?" Samantha exclaimed, slack-jawed as her eyes swiveled around the room. "Why are you even worrying? This is ridiculous."

"Ridiculous in a good way or bad way?" Anya immediately asked.

"Definitely in a good way!" Samantha laughed. "Anya, chill. You don't want to look so tense when everyone else is here."

But her words only deepened the groove between Anya's brows. "What do you think of the sign-in book? I labeled it as a celebrity autograph book like you suggested, but is it too gimmicky?"

"Not at all! People will think it's clever. Right, Tim?"

"Absolutely," he said firmly. "Anya, your party is going to kick-ass."

"You really think so?" Anya asked, her eyes swiveling between Samantha and Timothy. "You don't think it's too much?"

Samantha gripped Anya's shoulders and looked straight into her eyes. "Anya, take a deep breath." After a moment, Anya acquiesced, her eyes fluttering shut as she inhaled slowly. "And now, let it out gently." A long exhale. "Okay, good. Just remember you're the birthday star and tonight is your night. Everyone's going to absolutely love this."

Anya's eyes flew open. "I'm the birthday star," she repeated quietly, almost to herself. Another deep breath. "I'm the birthday star," she said again, louder and surer this time. "You're right—I can do this. *I'm* the star tonight. Daisy Taija's party can suck it."

Samantha's heart stuttered, but before she could say anything, she found herself stumbling back a little as Anya flung her arms around her. "Thank you," Anya whispered into her shoulder. "I know I've been a lot to put up with lately because I've been panicking so much about tonight. But thank God I have you in my corner—I'd have gone crazy otherwise."

"Of course," Samantha murmured, patting Anya's back and trying to ignore the sinking sensation in her gut.

———

THE GUESTS BEGAN trickling in, and soon, the party was in full swing. Samantha smiled as she watched Anya flit around, making sure to talk to everyone but never letting herself stay at any table for too long.

Even with all the attendees clad in their own Oscar-worthy regalia, the birthday girl was the belle of the ball, resplendent in her tight gold Balmain minidress. No one looking at Anya's bright smile would ever suspect she had to duck out to the bathroom every half an hour to unzip and give herself a literal breather while Samantha stood guard outside to make sure no one entered.

Anya was constantly besieged by well-wishers, but just past eight, Samantha finally managed to get her alone for a moment. "Hey, I think I'm going to head out now," she said quickly, hoping the urgency in her voice would convince Anya to let her off without further questions.

Frowning, Anya glanced at her Cartier watch. "But there's still an hour left. And some of us might be headed to an after-party afterward at Zouk."

"I'm so sorry to dip out. But my mom's not feeling well, so I should head back early." Technically true, but Samantha had made sure before she left that all the housework was done and dinner was ready so Ma could just rest.

Anya pouted. "Oh man. I hope she feels better soon. I'll see you—wait! Were you in all the group photos?"

Anya's face relaxed back into a smile when Samantha nodded. "Good. I'll be submitting the photos to all the society magazines, so the more people who appear in them, the better. I need to make sure people think my party is more popular than Daisy's."

Samantha swallowed. "Right. I was definitely in them."

"Cool! Thanks for coming tonight. Love ya!"

Samantha breathed a sigh of relief as she walked out of the Gallery, leaving the party and its two Oscar statues behind her. In just a few minutes, she'd be out of the hotel and on her way to Daisy's party—

A hand gripped her arm. "Sam, you're leaving already?" Timothy asked, his brows furrowed. "Is everything all right?"

The truth was on the tip of her tongue, but Samantha hesitated. She couldn't risk him telling Anya. "My mom's kind of unwell," she said instead. "So I'm gonna head home early."

Timothy's face fell. "I see."

"What's wrong—oh." Samantha's heart sank as Timothy's earlier words came to her. "Crap. You wanted to show me something, right?" She glanced at her phone's time display. "I think I can spare a few minutes . . . ?"

He paused, then shook his head. "It's all right. Your mom definitely comes first. Is there anything I can do?"

"No, really, I want to see your surprise," she insisted, tucking her phone back in her clutch to prove she meant her words.

"Nah, it's fine. It's not something that should be rushed. We can always enjoy it properly another time."

"But when would we find another time? Sentosa Island isn't easy to get to."

"I'm your personal driver, remember? That's why you keep me around," Timothy reminded her with a grin. "We can come to Sentosa anytime. Hey, let me give you a ride back to your place. It's the least I can do."

"No!—I mean, I think you should stay here to offer Anya moral support," she quickly added as Timothy shot her an odd look.

"Oh. Right."

Phew.

"But let me at least call you an Uber," he continued. "I don't want you traveling alone by yourself at night, especially when your house is so far away."

Samantha quickly shook her head. "No, no. Please don't. Evening traffic is so horrible that taking the subway will get me home faster if I leave now."

Frowning, Timothy opened his mouth, then closed it again. Finally, he sighed. "All right, be careful and call me when you get home. If you update me about your mom's situation, I can ask my family doctor for advice."

Timothy's whiskey-brown eyes were so piercing that Samantha was afraid he might see the untruth in hers if he looked too hard. They were standing close, too close. So close Samantha could feel the heat of his body emanating through his dress shirt, his sheer physicality wrapping around her until it was all she noticed.

Slowly, his eyes locked on hers, Timothy dipped his head lower. His breath ghosted across Samantha's face as he bridged the thin strip of space between them. His lips parted—

She wrenched her arm out of his grip and took a hasty step back, pretending not to notice the hurt that flashed across Tim's face. Her heart was pounding so hard she was sure he could hear the jerky, staccato beat vibrating through her skin.

For a few moments, neither of them said anything, the silence broken only by their heavy breathing. "I'm sorry," Timothy finally said, tugging his collar and looking everywhere but at her. "I didn't mean to."

"No, I'm sorry," Samantha managed, her heart growing cold. Of course Timothy didn't mean to—he'd just gotten out of a four-year relationship, so whatever the hell just happened must have simply been due to boredom and loneliness. "Anyway, I really have to go now."

"Right. But, uh, maybe we can do something together soon?" Timothy scrubbed a hand over his face. "Movie at my place?"

"You don't wanna spend the Golden Village gift card in our party gift bag? Anya spent really long deciding on the party favor, you know," Samantha joked, glad she was able to muster a teasing voice.

"Oh, yeah, we could. But there's this Laura Dern movie I think you would love and it isn't out in Singapore yet."

"Ah, your place it is then!" Samantha said, shifting from one foot to the other. Everything seemed fine on the surface, but the conversation felt like that between two people who'd just met. "Text me the details. And thanks for giving me a ride today!"

Shooting him one last smile, she made her way out of the hotel and to the cab stand, her heart thudding wildly the whole time. Her thumb rubbed circles in the spot where Timothy's hand had touched her, his palm still a ghostlike imprint on her skin.

24

Daisy's engagement party was also on Sentosa Island, in the über-wealthy Sentosa Cove enclave. A fifteen-minute cab ride later, Samantha found herself striding up a pebbled walkway—thankfully not as long as the one at Tim's place—toward a seafront mansion. As she neared the door, a high-pitched buzzing made her glance up: two drones whirred midair, each with a blinking red light on its bottom.

The hairs on Samantha's arms stood up. *Cameras.* Of course Daisy's family would have arranged for a cinematography team on such a special occasion, and *S* would have sent photographers too.

Samantha immediately ducked her head and raised her bag to cover her face as she quickened her footsteps. Thank God she had gone with a sizable Inés Figaredo clutch tonight. Getting caught on camera at Daisy's party would be a death sentence—if photos of her were published, Anya would find out immediately about her betrayal.

A butler in a *Downton Abbey*-esque uniform met Samantha at the door and ushered her into a massive room that appeared straight out of a tropical resort. The wooden shutters to the wrap-around patio were flung wide open, ushering in the tangy scent of the sea. Lush foliage spilled out of intricately carved urns and onto the vibrant floor mosaic. In the center of the room, a marble fountain bubbled away merrily, though its gurgling was barely audible over the babble of the party guests.

"Sam!" Daisy shrieked, rushing across the room and almost knocking Samantha over with the force of her bear hug. "It's so nice to see a familiar face! My mom and Pan Ling invited all their friends, and I've no idea who most of these people are."

Laughing, Samantha untangled herself from Daisy's coltish limbs. "I'm glad I'm able to rescue you then!" She shook her head admiringly as her eyes swept down the other woman's outfit. "Look at you—you're *stunning*."

Daisy beamed as she smoothed her long white dress. "Thank you! Pan Ling insisted I wear white so I look like some pure virgin." She rolled her eyes. "As if Lincoln and I didn't have sex in a nightclub's bathroom half a decade ago."

"The pearls are a nice touch." Samantha smirked at Daisy's necklace. "Very blushing bride of you."

Samantha's smirk faltered as her eyes caught on something over Daisy's shoulder. A man with an impressive-looking camera and an *S* lanyard hanging from his neck meandered around the room, drifting closer toward where she and Daisy stood.

Her heart hammering, Samantha shifted her body behind Daisy's and scanned the room as subtly as she could for more photographers. The back of an asymmetric bob flashed across her eyes, and Samantha froze. It was a hairstyle only someone with absolutely nothing to prove could get away with.

Samantha's breath hitched in her throat. This was it; this was what she had been waiting for.

"Daisy, is it okay if I go say hi to someone I know?"

Daisy pouted. "Ooookay. But you're obliged to come rescue me later from Pan Ling. Actually, I should go find her now before she scolds me for shirking my host duties." And with a final eye roll, she turned around and plunged into the crowd.

Samantha bit her lip as she stared after her friend's retreating profile. She probably ought to go with Daisy and provide moral support, but with so many photographers milling around, the last person she should be with was the party's guest of honor.

Even so, as she neared Missy, Samantha began to wish she had followed Daisy. Pan Ling sounded terrifying, but surely no one could be as scary as *S*'s famed editor—*no one*. Missy was wearing a black capelet over a sleeveless knit dress that Samantha recognized from Proenza Schouler's latest line; it was an outfit that looked rather out of place in Daisy's resort-like house, but that only made Missy seem even more intimidating.

Samantha's footsteps slowed as the crisp scent of Missy's fragrance drifted over. Maybe she should have dabbed on some perfume too. She didn't feel ready yet. She had to run to the bathroom and check her makeup and her hair and her outfit—

Taking a deep breath, Samantha forced herself to calm down. For once, Missy stood alone, studying the refreshment table. It had to be now; she might never get another chance to speak to *S*'s editor in private again. Before she could think further about what she was doing, before her resolve could abandon her, Samantha reached out and tapped Missy's shoulder.

Time stood still for an impossibly long moment as the editor turned around as though in slow motion. Missy arched a brow, her eyes sweeping down Samantha's body then back up to her face. "Yes? Can I help you?"

Up close, Missy's flinty eyes felt like an X-ray piercing straight to Samantha's core, picking up every blemish no matter how minute. There was a faint inkling of crow's-feet at the corners, but that only gave the editor an added sense of gravitas.

For the first time, Samantha became starkly aware of how much younger and less experienced she was compared to the woman scrutinizing her. Her nails dug into her palms. What had she been thinking—trying to pull the wool over Asia's most famous woman in both the publishing *and* fashion worlds? Someone who had rubbed shoulders with celebrities, dignitaries, and people far more illustrious than Samantha ever could be.

"Hello, I'm Samantha," she finally squeezed out, completely forgetting all the witty conversation openers she had prepared in anticipation of this meeting. "Uh, we met at a dinner party thrown by Tim's parents—I mean, Albert and Eileen Kingston—two months ago."

"Yes, the Peking duck entrée was phenomenal," Missy said, her expression polite but blank. Samantha could only take her word for it; she had been too busy ignoring Lucia's glower to even taste the food. Missy remembered the dinner, but did she remember the wine spill too?

"Tim mentioned he's known you for a long time," Samantha offered, hoping the mention of her friendship with Timothy would elevate her in Missy's eyes.

"Ah, Timothy. I practically watched that boy grow up."

The words were warm, but Missy delivered them so matter-of-factly it was impossible for Samantha to deduce what she was really thinking.

Samantha tried again, "So does that mean you've known his parents for very long?"

"I only met Albert through Eileen, but she and I are longtime friends. Back when we both worked at Christie's in Hong Kong, not much older than you are now, we even lived together for a year."

"You worked at Christie's? Were you in the acquisitions department like Eileen?"

"Oh no. You have to be truly passionate and knowledgeable about art like Eileen is to work in acquisitions. I worked in the publishing department instead, where I helped write the catalogs, brochures, and press releases. That gave me good editorial experience for my jobs in fashion publishing later on."

"My dream is to work in publishing too!" Samantha blurted. "In fact, it was reading magazines like *S* that made me want to write for a magazine."

Missy gave her a tight-lipped smile. "Yes, many girls think working at a magazine is very glamorous. But if you actually work here, you'll quickly realize this job isn't just about meeting celebrities and going to ritzy events. It's one thing to attend parties as a guest, which you're probably used to. But attending as a working professional is a different thing altogether."

Samantha's smile faltered. "That's not what I mean."

Giving no sign she heard Samantha, Missy nodded at a young woman in a simple silver sheath standing not far away. "That's Fiona, one of my writers. She gets to tell all her friends she attended the engagement party of the year, but she can't relax at all tonight because she needs to note down every single detail, interview the right people, and post photos onto *S*'s social media accounts with suitable captions. Then she has to write the article, liaise with our photographer about the graphics, and put everything up on our website before the other media outlets do. No one sees how much work we put into every piece of content to try to stay ahead of the pack."

Scorched by Missy's cool disapproval, Samantha couldn't bring herself to meet the other woman's gaze. Instead, her eyes landed on Missy's pursed lips, where the editor's caked-on nude lipstick had settled into every crease. Somehow, seeing those ridges and wrinkles gave Samantha a sudden burst of courage. *Missy is human too*, she reminded herself. *She's not some perfect, untouchable being.*

"I didn't mean to imply the work is easy, because I know it's not," Samantha managed, fighting to keep her voice steady. "When I was at *Tatler*, I saw for myself how hard everyone works, and I know it's the same at *S*. I'm not afraid of putting in the work needed."

Missy eyed her, her expression softening slightly. But there was still a touch of coolness in her voice as she asked, "*Was*? You don't work there anymore?"

"No. I'm now doing PR at Arrow Public Relations," Samantha replied, then couldn't resist adding: "It's under the same parent company as *S*, I believe."

"I thought working in publishing was your *dream*," the editor said with pointed air quotes. "Apparently, not anymore since you switched to PR."

The notion that Missy doubted her passion and commitment was too much for Samantha to bear—didn't the editor realize that Samantha was doing everything she could, including coming to this party, just to have a foot in *S*'s doorway?

"I wanted to keep writing, but there were barely any full-time positions available at all the magazines I applied to, including *S* and *Tatler*. So I—" She broke off, her stomach sinking as her brain caught up to her words.

How could she have been so stupid? A well-connected socialite would never have to suffer the indignity of going through a job search, much less failing at one—just take Tim and Anya, for instance. But she'd been so desperate to prove she wasn't lying about her editorial dream just to suck up to Missy that for a moment, her Fraud Squad role had completely slipped Samantha's mind.

Samantha hastily backtracked, "Uh, some family friends did offer me writing jobs, but I held off on those because I want to know I really deserve my bylines."

Missy tilted her head to one side. "You know, you kind of remind me of Timothy. He said something similar to me once."

Samantha smiled weakly. It *was* Timothy's words at the Apothecary that had inspired her lie.

"Well, it's not just you who had trouble finding a job in this industry now. Thanks to the ongoing recession, most people aren't thinking of buying designer goods these days, so the luxury sector—including luxury publications—has been hit."

"To be fair, even without a recession, most of your readers can't really afford the pieces in *S* anyway. I think they just like admiring and imagining themselves with those items. Kind of like a fantasy to reach for," Samantha said lightly, the way someone would when they are commenting on the weather or anything completely unrelated to themselves.

Missy tipped her champagne glass toward Samantha. "Very true. Aspirational content is exactly the whole premise of *S*. But in times like this, showing too much of that can come across as tone-deaf. We want to produce content more attuned to the current climate without compromising on the luxury and glamour we're known for."

The glimmers of an idea began to take shape in Samantha's mind. "What about balancing out the glamour with some grit? You can still keep all the aspirational content, but maybe add a fresh take that shows there's much more to socialites than just designer brands and glitzy parties."

There was a sinking feeling in Samantha's stomach as Missy narrowed her eyes, but the editor simply said, "And how do you suggest we do that?"

"*S* does an amazing job of showing the exciting, jet-setting lifestyles of socialites, but like you said, that might rub readers the wrong way right now," Samantha said carefully. "So I think it would help if *S* featured socialites talking about their jobs instead of their latest Maldives trip or designer purchase. You know, remind your readers that socialites also have careers and causes they care about, just like most people do."

Missy drummed her fingers against her champagne flute, every clink of her nails against the glass sending Samantha's nerves rocketing to even higher levels. The editor had one of the best poker faces Samantha had ever seen—it was impossible to tell if Missy was actually considering her suggestion or just deciding what was the most polite way to dismiss her.

"You might be onto something," Missy finally said. "We do have quite an interesting article coming out in our September issue that's along those lines, about how there's nothing fundamentally different between the society set and everyone else—well, I won't spoil the surprise now."

Missy paused. "I see one problem though. A lot of our society friends work in family businesses or as influencers. Absolutely nothing wrong with those, but I foresee a lot of cries of nepotism or complaints from readers about how being an influencer is not a real job."

Samantha scarcely dared to believe it—Missy had just given her the perfect opening to bring up her own career, one that would hopefully see a new development if this conversation went well.

"I get what you mean," Samantha said, tempering her voice so her excitement wouldn't show. "It's unfair people think being an influencer isn't a real job, when I've seen how hard they work behind the scenes. Why, my job depends on influencers. For my most recent project promoting Cassandra Ow's cookbook—"

"*Deluxe Eats*?" Missy gave her an appraising look. "One of my writers, May Le, covered the launch party. She said the media kit was well put together."

Samantha had to press her lips together to stop herself from smiling. From Missy, any word of praise was rarer than a Himalaya Birkin. "Thank you! But it was because of all the influencers who attended the party and promoted *Deluxe Eats* that it managed to land on Singapore's bestsellers list. So really, I have a lot of respect for them."

"You don't consider yourself an influencer? I think I've seen you in a few magazines."

Missy recognized *her*? "I love attending those events and meeting new friends like Daisy, but I don't think the public knows me. I'm not on any social media," Samantha said. To minimize any chances of someone from Samantha's past foiling their plans, Anya had made Samantha deactivate all her online profiles—a fresh slate for the creation of *Socialite Samantha Song*.

Missy murmured, "Interesting. It's quite rare to meet a young socialite like yourself with no social media presence."

"Honestly, I enjoy writing media kits for other people more than I enjoy writing Instagram captions for myself."

"You do have quite a bit of editorial experience, don't you? First at *Tatler* and now at Arrow," Missy mused. She looked straight at Samantha, a new gleam in her eyes. "Samantha, I know you are probably very busy with your PR job, but there's this new project at my magazine I think you might be a good fit for."

"What sort of project is this?" Samantha asked, proud of how calm she sounded despite how her heart rate just rocketed. Back when the Fraud Squad's scheme was just beginning, Anya had instructed: "Remember to always play it cool, as though you're used to glamour and wealth and won't be impressed by anything."

The editor took a quick look around their vicinity and lowered her voice. "As you know, *S* prides itself on being the voice of Singapore high society. We were the first in Singapore to come up with the idea of giving a socialite their own column, but there are some . . . shake-ups going on currently with As Seen by Argus. We're always looking for contributions from more of our society friends. And what you were saying gave me an idea for a new column, one that I envision as the ruminations of a Gen Z–millennial socialite. *Sex and the City*-style, except it will be more like *Career in the City*. I want to show readers how younger socialites can balance their social commitments with their day jobs, that they are not afraid of working hard and putting their own spin on the 'social-ite' label. Balance out the glamour with something grittier, like you said."

Samantha's eyes widened. She had been hoping for an interview or, at best, a feature in *S* that might raise her profile enough to secure an invite to the S Gala.

But Missy was offering her everything she had ever dreamed of . . . right here, right now.

"And you really want *me* to be your Carrie Bradshaw?"

Missy's mouth curved into a semblance of a smile. "Yes, I think you could be perfect for this. You have an interesting job that I don't see ruffling any feathers; you have editorial experience under your belt; and since you came up with this idea, I'm confident you will have good ideas for the column as well. Best of all, you are still an unknown entity, so the public doesn't hold any preconceived notions of you as they might for other young social-ites who have appeared in the tabloids or posted too many party photos on Instagram."

The last bit made Samantha think of something. "Is that why Argus is anonymous? So she wouldn't get judged by the public?"

"Well, that, and the fact that I doubt the other socialites would be happy with Argus about some of the things written in the col-umn," Missy said dryly. "Anyway, I will still need to see some writ-ing samples first, and if you decide this isn't aligned with what you want, there are some other young socialites I can reach out to, so no pressure to say yes."

Other young socialites like . . . Lucia Yen. "No, I'm definitely inter-ested," Samantha immediately said. "I'll send over some of my past work and also a list of ideas for how to make Glamour and Grit the best magazine column in Singapore." *Even better than As Seen by Argus.*

"Glamour and Grit?" Missy asked, arching one brow.

"Just an idea I had for the column title, but we can totally change it."

"No, I like it. Glamour and Grit it is," Missy said crisply. She passed Samantha her business card. "Here's my email. Send your samples and ideas to me and I'll get back to you with my thoughts."

As Samantha accepted the card, her eyes landed on Missy's nails. "I like your manicure. That's an American manicure, right?"

"Why, yes. I'm surprised you recognize it. Most people confuse the American with the French."

Samantha smiled. If there was one thing she might know more than anyone else here, it was nail design thanks to Ma. "I'll send over the materials you asked for within the next few days."

"Excellent." Missy scooped up her champagne glass. "Now if you'll excuse me, I should go check up on Fiona and see how she's doing. She's a sweet girl but tends to lose her head around celebrities. Since there are plenty of them here, I'm sure her mind's all in a whirl."

The moment Missy walked out of view, Samantha collapsed against the wall. Adrenaline had carried her through the conversation—an out-of-body experience where it felt like she was watching from afar someone else charm the editor, someone infinitely more polished and charismatic than her actual self. Only now was Samantha processing the toll the past twenty minutes had taken on her: the dryness in her mouth, the stiffness in her fingers from where she had been unconsciously clenching her hands, the ache in her neck from pulling herself up to her fullest height to try to match Missy's six-foot frame.

Samantha took a deep breath, remaining still as the air wound through her until she could feel her body loosening. As her hands tightened around Missy's business card, the edges dug into her flesh, the sting breaking through her haze as she registered the enormity of what had just happened.

Singapore's most powerful editor had just asked *her*, Samantha Song, to write for the country's most famous magazine. There was the matter of the writing samples she had to submit, but her editorial skills had never been something Samantha doubted. And as for coming up with column ideas of how to balance glamour and grit—who better to write about that than someone actually straddling two different worlds?

Her biggest dream was finally on the verge of coming true, and all Samantha wanted to do was celebrate it with the people she loved most. Automatically, she reached for her phone, but her finger stilled on the first button on her speed dial. Her heart slowly sank. This was the happiest thing to have happened to her in a long time and she couldn't even share it with Raina, the first person she'd confided her *S* dream to years ago back in secondary school. Who else could she tell? Not Anya, who would definitely ask for details about the Missy run-in and be furious once she learned Samantha had gone to Daisy's party.

And Timothy—he had never once been anything but completely sincere and up-front with her. She hated the thought of deceiving Anya, but somehow, it was his reaction she truly dreaded. Already, Samantha could picture Timothy's whiskey-brown eyes growing dark with hurt and anger upon discovering her lie.

25

True to his word, Timothy contacted Samantha the day after Anya's party to plan their movie session—an unexpectedly difficult task, since not only had Samantha been kept busy with putting together the editorial samples Missy asked for, but her work assignments had also grown to mountainous proportions in recent weeks. At the *Deluxe Eats* party, Genie Tsai, Cassandra's friend and owner of a plant-based food company, had approached Samantha about spearheading the marketing campaign for Alter Meatgo's latest vegan product—a request her manager Heather had only been too happy to approve in light of *Deluxe Eats*'s roaring success.

In the end, Samantha and Timothy settled on Wednesday night—the only evening that week when she had neither a work nor social commitment. As she followed Timothy into his house, she couldn't help wondering when was the last time she'd reached home before nine and gotten dinner with her mother. They barely even saw each other anymore since Ma was always asleep by the time Samantha came back and at work before Samantha woke up the next day.

But the unease worming through Samantha was swiftly dashed as she stepped into the Kingstons' home cinema. Her eyes widening as she tilted her head back to take in the ceiling frieze of a dozen sculpted angels. "You know, when you said movie at your place, I was expecting more of a Netflix-on-your-laptop situation, not . . . this," she breathed, eyes tracing the arabesques carved into the walls.

Those, combined with the soft cove lighting, plush carpet, and cozy-looking seats, sent flutters through Samantha's stomach. It was a good thing they weren't watching a romance movie. *That*, in such an intimate setting, would have been too much. Too dangerous.

Timothy chuckled. "It's definitely convenient, but I still prefer going to public cinemas. It's fun seeing everyone reacting at the same time to the same scene. Anyway, make yourself comfortable," he said, walking toward the minibar in the back of the room. "I'm going to fix us some popcorn and drinks."

"Being able to skip the ads is definitely a perk of having your own cinema. I usually finish half the popcorn before the movie even starts," Samantha quipped, but her expression faltered as she registered the seat layout.

In front of the massive screen were three rows of overstuffed velvet chairs. Each row had one love seat in the middle, flanked by two single seats on each side. If she chose a single seat on the side, that would look weird since everyone knew the center seats were the best. But if she chose the love seat, would Timothy read too much into it? Was *she* reading too much into it?

"What's up?" Timothy called out over the crackling of the popcorn machine. "Why are you just standing there?"

"Nope, nothing wrong. All's great," Samantha quickly said. She gritted her teeth and slid into the couple seat in the last row, pressing her body close to the side of her chair.

"Just scan the QR code on the seat's arm and it should direct you to the film options we have. The Laura Dern one is probably under *New Releases*."

Before she could do so, Samantha's phone chimed. She immediately whipped it out of her pocket, her heart thundering—maybe it was Missy finally emailing about whether she had been approved for the column. A wave of disappointment swept through her as two messages from Anya popped up instead. These texts must be the latest updates about Rocky and Ollie from the zoo that she had been steadily forwarding Samantha and Tim. After remembering Anya's love for animals, Samantha had talked Timothy into getting her a joint gift from Singapore Zoo. When they presented her with a certificate declaring her the sponsor of two baby otters, Anya's face had lit up with a look of unadulterated joy that had been incredible to behold.

What's this? the first message read.

The second message was a photo that took a few moments to load. Samantha's heart lurched when it finally did.

A grainy screenshot with the letter *S* undulating in the top right corner.

Samantha's fingers were so shaky it took her a couple of tries to enlarge the screenshot. But even before she read the title, she already knew what it would say: IT GIRL DAISY TAIJA CELEBRATES ENGAGEMENT TO TYCOON'S SON LINCOLN PAN. The masthead image was slightly pixelated, but the figure in one corner—head thrown back in laughter mid-conversation, curly hair swept behind one ear, wearing a Selkie off-shoulder dress on loan from Anya—was undeniably her. She remembered this moment: She had been telling Daisy about Missy's offer, so overjoyed in that instant she had completely forgotten her usual caution around photographers.

And now, her carelessness gave Anya irrefutable proof of her presence at Daisy's party, of her lie.

Samantha sagged in her seat, her breath rushing out of her in a panicked gust and filling the room. Too late, she heard how her sigh rang out unnaturally loud in the silence. Sometime as she was reading the message, the popcorn machine had stopped, and now Timothy was asking, "What's wrong?"

Reluctantly, Samantha turned around in her chair to face him. His brows were furrowed in concern, and beneath them, his eyes were soft and gentle. He wouldn't be looking at her like that once he discovered her deception.

She attempted a smile, but suspected it came out shakier than she'd like. "Promise not to be mad if I tell you?"

Timothy's gaze sharpened as he walked over to her. "No. But I promise to hear you out."

Samantha scrambled out of her seat. She wanted to be eye to eye, or at least eye to chest with Timothy's six-foot-three frame as she confessed her lie—a vain attempt to compensate for how small she felt on the inside.

While she spoke, her voice steadily shrank as Timothy's face steadily darkened, the hard set of his features suddenly making him look much more like his father. When she finished, he stared at her for a painfully long moment, before saying in a voice devoid of emotion, "Samantha, what the hell."

Samantha tried not to flinch at the sound of her full name coming out of his mouth. He had never called her Samantha, not even at their first meeting in Enzo. Timothy continued, a bitter tinge creeping into his voice. "I feel like a fucking idiot now. I can't believe I wanted to drive you home and even called you to check on your mom and ask if I should send my family doctor over. I can't believe I cared so much when you were just stringing me along. You were probably laughing at my naivety the whole time."

Hard as it was, Samantha forced herself to hold his gaze. "I'm sorry," she whispered. She'd seen Timothy frustrated on occasion, but never at her. "I know I was wrong to lie, but how can you possibly think I don't care about you?"

"*I guess I could spare you a few minutes*? I don't want to just be someone you fit into your life when it's convenient for you." His lips twisted into a wry smile, its rueful edge making Samantha's heart sink. "You said you love watching sunsets, so I was gonna show you my favorite spot on Sentosa that offers the best sunset views. I even stowed a blanket and your favorite red wine in my car. I was so excited about everything, but the whole time, you were lying straight to my face."

Timothy closed his eyes and took a deep breath. When he spoke again, his voice was back to its tight and controlled state. "I know we only started hanging out because of the Fraud Squad, but I thought we actually meant something to each other."

If anything, this calm and guarded version of Timothy made Samantha feel even worse. It was *her* lies that had sown this new distance between them, that made him feel like he had to hold back around her. "I'm sorry," she repeated quietly. At this point, Timothy looked like he didn't even want to be near her, much less ever watch a sunset with her. "I just didn't know what to do about Anya and panicked."

There was a shaving nick on Timothy's right cheek she hadn't noticed earlier; it throbbed as he clenched his jaw. "If you had just told me the truth from the beginning, we could have worked together to figure something out. I thought you trusted me."

"Of course I trust you! I just didn't want to drag you into this and put you in a tough spot since you're also Anya's friend."

Timothy was silent for a beat, then looked her straight in the eye, and said, "I am Anya's friend, but it's not the same with you."

There was a sudden intensity in Timothy's gaze that made Samantha's breath catch in her throat. She took a hasty step back, her legs knocking into the edge of her seat. There was nowhere for her to go.

"Samantha—" Timothy began, then lapsed into silence again. Samantha swallowed, every nerve in her body thrumming with an emotion she couldn't quite name. His eyes were like two pools she could feel herself sinking into.

Timothy exhaled deeply. "Samantha, I don't know how to be just friends with you."

Before his words had fully sunken in, his face moved closer; Samantha could see a wordless question flickering in the depths of his dark eyes. Without knowing exactly what he was asking, she gave a small nod. The tiniest of movements, but it was enough to send Timothy surging forward, and suddenly, his lips were on hers.

Heat exploded in her stomach as Timothy—the taste of his lips, the musk of his cologne mixed with a natural scent that was uniquely his, his lashes fluttering against her cheeks—drifted into focus. At some point, her blouse had ridden up, or maybe Timothy snuck his hand beneath it. His palm seared the small of her back, pressing her tightly against him as though he wanted nothing more than to meld their two bodies into one. Every inch of her skin felt one spark away from dissolving into nothingness. Only the weight of his mouth against hers and his fingers on her waist tethered her to reality.

"God, Samantha." This time, far from minding, she relished the way her full name sounded in his voice, the way he drew out the three syllables into infinity. "I've wanted to do this for so long. It was driving me nuts."

As Timothy reached up to cup her face, something glinted on his left wrist—a pinprick of light that pierced Samantha's half-closed eyes. Her brain seemed to be working at half its usual speed, so it was a few moments before she identified it.

The watch from Lucia.

The bubble shattered. "Tim, wait," Samantha tried saying, but her words were muffled against his mouth.

"Mm-hmm?" Timothy muttered, nibbling on the plump flesh of her lower lip.

Somehow, Samantha managed to draw away from him. "I don't want to be your rebound." She could hear her voice shaking as Timothy's eyes sharpened on her face, but forced herself to continue. "I don't want you to kiss me just because you got bored of your relationship with Lucia and felt like trying something new."

"Bloody hell, Samantha." The sudden edge in Timothy's voice made her jerk back. "Is that what you think of me? My feelings for you are completely unrelated to my history with Lucia. She and I have been having problems for quite some time but stayed together because it seemed like the easy thing to do." His Adam's apple pulsed as he swallowed. "But then, I met you and you showed me what I actually want. So even if you don't feel the same way as I do, please don't assume the worst of my feelings for you."

Something in Samantha lightened. She took Timothy's hands in hers, her thumbs gliding over the lines in his palms. "Of course I feel the same way."

Before she could say anything else, he was wrapping his arms around her once more. This time, his touch was gentler, more tentative, as though her body were a privilege that could be withdrawn at any moment. "Sam, you have no idea how happy that makes me."

For a few seconds, Samantha allowed herself to simply savor the warmth of Timothy's breath against her neck and the softness of his lips against her skin. The moment felt so perfect she almost couldn't bear asking, "But what about your parents?"

Timothy drew back to look her in the eye, but kept his forehead pressed against hers. "Are you seriously thinking of my parents right now?" he asked teasingly.

"I don't know if they would be happy with this . . . with *me*," Samantha admitted. "They have such big hopes for you, so surely someone like Lucia is more suitable for the person they expect you to be. Unlike her, there's nothing I can do to help you with your career or anything else."

Smiling, Timothy shook his head. "My parents might be hard on me, but that's because they want me to be so successful in my career that no one can find fault with me in other ways like my relationships. That's why they never cared that I remained friends with Anya." His voice gentled. "Besides, you're helping me just by being yourself. For the past year, I've been suffocated by people's expectations. Everyone wants me to be Timothy Kingston. Everyone except you. Who you are is exactly what I need."

He let out a small "oomph" as Samantha surged up to kiss him. When they broke apart, he let out a breathless chuckle. "What was that all about?"

"For being the sweetest silver-tongued man I know."

He looked her straight in the eye. "I meant every word I said."

Samantha grinned. "I know, and that's why I kissed you."

She reached up to circle her arms around Timothy's neck, clasping her hands together at the bottom of his nape. Her back arched as Timothy's interlaced fingers tightened around her waist. His broad palms, splayed across the small of her back, made Samantha feel almost fragile.

The two of them stood chest to chest, faces a hair's breadth apart, bright eyes reflecting the flickering light from the movie screen.

26

On the way home from Timothy's house, Samantha could not stop touching her lower lip as her mind ran through the afternoon's events over and over again. Timothy had offered to drive her home or at least call her an Uber, but a long bus ride gave her the time she needed to process everything.

The back of Samantha's neck warmed, as though Timothy's mouth were still pressed there, against the sensitive spot that he had been much too smug about discovering. And to think she had been nervous about the movie seating arrangement! In the end, she'd spent the entire film curled up in Timothy's lap, feeling safe and snug as he occasionally dipped his head to trail kisses against her neck, his stubble scratching pleasantly along her skin.

The afternoon went so well that the last thing Samantha wanted to think of was how unpleasantly it had begun, but Anya loomed in her head like a constant shadow. Her insides writhed with guilt every time she imagined how hurt, how *betrayed* Anya must have felt when she saw those photos of Daisy's party.

When Samantha finally mustered the courage to dial Anya's number, the call connected at once, as though Anya had been waiting for it. However, Anya's end of the line remained ominously silent, so Samantha gritted her teeth and forged ahead.

"Anya, I'm so sorry I lied to you. I never meant to hurt you. Please believe me." An old woman sitting beside Samantha shot her a curious look that she ignored.

"Why didn't you tell me about Daisy's party?" Anya asked in a calm voice that only unsettled Samantha further.

"You were so upset about Daisy's party being on the same night, and I didn't know how to tell you—"

"How did you even get an invitation? Didn't you only meet her a few weeks ago?"

"Um, I guess we just hit it off pretty quickly." Samantha bit her lip. "Listen, I'm really sorry. I should have been honest, but I didn't want to stress you out more when you were already so nervous about your party."

For the first time in the call, Anya's cool and steely facade broke as she sighed. "It just feels like you went to Daisy's party because you thought it'd be better than mine."

Samantha's heart clenched. "That's not true at all!" Her exclamation drew a loud tut from her seatmate, which she pretended not to hear. But she did turn to face the window and lower her voice. "I made sure to go to your party first and only caught the last bit of Daisy's. Yours was definitely my top priority and I thought everything about it was incredible."

Another sigh, but heavier this time. "Seems like you're the only one who thinks so. I see Daisy's party featured everywhere, and *S* even called it the party of the year. Meanwhile, only *8 Days* mentioned mine in a tiny section on their website. And it doesn't even count since they aren't a society magazine."

"But there were so many media reps at your party."

"That's no guarantee they would feature it. I called up all my contacts at the society magazines, and only *ICON* said they might include it in an online roundup of themed parties. At least they like my Oscars theme, I guess."

"Your theme was brilliant, so I'm sure the other magazines will come around," Samantha said brightly to mask her doubt. Digital publishing moved so fast that the dearth of immediate coverage was practically a death knell for Anya's party.

"I guess . . ." Anya said, also without much conviction. "Anyway, was Daisy's party really as amazing as it was made out to be?"

Samantha knew better than to tell the truth. "Uh, it was okay. I think most of the people there were friends of Daisy's mom or mother-in-law."

Anya let out a small snort. "That explains why all the magazines are fawning over her party. Both women are very well-known on the Asian social circuit."

Samantha decided it was time to change the subject. "Oh, guess what—I ran into Missy that night!"

"No way! What happened? Did she say anything about the wine spill at Timothy's house?"

"No, but something even crazier happened."

"Whoa. What is it?"

Relief swept through Samantha. At last, she and Anya were falling back into their usual gossipy mode. "If I tell you, will you find it in your heart to forgive me?"

Thankfully, Anya laughed. "Only if you don't keep any more secrets from me!"

Samantha paused. "Actually, there's still something else . . ."

"What is it? Does it have anything to do with our Fraud Squad scheme?"

"Kind of . . . but not in the way you imagine."

"*Samantha Song!*" Anya screeched. "Stop toying with me and spill it."

Samantha couldn't help but smile at Anya's demanding tone. "Well, it's about Tim . . ." She let her voice trail off, the silence saying what she didn't quite know how to put into words.

There was a sharp intake of breath. "No way. Are you two—"

"Yes way." Samantha giggled. "We only just got together"—she drew the phone away from her ear to check the time—"three hours ago. You're the first to know."

Just for a moment, Samantha felt a pang. In the past, Raina would have been the first person she ran screaming to about this news. Rai would probably smirk and say in the most self-satisfied manner, "I told you so. Didn't I say at brunch ages ago something might happen?" And Samantha would roll her eyes but laugh. "Yes, yes, wise prophet Rai."

But it was Anya's voice crackling against her ear right now: "What an honor—at least I'm the first to know *something*. But wow. I've so many questions."

Since they only just made up, Samantha decided to gloss over the jab. Nestling her head into a more comfortable position against the bus window, she told Anya, "Fire away."

"Firstly, what about Lucia? Tim might have broken up with her already, but you know there's no way she will take this well, and she's going to take it out on you."

Samantha's good mood rapidly evaporated. "I know, but I'm hoping she won't find out. Tim and I agreed to lay low for a bit."

"I'll be surprised if she doesn't already suspect you're the reason behind her breakup, given how much time you and Tim have been spending together."

"But she can't know that—Tim and I have never gone to any public event together. And come on, what can Lucia do to me? She isn't some sort of Mafia boss."

There was a pause, and then Anya said quietly, "Lucia and I

used to be friends, but she immediately cut me off after my parents' divorce. And because she's so popular, most people in our circle followed her lead."

Samantha sucked in a breath. "That's awful. I'm glad Tim stuck by your side."

"Yeah, I'm really grateful for his friendship. But my point is, Lucia is brutal. She needs Tim to complete the image of the power couple she has in her head, so I'd watch my back if I were you."

The bus rolled to a stop. Samantha peered out of the window as the familiar outline of her block of flats swam into view. She stood up as the doors opened, promptly ushering in a wave of hot summer evening air. "I guess I have to make sure Lucia never finds out then," she said, unsure if the sweat beading on her temple is from the heat or from nerves.

On the other end of the line, Anya said, "For your sake, Sam, I hope so too." She paused. "Anyway, what were you saying about Missy?"

S's office looked so similar to *Singapore Tatler*'s that Samantha was struck by a heady sense of déjà vu the moment she walked in. The same style of animal-print throw pillows lined the couch, while stiff-spined coffee-table books from fashion houses stood next to a vase of orchids on the glass table. Someone had taken care to select pink flowers to match the cover of *Yves Saint Laurent Catwalk*.

The nostalgia intensified when Samantha saw the pile of PR packages on the semicircular reception desk. At *Tatler*, the last workday of every month had been her favorite because that was when the interns were given whatever brand products the full-timers didn't keep for themselves. While that wasn't comparable to the treatment she received now, with brands reaching out to her directly to offer gifts, there was something precious about the excitement she felt back then, vying with the other interns good-naturedly for the most covetable items.

The receptionist, who sported a pixie cut and fashionable neon eyeliner, looked up lazily at the sound of Samantha's footsteps. "Um, do you have an appoint—" Her yellow-lined eyes widened. "You're Samantha, right? Samantha Song?"

"Yes. Here to meet Missy," she replied, fighting to hide a smile. She was now someone who could make private appointments with the woman widely referred to as Asia's Commander in Chanel. A couple of days ago, Missy had finally reached out and put her out of her misery with a characteristically crisp phone call: "Samantha, I enjoy your writing and ideas. When can you come in so we can discuss further?"

The receptionist scrambled to her feet and gestured at the couch. "Please, take a seat. Missy will be out shortly. Can I get you anything? Coffee? Tea? Sparkling water?"

"I'm good, thank you," Samantha said, walking over to the couch. So this was what it felt like to be a VIP.

Trying her best to ignore the receptionist's unsubtle peeks, Samantha looked over at the wall of photo frames behind the reception desk, each containing a different *S* cover. Smack in the middle was the cover that had launched *S* to mainstream popularity—the one boasting Argus's debut. The subtitle, **A SINGAPORE SOCIALITE SPILLS ALL ABOUT HIGH SOCIETY**, was on everyone's minds and tongues the day that issue came out nearly a year ago.

Samantha sat up straighter. One day, it could be *her* column debut framed up on the wall and taking Singapore by storm.

"Samantha, hello," Missy said, appearing around a corner and trailed by a younger woman with a high ponytail and a smattering of freckles across her cheeks. It took Samantha a moment to place her as the *S* writer at Daisy's engagement party.

"Hi, Missy, lovely to see you again," Samantha said, standing up for the customary air-kiss. Her eyes caught on the Karl Lagerfeld leather purse hanging off Missy's arm. The editor looked like she had places to be, places that didn't involve sticking around for a Glamour and Grit brainstorming meeting.

As though she knew what Samantha was thinking, Missy said, "Unfortunately, I've a dinner meeting that got scheduled at the last minute. However, I think your column's debut would be perfect for our October issue, which doesn't leave us with much time, so I've assigned Fiona to help you with it." The young woman gave a shy little wave. "I can't wait to hear the results of your discussion."

Before Samantha could react, Missy gave her another air-kiss and disappeared as quickly as she had arrived, leaving behind a nervously smiling Fiona. "Hi, it's so wonderful to meet you. I'm Fiona. Oh, but Missy's already said that, hasn't she? Um, I guess we should go somewhere quiet to brainstorm?"

Samantha squashed down her disappointment that her cozy one-on-one with Missy was no longer happening. "Sure, lead the way."

En route, they passed by rows of heads bent over laptops and desks piled high with empty coffee cups and Red Bull cans.

"Wow, I can't believe you have a full office after six on a Friday," Samantha marveled. "No wonder *S* is at the top of the magazine game."

Fiona giggled. "Yeah, we are always busy, but even more so now that the big do is right around the corner."

Samantha startled as the words sank in. That's right—the S Gala was only two weeks away. All the invitations would have been sent out already, which meant she hadn't gotten one. Then again, she didn't need the gala anymore since she had already achieved her goal of writing for *S*.

Even so, Samantha couldn't help the disappointment that welled up in her—it would have been a once-in-a-lifetime opportunity to attend an event like that.

"We're lucky I managed to book this room," Fiona said, pushing open the door to an empty conference room. "Because everyone's working overtime these days, all the meeting spaces are getting snapped up fast."

Samantha slid into one of the swivel chairs. "Yeah, seems like it's crunch time for you and the whole team."

Fiona's eyes widened. "Oh, you don't have to doubt my commitment! Your column is my top priority. You can feel free to call, text, or email me whenever, wherever. I'm determined to make Glamour and Grit a success, and I want to help in any way I can. Whether that's brainstorming article ideas, or helping you choose graphics, or even doing some of the writing—"

"Wait. You want to ghostwrite for me? Did Missy ask you to?" Samantha said, her heart sinking. Did the editor doubt her capabilities after all? Did she think Samantha's writing couldn't measure up to Argus's sharpness and wit?

Fiona's expression faltered. "No, no! Missy didn't say anything. It's just . . . if you're really busy and there's a deadline coming up, I'm happy to step in." She laughed weakly. "Things move really fast in the publishing world, so everything's always in a bit of a time crunch."

"I know that," Samantha said, her words coming out sharper than she'd intended. "I used to work at *Tatler*, so I know what magazine publishing is like. I can handle the deadlines."

Fiona's freckles stood out even more as her face flushed. "Oh no, I totally didn't mean to imply you couldn't. But since Missy said your column is my top priority, I figured I should make things as easy for you as possible since you also have a full-time job."

The knot in Samantha's chest eased; Missy was simply trying to look out for her. But Fiona's assurances still couldn't dispel Samantha's doubts fully.

"So, what's the arrangement like with Argus?" she asked in her most casual voice. "Does Argus write it herself, or is it ghostwritten?"

Fiona shrugged. "No idea."

"Missy has never assigned you to help her before?"

"I don't know anything about her column. None of the writers do. Whoever Argus is works directly with Missy. She sends the article to Missy every month, Missy does whatever she has to do, and voilà! It gets published in every issue like clockwork."

"Wow. How come Argus gets personal attention from Missy and I don't?" Samantha joked, but her playful tone sounded hollow to her ears. Was she doomed to play second fiddle to Argus?

Her stab at levity must have been even weaker than Samantha imagined, for a panicked look immediately crossed Fiona's face. "Oh no! I wasn't trying to imply you aren't good enough, because you totally are. I don't think it has anything to do with who you are."

Wringing her hands, Fiona glanced at the row of bent heads on the other side of the conference room's glass walls, then back at Samantha. She leaned forward and whispered, "If it makes you feel any better, I think Argus is Missy."

For a few moments, Samantha could only stare at Fiona agog. Then she narrowed her eyes. "What makes you think that?"

"Well, Argus obviously knows a lot about the socialite lifestyle, and it's Missy's job to know everything going on in high society."

"But many socialites are gossipy. It wouldn't be hard to keep up with the grapevine."

"Right, but why would any socialite want to write this column?" Fiona countered, her voice growing stronger. "They obviously don't need the money, and neither are they doing it for recognition since Argus is so careful to hide her identity."

"Maybe they have an agenda against the other socialites and want to stir things up?"

Fiona shook her head. "Argus must have irked at least half of the society set by now—no smart socialite would risk so much just to start some rumors. If she ever gets exposed, it's the end of her. Can you imagine having the most influential people in Singapore turn against you? I would *die*."

"So would I," Samantha conceded, grimacing at the very thought. "But what's Missy's motive?"

Fiona spread her arms open. "Business, of course! Just a year ago, *S* was like any other fashion-luxury magazine, and you know how saturated the industry is. So Missy comes up with the idea for this society column that she knows will grab people's attention, *but* she also knows it will be career and social suicide for her to put her own name on it. Lo and behold, she invents a persona for herself and writes under the Argus pen name. It all fits, doesn't it?"

Samantha leaned back in her chair, looking at the other woman with a newfound respect. Fiona had just given her a lot to think about.

CHAPTER

28

It was close to 9:00 p.m. when Samantha reached home, her stomach rumbling like a freight train. She had ended up skipping dinner because her brainstorm session with Fiona was going so well she couldn't bear to stop. They had not only hammered out a solid outline for the first column and possible ideas for the subsequent few, but also made arrangements to get her byline photo taken next week.

"Maaaa! What's for dinner?" Samantha called from the doorway as she pried the buckles off her flats.

Her mother rushed up to her. "Something came for—"

"Can this wait? I'm starving. Do we still have any leftovers?"

"There's some soup, but never mind that," her mother said impatiently. She waved a small piece of paper. "Sam, what's this?"

Sighing, Samantha kicked off her shoes and flicked an eye over the document. "If it's more tax forms, I'll look at—" She stilled as her eyes landed on a familiar insignia: a black-and-gold loopy *S* undulating at the top of the paper like a snake.

All thoughts of her growling stomach forgotten, Samantha

grabbed the card out of her mother's hands and scanned it, the words flying past her eyes as her heart pounded in her chest.

Dear Ms. Samantha Song,

Merlion Media requests the pleasure of your company at the fifth annual S Gala to celebrate a decade of S being the authoritative voice in Asian fashion, beauty, and society.

Time: Friday. Eleventh of August. At seven o' clock in the evening.

Place: John Jacob Ballroom, The St. Regis Singapore.

Dress code: "Supernova." Black tie.

Kindly RSVP to gala@smagazine.com. We look forward to seeing you there.

It took a few moments for the words to sink in. *Oh. My. God.* Samantha brushed a finger against the dark gold embossed script, cast in sharp relief against the bone-white paper, then read them again, more slowly this time: *Merlion Media requests the pleasure of your company at the fifth annual S Gala* . . .

Samantha flipped the card around, scrutinizing every groove of the raised script and every curve of the *S* logo. This must be a mistake, or a prank, or a hallucination from drinking too much coffee lately while working on the Alter Meatgo project.

But the thick and creamy card was a solid weight in her hands, and when she turned it back around again, it was still her name at the top. This was *real*. She was actually going to Singapore's most legendary social event—something she thought she could only ever read about.

"So what's this about?" She startled as her mother poked her head over Samantha's shoulder to peer at the card, her voice booming in Samantha's ear. "A party? Is this an Arrow event? Surely not," Ma answered her own question before Samantha could. "It must be a big deal since a courier hand delivered this to our flat today."

Samantha snorted. "Yeah, no way Arrow has that kind of money. This is from *S*, the magazine. They're inviting me to their annual gala."

Ma scrunched up her face. "*S*? The one you've always wanted to work at?"

"That's the one! In fact, I think they invited me to the gala because I'm now writing for them."

"You're writing for them? Wait a minute . . ." Ma breathed in sharply. "Did Arrow *fire* you?"

Laughter bubbled out of Samantha's mouth. "Far from it, actually. I'll be writing about my Arrow projects for my column."

Ma's horrified expression gave way to confusion. "How did that happen?"

"I ran into *S*'s editor at a party and pitched an idea to her, and she ended up loving it so much she wanted to turn it into a whole series of articles. We agreed on six months' worth for a start, with the potential of expanding it if the response is good." *And it'd better be good.*

Her mother frowned. "So you're holding two jobs now?"

"*That's* what you choose to focus on?" Samantha asked, stung by her mother's lack of interest. "Not that I managed to impress Singapore's toughest editor?"

"Of course I'm happy for you, but you know I don't like to see you working so hard." The older woman laid a gentle hand on Samantha's shoulder. "We aren't out of the doghouse, Sam, but you don't need to take on two jobs."

"Ma, I'm not doing this for money!" Samantha laughed. "I mean, yes, the additional income is nice, but this is my dream writing gig. Even better, it taps into my Arrow work, which is awesome because I really enjoy doing PR now. I've some cool projects lined up with high-profile clients, and my manager has been very happy with me lately. This is the best of both worlds!"

Ma's brows remained furrowed. "But between Arrow and this column, where are you even going to find the time to relax? When was the last time you and I have had a proper conversation? And don't think I haven't noticed that you and Raina haven't been hanging out lately. And what about meeting boys and going on dates?"

Samantha squirmed as every question coming out of her mother's mouth hit her like a rock. But quickly, her guilt gave way to anger; why couldn't both her mother and Raina just be happy for her success?

"What century are we living in where you would rather I prioritize men over my career?" she retorted, seizing on the only thing her mother said that she could justifiably be annoyed about. "I don't want to go on dates. I already have a boy—"

She stopped herself, but it was too late, for her mother pounced on her slipup at once. "You have a *boyfriend*?" she screeched. "Samantha Song! Since when did you start keeping secrets from your own mother?"

Was she imagining the hurt in Ma's voice? But Samantha couldn't think much further, for the questions kept coming: "Who is this boy? I hope he's better than that guy you went out with in uni. Remy, was it? Your dates used to end so late and he could never afford to send you back in a cab." Ma pursed her lips. "Girls shouldn't be taking public transport alone at night."

"Remy was just a student. And you know how expensive cab rides get at night with those surcharges."

"Yes, but our neighborhood really isn't safe. Why, just the other day, Madam Pang swore she saw a gang fight break out at the void deck of Block 513!" Ma gave a little shudder. "But never mind that! I want to hear all about your new boyfriend."

My boyfriend. Samantha couldn't stop a smile from slipping out. "His name is Tim."

"Tim who? I hope he has a good last name. Samantha doesn't go well with some surnames."

"Kingston. Timothy Kingston." Samantha's mouth twitched at the unintentional James Bond parody. Tim could probably pull off Bond's suited looks very well, and he had the British accent to match.

"Timothy *Kingston*?" Her mother pursed her lips. "Samantha, those white boys aren't good news. All they think about is sex, sex, sex."

"Ma!" Samantha's cheeks heated up. "Tim isn't like that at all." She paused. "Besides, he's half-Chinese."

Her mother threw her hands up in exasperation. "Yes, but he's also half-white. And I know what those white boys are like. They just want to get into your pants and ditch you once you give them what they want. You should stop seeing him, Samantha. Let me fix you up with a nice Chinese boy."

"I guarantee you, that's not what Tim is trying to do—"

Scoffing, her mother shook her head. "Samantha, you're so naive. You need to listen to me. That boy is clearly just using you—"

"Tim's dad is a freaking billionaire!" Samantha snapped. "He doesn't need to use me for anything, okay?"

A deafening silence descended. Her eyes wide like saucers, Ma opened her mouth, then closed it again. Samantha wanted to kick herself. Why oh why did she have to blurt *that* out?

Her mother finally found her voice. "*You're* dating a billionaire's son?" she whispered, as if afraid the neighbors were listening in. "Surely he's not related to the Kingstons of the Kingston Management Group?"

Samantha didn't say anything, but her silence was all the confirmation her mother needed. "Oh, Sammy, I knew something was going on! I thought your skin has been looking extra glowy lately. Only a woman in love could look like that."

"No, Ma. Only a woman religiously applying Crème de la Mer could look like that," Samantha deadpanned. Ever since she became a mainstay on the high-society circuit, luxury brands such as La Mer were constantly reaching out to offer free gifts. She would give them Timothy's address so that none of the PR ladies working at those brands would wonder why they were sending face cream that cost $150 per ounce to someone who lived in public housing. "You know, there's plenty of the face cream to go around. Are you sure you don't want to try some?"

"Oh no. You're still young and attractive, but I'm already an old auntie," Ma immediately said, trotting out the same line she always used whenever Samantha offered her the new cosmetics she'd received. "It's not like *I* need to look good so I can attract a husband."

Samantha pursed her mouth. Why was her mother's mind always assessing everything through how beneficial it would be for Samantha's marriage prospects?

"Besides, the ladies who go to my salon don't like it when we look too good," her mother went on conspiratorially. "You know Xiao Mei, that very pretty young girl who just started working here? She works so fast, but none of our customers like her much." She touched her face absently. "No, no need to waste your skin care on me. Save it for yourself."

Even so, Samantha's revelation about Timothy seemed to have done what no amount of La Mer moisturizing cream could. Her mother instantly looked ten years younger, the lines in her face smoothing out as she beamed. "Sammy, you'll be set for life now. Timothy can take care of you so you never have to go through what I did."

Samantha's chest tightened. There it was—the real reason she hadn't said anything about Timothy to her mother in the first place. Somewhere along the way, as she had gotten to know, then befriend him, she had found herself falling not for Timothy Kingston, the billionaire's son, but for *Tim*—the man who had demonstrated over and over again that he cared for her in a way money couldn't buy. But in the blink of an eye, all of that had been sullied with a dirty, mercenary touch. All those memories and feelings reduced to nothing but dollar signs.

"Ma, you're blowing this way out of proportion," Samantha said, fighting to keep her voice even. "We've only been dating for a while, and I'm not counting on him to support me when I have my own career."

Her mother clucked her tongue. "You've been hanging out way too much with Raina. Where did you get all these silly notions from? What's wrong with wanting a man to take care of you? You young people are so strange—it's like you don't want to make life easier for yourselves."

At the mention of Raina, Samantha's heart squeezed further. She had reached out a few times after their Atlas brunch debacle, but Raina's responses were so curt their conversations never got far.

"Please stop with these ridiculous fantasies. Tim and I just started dating."

"But this is a very good start, no? I bet *he* can afford to pick you up and send you home after dates in a car. Oh! What if Tim gives you a car?" Ma wagged her finger. "Make sure he gives you lots of presents—a boy like him can surely afford it. Did I tell you about this story I read the other day—a rich man in China proposed with an orange Lamborghini, but his girlfriend rejected it." Her eyes widened. "*Rejected* a Lamborghini, can you believe it?"

"Yes, I can," she said shortly. "Anyway, I don't need a Lambo or any other car. I don't even have a driver's license."

"Silly girl! That's what chauffeurs are for."

It took everything in Samantha to control herself. "You know,

I think I'm gonna go now." Without waiting for a response, she turned around and began walking toward her room.

Her mother's footsteps pounded after her. "Sammy, where are you going? What about dinner? I still have a lot of questions about Tim!"

"I'm going to my room to call him," she called over her shoulder, not trusting herself to control her temper if she faced her mother now.

Her mother's footsteps stilled. "Yes, that's a good idea. I'll turn the TV off so you can have full peace and quiet for your call. Remember to ask how his parents are!"

29

Rolling her eyes, Samantha shut her room door, impressed by how she hadn't given in to the urge to simply slam it. She collapsed onto her bed, pulled out her phone, and sent a three-way video call invitation to Timothy and Anya. *They* would be able to celebrate her news without losing their heads.

After a few moments, Anya's video square flickered into life. "Sup, girl!"

"Hey! I've something to tell you, but let's wait for Tim to— speak of the devil." Samantha's heart fluttered as Timothy popped up on screen. Even her phone's poor resolution could not hide his ridiculously good looks or bright smile. And this man was *hers*.

"Hey, you two," Timothy said, then softened his voice, his eyes swinging to the bottom of his screen. "Babe, I miss you."

The full force of his gaze struck Samantha even through the spiderweb of cracks across her screen. She glanced toward her door, then back at her phone. "I miss you too," she said softly, the flutters in her intensifying. How wonderful it was to be able to say things like that out loud, no longer worrying he was with someone else or might not feel the same way.

"Why are you whispering?"

"I don't want my mom to overhear."

"I doubt she would, since she didn't even overhear your sounds from last—"

"Okay, time out," Anya said loudly. "Don't make me feel like a third wheel."

"Sorry," Samantha said, duly chastised.

"Yeah, sorry," Timothy echoed, though he was smiling too smugly for anyone to take his apology seriously.

Anya rolled her eyes. "Anyway, Sam, what did you want to tell us?"

"I've got some big news. Any guesses?"

"You're pregnant," Anya immediately said.

"Anya!" Samantha yelped, then quickly lowered her voice. "Don't even joke about that."

"Yeah, please don't," Timothy said, looking slightly queasy.

"Give us a hint then."

"It's something to do with a party."

Anya leaned so close to her phone that her eyes took up half the screen. "Did *S* say they're going to feature my birthday party?" she demanded.

Samantha tried not to wince. "Uh, no . . . but it's something to do with *S*."

"*S* is going to feature an event you organized for Arrow?" Timothy suggested.

"That's not big news. They already featured Cassandra's party."

There was a sharp intake of breath from Anya. "Don't tell me you got invited to the S Gala?"

Samantha beamed. "Bingo! I just found out ten minutes ago."

Timothy squinted. "Wait, slow down. Did I just hear you say you received an invitation to the S Gala?"

"Yeah, it was delivered to my house today."

Timothy blinked. "Oh, wow. That's . . . yeah, wow. That's unexpected."

"Right! There's only, what, less than two weeks to the gala? I thought all the invitations would have been sent out long ago. But lo and behold, one arrives at my flat at the eleventh hour."

"This is the best kind of surprise!" Anya exclaimed. "Sam, congrats! You must be ecstatic."

"But do you even need to go to the gala anymore?" Timothy asked, frowning. "You've already achieved your Fraud Squad goal. You don't need the gala to establish your credentials for writing a society column."

"But what about *your* Fraud Squad goal?" Samantha threw back. "I thought you wanted to prove a point to your parents with my presence at the gala. You know, show them we don't have to be pigeonholed by the background we're born with."

"Actually, they just found out they'll be missing the gala this year. My father has an important meeting in Dubai that weekend, and he wants my mother there with him. Since the gala no longer has anything to do with our Fraud Squad scheme, are you sure you even want to go?"

"Of course I want to go! This is the biggest event on Singapore's social calendar."

Timothy wrinkled his nose. "I've gone every year since the gala began, and it's honestly not that fun. Everyone's just trying to humblebrag, and you'll have to be on your best behavior at all times."

"It's only for one night—I'm sure I'll live," Samantha said lightly, but her flutters had all disappeared. At Enzo, Timothy had mentioned Lucia prided herself on being invited every year—of course, the two of them would have gone together in the past. But why didn't he seem excited now about going with *her*?

You aren't his type, whispered Lucia's voice in her head. A lump welled up Samantha's throat. Everything that was still so new and exciting for her was already *been there, done that* for Tim and Lucia. He had suggested they keep their relationship low-key so it wouldn't incur Lucia's wrath, but what if he was just embarrassed to be seen with her in front of his glamorous ex and the rest of high society?

Anya jumped in, "Tim, how could anyone possibly turn down an invitation from *S*? That's a surefire way to get on the committee's bad side, and Sam can't piss off her new boss."

Samantha pushed herself up into a sitting position, eager to focus on anything that wasn't Tim's lukewarm response. "You know what's weird? I literally saw Missy just a few hours ago and she didn't say a single word about this. Not even a hint, or an 'I guess I'll be seeing you at the gala.'"

"Probably because she didn't want to spoil the surprise," Anya replied, grinning. "Wasn't it more magical finding out for yourself as you opened the invitation at home?"

A new thought struck Samantha. "How did *S* even know where to send it to?"

"You must have given them your particulars at some point when you signed the contract," Anya suggested, then realization dawned on her face. "Oh, don't worry! Everyone at *S* is too busy working on the gala to bother looking up your address. And they clearly haven't, because there's no way they'd invite you if they found out you stay in an HDB flat."

"Yeah, you're right." Samantha sank back against her pillow, her heart rate mellowing. It was a close shave, but thankfully, no harm was done. The last thing she needed was for Argus to catch wind of a slipup and blow her cover just when everything was finally falling into place.

"Oh, babe, how did your meeting with Missy go?" Timothy asked. "Tell us about what you came up with for your column."

Samantha perked up; at least Tim seemed more enthusiastic now. "The meeting went really well, although Missy couldn't make it. Oh! That reminds me—" She hesitated. What if either of them accidentally told someone else about Fiona's hypothesis? The news would soon spread like wildfire through Singapore's tight-knit high society. And if Missy ended up tracing the source back to her—Samantha swallowed.

Timothy raised an eyebrow. "Yeah?"

Samantha cleared her throat. "Uh, I was gonna ask if you guys think I should reach out to Missy and thank her."

"For the column?"

"No, for the gala invitation."

"Definitely not," Anya said immediately. "The September issue is the biggest and most important issue of the entire year, and traditionally unveiled at the gala. And with only eight days left, she'll be ridiculously busy now trying to complete everything in time. You shouldn't bother her."

"You're right. Wow, I still can't believe I'm actually going to the freaking S Gala. Every year, I would read all the event reports, look at the photos, study the best-dressed list . . . And this year, *I'm* going to be there . . . I can't even describe how I feel."

Anya let out a small sigh. "Aw, I wish I got invited, too, and could go with you two. But, important question: What will you be wearing? I don't think I can lend you anything for this. Everyone there is going to be wearing dresses from *next* season."

"Damn, I haven't even considered that." Just getting invited to the S Gala was such an insurmountable task that Samantha had barely thought about what would come after. Where in the world was she going to find a designer gown from next season? What about accessories, hair, and makeup? And how should she get there? Would everyone else arrive in chauffeured limousines?

Timothy cut in with a small cough. "About that—don't worry.

I'll take care of everything. I'm going to make sure you have the best night of your life."

WHEN TIMOTHY SAID he was going to take care of things, Samantha hadn't expected his plan would entail spending an entire afternoon in Mode Luxure, a fashion showroom in Orchard he described as a hidden gem only a rarified group of society ladies like his mother knew about.

As Timothy pushed open the store's beveled glass door, Samantha's breath caught in her throat. No wonder Mode Luxure was one of Eileen Kingston's go-to shopping spots.

Lined against the paneled walls were racks after racks of the most stunning outfits: gowns and cocktail dresses and pantsuits and capes, dripping with diamonds, pearls, intricate embroidery, and top-notch beadwork. Soaring up to the gold leaf ceiling were built-in suede shelves, holding shoes of all kinds and a comprehensive selection of designer bags ranging from Judith Leiber novelty clutches to petite Jacquemus bags that couldn't hold more than a toothpick. Trays of fine jewelry and watches, housed in lacquered cases, glistened in the chandelier light.

A wiry man with a receding hairline bounced up to them. "Good afternoon, Timothy! And you must be Samantha. Lovely to meet you! I'm Franc. Come, take a seat," he said, waving at a cluster of tufted poufs. His assistant, a woman with a severe chin bob, brought over a tray of petit fours and glasses of champagne that Samantha didn't hesitate to help herself to.

Franc locked the door before joining Samantha and Timothy. Catching her look of surprise, he explained, "Mode Luxure accommodates only one client at a time so our clients can shop in peace."

Samantha immediately smoothed out her expression and gave

a cool nod, hoping she appeared like she shopped in private ateliers all the time.

Franc took the remaining seat and leaned forward, his eyes gleaming. "Samantha, 'Mode Luxure' is French for 'lust for fashion.' There are many stores out there who say they want to help you find an outfit you *love*, but 'love' is too soft, too placid. I want to help you find something you truly *lust* after, a dress that would make your jaw drop, make you want to rip it off the mannequin, and make every other female at the party want to rip it off your body because they wished they were wearing it instead."

Samantha had a sudden image of Franc standing in front of a mirror, solemnly rehearsing his little spiel over and over again. Poor guy. It was such a shame Mode Luxure was so frightfully exclusive that Franc would rarely have anyone new to try his pitch out on.

Samantha fought back a grin. "I absolutely agree with you, and that's why I'm here."

Franc smoothed back his comb-over. "First, tell me: What is your vision for your outfit?"

"The dress code is 'Supernova'—a powerful stellar explosion—so I was thinking something with sequins and glitter."

Franc wagged a finger. "Let's tread lightly here. Too much sequins and glitter can end up looking very cheap."

"Yes, of course," Samantha said as nonchalantly as she could, hoping her embarrassment didn't show.

"Don't worry, I'm confident we can find the perfect dress that has the bling factor you desire without looking like a Cirque du Soleil outfit. Now, let's talk details. Sleeves, no sleeves, or off-shoulder? What kind of neckline do you want? What kind of hemline? And what about waistline? Any color preferences? Any materials you like or dislike?"

Samantha's head swam; Franc had lost her somewhere after

"neckline." "Uh, I'd prefer something with sleeves. And I guess any neckline would do, as long as it's not too high neck, or slashed to my navel. And hemline, uh—" She exhaled deeply. "Actually, I trust your judgment completely, so pick whatever you think works best on me."

Franc rubbed his hands together. "This is exactly what every artist wants—a blank canvas! You just sit back and relax while I prepare your dressing room. And let me know if you want more champagne!"

The moment Franc and his assistant were out of earshot, Samantha turned to Timothy. His shoulders were hunched around his ears, a deer-in-the-headlights expression on his face as he took in the mountain of clothes looming over them from all directions.

Taking pity on him, Samantha suggested, "Babe, why don't you take a walk around town? I'll text you when I'm done, but it shouldn't take long."

Timothy straightened up. "Don't worry about me," he said, wrapping an arm around her and pulling her close. "Since this is your first try-on, I want to be here for moral support. I even brought a book along. I'm left with about a hundred pages, so I'll probably finish around the same time you do."

Samantha kissed his cheek. "Someone's a fast reader."

Timothy turned his face so his lips were against hers. "I'm sure most people can read a hundred pages in three hours," he whispered, his breath skating across her skin. Somehow, Samantha got the feeling his mind wasn't on books anymore, for neither was hers.

Reluctantly, Samantha pulled back, reminding herself that Franc and his assistant were just steps away. "Three hours? Don't exaggerate. I think I'll be in and out within thirty minutes at most."

"Babe, you're in for a rude awakening. Franc will put you

through your paces all right. Not gonna lie, I think some of his methods are bonkers—he likes to say you need to develop a spiritual connection with an item before you buy it. But his attention to detail is also why he's the go-to stylist for my mother and her friends. In fact, he's also going to talk to my mother's makeup artist, manicurist, and hairstylist to make sure their designs complement your outfit."

"Spiritual connection?" Samantha scoffed. "I just want something that makes me look good."

Timothy smiled. "In that case, we can be out of here in under five minutes. You'll look beautiful in anything," he said, eyes falling to her lips again.

Samantha was determined not to give in to his sweet-talking this time. "Honestly, all the dresses here are so beautiful I'll be happy to wear any one of them. I'm a fast shopper, you'll see."

"Everyone's a fast shopper until they run up against Franc."

Right on cue, Franc reappeared. "Samantha, the dressing suite is ready for you. Please come with me. Timothy, make yourself comfortable here. There's more champagne and also some delightful chocolate truffles imported straight from Belgium. And if you need me, just ring this bell."

"Good luck and stay strong," Timothy whispered, giving Samantha's hands a tight squeeze. "I'll be right here if you need anything."

Smiling to herself, Samantha followed Franc. Timothy was the sweetest, but did he have to make a simple try-on sound like guerilla warfare—

Her eyes widened as she stepped into the dressing suite. The whole place was the size of bedroom, half of it taken up by a rack that sagged beneath the weight of two dozen couture confections. Several had such complicated, BDSM-style laces and straps that just putting one on would take at least ten minutes. The entire rack would probably take upwards of two hours, and that wasn't even including shoes or accessories.

Franc clasped his hands behind his back. "Samantha, I have a very thorough system for doing things. For each dress you try on, I want you to walk a lap around this suite so that I can see how it drapes against your body in motion. And if it's a piece we think has potential, you'll repeat your walk in three different pairs of shoes so we can see how the height of your heels affects the gown's movement. And after dress and shoes, we'll need to pick accessories—my favorite part! Rings, necklaces, bracelets, watches, clutches, maybe even gloves and veils! No such thing as moderation in my shop, so the sky's the limit!"

Raina's words pushed themselves into Samantha's mind: *Since when are you so comfortable spending so much money? Money that's not even yours.* Samantha hitched her smile up a notch. "Sounds good," she said brightly over Raina's voice needling her in her head. Tim was the one who had offered to cover today's shopping expedition. Besides, the S Gala was a once-in-a-lifetime event; it wasn't as though she went around splashing his cash every day.

"And once we've decided on your outfit, we have to tailor everything until it suits you perfectly! Some clients think the hard part's over once the outfit's been chosen, but I respectfully disagree—I believe customization is just as, if not more, important. No matter how long it takes, we have to make sure the necklaces hug your décolletage perfectly, the length of the gown is just right, and everything fits you like a second skin."

Samantha stared agog, first at a beaming Franc, then at the profusion of couture surrounding her. Turned out Timothy hadn't been exaggerating after all.

30

"Sam, you really should go to bed soon! Tomorrow's the big day!" Ma chided, setting down a plate of cut apples on the dining table next to Samantha's laptop and sliding into the chair beside her daughter's.

Samantha rubbed her eyes and peered blearily at her computer. "I'll go to bed as soon as I'm done with this article. The deadline *S* gave me is coming up, but I have the worst case of writer's block right now." Did Argus ever get writer's block, too, or was she so confident about the reception her articles would receive that the words just poured out?

After a beat of silence, Ma asked, "So . . . are you all prepared for tomorrow?" Her tone was light, but Samantha caught the unmistakable eagerness underlying her words.

"Yeah. The store delivered my dress and accessories straight to Tim's place since that's where I'm getting ready," Samantha replied absently as she reread the pithy opening paragraph of her article. Her words were decent, but what she really wanted—no, needed—was for Glamour and Grit to be so incredible that it would blow everyone's socks off. The way As Seen by Argus did. That both were socialite-penned columns made them ripe for comparison, and she *had* to come out on top if she wanted hers to stick around.

"Sammy? Samantha?"

Samantha's head jerked toward her mother. "Huh?"

Wearing a faintly exasperated expression, her mother sighed. "You didn't even hear me because you were so focused on writing. Tomorrow could change your life forever, and you're still up working instead of getting your beauty sleep. You work much too hard, and for what? The amount of money *S* is paying you for that article won't even cover the cost of just one of the shoes you're wearing tomorrow."

Samantha did some quick calculations and realized her mother was right—at the rate of fifty cents per word, she would have to write over sixteen hundred words to pay for those Sergio Rossi heels.

"Speaking of shoes, it's so nice that Timothy's paying for everything—dress, jewelry, bag! All from designer brands and specially tailored for you too. How much do you think everything cost?"

Samantha stiffened. *Do not feel guilty, do not feel guilty.* After all, Tim had offered to pay. "Uh, none of them had price tags because they're from next season."

"He's so generous," Ma said, and even without looking, Samantha could tell her mother was smiling. "And oh my, those flowers he sent the other day—I've never seen anything more beautiful!"

Samantha's gaze followed her mother's to the box of Venus et Fleur white roses taking up almost the entire coffee table. Each petal was so perfect she'd thought the flowers were fake when she first saw them. "Yeah, they are," she said softly, her eyes drawn to the card attached to the box. It was too far away for her to read it, but she already knew all the words by heart.

Flowers for my beloved girl. This arrangement is called the Eternal

Melody and reminded me of you, Miss Song. Samantha had always been slightly self-conscious about how common her last name was, but Timothy managed to transform it into something precious, something worth celebrating.

"I went on Venus's website to find how much the whole arrangement costs. Guess how much?"

Samantha dragged her eyes away from the flowers to focus on her computer again. "No idea."

"That's why I'm asking you to guess!"

"I'm not really interested, so why don't you just tell me?"

"Thirteen hundred dollars! Can you believe it? More than half my monthly salary on something that's going to die within a year."

That caught Samantha's attention. "Oh my God," she said faintly. How was she supposed to gift Timothy anything in the future, knowing she could never afford anything close to thirteen freaking hundred dollars? She would never be able to give him a designer watch like Lucia had.

"If he's buying such expensive gifts for you now, imagine what he will give you once you two have been dating for a while. Didn't he also pay for all your beauty treatments this week?"

"Those? Nah, my friend Daisy treated me. She's attending the gala, too, with her fiancé."

"Daisy? I don't think I've met her before. Is she a new friend?"

"Yep. She actually said I'm doing *her* a favor because she wants a spa buddy to help her decide which treatments to do for her wedding next year." That had made it easier to accept Daisy's offer, and Samantha made sure to uphold her end by drawing up a detailed Excel spreadsheet that reviewed every treatment against twenty criteria. It wouldn't compare to Daisy's generosity, but at least Samantha could take heart in the knowledge that she had done all she could to repay her friend.

"If she's looking for more people, why not call Raina? Make it a fun girls' activity."

Samantha looked down in case something showed in her expression and tipped her mother off. "Yeah, I asked Raina. She wanted to come, but she's too busy these days." Which was only half a lie. Raina had sounded genuinely pleased to hear from her and excited about a spa day together, until Samantha disclosed everything would be paid for and done with Daisy. The conversation broke down after Raina's reply: *Let me know when you're ready to do something without your socialite friends and their money.*

Ma's tone turned thoughtful. "Daisy's helping you with the beauty treatments, and Tim's taking care of your outfit, is that right?"

"Yup."

"And what about hair and makeup?"

"I'm getting those done at Timothy's place too. His mom keeps a makeup artist and hairstylist on retainer."

"Sammy." Ma waited until Samantha was looking at her before she leaned forward, eyes glittering as she asked, "Sammy, why don't *I* do your manicure?"

Samantha blinked. "What? You've never offered that before. When I used to ask, you always said your materials were too expensive to be used on me."

"That's completely different. Everything's from the salon, so I can't just use them for a school formal."

"How's this any different? It will still be for a personal cause."

"Because this isn't just some small school dance!" Ma threw her hands up. "Ever since you got your invitation, I've been reading up on the S Gala, and I now know it's Singapore's grandest event of the year. Did you know, last year's gala was attended by members of the Macau royal family—"

"Monaco," Samantha muttered. "And of course I know."

"And *my* daughter is going this year, so of course I must do everything I can to help you prepare for your big moment. But it's not like I can afford to buy you a nice dress, or teach you what's the right fork to use for dessert—*I* don't even know that," her mother said with a laugh that was a shade too bright. "And you already have your friends helping you . . . but I want to help, too, and doing your nails is the only way I know how."

Samantha shifted in her chair. "Ma, I really appreciate your offer," she said as gently as she could. "But Tim's already arranged a manicurist for me tomorrow. It's a woman his mom's been using for over a decade."

Her mother jutted her chin out. "That's very nice of him. But you know, my skills are up there too. I've helped many women get ready for parties before."

"But this isn't just any party. Like you said, the S Gala is the grandest event of the year. The nail polish Daisy's using contains real diamond dust."

Her mother's smile dimmed. "Of course, I understand," she said quietly. "I'm sure Eileen Kingston only uses the best of the best, and I definitely can't offer diamond nail polish."

Her mother's weak attempt at humor made Samantha's stomach twist into knots. Ma had never seemed so downtrodden before, and *she* was responsible for it.

Before she could regret it, Samantha heard herself saying, "Ma, actually, I think your suggestion is great! I would love to get an An Jie original design for the gala."

Her mother shook her head. "Oh no. Don't say that for my sake. It's your big night and you should do whatever's best for you. I just want you to have the best time of your life."

"I'm not saying that for your sake," Samantha insisted. "Come on, I've been asking you for a manicure for years! There's nothing I would love more."

"Are you sure about this?" her mother asked, still looking unconvinced.

"Maaaaa, don't make me beg."

Finally, her mother smiled. "To be honest, the moment you showed me that photo of your dress, I started thinking of a nail design and I think I've now—"

"Nailed it?" Samantha quipped.

When Ma merely gave her a blank stare, she sighed. "Never mind. Anyway, what's your brilliant idea?"

"I want your nails to match the crystals on your dress, so I'm planning on using Swarovski crystals—"

Samantha furrowed her brows. "Uh, don't go overboard with those. Too much will just end up making me look tacky, like I'm a . . . Cirque du Soleil performer or something."

"Don't worry! I'll make sure you have the best manicure there. And if anyone asks, you can tell them your ma did it and even give them my business card!"

"I can't do that. If I want to fit in at the gala, I need everyone to think my mother is a tai tai, too, not someone who does manicures for one."

The moment the words left her mouth, Samantha wished she could take them back. Ma flinched like she had been hit. Outside, the evening air thrummed with the chirping of cicadas, but in their flat, a heavy silence hung in the air like a grenade. Samantha's mouth dried, her mind racing for something she could say to rescue the situation, but all she could think of was how much she wanted to kick herself for putting that wounded look on her mother's face.

"You know I was only joking, Sam," Ma finally said with a small smile that fooled neither of them. "Of course I don't expect you to do that. Besides, now that you're with Tim, you're well on your way to becoming a tai tai yourself, eh?"

"Let's not get too ahead of ourselves here," Samantha said, her guilt instantly erased by a familiar flicker of annoyance. "Can we do the manicure tomorrow? I want to finish up this article before bed." Without waiting for a response, she turned away from her mother and faced her laptop.

"Of course, of course." Ma's knees creaked as she pushed herself out of the chair. "There are some nail art tools I have to get from the salon first. You've taken tomorrow off work, right? I'll come home during my lunch break tomorrow and do your nails then. Oh!" She wagged a finger at Samantha. "Remember to sleep facing up so that your face isn't pressed against the pillow. The last thing you want is pimples on your big day. You must look your best for everyone at the gala, especially Timothy."

Samantha forced herself to simply nod in response. If she opened her mouth, she didn't trust herself not to say something she might regret.

31

The lobby of the St. Regis hotel was filled with bleary-eyed tourists tugging massive suitcases, and bellhops weaving between them with luggage carts. But once Samantha and Timothy made their way up a winding staircase, its lush carpet filigreed with sparkling crystals, they found themselves in another universe altogether.

In the voluminous foyer outside the John Jacob Ballroom, two hundred luminaries milled about like peacocks, each proudly displaying their own "Supernova"-inspired plumage. Samantha rolled her shoulders back and tipped her chin up. *I am one of them now.*

Crystal embellishments and paillette hand embroidery twinkled like stars against the midnight-blue silk of her Zuhair Murad gown—yes, from *next* season. It hugged Samantha's curves as though someone had carved out a piece of the night sky and poured it over her body, but was hemmed to just the right length so it wouldn't get in the way of her four-inch Sergio Rossi stilettos.

Rings shaped like shooting stars from Chanel's Comète collection glistened on Samantha's fingers, while a Jennifer Behr diamond headband held her updo in place. With her smoky eye shadow and lipstick such a deep crimson it appeared almost black, she was Franc's vision of a moon goddess come to life.

"Samantha!" society maven Kate Low exclaimed, floating up in a glittery robe bedazzled with colorful jewels. She was trailed by three bodyguards who kept a careful watch on her dramatic double-wrap necklace that dripped into her cleavage. "You look amazing. You're wearing Zuhair Murad, aren't you? I don't know this exact piece, but I can recognize his designs anywhere."

Laughing, Samantha returned Kate's air-kiss greeting. "You're one to talk. You look absolutely incredible. Your necklace—wow!"

"Please, you have the best accessory of all—the most handsome guy in this room! Talk about arm candy," Kate fired back good-naturedly, shooting Timothy a small wink.

"Oh, we aren't together," Samantha quickly said, stepping away from Timothy. "We were just saying hi to each other." This was the first time since Cassandra's party that she, Tim, and Lucia would be in the same room, and the last thing Samantha wanted was for Lucia to find out about their relationship and potentially make a scene in front of two hundred of Asia's most important people.

"Well, I need to go say hi to a few more people," Kate said. "But let's definitely reconnect again in the ballroom."

Once the older woman was out of earshot, Samantha smirked at Timothy. "How does it feel to be hit on by *the* Kate Low?"

"Babe, I think she's old enough to be my gran. Kate Low enjoys her cougar act, but only Keith will get excited over it. She's right about one thing though."

"That you're the most handsome guy in this room?" Samantha suggested coyly. An unexplainable pang hit her as she took in his debonair appearance. Timothy cut a svelte figure in a black Saint Laurent suit that showed off his broad shoulders, lean body, and long legs, topped off with a dark blue bow he had chosen to match Samantha's dress. For once, there was nary a wrinkle or crease anywhere on him, but the perfection made him seem more like a Kingston and less like himself.

When it was just the two of them alone, she could forget he hailed from a background so far above her own, but that was much harder to block out here tonight.

"No, that you look amazing. I wish you could see yourself through my eyes."

A hot flush of pleasure ran through Samantha. Timothy's eyes darkened as they traced the blush spreading from her cheeks down to her chest. "Thank you," she said, drawing his eyes back up to her face. "But this is all because of you—the dress, accessories, everything." She could hear her voice growing smaller. "I don't know how to thank you enough."

"Don't thank me like we're strangers," he said gruffly. "I wanted to do this for you. I *want* to give you everything you desire."

Samantha's smile stiffened. *Make sure he gives you lots of presents— a boy like him can surely afford it.*

But tonight was too special to waste even a single minute on unpleasant thoughts, so Samantha forced her mother's voice out of her head and said brightly, "I don't think I'll ever be this dressed up again, so I want something to remember this night by. Let's go hit up the photo booths."

"Sure. Which one though?"

Samantha scanned the offerings available. There was an official red carpet where guests were jostling for prime positions, but the gala's sponsors had each set up photo booths of their own. The BMW booth displayed a fire-engine red car Samantha didn't recognize but could only presume was extremely coveted, judging from the male guests clustered around it. Or perhaps they were simply enthralled by the two female models posing on the car's bonnet in skintight dresses.

Meanwhile, the female socialites' attention was gripped by the Armani booth, where a line of male models stood, clad in suit jackets and nothing on beneath. Samantha stifled a giggle as Ayeling Mei, who was around Ma's age, let loose a most undignified cackle at the sight of the models' rippling six-packs. At least there was equal opportunity ogling.

"Maybe the Van Cleef and Arpels booth? Apparently, we can even get our fortunes told by a professional psychic—a nod to the brand's lucky four-leaf clover motif," Samantha read aloud from the signage.

"Yeah, let's do that. But we should sign in first."

"You're the boss," Samantha quipped. Thank God she had Tim with her. He looked completely unfazed as he navigated the throngs like a pro, turning back every few steps to check on her. He was usually so reticent about his background that it sometimes slipped Samantha's mind he had grown up in the heart of Singapore's elite set.

They joined the end of a snaking line in front of the registration table. "You can go find Daisy while I sign us in," Timothy offered.

"Okay. Behave yourself while I'm gone," she joked before slipping away.

For the next few minutes, Samantha wandered around the foyer, exchanging pleasantries with the socialites she recognized, her smile widening with every compliment that came her way. It was a while before she spotted Daisy with her fiancé, Lincoln. Daisy's black-and-white gown was perfectly elegant, but rather boring compared to the magenta tulle confection she had gushed about at their glycolic peel treatment last week.

Samantha was about to make her way over, but Daisy caught her eye and jerked her head surreptitiously toward the middle-aged woman beside her, who had a possessive hand wrapped around Lincoln's arm. Pan Ling's gray hair was swept into a towering pompadour, and her high-necked black-and-white coatdress made her look like the place fun went to die. Poor Daisy—her mother-in-law must have forced her to change into that dull design to match hers.

After shooting her friend a sympathetic smile, Samantha turned around, her eyes landing on the towering stack of *S*'s September issue placed on a table in one corner. The September issue was always the marquee product of any magazine, and *S*'s in particular was always chock-full of the most stunning editorials and shoots. But right now, the issues lay there forgotten as all the guests busied themselves with making their rounds, posing for photos, and sizing up one another's outfits.

"Sam, guess what—we're sitting right next to each other!" Timothy exclaimed, striding over to Samantha. With his long legs, he was by her side in the blink of an eye.

"Really? But we aren't even each other's plus-ones."

"I'm surprised, too, since we were invited separately. But I'm definitely not complaining about this coincidence."

"Me neither." At least this meant she could be with him the whole night, instead of torturing herself wondering what Timothy thought of his ex-girlfriend up onstage.

"How's Daisy?"

"She's occupied now, so I thought I'd check out the September issue instead," Samantha said, leaning forward to grab a copy. The issue would hit the newsstands tomorrow morning, but half the fun of being a top socialite was the early-access perks her new status offered.

Timothy grasped her outstretched arm. "Wait."

Samantha looked up at him. "Yeah?"

He ran a hand through his hair. "There's something I need to tell you about the mag—"

"Good evening, you two!" Fiona chirped, walking up to join them.

"Fiona, hi! You look fabulous," Samantha said, reaching out to hug her. In her gold beaded frock, Fiona could have passed as one of the gala guests if not for the lanyard around her neck and the headset curved around her ears.

Her smile suddenly slightly shy, Fiona tucked a lock of hair behind her ears. "Thank you, Samantha. You look absolutely beautiful too. In fact, that's why I came to look for you. As you probably know, our October issue every year features a roundup of our best-dressed gala guests. My colleagues and I simply adore your whole look—it fits the theme perfectly! Would you be all right if we include you on the list?"

Samantha's heart soared. "Of course! I'd love that." To think she would be appearing on the best-dressed list she had spent so much time poring over in previous years.

"And, Timothy, you look wonderful as well. I'm sorry your parents can't join us tonight. Would you mind if I steal Samantha away for a few minutes? It's better to get the photos of her outfit now before the night gets even crazier!"

Timothy smiled. "Of course." He turned to Samantha, his eyes twinkling. "Enjoy yourself. Come find me in the ballroom when you're done. We're at Table Eight."

As she followed Fiona, Samantha couldn't stop smiling. Not even twenty minutes at the gala and she had already been singled out in a hall full of Asia's most stunning and influential people by the gatekeepers of Singapore's poshest publication. This evening was off to a perfect start.

AFTER PHOTOGRAPHERS HAD captured her from every possible angle and Fiona had fastidiously noted every designer and detail of her outfit, Samantha was ushered into the John Jacob Ballroom.

Two dozen tables filled most of the floor space, packed with a veritable who's who of the Asia-Pacific. At the center of every table stood a perfect sphere of hydrangeas dyed a bold gold, luminescent from the flames of the surrounding ring of white votives. Against the ink-black tablecloth, their petals glistened like clusters of stars. A canopy of gold-and-silver star streamers dripped from the ceiling, shimmering under the crystal chandeliers and raining constellations across the walls. Embedded in the soaring ceiling were romantic skylights through which swaths of the night sky could be glimpsed.

Samantha found Timothy easily, since Table Eight was placed right in front of the stage and clearly visible from every corner of the ballroom. Thank God for him, because everyone else at the table, despite their pleasant demeanors and friendly greetings, left her quaking in her heels.

Seated on her other side were Celeste and Adrian Beh of Beh Holdings. Known for their sartorial statements, they did not disappoint on this occasion: she in a two-tone gunmetal-and-silver-sequined jumpsuit vaguely reminiscent of a disco ball; he in a tuxedo that was all business in the front and party in the back, featuring a hand-painted replication of Van Gogh's *The Starry Night* on his jacket. Rounding off their table were a Korean pop star, Singapore's ambassador to Turkey, the founder of Southeast Asia's leading luxury travel site, a Thai princess, and the prime minister's personal lawyer.

A morbid thought flitted into Samantha's mind, coalescing before she could push it away. *What would happen if a meteor crashed into the ballroom and obliterated everyone here?* The notion was so outrageous she decided to entertain it. For starters, dozens of companies would see their stocks plunge overnight; several nations would fall into disarray as they rushed to figure out their monar-chical and political succession plans; and millions of fans would be heartbroken at the loss of their favorite celebrity.

But what about me?

Next to Samantha, Celeste Beh was fingering her aquamarine necklace and blithely telling the table at large, "My astrologer told me my rising sign makes me too aggressive, so I've been wearing calming crystals more often lately."

Everyone nodded like they knew what a rising sign was, but Samantha could only stare blankly at the floral centerpiece. She might be at the top of Singapore high society now, shopping at designer boutiques, attending fancy parties, and being fawned over by others. But would most people even give her the time of day if they knew her from her days of splitting the $4.99 toast set at Madam Pang's kopitiam with Raina?

A sharp spike of guilt shot through Samantha. How could she have pushed away Raina, the one person who always had her back? And how could she have been so curt with Ma last night, so un-grateful after everything she had done for her? Ma was working a ten-hour shift today but still gave up her lunch break to painstak-ingly glue Swarovski crystals on Samantha's nails. Even right now, while Samantha was sitting down to a five-star dinner, her mother was probably still stuck at the salon.

"Sam, you all right?" Timothy asked softly, squeezing her right hand beneath the table, the gesture hidden under the thick black tablecloth.

Samantha startled, the heat of Timothy's palm seeping into hers. As her eyes met his, the weight in her heart eased slightly. Tim was the only person in this entire ballroom who knew her from the pre–Fraud Squad days, who liked her for the person she really was and not the It girl she had transformed into.

"Yeah, I'm okay," she whispered back.

He let go of her hand as a sharp screech of microphone feedback pierced the room, drawing every eye to the stage. Missy stood behind the speaker's podium, dressed in a silk faille navy suit and towering over the podium in her platform boots. A three-tiered chandelier earring dangled from her left ear, shown off to great effect by her asymmetric bob. Backdropped by a massive LED screen display of the gala's banner, she smiled coolly at the audience, making no mention of nor apology for the auditory disruption; Samantha instantly loved her all the more for it. What was it like being *that* self-assured?

In no time at all, the massive ballroom was completely silent, all two hundred pairs of eyes trained on the woman onstage. "Your Excellencies, distinguished guests, ladies, and gentlemen, a very warm welcome to you all," Missy began. "We're always looking for an opportunity to throw a party, and tonight, we have two incredible milestones to celebrate. This year marks not only the fifth edition of our gala, but also the tenth anniversary of *S*!"

At that, the ballroom burst into an ovation so thunderous that Samantha wondered if the hotel guests in the lobby below could hear. When the applause finally died down, Missy continued smoothly, "Since its inception a decade ago, *S* has never shied away from pushing the boundaries of society journalism and reaching for new frontiers. Things move fast in this industry, but we always seek to disrupt the status quo. We don't just report trends—we create them. And we are committed to shining even brighter in the years to come, much like the powerful celestial phenomenon that inspired this year's gala theme."

Samantha straightened up in her seat. No longer was she just a casual reader admiring the magazine from afar; now, she had a *real* part to play in building up *S*'s profile and legacy. As though he could sense her thoughts, Timothy bumped his fist against hers beneath the table.

"This brings me to the highlight of tonight. As you all know, the September issue represents the pinnacle of any publication's year. While Singapore doesn't have the four seasons, being hot and humid all year round"—the crowd tittered—"September has traditionally marked the end of summer and the beginning of fall, a time of new starts and fresh inspiration, of rejuvenation and growth. And that invigorating zeal is captured perfectly in our September issue."

A heavy hush descended over the crowd as the LED screen behind Missy faded suspensefully into darkness. "Tomorrow, this year's September issue will be revealed to the public. But tonight, you will be the first in Singapore to learn about all the hottest trends, must-haves, and zeitgeist of the new season. I present to you: this year's September issue!" Missy announced, sweeping her arms ceremoniously outwards as the screen lit up with an image of the much-fanfared issue cover.

32

There was a chorus of scraping chairs as all two hundred guests leaned forward in unison. The next moment, whispers broke out across the ballroom.

At first, Samantha thought everyone was simply marveling at *S*'s coup in landing Hollywood darling Gemma Chan as the cover star. It was only when Celeste Beh screeched, "As Seen by Argus is no more?" that Samantha noticed the subtitle tucked away in the cover's bottom right corner: *Argus ponders fate and free will in their final column—don't miss it!*

Samantha's eyes widened, her mind racing to process this unexpected development. So *this* was why Missy had engaged her to write a new column. But why would *S* end As Seen by Argus when it was what the magazine was best known for?

Missy coughed lightly into the microphone, a coy half smile playing about her mouth as she surveyed the commotion her reveal had caused. "A copy of the September issue is included in every gift bag, so be sure to pick one up on your way out," she said smoothly. "I will now pass the time to our event host and one of *S*'s dear society friends, Lucia Yen."

Scattered applause echoed through the ballroom as Lucia sauntered onstage, smiling widely and waving at the audience as though everyone had gathered here for her. Her appliquéd gold gown clung to her statuesque figure and revealed strategic ribbons of skin along her torso.

You aren't his type. The words rang out loud and clear in Samantha's head, twisting her stomach into knots. Against her better judgment, she snuck a peek at Timothy, driven by a masochistic need to see his reaction to the woman who had been by his side for four years.

But if anything, Timothy looked even queasier than she felt, his brows knit together and lips pressed into a thin line. The air-conditioning was so strong Samantha had stuffed her hands under her thighs to warm them, but tiny drops of sweat dotted Timothy's forehead and above his lips.

"You okay?" she whispered.

Timothy's head jerked toward her. "Of course," he said quickly. "Why wouldn't I be?"

Before Samantha could respond, Lucia's singsong voice rang through the ballroom. "A very warm welcome to one and all. My name is Lucia Yen, and I am absolutely delighted to be your host for tonight. Appetizers will be served soon, but in the meantime, I thought we could play a fun little predinner game. Since this is the fifth S Gala, I'm looking for five people to say what they're most excited to see in this year's September issue."

For a few moments, everyone was completely silent. Then Lucia added, "And did I mention—every participant will get a gift voucher from Viva la Spa, the gala's official beauty sponsor."

Instantly, hands shot up all over the ballroom. Fiona scurried about, holding out a microphone to those lucky enough to be picked.

"I can't wait to read more about how Gemma Chan is championing Asian representation."

"I'm excited to learn about the fall and winter fashion trends this season—I want to know if it's true plaid is dead."

"I'd love to get recommendations for where's the best place to bring my kids for the September school holidays."

"I want to get holiday present inspo from the gift guides."

Celeste Beh inhaled audibly when she was the final person to be called upon. "I think I speak for most people when I say that my favorite S feature is As Seen by Argus. And I'm *so* disappointed the column's only been around for twelve issues. I want more of her juicy tales and observations!"

Three tables over, Gabriella Yeo, the OG Chinese supermodel, shouted, "Amen, sister!" drawing a smattering of laughter from the guests.

A smile slithered across Lucia's face. "Celeste, you read my mind—I was hoping someone would mention Argus," she purred. "Every time a new issue comes out, the first thing on everyone's minds is what our favorite columnist has to say. And as the September cover promised, this last article really is one not to be missed. It's rather different from the usual content, but like Missy said earlier, S is all about challenging the status quo and setting trends. And since everyone here is a dear friend of the magazine, I'm going to give you all a special dinner treat and read you an excerpt from As Seen by Argus's grand finale."

On the LED screen, Gemma Chan's smoldering beauty faded away into the distinctive As Seen by Argus masthead—an abstract rendering of a giant eye. The title, **WHAT PLAYING PYGMALION TAUGHT ME**, headed a wall of text.

Samantha looked down at her empty plate as Lucia cleared her throat. If only the appetizers would arrive already. She could handle seeing only so much of Tim's ex in one go.

Lucia began reading out loud from the screen, her clear and melodious voice ringing through the ballroom:

The ancient Greeks believed life was predetermined, even going to the extent of anthropomorphizing this lofty concept with the Moirai, or the Fates—three old women said to dictate and govern any human's destiny, setting out an individual's life path at birth. Achilles was always going to be the hero of the Trojan War as prophesized, despite all his mother's attempts to shield him from this fate—his background as a demigod through whose veins runs the blood of Zeus would have never allowed room for deviation. Sure, he was offered the choice to go to war and die young as a hero, or stay behind and fade into obscurity, but it was a Hobson's choice at best, and ultimately, the only options available ensured he would choose the one that fulfilled his destiny.

Not to compare myself to a mythical demigod hero, but sometimes, it is hard not to also feel like I as a person didn't matter as much as the role I was born into: the only child who could continue the trajectory my family had pursued for generations. It's akin to being a fashion model with a facade that's pleasing to behold, but essentially a blank canvas for someone else's vision—one that I'm taught to accept blindly even if I don't agree with it. But at the same time, it is hard to reconcile my feeling of being stuck in a cage with the uncomfortable truth that this is—in all fairness—an incredible gilded cage, one that would scream "freedom" to many others.

High society has always been a jealously guarded arena, with entry permitted only to the select few who meet some arbitrary standard of wealth and reputation. These "elites," including myself, are then expected to maintain said arbitrary standard by pursuing a list of predetermined roles, paths, and activities available only to this group through a combination of nepotism and gatekeeping. It becomes an entrenched system of more privileges for the privileged, thus marking clearer distinctions between ourselves and everyone else.

But the truth is: Status means absolutely nothing except for the self-congratulatory significance people choose to inscribe it with. Kudos to those who fought to get to where they are today, but most of us came by our status through a decidedly non-meritorious lottery of being born into the "right" family—and what's so laudable about that?

But what if I could turn all that on its head? What if I could prove what I suspected all along—that the emphasis from people around me on preserving lineages and upholding class distinctions stems from fear, a simmering concern that their positions at the top aren't as secure as they would like? And from there bloomed an idea, one that took on more definition the more thought I gave to it: What if I turned an ordinary working-class person into a socialite?

Now, this pauper-into-princess idea has been around since time immemorial. Pygmalion is a sculptor in Greek mythology who made a statue so beautiful he had it brought to life. Hey, ancient Greece was a different time, but the Pygmalion concept has lived on in stories closer to our age: Have you heard of *My Fair Lady* or *Pretty Woman*? In both these *little-known* films, an ordinary woman is radically transformed so she can assimilate into elite society. Some might call this deception, and there is an undeniably sexist element to those plots where the man is portrayed as the woman's savior, but I've always admired how the women in those movies assertively leveraged a system that would have worked against them otherwise.

And one night, the line between fiction and reality blurred when I met Melody (not her real name) at a Clarke Quay lounge—

Something poked at the edges of Samantha's mind, like a Polaroid photo just beginning to take on color. Her eyes snapped to the screen as a chill crawled down her spine. There was a dull ringing in her ears, and through it, she could just about make out Lucia's voice, rather hazy as though it was coming from underwater.

> Hailing from a working-class background, Melody was a clean slab of clay that could be transformed into a true "society star," or whatever the established standards for one were—precisely the standards I aim to dispel.

It took a few seconds for the words to sink in, a few seconds of blissful ignorance that ended all too soon. Something in Samantha cracked wide open, a splintering of everything she thought she knew. In a daze, she turned to Timothy, who looked just as stricken as she felt.

TIMOTHY RECOVERED FIRST. "Sam," he said in a low, tight voice, his fingers curling around hers beneath the table. Samantha could only stare back at him, too stunned to even shake off his grip. She waited for him to continue, but after a moment, his mouth clamped shut, apparently as lost for words as she was.

Set against his paled face, Timothy's brown eyes were like two bullets boring into hers. People always said eyes were the windows to someone's soul, so how could she have gazed into Timothy's so many times and never had a clue he had been carrying such a cruel secret all along? That every time he looked at her like she was the only person in the world, all he really saw was how to exploit her for his stupid, *stupid* column.

A cacophony of voices erupted throughout the ballroom, sucking up all the air and pounding in Samantha's head like a jackhammer. But the babble seemed to be emanating from a great distance. Dimly, she was aware of Celeste slapping the table and exclaiming, "Gosh, this S Gala is the most entertaining one yet! Who do y'all think this Melody chick is?" The glee in her voice was so obvious it made Samantha's stomach turn.

But suddenly, the table turned quiet. Disarmingly so. Samantha looked up. Straight into Lucia's pretty, predatory eyes; her gleaming red lips sliced open into a sugary-sweet smile. At some point, Lucia had stridden offstage and was now standing so close her Chanel No. 5 perfume coiled around Samantha like a snake. One hand rested on the back of Samantha's chair, sending an eruption of goose bumps over Samantha's skin as she imagined Lucia's long nails sinking into her neck.

"I have another surprise," Lucia announced, her microphone-amplified voice reverberating around the now silent ballroom. "The Melody from the column is in this very ballroom, and she's none other than this woman sitting right here, Miss Samantha Song!"

Blood thundered in Samantha's ears. Her body felt like it was being suffocated in heat despite the chills running down her spine. Timothy's grip on her hand under the table slackened, but she could still feel the sticky sheen of sweat on his palm. Beside her, Celeste let out a sharp gasp, then quickly turned it into a cough that fooled no one. The ballroom that had seemed so massive to Samantha mere moments ago now felt like it was pressing down on all sides, threatening to bury her alive.

"Samantha, Melody—whichever you prefer—I understand you work an entry-level job and live with your single mother in an HDB flat. Did you ever imagine you would end up at the S Gala one day?"

No . . . No, no, no. Terror swept through Samantha, turning her brain to mush and her tongue to rock in her mouth. Lucia's eyes, ringed with heavy coatings of mascara, glinted with malicious triumph as she waited for a response. Every fiber of Samantha's being screamed at her to look away, but she didn't dare to. Because focusing on Lucia meant she could at least put off facing everyone else for just a bit longer. Timothy, still and silent like a statue next to her; the other guests, who had thought she was one of them; Fiona, who had admired her so openly; Daisy, who had been so excited to know her better; and Missy—Samantha's heart lurched.

"Well, Samantha, would you agree with Argus that you're now a true *society star*?" Lucia prompted, her pointed air quotes sizzling in the air like smoke over flames.

Try as she might, Samantha couldn't pull together a lucid train of thought, couldn't string words together into a coherent line. Her body felt frozen in place by two hundred pairs of eyes, the judgment from them so visceral she could almost taste it in the still air. Maybe if she didn't move, she could pretend she was simply trapped in a nightmare that would end soon.

Then, from the corner of her eye, Samantha saw a hand, its wrist encircled with an Alexander Shorokhoff watch, rise into the air like a mirage.

"Lucia, if I might just say something," Timothy began. And without waiting for Lucia's response, he reached out to take the microphone from her and cleared his throat. "I think Argus makes a really good point about how the standards of determining a society star are completely arbitrary and rather meaningless. How does being a socialite matter in any way? I, for one, am much more interested in hearing about the work that everyone's doing than in their family backgrounds. For instance, I would love to learn more about what inspired Mr. Rajaratnam"—he gestured at the Indian man beside him, who looked momentarily startled before straightening up and nodding attentively—"to give up his high-paying engineering job to go into entrepreneurship and start his own travel site."

Timothy's voice snapped Samantha out of her dreamlike haze. How did he manage to sound so composed, when she could feel his leg shaking beside hers? Then a burst of white-hot fury: How *dare* he sound so composed, when he had just ruined her life?

Timothy pushed the microphone back toward Lucia. A shadow passed over Lucia's face as her fingers closed around the microphone, but it disappeared nearly as soon as it arrived. The next moment, her bright smile was back in place.

"Thanks for sharing that fascinating insight with us, Timothy," Lucia said smoothly, although Samantha thought she could detect an almost imperceptible hesitation before his name. "Mr. Rajaratnam, we would all love to know your zero-to-hero business story. But I'm sure this interesting interlude has worked up everyone's appetite, so we'll be serving appetizers before hearing from him! For those who have indicated dietary restrictions, we've taken those into account and you should receive a suitable replacement."

A plate was set down in front of Samantha. "Serrano ham and membrillo crostini," the waiter announced.

The slivers of ham glistened ruby pink beneath the light of the flickering votives. Acid pooled in Samantha's stomach. Regardless of how pretty they looked beneath the garnishes, they were still nothing more than limp, dead flesh. And regardless of how dressed up she was in her elaborate gown and accessories, everyone here knew she was a fraud who didn't belong.

Samantha's head shot up as Celeste Beh let out a loud gasp. "Oh, Timothy!" she exclaimed, clapping a hand to her mouth.

Samantha felt Timothy freeze next to her and guessed the same thought that just struck her must have occurred to him as well. By standing up for her, he had given himself away. Celeste had guessed Argus's identity, and given the stronghold she had in Singapore's gossip network, soon everyone else would know too.

Despite her anger toward him, Samantha's heart clenched in

fear on Timothy's behalf. Many people here had been called out in As Seen by Argus before, and most of them knew Albert and Eileen Kingston. The couple would be mortified if their friends and business partners found out that their only son was responsible for the anonymous criticism, and what would they do to Timothy then?

"Timothy, you are so sweet—standing up for someone you don't even know!" Celeste cooed. Beaming, she looked around the table. "I've known Timothy's parents for many, many years, and the Kingstons have sure raised a fine young gentleman, haven't they?"

Samantha was sure she must have heard wrong. Timothy was being *praised*? And how could Celeste possibly think the two of them didn't know each other when—*oh*. Samantha felt like someone had just thrown cold water over her. Since he didn't want to run into Lucia, Timothy had never actually accompanied her to a public event, always having Anya go as Samantha's plus-one instead. Even tonight, the two of them had kept their interactions low-key so they didn't attract Lucia's attention.

A fat lot of help that was.

Around their table, everyone was nodding along to Celeste's words. A short, ruddy-faced man visibly perked up. "Your father is Albert Kingston?" he asked Timothy, the eagerness in his voice so obvious it would have made Samantha embarrassed for him if she had any mortification to spare. "That man has the Midas touch— he's my business idol! I'm Steve Larkin, by the way. I started a private-jet-sharing business and would love to discuss some partnership ideas with your father and you. Looks like KMG is in good hands, eh?" He gave Timothy a friendly punch in the shoulder that Timothy accepted with a tight-lipped smile.

All around Samantha, the conversation was beginning to pick up again, interspersed with the clinking of utensils. But she had no desire to eat anything or talk to anyone. And she had no desire to look at Timothy, who had been steadily trying to catch her eye for the past few minutes, his gaze scorching her skin.

Because now, she knew how Lucia had found out everything. She could feel the outline of Timothy's watch pressing against her arm like a scalding poker.

Samantha's chest constricted until she felt like it might cave in, her body overcome with the urge to shrink into itself, to put as much distance as possible between her and Timothy.

So, as everyone else tucked into their crostini, Samantha leapt to her feet. The entire table looked up, and Celeste opened her mouth, but before anyone could say anything, Samantha was running straight for the door, as fast as her Sergio Rossi stilettos and figure-hugging Zuhair Murad gown would allow.

33

As Samantha burst through the door and into the blessedly empty foyer, she could hear footsteps pounding behind her, muffled by the thick carpeting.

Thanks to her four-inch heels, Timothy caught up to her easily. He grasped her arm and pulled her around to face him. "Sam, please. Let me explain." His hair was plastered to the side of his head with sweat, and his dress shirt—having come untucked at some point—flapped in sync with his heaving chest.

Samantha ripped her arm out of his grip and scoffed out an incredulous laugh. "What explanation can you possibly give for humiliating me like that?"

Timothy flinched. "I—I wasn't trying to humiliate you."

"Are you kidding me? Were you not the one who wrote that stupid article?"

Timothy raised his hands in a placating gesture that made Samantha grit her teeth. "I did write it, but the point was never to humiliate you. You were the one who said I could use your high-society transformation to prove my point!"

In a flash, Samantha heard herself declaring over the sound of clinking wineglasses all those months ago at Enzo: "Feel free to present me to your parents as evidence, case study—whatever."

Samantha's heart sank. "So you've been getting close to me all along just to use me as fodder for your column."

"Of course not!" Timothy exclaimed, looking aghast at the very thought. "When you suggested the Fraud Squad plan at Enzo, it didn't even cross my mind then to put it into my column. At that point, I really was just thinking of proving a point to my parents and Lucia. It was actually something you said a few weeks ago that gave me the idea to write about our scheme."

Fury spiked through Samantha, so potent she could barely get her words out. "Don't you *dare* turn this around on me."

"I'm not! I'm telling the truth. After you ripped into Argus—into me—for writing so shallowly, I couldn't stop thinking about it and realized you were right. So when Missy asked if I wanted to continue as Argus even after my sabbatical ends, I decided not to. But I wanted to wrap up my column with something more meaningful." Timothy looked down and away, his voice growing small. "Something that would show I'm not actually mean or superficial."

Samantha's hands balled into fists. How dare he use *her* words to defend himself? "And you couldn't have at least given me a heads-up? Did you seriously not think I wouldn't put two and two together when I saw your article tonight?" Her eyes widened. "So *that's* why you didn't want me to come. And I thought it was because you were embarrassed to be seen with me in high society . . ."

"What?" Timothy jolted toward Samantha, then seemed to think better of it and pulled back. "I will never, ever be embarrassed by you," he said, looking Samantha straight in the eye, his voice the steadiest it had been all conversation. "If anything, I'm the lucky one to have you in my life."

For a moment, as their gazes locked, something in Samantha wavered, but she steeled herself. Telling his audience what they wanted to hear was exactly how Timothy made a name for himself as Argus.

"It warms my heart that you think so highly of me but not enough to tell me you're the infamous Argus," she said, her voice ice-cold. "So Lucia's an important enough girlfriend for you to confide your Argus identity to but I'm not?"

Timothy lowered his eyes, his neck straining against the tight knot of his bow tie as he swallowed. "That's not the case at all."

Samantha waited, but when it became clear no elaboration was coming, her expression hardened. "Then explain why you trusted Lucia with the truth but not me."

"It has nothing to do with trust." Timothy looked up, his cheeks flushed. "I was embarrassed, okay? I had your dream job, and after what you said at Enzo about how only socialites get to write for society magazines, how was I supposed to say anything? Especially when I didn't even get the column through merit but through nepotism."

"Nepotism? There's no way your parents helped you with this."

Timothy smiled wanly. "Of course they didn't, but Missy did. At the start of my sabbatical, we were talking at a party, and when I mentioned I was looking for something creative to do, she offered me the opportunity to write for *S*. She didn't know I was going behind my parents' back, and even agreed to let me use a pseudonym when I said I didn't want my Kingston background to influence how the public viewed my work."

"*Wow*. I bet you felt so proud of yourself for trying not to be a stereotypical rich kid coasting off Daddy's name." Samantha poured every ounce of venom she could muster into her words, satisfaction surging within her as Timothy's face paled.

But frustratingly, he didn't rise to her bait. Quietly, he said, "I was already embarrassed about how I got the job, and after you called Argus mean and shallow, there was no way I could admit I was him. Since you said you didn't plan on reading the column anymore, I figured I never had to say anything about it, especially when this issue would be my last. But after you got invited to the gala, I realized you would be coming face-to-face with my column. I tried fessing up, but I didn't know how to bring it up, and the longer I put it off, the harder it became . . ." His voice trailed off as though he'd finally realized how weak his words were.

Samantha scoffed. If only he had realized it sooner. "You were embarrassed about being Argus so you decided to embarrass *me* instead?"

"I was never trying to embarrass you! I thought I was writing about something that would also help you. I thought my article's message was one we both felt strongly about."

Timothy's eyes were guileless and earnest. His words came out a little too fast, but his voice was unequivocally sincere. Samantha's blood ran cold. He *genuinely* believed he was doing a good deed with this article and all the previous ones, too, driven by a misguided sense of justice to expose everything he found pretentious and seedy about the world he had grown up in.

"I said you could use my transformation to prove a point to your parents, but you didn't have to let everyone else know. All the people in that ballroom now see me as nothing more than a cheap joke thanks to your article. To them, I'm just the pathetic Melody chick who lives in public housing with her single mom."

"That was never supposed to happen," Timothy said, his voice so soft Samantha had to lean forward to catch it. "No one was supposed to find out it was you. The only people I planned on telling were my parents when I finally feel ready to share my column with them."

"*Stop lying!*" The two words tore out of Samantha's mouth, fueled by so much anger her voice cracked at the end. "You clearly had a wonderful time telling Lucia everything. How else could she have known I was Melody, or found out so many details of my personal life?" Her mouth tasted like acid. All she could think of was the two childhood lovers meeting up behind her back, trading stories of her working-class background and laughing at her naivety.

Timothy's eyes widened as he raised his hands, as though her anger were a physical force he could ward off. "I don't know! Back when I was with Lucia, I did tell her about my column, but I never said a single word about you or about our Fraud Squad scheme to her. I swear! We were already on a break then."

"What about your watch then?" Samantha shouted, a dangerous prickling in the back of her eyes. "Why are you still wearing Lucia's gift if you don't care about her?" A hotel employee passing by gave her a wary glance before scuttering away, but screw what people thought. Her reputation was already shot to pieces. And it felt good to shout, her anger the only thing keeping her tears at bay.

She wouldn't waste her tears on *him*.

"My watch?" Timothy echoed, blinking down at his wrist as though noticing the watch for the first time. "When I put it on, I wasn't even thinking of who gave it to me. I just thought the celestial design fits 'Supernova,' kind of like why you're wearing star-shaped jewelry."

Timothy took a step toward her, his hands splayed in front of him like he was approaching a skittish animal. "Sam, this watch doesn't mean anything to me. Lucia doesn't mean anything to me. I swear I didn't tell her anything about you, and I've no idea how she discovered you were Melody. I regret everything I did, and if there's anything I can do to show how sorry I am, I'll do it without hesitation."

Samantha's skin crawled as Ma's words pierced her mind: *They think they don't have to feel guilty as long as they throw money at me.*

She hugged her arms to her chest and asked quietly, "Did you really have feelings for me, or were you only nice to me because you felt bad about the shit you were pulling behind my back? All the gifts you sent me and the sweet things you said and even this outfit I'm wearing now—did you give me those to soothe your guilt?"

"Did I have feelings?" Timothy repeated with an incredulous little laugh. He dropped his hands back down. "Sam, I loved you. I *love* you. More than anything I could have said or given you."

Samantha froze. This was the first time either of them had ever said those three words to the other. If she had heard them just half an hour ago, she would have been the happiest girl in the world. Now they meant nothing.

"Please, you have to believe me."

Samantha shook her head. She didn't know what to believe anymore.

"I never wanted to hurt you—"

"But you did," Samantha interrupted, lowering her arms and staring Timothy squarely in the eyes. She wanted him to remember every word she said next. "You used me and you humiliated me. You think you're so much better than your parents, but you're just like them—so comfortable in your ivory tower you think the world is yours for the taking and everyone else only matters in terms of what they can do for you. All you ever thought about was yourself."

Timothy recoiled like he had been slapped. His skin was covered with a sheen of sweat, his shirt turning translucent in patches as it clung to his body. But beneath the hallway's chandeliers, he still glowed. *The golden boy.* He was a Kingston, so protected by his status that he simply floated through life, never once imagining others might not enjoy the same safety net he did. Of course, he wouldn't consider how his column might affect anyone else, as long as it made him feel good about himself.

Samantha smiled grimly. "You know what, Timothy?" she continued, so cheerily that his expression grew wary. "I don't even know why you have such a chip on your shoulder when it comes to your family. You only got your column in the first place because of your parents' friend. On your own, you are *nothing.*"

"Do you mean that?" he asked quietly as his eyes searched her face, as though looking for a glimpse of the woman he had fallen in love with. Samantha hoped he didn't find her; Timothy wasn't the man she thought she knew, and she no longer wanted to be the woman he knew—the one he had assumed would be okay with being walked over like a doormat.

Samantha dug her fingers into her palms, the pinpricks of pain steadying her enough to say, "Did you think I actually liked you? If not for your family background, would *anyone* even like you?" She savored the bite of every word leaving her mouth and the steady blanching of Timothy's face. "I only pretended to because I needed your help to get into high society and impress Missy. So you see, this whole time, I've been using you too."

Timothy stared at her, his face ashen. But swiftly, his expression hardened. For one foolhardy moment, Samantha was tempted to reach forward and smooth out the hard set of his jaw with her own hands, to poke at his stoic mask until the Tim she knew shone through the cracks. She wanted to tell him she didn't mean what she had said so carelessly in her anger, that while her initial desire to know him might have been selfishly motivated, she ended up genuinely loving him. First simply for who he was as a person—as *Tim*—then as a friend, and then as a lover.

The words were on the tip of Samantha's tongue, but the coldness in Timothy's expression forbade her from saying them, and her own heart chilled in return. The two of them stared at each other as though seeing the other person clearly for the first time, unsaid volumes stretching into the heavy silence between them.

Then Timothy opened his mouth, and Samantha's heart stuttered. For all her put-on bravado, she wasn't ready to hear the unkind things he had to say in return. She couldn't let him hurt her twice in one evening.

So, for the second time tonight, Samantha turned and ran. But this time, Timothy did not chase after her.

Samantha braced her hands against the cool marble counter in the ladies' room. There was something about hotel bathrooms that made them a perfect sanctuary, an oasis of lemon-fragranced calm in a building crawling with people.

But the inside of her mind was a different story—a swirling chaos of hurt and anger. The judgment and scorn in the other guests' eyes, the malicious glee in Lucia's, the mingled apology and distance in Timothy's. All those coalesced into an overwhelming mess that made her head and heart ache—she couldn't tell which hurt more.

The bathroom door opened, swinging so smoothly on its hinges that it hardly made a sound. Against all reason, Samantha's heart leapt within its cage—Timothy had come back for her after all. They could still talk it out; they might still be able to fix things.

But a trace of Chanel No. 5 snaked into the space, overpowering the bathroom's citrus-scented air freshener. Samantha's skin crawled as she slowly turned around to face the intruder.

"So, this is where you ran off to," Lucia said, her eyes dancing with merriment as they raked across Samantha's disheveled appearance, lingering pointedly on the curls that had fallen out of her hairdo and the redness rimming her eyes.

"Why did you do that?" Samantha bit out, though not nearly as cuttingly as she would have liked. As always, Lucia looked like the epitome of taste and good breeding and everything Samantha had ever wanted to be. The kind of woman who belonged in Timothy's world, the kind he would have never dared to treat as callously as he had treated her.

All traces of faux niceties disappeared from Lucia's face as her upper lip curled. "You know perfectly well it's because of Timothy. What else do you have that I could possibly want?"

"It's not my fault he likes me—"

Lucia rolled her eyes. "Oh, please. Timothy doesn't *like* you. You just intrigued him because you're so different from the kind of woman he's used to. But whatever you two had going on can never compare to what he and I had. We were together for more than *four years*. His parents loved me and mine loved him. Everyone knew it was only a matter of time before he proposed."

Samantha couldn't help but laugh. "Lucia, you two were on a break when I met him and then broke up. Save your perfect love story for your fantasies."

Lucia's face darkened. "We would have gotten back together once you were out of the picture. But you proved surprisingly hard to crack." Her scarlet lips curved into a smirk. "Until an unexpected tidbit about your little Fraud Squad scheme fell into my lap, and I saw the perfect opportunity to make sure you and Timothy had no future together. As the gala host, I was given a few spare invitations, so I sent you one. Didn't you wonder why a nobody like you was seated at the best table? News flash—I changed the seating plan to make sure you and Timothy were beside each other so I could watch the expressions on both your faces when his betrayal was revealed. Even better, your prime seat made sure everyone else got a great view too."

Samantha's breath caught in her throat. All her earlier pride over being invited to the S Gala now seemed so laughably naive. The invitation hadn't been a mark of high society's approval but a harbinger of her biggest humiliation.

But a thread of red-hot anger burst through the dull shock: Timothy—*he* had given Lucia her address. *He* was how the invitation had shown up at her flat, setting in motion a chain of events that led to tonight.

"Honestly, you and Timothy deserve each other," Samantha choked out, her voice trembling slightly. "Congratulations—I hope he makes you very happy."

Lucia smirked, but there was an odd fragility lingering beneath her expression. "I know you think I'm pathetic, still pining after some guy who can't even be bothered to reply to my texts. But do you think I actually want to be like this?" She jutted her chin out. "For God's sake, I'm *Lucia Yen*. I can have any guy I want."

Then her shoulders sagged. "But my parents adore Timothy, absolutely adore him. He's the most eligible man of our generation, which makes him the perfect son-in-law in their eyes." She let out a dry chuckle. "You know, sometimes I get so frustrated with him when he complains about how his parents force him to work at KMG—meanwhile, my parents don't even want me to join the family company because *my* career doesn't matter. As a woman, my biggest accomplishment will be who I marry and how successful *he* is."

Against her will, Samantha felt a glimmer of sympathy for the other woman. Earlier tonight, she had thought Lucia's gold dress was absolutely beautiful, made even more so by her gold jewelry. But now, all the gold and trinkets just made her seem like a trophy— someone who simply had to look good on a man's arm and not much else.

"Maybe Timothy and I would have stayed together if my parents let me study overseas with him," Lucia mused, a touch of wistfulness in her voice. "But they kept me in Singapore, where I could spend more time buttering up his parents instead and learning how to be a society lady. We dated long-distance for three years, and when he came back, it felt like university had changed him so much. We have always both been disgruntled with how strict and old-fashioned our parents can be, but suddenly he *really* wanted to get out of all this and couldn't understand why I complain but still put up with my parents' demands."

Lucia rolled her eyes. "Easy for him to say. He gets away with things because, at the end of the day, he is the only child and a son to boot, but I have three older brothers, and my parents made it clear to me that my inheritance depends on how good my marriage is for the whole family."

So that was why Lucia had always pushed Timothy to join his father's hedge fund. "Does that mean you never actually loved him?" Samantha asked. She might be furious with him now, but her chest still tightened at the thought that Timothy had been strung along for four years by a woman who saw him merely as the key to unlocking her inheritance.

Scoffing, Lucia shook her head. "You still don't get it, do you? Feelings and sentiment don't matter in my world, where it's all about getting what you want using whatever means you have. That's something Timothy and I both understand very well. I'm sure he told you a bunch of sweet nothings, but he didn't shy away from using your story for his benefit, did he?"

Samantha grappled for a response, but her tongue felt like deadweight in her parched mouth. There was no comeback she could offer against the cold, bitter truth.

Lucia's voice sharpened. "Your naivety only shows me you don't have what it takes to be a part of Timothy's world. In fact, he was probably only attracted to you because your starry-eyed innocence offered him an escape from all the pressures of high society."

Samantha's throat tightened; suddenly, the diamond choker around her neck felt like it was actually choking her. Her Zuhair Murad gown that had scored her a spot on *S*'s best-dressed list barely an hour ago now seemed like a cheap and dowdy stage costume. Lucia was right—at the end of the day, she had only been playing dress-up in a fantasy role bought with Kingston money, never fully assimilated into Timothy and Lucia's world with its Byzantine rules that she could not understand.

Lucia peered at the mirror and finger combed her bangs, her face impassive as the hair fell perfectly into place. Finally, she turned to Samantha and said coolly, "If you'll excuse me, the dinner service is drawing to a close and I must resume my hosting duties. See yourself out, won't you?" And without a second look, she swept out of the ladies' room, the lingering trace of Chanel No. 5 beneath the air freshener the only sign she was ever there.

Samantha's body deflated the moment the door swung closed. She propped her hands on the bathroom counter and looked into the mirror. Even the warm and flattering bathroom lights couldn't disguise her gaunt expression and puffy eyes. She looked like a wreck. She *felt* like it too.

Something gnawed at the back of her mind like a persistent itch. She'd thought it was Timothy who told Lucia everything, but Lucia just said he hadn't even been responding to her texts.

And how did Lucia know they called themselves the Fraud Squad?

Samantha stiffened. She watched her eyes widen in the mirror as the final pieces fell into place. *No, it can't be* . . . Her body felt weak and jittery all over, as though she'd just been submerged in an ice bath. Then again, ugly truths had a way of feeling like one.

Inhaling deeply, Samantha forced herself to straighten up. From the depths of her clutch, she retrieved her phone, scrolled down to a familiar contact, and typed: Hey, can we talk?

Her fingers hovered over the "Send" button. The message was perfectly cordial, which was exactly what she did *not* want. If nothing else, the past hour had shown her that in this world, any semblance of niceness was often mistaken for weakness—an invitation for others to step all over her. She'd had enough of that for a lifetime.

Samantha took a deep breath, feeling a detached sense of purposeful calm settle over her. Hurt still lingered, licking her heart like flames, but there was something else lurking, something that felt deliciously like anger. It buoyed her as she tucked her phone back into her clutch, kept her legs moving toward the cab stand, made her feel in control for once. Another confrontation awaited, and this time, she would call the shots.

35

Anya's eyes widened at the sight of Samantha on her doorstep, still in her Zuhair Murad ball gown.

"Sam, what are you doing here? The gala couldn't have already ended."

Samantha met her gaze levelly. "Can I come in?"

Anya hesitated for a moment, then said, "Sure," stepping back to let Samantha into her house. In silence, they made their way to Anya's room.

As they each took one of the armchairs by the bay window, Anya smacked her forehead. "Shit, where are my manners? Do you want something to drink? Or maybe something to eat? The portion sizes at these fancy events are always tiny, so I bet you're really hungry. Oh, but I heard *S* sets up a dim sum supper bar at the gala every year, and the lobster siew mai is apparently to die for. But I'm sure you know that since you've been reading about it for years. Did you manage to—"

Samantha cut her off. "Anya, I don't care about dim sum. I care about why you teamed up with Lucia to humiliate me."

Anya's jaw dropped. "*Lucia*?" she echoed, her expression one of utter disgust. "What are you talking about? You know the two of us can't stand each other!"

Anya sounded so sure and offended that a prickle of doubt crept into Samantha's mind, but she steeled herself. She had already been fooled once tonight by the one person she never would have expected to betray her. Fool her twice, shame on her.

"You clearly hate me more to go behind my back and ruin my life," Samantha said coolly. "Thanks for telling Lucia everything about our Fraud Squad plan and about Timothy's article. I should have guessed that as his best friend, you would know about his column."

"*That's* your evidence? That just because I know about Tim's Argus alter ego, *I* was the one who told Lucia about his article? Don't you think it's more likely Lucia got the info straight from him?" Anya raised an eyebrow. "I think you're letting your feelings for Tim cloud your judgment here."

The last thing Samantha wanted to do was think about her feelings for Timothy. "It's also many other things all fitting together. Like how the gala invitation was delivered to my flat, and you're the only person besides Tim I gave my address to so you could send your clothes over. And how you told me not to thank Missy for the invitation because you knew she had absolutely no idea about it."

Anya's face turned white. Hunching her shoulders, she brought her legs up and hugged them close to her body, suddenly looking like a small child in her oversized armchair. That was all the answer Samantha needed. Her voice grew stronger even as her heart sank. "It's obvious that you were the one who told Lucia everything. I understand why she hates me, but what did I ever do to you?"

Anya pressed her lips together and stared down at her bare feet.

Samantha's voice sharpened. "If you're going to ruin my life, at least have the decency to not gaslight me."

"I was jealous, okay?" Anya mumbled, in such a low voice Samantha thought she must have misheard.

"Jealous? You were jealous of *me*?"

Anya's response was the tiniest jerk of her head.

Samantha laughed in disbelief. "What could you possibly envy about me?" She swept a hand around the room. "Just your walk-in closet alone is basically the size of my entire flat. You have everything I could ever want, everything *anyone* could possibly want."

"That's not true!" Anya burst out, finally lifting her eyes to Samantha's face. "What I want most is exactly what I don't have. I was the one who gave you the clothes and accessories and advice. But suddenly, it was *you* being invited to exclusive parties like Daisy's and getting featured by the magazines I've always wanted to be in. And Tim was *my* best friend, one of the only people who stuck by me. But once you two got together, he barely had any time for me. Not to mention, you were doing so well at Arrow, even winning over those snooty society ladies who have always looked down on my mom and me. You had *everything* going for you."

Samantha recoiled at the sudden vehemence in Anya's voice. "Why are you even comparing yourself to me? You know what my family situation is like, so how can you blame me for trying to improve my life?"

Anya glared at her with watery eyes. "At least you have the opportunity to fake a persona and reinvent yourself! But I'm stuck under the shadow of my mother's reputation forever." Her voice quivered. "Do you know how painful it is to be on the fringes, looking into a world that I used to be a part of? And for the past few months, I had to stand by one side and watch as you got everything I've always wanted."

"So you decided to make sure I couldn't have what you didn't?"

The anger disappeared from Anya's face as she shrank back in her armchair, her body folding into itself. "I thought you were getting too big for your boots. I hate Lucia, but at that time, I resented you even more. I knew Lucia had access to the S Gala as the host, so I tipped her off about everything. But I just thought we would be bringing you down a few pegs . . . I never wanted to publicly humiliate you."

Anya wrung her hands, a plaintive note creeping into her voice. "When Lucia told me her full plan, I tried to back out of it. I really did. But by that point, she already knew everything and she was going ahead with or without me. There was nothing I could do."

Samantha dragged her eyes away from Anya's trembling bottom lip. She would *not* allow herself to feel sorry for someone who had betrayed her. "But why did you even help me in the first place if you don't want me to become a socialite?"

"Because I didn't think you'd have any staying power. I know better than anyone else how hard it is to climb up the social ladder, so I never expected you would actually succeed. Around other socialites, even those who are still my friends, I've always felt inferior to them because of who my mom is. But you were always so impressed with my lifestyle, with my tales of parties and jet-setting and living the high life."

"That's why you offered to help me, because it would make you feel better about yourself as you showed me the ropes," Samantha finished quietly, a sinking feeling in her stomach. She and Anya spent every lunch break together, swung by each other's desks at least half a dozen times every day to gossip, and even commiserated over being from single-parent households. Just a month ago, they had been huddled up in these exact armchairs, both with such grand plans for their futures. Now, Samantha barely recognized the woman sitting opposite her.

Her heart clenched. Was this what Raina had felt like as they sat in the leather banquettes at Atlas?

Samantha stood up and smoothed her gown. "I don't think there's anything more for us to say to each other. I'll return all your clothes tomorrow."

Anya looked up at her with red-rimmed eyes. After a moment, she asked in a small voice, "Do you need me to walk you out?"

Samantha shook her head. Any niceties now seemed like a mockery of how close they had been once upon a time.

On the bus ride home, Samantha propped her head against the window, the coldness of the glass a welcome respite for her throbbing head. She ignored the curious stares from the other passengers as they eyed her long gown and elaborate hairdo. Had it really just been a few hours ago that she was getting preened and pruned in Eileen Kingston's vanity room? She had felt on top of the world when she had slipped on the beautiful Zuhair Murad gown, when Timothy had looked at her like she was everything he had ever wanted, when she had sat among the gala guests and felt like she belonged.

And now, she was nothing more than high-society roadkill. A cheap anecdote to be laughed at over dim sum for Singapore's elites; a cautionary tale about what could happen if you tried flying too close to the sun.

Samantha's lips twisted into a bitter smile. Argus—*Timothy*—shouldn't have written about Pygmalion, not when her story was more like that of Icarus, who had dared to dream too big and paid the price for his wild ambition.

Samantha pushed open the door quietly, praying her mother would be in bed. But no such luck, for Ma was sprawled on the couch with the television turned on and her feet propped up on the coffee table. One hand was buried in a tub of melon seeds, and judging from the small mound of seed shells on the table, she had probably been watching her Mediacorp shows for the past couple of hours.

Ma glanced up as the door creaked open. "Sam, what are you doing home so early? Didn't you want to stay out late with Timothy after the gala?"

At the mention of Timothy's name, Samantha pressed her lips together. If she opened her mouth now, she might just start crying.

Her mother's gaze sharpened. "Did something happen between you and him?" Without waiting for a response, she abandoned her tub of melon seeds on the table and was over by Samantha's side in seconds. Placing a firm hand on her daughter's elbow, she steered the younger woman toward the couch. "Sit," she said, her tone brokering no room for dissent.

Silently, Samantha acquiesced. After the night she had, she didn't have it in her to resist.

Ma turned the television off before fixing her eyes on Samantha's face. A de-shelled melon seed clinging to the corner of her mouth fell off as she pursed her lips. "Samantha, if you and Timothy had a fight, it doesn't hurt to be the bigger person. You have to understand that he's probably used to getting what he wants, so give him some time to come around."

A wave of bitterness seared Samantha, so strong she could choke on its acridity. "Be the bigger person?" she repeated with an incredulous laugh. "After he humiliated me tonight in front of everyone?"

Her mother's eyes widened. "Samantha, what are you talking about? What did Timothy do to you? You can tell me—I'm your mother."

"Right, my *mother*. Which is why you care so much more about protecting his feelings than you do about mine. You don't even care about how he treats me."

Her mother sputtered. "Of course I care! I'm always asking you about him."

"About what he buys me and how much he spends on me and where he takes me for dates! But you never asked me how he makes me feel."

Her mother's expression faltered. "I just always assumed he makes you happy—"

"Because he spends so much on me?" Samantha chuckled humorlessly as she shook her head. "I think we have very different ways of measuring happiness in a relationship. I know you want a rich son-in-law, but I'm sorry I can't give that to you. Turns out I don't have what it takes to be a part of Timothy's world."

A beat of silence passed, then her mother's face crumpled and she reached for Samantha's hand. For a moment, Samantha considered resisting the gesture, but she couldn't muster the energy for such a meaningless rebellion.

Her mother's voice was much softer as she said, "Sam, I'm sorry if I ever gave you the wrong impression, but you are always, *always* the person I love and care about most. Please tell me what happened. Maybe I can help."

Samantha's breath hitched, and something warm trickled down her cheeks. She brushed at it roughly, but her fingers came away wet and tinged black with Burberry mascara ink. Of all the people who could have cracked her tonight, who knew it would be her mother?

Ma—a watery blur—made a move to touch Samantha's face but seemed to reconsider. She stuffed her hand beneath her right thigh as if to prevent it from springing up again. Her eyes swiveled around the living room, as though hoping the walls contained a script for what to say to her crying daughter, before stilling on the coffee table. Then, very casually, Ma picked up the box of Venus et Fleur roses—their petals still snow white and perfect—and nudged it out of sight behind the sofa.

Samantha tore her eyes away from where they had been following her mother's movements. Her chest coiled tight the way it always did whenever she thought of Timothy now. But amid the knots that twisted her insides, a small warmth bloomed: Her mother was still looking out for her.

"Do you want to tell me what happened?" Ma prompted gently, her hands folded together in her lap.

Samantha shook her head. Recounting her humiliation would only break her mother's heart. "Ma, can you just hold me for a bit?" she whispered.

"Of course," her mother immediately said, looking pained Samantha even had to ask. She opened her arms into a circle for Samantha to nestle into.

The position was a little awkward, especially with the voluminous folds of Samantha's gown taking up most of the space on their two-seater couch. Through the thin upholstery, Samantha could feel an unwieldy spring poking against her back, and her neck was starting to cramp. But none of that mattered. In Ma's arms was the first place all evening she'd allowed herself to relax.

Samantha closed her eyes, breathing in her mother's unique scent—a mix of her drugstore deodorant, the polish fumes from her nail salon, and a not unpleasant smell of sweat dried under air-conditioning. She felt Ma remove her diamond headband with the gentlest touch—as though she were afraid Samantha might crumble beneath her fingertips—then start combing through her hair with her fingers, carefully separating each curl from the others.

Samantha's breathing shallowed. All of a sudden, she was fifteen again, Ba had just passed away, and she and Ma suddenly found themselves with no one else to depend on but each other. In the months after the funeral, she had crept into her mother's bed every night, letting the warmth of Ma's body and her quiet breathing reassure her she wasn't all alone.

The silence was broken by her mother's tentative voice. "Sam, I never want you to feel like I don't care about you. Yes, I've been pushing you to be with a rich man, but it's only because I care so much about you."

Samantha let out a sound halfway between a laugh and a snort.

"No, I mean it," her mother insisted. "It was never because I wanted to be some billionaire's mother-in-law. My life isn't easy, yes, but I've made peace with it. All I want is for you to have a secure future and never worry about money again. I want you to avoid everything I went through—"

Ma's voice cracked. A deep breath, then: "I had to pawn my

wedding ring and all the jewelry my mom left me to pay off your dad's medical bills. I had to get down on my knees to beg the loan sharks for an extension. Now, I wash and prune other women's feet for a living." Her hand on Samantha's head quivered. "There's not been a single day that I haven't been scared you might end up just like me."

Samantha's eyes grew hot. She wanted to lift her head to look at her mother, but the moment felt too heavy for any abrupt motion. She settled for searching Ma's face in the reflection of the darkened television screen, but all she could see was the older woman's bowed head with its streaks of white, and a fluttering of fingers as she continued stroking Samantha's hair.

"I was scared too," Samantha heard herself admit. It surprised her how good it felt to finally say those four words out loud—something she had never done in front of her mother. Growing up, she had been so careful not to add to Ma's worries that she never permitted herself to reveal anything unhappy, not even when she had been bullied in school for her hand-me-downs and school lunch subsidies. She had either kept everything to herself or confided in Raina instead.

"I still am. But not about ending up like you, per se. I was just scared I would never be able to get out of the rut Ba's death and debt left us in." Samantha's eyes caught on the magazines piled on the coffee table. "I guess that's why I fell in love with magazines. Those socialites—their lives always seemed so perfect and untroubled that I . . . couldn't help but want to be as close to that world as possible."

"Sammy . . ." Her mother sighed, the couch's faux-leather cover crackling as she shifted in her seat. "I'm so sorry. You were so young when those things happened, and I wasn't able to protect you."

"Ma, please don't say that. You have nothing to apologize for,"

Samantha whispered, flicking her eyes down when she heard her mother's breath hitch. She hadn't cried in front of Ma in years, but she didn't think she had ever seen her mother cry, either, not even at the funeral. There had only been once, an early morning three months after Ba's passing, when she heard what sounded like muffled sobbing coming from Ma's room. But the door was locked, and since nothing seemed abnormal afterward—her mother rushed off to work and then came back ten hours later to whip up dinner—Samantha never pressed the issue.

"I don't blame you for anything," Samantha continued despite the lump that had swelled in her throat. Why had she never thought to ask her mother how *she* was doing? "I know you did your best to keep our family together. You are why we made it past those difficult years."

Ma sighed so deeply that Samantha felt the top of her hairdo rustle from the exhalation. "Maybe, but I still feel so guilty you never had any of the nice things other girls had. And it still breaks my heart to see you working so hard, coming back so late every night from the office. Even back in uni, you were juggling a part-time job while keeping up your grades for your scholarship. I just want you to be able to relax for once and let someone else take care of you. Maybe you think I'm too materialistic, but to me, having money means having security and stability, and giving money means showing love."

"Ma . . ." Samantha pushed herself upright and reached out to clasp her mother's hands. "I get that you're trying to look out for me," she said gently, "and I appreciate it. I really, really do."

She glanced down at their interlaced hands. They sported matching manicures, but for completely different reasons—Ma's was part of her workplace uniform, the rhinestones and long tips often getting in the way of household chores; hers was the only gift Ma knew how to give her.

"But we don't ever need to depend on a man, or anyone else. You inspire me so much—single-handedly raising me after Ba passed away while also working such a demanding job." Samantha's voice cracked. "I want to be like *you*."

Ma opened her mouth, but Samantha forged ahead, "I know what you're going to say. You're going to tell me I should never end up like you and I should strive for a better life." Her hands tightened around her mother's. "But, Ma, there's nothing shameful about your job. It puts food on the table, takes care of the bills, and helps pay off the debt. And while I do want to build a better life for the both of us, I want to do it the way you did—as a strong, independent woman who won't take shit from anyone."

Ma's jaw slackened, but Samantha didn't think her wide-eyed expression had anything to do with the cursing. Feeling braver, she continued, "I would rather be like you, someone who made the most of the cards life dealt her than rely on my husband and risk losing everything because of a decision he made."

There was a long silence. Ma appeared frozen but for the barely perceptible tremble of her hands and a slight twitch in the crook of her jaw.

But finally, she released a long breath. Staring straight into Samantha's eyes, Ma said gravely, "Sam, you need to know that I never, *ever* want you to be with someone who doesn't treat you well. I don't care if Timothy's a Kingston or even a king—if he makes you sad, then he will have me to deal with. Above all else, I just want you to be happy, and if that's with a not-so-rich man, or if you want to be single for life and end up with twenty dogs, I will accept it. But don't expect me to help take care of them—you know dogs scare me."

A laugh escaped Samantha. "Sounds good, Ma. I'll remember to get cats instead."

Her mother's mouth curved up slightly. "It's good to see you smile again," she said, rubbing her thumb against Samantha's wrist. Then she let go and pushed herself off the couch, careful to keep her weight off her weak left wrist. "How about I bring you some comfy clothes so you can change out of this dress? Singapore is so hot these days, so what you need right now is a tank top and some cool cotton shorts."

As Ma walked away, Samantha almost called out to her to come back. All she wanted was to hide away in her mother's embrace, but she knew she had to face the music at some point.

Steeling herself, she groped in her Valentino clutch for her phone. Samantha stared at the dark screen for a few moments, wanting to drag out this last bit of calm before the storm hit.

The moment she switched her phone on, it started vibrating furiously as a cascade of notifications trickled in. Ten missed calls: one from Anya, three from Daisy, and six from Timothy.

Also, two new emails and three new text messages:

EllieA@smagazine.com: Good evening, Samantha. I hope this email finds you well. Kindly use the link below to schedule a meeting with Missy to discuss your column, Glamour and Grit. Thanks and happy weekend, Ellie Ang (Executive Assistant to Missy Tanaka, Editor in Chief, S).

Genie@altermeatgo.com: Samantha, I need to speak to you asap about our contract for Meatless Grub™. Let's set up a meeting for early next week. Best regards, Genie.

Winston: Samantha, it's come to Bulgari's attention that your profile might not be the most suitable for their brand image, so I'm afraid I'll have to pull your piece from the advertorial. Sorry.

Daisy: Sam! Are you okay? I'm so worried about you. Please call me when you see this.

And the one she had been anticipating and dreading in equal measures:

Tim: Sam, I don't blame you for ignoring me. I'm an asshole. But I meant everything I've ever said to you—I never told Lucia a single thing.

I don't know how she found out about it, but I'm investigating that. About that article—I was stupid; I thought no one would discover your identity and nothing would happen to you. I know nothing excuses what an asshole I was, but I just want you to know I really do love you and you're the last person I'd ever want to hurt. I'm so sorry about everything. Please call me back if you can. I don't want this to be our final memory of each other.

Samantha stared at her phone screen. She wanted to pick up the phone and call him, scream at him, and rage at him. She wanted to tell him that despite his attempts to rescue the situation, the damage had been done, that there were some messes no amount of money or power could fix. She wanted to confess that she loved him, too, and it was that which made the betrayal hurt all the more.

Samantha's thumb hovered over the "Delete Message" option, but after a moment, she simply closed it instead. Tonight, she wasn't ready to deal with him, not when the hurt and anger were still so raw, the memory of the gala still a fresh wound. For now, there was only one person she wanted to talk to—the person who had been there for her since the beginning when she was just plain old Sam.

Her heart in her throat, she typed:

Rai, I know you're mad at me, but can we talk? Something happened and I could really use a friend.

Her hand tightened around the phone as three little dots appeared on the screen. It felt like an eternity before a response came.

Raina: Cabbing over right now.

37

Twenty minutes later, Raina texted to say she had reached her HDB block, so Samantha made her way down. The void deck's decor was sparse, and the only furniture in the whole space was a couple of bins, a bicycle rack filled with wheelless bicycles—wheel theft was a serious issue in the neighborhood—and a single hexagonal table.

Usually, chain-smoking old men monopolized the table, whiling their afternoons away gossiping loudly and playing Chinese chess. But now, close to midnight, the only person there was Raina—Samantha's eyes widened as she neared. Her best friend was sitting right across from . . . Daisy, both with their backs turned toward her.

The pair couldn't look more different if they tried. Even though it was a muggy summer evening, Raina was wearing her trusty pin-covered denim jacket like always. Meanwhile, Daisy was still in her gala sheath, seemingly unaware that one of her sleeves trailed dangerously close to a mound of cigarette ashes left behind on the table.

As Samantha neared the duo, she could hear Daisy saying,

"You're totally rocking the girl power vibe with your pins. What do you think of Dior's *We Should All Be Feminists* collection?"

"I think it's cool that such a big brand is talking about such an important issue," Raina said. "But it feels kind of like slacktivism to me. Catchy slogan, but doesn't make up for the fact that Dior's still only using size zero models. Pretty skewed sense of female empowerment if you ask me."

Daisy nodded. "Totally! It's so performative. One guy I know straight up told me he only wears Dior's feminist collection to 'impress the chicks.'"

"Sexist pig," Samantha muttered as she came up behind them.

Both Raina and Daisy jumped in their seats and turned around. Daisy clapped a hand to her chest. "Sam, you totally scared me! You're like some insane ninja."

Raina scooted down the table and pulled Samantha down into her vacated seat. "How are you?" she asked, her eyes roaming Samantha's face. "What happened? Your text freaked me out."

"Got backstabbed, but could be worse," Samantha said lightly, trying for a nonchalant shrug. But to her horror, she heard a dangerous wobble in her voice.

Raina pressed her lips into a thin line. "Tell me who I have to fight. No one screws over my best friend and gets away with it."

My best friend. Tears pricked the back of Samantha's eyes as her heart flooded with warmth.

"Sam, oh no, don't cry," Daisy exclaimed in distress. She rummaged around in her clutch. "Hang on, I've got some scented wipes here. They're really soft so they won't pull at the skin beneath your eyes. Do you know, the skin there is really thin, so that's how people get eye bags and dark circles?"

Another laugh spewed out of Samantha's mouth even as more tears welled up in her eyes. She was persona non grata in Singapore high society, looked down on by just about everyone. But here was Raina, who had had her back since day one, as well as Daisy, risking her own fledgling reputation to be by her side.

"Sam, I'm serious—crying can totally clog your pores. Drat!" Daisy snapped her clutch closed with a huff. "I just remembered I used it at the gala to rub off the lipstick on Lincoln's face after I kissed him. I must have forgotten to put it back in my clutch."

Samantha wiped her tears away—roughly at first, then gentled her dabbing after Daisy shot her a scandalized look. "Isn't there still an hour till the gala ends? You're missing out on the famous dim sum supper."

Daisy pulled a face. "As if I could bring myself to remain there after what happened. I wanted to go after you, but Tim beat me to it. But when he came back into the ballroom alone, I figured something happened between you two, so I went up to him. He gave me your address and asked me to check up on you."

Samantha smiled weakly. "Well, you found me." Would there ever come a day when her heart wouldn't pound just at the mention of Timothy's name?

"Credit goes to Raina. I've never been in this area before, so I got quite lost at first."

Raina smirked. "I'd just gotten out of my cab when I saw this woman wandering around in this ball gown. She came up to me and asked me for directions to your flat, so I guessed she came from the S Gala too."

Daisy placed a hand tentatively on Samantha's. "Sam, I know you might not want to talk about what happened back at the gala. But I think telling us will make it easier to figure out a solution together."

Raina nodded. "I agree. Daisy has filled me in on some of it, but I'm still kind of confused. Lucia's obviously an asshole, but how did she know so much about what you were up to?"

Samantha hesitated, but Raina and Daisy were both looking at her with kind, sympathetic eyes. Well, Daisy's were; Raina just looked like she was ready to commit murder. She hadn't wanted to worry her mother with the details, but maybe sharing them with her friends would help.

Samantha took a deep breath, then filled Raina and Daisy in on what happened. When she finished, there was a moment of silence before they erupted.

"I never liked Anya much, but I didn't think she would be a backstabber either," Raina said grimly.

Daisy tapped one manicured finger against her chin. "I don't know who's worse—Lucia or Anya. I mean, Lucia is obviously horrible, but—"

"Definitely Anya," Raina said. "Lucia's an asshole, but at least she didn't try to hide it."

Daisy turned to Samantha. "Smart of you, Sam, to figure out what Anya did." Samantha bit her lip; she would have given anything to be wrong.

"Actually," Raina interjected, "I think the biggest culprit here is Timothy."

Samantha's head jerked up, a fierce pang rocking her heart. Raina wasn't wrong, but to hear someone else vocalize what she herself thought made Timothy's betrayal seem even more real. But at the same time, a weight in Samantha's chest eased—her best friend was one of the few people who wouldn't automatically excuse Timothy and take his side just because he was a Kingston.

Daisy winced. "I can't believe he wrote that article . . . I can't believe he's Argus! Holy shit, I can't believe Argus is a dude! That's a plot twist I don't think any of us saw coming." She paused. "Still, he wasn't the one who embarrassed Sam in front of everyone. Anya was the one who told Lucia everything, and Lucia was the one who exposed it—"

"And Timothy was the one who gave them the material to do so," Raina retorted. "If he hadn't written that article, there wouldn't be anything for Lucia to expose."

"But Lucia and Anya were acting out of pure malice; Timothy wasn't," Daisy protested. "He made a stupid mistake, but he was never deliberately trying to hurt Sam."

Raina frowned. "I think what Lucia and Anya did was despicable, but I hate it when men can get away with the shit they do while women take the full brunt of the blame. Timothy messed up, and he should be held accountable. Sam, what are you going to do about him?"

Samantha ran a shaking hand through her hair. "I—I don't know."

"I say you should just pretend he never existed," Raina said, her eyes blazing. "Forget about him and move on. It's outrageous he gets to walk away from this whole mess scot-free while you suffer."

"I think Timothy's suffering too," Daisy said quietly. "At the gala, he looked like an absolute wreck. He was literally begging me to let him know how you were doing if I managed to speak to you. Not that I would," she quickly added as Samantha's head snapped up. "I won't tell him anything you don't want me to, Sam. But maybe you should hear him out. At least get some closure on this whole mess."

With every word her friends exchanged, Samantha shrank farther back in her seat. Her head was torn; her heart even more so.

"Closure?" Raina snorted. "That's how it always goes in those TV dramas: a couple breaks up, one of them says they want closure, so they meet up and talk. But then they start making out, and then making up. And before you know it, they wind up married with three kids and a dog, and still squabble over whose turn it is to wash the dishes."

"You say that like it's a bad thing. Everyone knows arguing about dishes is foreplay." Daisy's lips twitched. "Choreplay."

Raina rolled her eyes but gave a small smile. "My point is, people only ask for closure when there are unanswered questions. But it's pretty clear here what happened."

Daisy shrugged. "Maybe, but I still don't think cutting Timothy out completely is the answer. Sam, what do you think?"

Samantha gnawed on her lower lip. "I don't think I'm in the right frame of mind to be thinking about him. Honestly, I'd rather think about my career."

"Attagirl!" Raina exclaimed, slapping the table. "Who cares about men? Arrow over bros, amirite?"

"Missy over missing Tim!" Daisy chimed in.

"Public relations over romantic relations!"

"*S* over Tim's ass!"

Samantha groaned but felt her mouth tug up. "I love you guys, but those are terrible."

Raina's expression turned serious again. "I know things might be not so great now with your career, but you can totally still turn things around."

"'Not so great' is an understatement," Samantha said glumly, leaning forward and propping her chin on her hands. "Now that I'm the laughingstock of Singapore high society, how can I ever write for a luxury magazine again? And it's not just Glamour and Grit I'm worried about. I have PR projects at Arrow lined up with some socialites, but there's no way any of them would want to work with me now. How can I help them build their public image when my own is in the dumps?"

Daisy grimaced. "Nothing's set in stone yet, so don't count your chickens before they hatch!" She tilted her head to one side. "No, wait, chickens hatching is a good thing. And I know you're going to end up with a . . . thriving flock."

Samantha cracked a small smile. "Great metaphor, but the signs don't look good. I'm scheduled to meet Missy and Genie Tsai separately next week, probably so they can fire me in person. None of my other clients have reached out yet, but I think it's because most of them weren't at the gala. Still, it's only a matter of time before they hear of my social pariahdom."

Just then, Daisy's phone chimed. She looked down at it, then back up with an apologetic expression. "I'm so, so sorry, but I really have to go. The gala ended, and I'm supposed to fly to China with Pan Ling for a wedding cheongsam fitting. Sam, trust me, there's nothing I want more than to be here for you. But Pan Ling will—"

Samantha waved her off. "Don't be silly! You should go," she said, reaching over to hug Daisy tightly. "Thank you so much for everything. This means a lot to me, it really does. And good luck with your mother-in-law."

"Thanks, I'll need it," Daisy said grimly, before softening her tone. "And hey, let me know what you decide to do, okay? I'll support whatever choice you make."

Samantha and Raina watched as Daisy made her way to a car waiting by the curb. "I like her," Raina suddenly said. "She seems like a good sort."

Samantha turned to her with a small grin. "Really? But you never wanted to hang out with her when I asked."

Raina scratched her nose. "About that . . . I thought you were ditching me for your cooler friends, and I felt like I was losing you. But it wasn't fair for me to take my jealousy out on you. You're free to be friends with whomever you want."

Samantha shook her head. "No, I'm the one who should apologize. Rai, you were right—I was so consumed with the Fraud Squad and so focused on making it in high society to impress Missy that I lost sight of who I really am and the people most important to me. No matter who I meet or where I end up in life, you will *always* be my best friend."

For a moment, Raina didn't say anything. Then she shoved Samantha's shoulder. "Stop it with the mushiness. That's not like us."

Laughing, Samantha raised her hands. "Fine, fine. But I meant what I said."

"So did I." Raina grinned. "I would love to hang out with you and Daisy sometime . . . if that's okay?"

"Of course that's okay! You two get along so well. Once Daisy's back from China, I'll text her and ask when she's free to hang out."

"Great! Just . . . can we not do a glycolic peel, please? I looked up what it was when you told me about it last time, and it sounds *horrifying*." Raina's eyes widened comically. "Apparently, it uses acid to strip skin off your face. I happen to like my skin where it is."

"It's not as bad as it sounds; it did wonders for my pores. But I hear you. Why don't we hit up the new National Gallery exhibition instead? I heard Rothko is their artist of the month."

"More art?" Raina's face blanched. "You know what, the glycolic peel sounds pretty good after all."

38

As Samantha walked into the *S* office, the receptionist glanced up. Her eyes—lined with a poison-green color this time—widened briefly before she caught herself and schooled her face back into a blank expression. "Oh. It's you," she said flatly. "Missy's expecting you in her office. Down the hallway, then turn left. Last door there." Without waiting for a response, she returned her attention to her computer.

Samantha swallowed. The receptionist's attitude wasn't surprising—everyone working at *S* had probably heard about what happened at the gala—but what was surprising was the hurt she felt. She had an entire weekend to come to terms with how her fall from grace would change the way people treated her, but facing those changes in real life was much easier said than done.

Finding Missy's office was easy—probably the easiest step of this whole affair. After getting the go-ahead from Ellie, the editor's assistant, Samantha took a deep breath and pushed open the door.

Missy rose from her seat as Samantha walked in. "It's lovely to see you, Samantha. Take a seat," she said, gesturing toward a beige wingback in front of her desk.

The office was so massive that the walk up to the desk felt like an airport runway. Samantha could feel Missy scrutinizing her and quickened her footsteps, hunching over once she was seated to hide as much of her body as possible behind the walnut desk. Since she'd returned all of Anya's clothes the day after the gala, this was the first time Samantha was meeting Missy in her own things—a red Cotton On dress that had been a pre-Fraud Squad favorite, paired with plain black pumps for extra height to boost her confidence. Her curls, despite her best effort to tame them, were flying wild today. Meanwhile, in a chic three-piece paisley suit, Missy looked like she had stepped out from the pages of her magazine.

"Would you like anything to drink?"

"Just water, please," Samantha said in a voice just as courteous as Missy's, though there was so much adrenaline coursing through her that she wanted to scream. She wished the editor would just skip the niceties and put her out of her misery by firing her already.

"Let me grab two glasses."

As Missy rummaged through the shelf behind her, Samantha took the opportunity to examine her office; she would never be this close to *S*'s inner sanctum again. The room was filled with practical wooden furniture and metal light fixtures, brightened up slightly by a lone vase of purple flowers on the window ledge. In one corner hummed a Shiseido mini-fridge that held bottles of Perrier instead of skin care.

But the walls more than made up for the minimalist decor. One was plastered with photos of Missy and other socialites—there was one of her with Albert and Eileen, and several more of just Missy and Eileen. Another wall bore copies of every single one of Missy's editor's letters for *S*. And every inch of the wall behind her desk was plastered with two hundred pieces of A6-size paper—the mock-up of *S*'s October issue.

As if guided by some higher force, Samantha found her eyes drawn to one piece in particular, placed in the bottom left corner of the collage. **GLAMOUR AND GRIT**, its heading read. Or at least it used to, before it had been crossed out by a thick black marker. Next to it, someone had scribbled, *TSW?*

Samantha's heart sank. What was supposed to be her big debut had been Sharpied into oblivion.

She tore her eyes away from the wall as Missy set a glass of water in front of her. "I'm afraid my kettle isn't working today."

"That's all right," Samantha replied, taking a careful sip. The water tasted as lukewarm as she felt.

Missy leaned forward, propping her elbows on her desk. "You must be wondering why I called you here."

Samantha put the glass back down and took a deep breath. "Missy, I'm really sorry—"

Missy raised an eyebrow. "Sorry? What do you have to be sorry for?"

Beads of sweat wormed down the back of Samantha's neck. "I'm sorry for not being more up-front about my identity. Lucia was right—based on my real background, I would never have been invited to the S Gala. But I swear I never meant to embarrass you or *S*."

"So, you lied about your identity?"

"I never lied about it . . ." Samantha shifted in her seat. "But whenever people assumed I was a socialite, I just let them continue thinking that."

Missy fixed her with a long look. Then, to Samantha's astonishment, the corners of the editor's mouth rose into a smirk. "Well, then, what's the problem?"

Samantha blinked. "What?"

"You didn't lie, you didn't commit fraud—though I did hear about your Fraud Squad experiment from Timothy afterward, and I must say, that's quite a catchy name. You simply worked with what you've got."

Missy paused. "You know, Samantha, you kind of remind me of myself."

Wide-eyed, Samantha pointed at herself. "Me? But I'm just a small fry compared to you."

"Well, like you, I also had to take a detour to arrive at where I'm at now." Missy leaned back in her chair and raked a hand through her bob. "My parents never wanted me to go into fashion—they found the industry too frivolous and wanted me to do something that was still . . . ladylike but more cultured and proper. In the end, I agreed to accept a job at Christie's; I figured it could be a good launchpad since the art and fashion worlds are so intertwined."

"Oh!" Samantha exclaimed softly. "That's kind of why I joined Arrow. I thought that being under Merlion Media might make it easier to transfer to *S* down the road."

"Right, but while I was at Christie's, I realized making the switch was far from easy. People in fashion thought those in art were too snobby, while artists think fashion is too shallow and materialistic. I pushed for a lot of collaborations between the two fields, like fashion photo shoots inspired by paintings, exhibits of haute couture from Schiaparelli and Gaultier, and even helped launch a Christie's fellowship to support young designers. But it took years before public perception finally started to change and I gained the respect of the fashion world. I only jumped to fashion in my thirties, which is usually considered far too late for such an ageist industry, but I haven't looked back since."

Samantha sat there quietly, her head in a whirl. Even Missy, who had worked her way up to become *Prestige Hong Kong*'s fashion director, then deputy editor of *Vogue China*, and now editor in chief of *S*, once felt like she had something to prove too. The woman commonly called Asia's Commander in Chanel always seemed so untouchable that it was hard for Samantha to fathom that the older woman could have once been plagued by insecurities and fears as well.

The same ones she herself had.

Even so, Samantha's heart was still in her throat as she dared herself to ask, "Does that mean you aren't upset about the whole Fraud Squad matter?"

Missy's mouth flattened into a thin line. "Oh, I'm upset all right," she said grimly. "But not with you. Lucia should have never pulled that little stunt. When she veered off script and asked the guests to name things they liked about *S*, I thought that was a good piece of improv. But I was a lot less pleased when I found out why she did that."

Samantha's heart lifted slightly. "I'm still sorry, though, about causing you and *S* so much trouble."

Missy held up a hand. "Firstly, Samantha, never apologize for something you aren't at fault for. Women need to stop saying 'sorry' so much. And believe me—you aren't the one people think poorly of. Lucia won't be hosting the S Gala again, or any other high-profile events for the foreseeable future."

Samantha jolted upright, the pressure in her chest easing as though she'd just taken a big gulp of air after being underwater for too long. A second too late, she realized her $11.99 polyester dress was now on full display. The urge to hunch over again swept through her—

Oh, who cares! Her entire body was suddenly lighter and looser now, as though a physical weight on her shoulders had been lifted at last.

"Anyway," Missy continued, "I didn't ask you here today just to tell you this. I also wanted to talk about Glamour and Grit."

"Right, that." Samantha's shoulders slumped again. "After what happened at the gala, I doubt anyone will take me seriously anymore. I understand the column will have to be scrapped, and I'm sorry for leaving you and the magazine in a lurch like that. I know there isn't much time to find a replacement before the issue goes to print."

Missy steepled her hands. "You're right that we're scrapping *Glamour and Grit*."

Even though she'd been expecting it, Samantha's stomach still dropped. She tucked a piece of hair behind her ear and took a deep breath before saying, "Of course, I completely understand why—"

Missy held up a hand. "You didn't let me finish. The reason why *Glamour and Grit* no longer exists is because . . . it's been re-named *The Socialite Whisperer*."

TSW! Samantha could barely get her next words out. "And *I* am the socialite whisperer?"

Missy nodded. "Here's what I envision for TSW—you'll write about your PR projects and how you help socialites cultivate their personal and professional branding. In short, I see you serving as a bridge between the public and high society. At the same time, we can still achieve what we wanted to do with *Glamour and Grit* by showing readers that socialites can have their own ambitions and passions, like Genie Tsai with her vegan meat business, or your other client, Meera Abdul, and the keto bakery she just opened."

"That's a wonderful idea!" However, the spark of excitement growing within Samantha dimmed as a thought struck her. "But I don't think any of the socialites even want to work with me anymore." She cast her eyes down on her lap. "They all think I'm some kind of fraud."

"I think the email I sent out right after the gala will ensure that's not the case."

Samantha's head shot up. "What email?"

"The one where I told all the gala guests that you are a PR professional focusing on a luxury niche. You decided that the best way to understand what your upscale clientele wants is to go behind the scenes and see things from their perspective, which was why you agreed to help Argus out with the social experiment. But you must have seen my email since you are on the gala mailing list, no?"

"Uh, I must have missed it," Samantha said as casually as she could. While doing the best-dressed list photo shoot at the gala, Fiona had told her that *S* would be emailing the guests all the raw red-carpet photos. So the first thing Samantha had done after the debacle was to unsubscribe from the mailing list; she didn't want to receive reminders of the worst night of her life.

Then Missy's words sank in. "Hang on. So all the guests think I only tried to pass myself off as a socialite because I was doing user research for my PR work?"

"Yes, that was the gist of the email. And the damage control worked beautifully—many guests emailed back to praise your dedication, and several wanted your contact details. I told them I would get back to them after checking with you."

In that moment, Samantha could have cried with relief. It felt like a weight had finally been lifted off her shoulders. Instead of castigating her as a pathetic social climber, people actually thought she had done something worthy of praise.

"Thank you for writing that email." She made sure to look Missy in the eye so the older woman could understand the full depth of her gratitude. "Seriously, thank you so much."

Missy paused. "While the email came from me, I can't take credit for the idea. The gala might be in *S*'s name, but all the funding and backing came from its parent company, and a decision like this beyond the editorial scope is outside of my jurisdiction."

Samantha's mouth dried. Only someone more powerful than Missy, someone even higher up Merlion Media's chain of command, could have the authority to send out that email. And there was only one person it could be.

"But enough about that, Samantha. What I want to know is, are you still interested in doing the column?"

"Of course I am! I'm one hundred percent interested." Samantha paused. "But . . . are you giving me this opportunity because you feel sorry for me?"

Samantha's voice faltered as Missy fixed her with a long, level look. "I run Singapore's top magazine," the editor said coolly. "Every decision I make is only with business in mind, and I don't let my personal feelings interfere with my job."

"I didn't mean to imply anything," Samantha quickly said. "I'm just . . . so blown away right now. I came into this meeting thinking I'd messed everything up, and it's only just sinking in for me that things aren't as bad as I feared."

At that, Missy's voice gentled. "I've actually been toying with the idea of a column like TSW for quite some time now, ever since I heard that *Elle*'s new strategy is to have more down-to-earth human-interest content. And like I told you at Daisy's party, my readers are getting tired of seeing the same extravagance over and over again. So I'm hoping that having a nonsocialite like you run a column will strike a happy medium that pleases my readers but still retains *S*'s focus on high society."

Samantha pressed her lips together to hide a smile. "Sounds like the perfect role for me. I just hope Arrow will give me permission to write about my job."

"Since Arrow and *S* both belong to Merlion, that made it easy for me to contact Arrow's leadership over the weekend to do a soft pitch, and they're completely on board. They think this column will help the agency foster the right reputation for targeting a more high-end market. In fact, they also mentioned expanding your project scope beyond just the food and beverages sector so you can have a wider spread of projects to write about. And I can't imagine your clients will have a problem with that. People know being featured in *S* is the best publicity they could possibly have, and they won't even have to pay for this."

"That's amazing! I really enjoy doing PR, so this is a great way to combine that with my love for magazine writing."

"Precisely. You know, instead of being Carrie Bradshaw, I see you more as your namesake in *Sex and the City*. Didn't Samantha in the show run her own PR agency? Who knows—that could be you someday."

Samantha almost laughed. After all the hoops she had jumped through with the Fraud Squad and the pretenses she had pulled, in the end, what redeemed her was actually the very aspect of her identity she had been trying to hide—her working-class background that made her as far from a blue-blooded society lady as one could be. Maybe she never needed the Fraud Squad's scheme in the first place. Maybe she would have found another way into *S* eventually, one that didn't involve trying to be someone she was not.

Daisy: You can do this! Stay strong, girl.

Raina: Let us know how it goes. We're here for you no matter what.

A smile slid across Samantha's face as she read her friends' messages. She clutched her phone tighter, hoping their conviction would seep into her by osmosis. Then, taking a deep breath, she tucked her phone back in her bag and stepped into the kopitiam. At 3:20 p.m. on a Tuesday, it was blissfully empty.

Not quite empty. Samantha's steps faltered. She had deliberately arrived ten minutes early to give herself time to settle in before he did, but somehow Timothy had chosen today to be on time—no, *early*—for once.

He was at the table farthest from the entrance, back turned toward her—a small mercy, since it meant he wouldn't catch her staring. The tilt of his shoulders, the set of his back, the tendril of hair that curled just so at the bottom of his nape—everything was so familiar that her heart ached.

"Sam!" Madam Pang called out from behind the counter. Her white hair framed her tanned wrinkled face like a halo. "You naughty girl, why are you here on a weekday afternoon? Skiving off work?"

Timothy's shoulders jerked and his head shot up. As he turned around, Samantha saw what she hadn't seen from the back—the gaunt look to his cheeks, dark circles beneath his eyes, and a five-o'clock shadow that she hadn't seen since the day they got together. He had promised to stay clean-shaven after she got stubble burn because they were kissing too much.

Good lord, Ma was right—she *was* too sentimental.

Samantha forced herself to look at Madam Pang instead. "My project is moving ahead of schedule, so my boss let me work from home today. I'm just popping in to meet a . . . friend."

"Your regular order then?"

"Just a kopi c. I don't think I'm staying for long."

After Madam Pang shot her a thumbs-up to confirm the order, Samantha made her way to Timothy's table, her footsteps so heavy they felt like lead. He quickly got to his feet as she approached.

For a moment, they simply stared at each other. Then, Timothy offered a small smile. "Hey, you," he said softly and opened his arms.

Samantha hesitated for a moment before giving in to his embrace. As Timothy's arms closed around her, her head naturally nestled into the crook of his neck. She couldn't help but lean in, a strong, intoxicating whiff of his cologne rushing up her nose.

Damn muscle memory. Samantha quickly pulled back and busied herself with settling into the rickety plastic chair so she wouldn't have to look at him.

There was a plate of kaya toast on the table—golden-brown custard and yellow butter melting over the white bread. "Great choice. This is my favorite thing to get here," Samantha commented, then wanted to cringe. It was a new low to be making small talk about food.

"That's why I got it, since you said this is what you would always get during your brunches with Raina. I figured we could split it?" Timothy offered, his voice rising hopefully toward the end.

Samantha was glad her voice sounded strong as she said, "I've already ordered coffee. I didn't think our meeting would last that long."

There was a moment of silence before Timothy shrugged and pulled the plate toward him. "That's fine. No big deal. I'll just eat it myself." He rooted around the utensil canister for a while before finally finding a set of fork and knife that wasn't too chipped.

"I know this isn't a place you would usually go to," Samantha said, slightly embarrassed and hating herself for feeling that way. "The cutlery's pretty old, and it's really hot because there's no AC . . ."

"No, no," Timothy immediately said. "I'm really excited to check out this place since it's one of your favorites." As though to prove it, he took a big bite out of his kaya toast. Some of the melting butter slid out and dribbled down his lips, making them look glossier. Fuller.

Samantha tore her eyes away. She could still remember what those lips felt like against hers. Thankfully, Madam Pang arrived then, setting a steaming cup of black coffee and a little saucer of evaporated milk on the table. "Your kopi c. Enjoy!"

Once Madam Pang was out of earshot, Timothy said in slight surprise, "I didn't think this place offered table service. I had to pick up the kaya toast from the counter myself."

Samantha sipped her coffee. "They don't, but I'm a regular and Madam Pang basically watched me grow up."

Timothy's mouth curved into a smile. "So, you're a VIP here then?"

VIP. The term flooded Samantha with memories—none of them positive—but she settled for a shrug. "Madam Pang is just really nice, especially to her regulars. In the weeks after my dad passed away, she would bring my mom and me the leftover pastries every day. Small, neighborhood places like this have a strong *kampong* spirit, you know?"

Timothy nodded. "I get it." He peered into her cup. "So, what's a kopi c?" he asked, his tongue twisted awkwardly around the Malay term.

Samantha stared at him. "Seriously? You've never had one before?"

"No. I usually get my coffee from Starbucks. I don't really know what all the different kopitiam coffee names stand for— kopi, kopi o, kopi gao . . ." Timothy let out an embarrassed chuckle. "I know, I'm a pretty sheltered Singaporean."

"Oh boy, you're missing out. You need to get out of your imported–coffee bean bubble once in a while and enjoy the wonder that is no-frills coffee at cheap neighborhood shops." Samantha ripped open a pack of sugar and stirred it into her drink. "A kopi c is black coffee with evaporated milk and sugar. A kopi is black coffee with condensed milk, kopi o is—"

Samantha stopped and shot Timothy a stern look. "We aren't meeting for a kopi lesson."

"We're not," Timothy agreed. He braced his hands on the table as though steeling himself for what would come next. "Honestly, I'm surprised you even agreed to meet me. I thought I was dreaming when you finally responded after ignoring my calls and messages for days."

Samantha kept her eyes on his face as she said, "I wanted to ask you something."

"Yeah?"

"Did your parents have something to do with the email Missy sent out to the gala guests?"

Timothy was silent for a moment, then said, "Yes, but you weren't supposed to know."

"Well, I'm grateful to your parents for intervening and doing damage control. The email basically saved my career." Samantha paused. "What about your career though? I'm guessing your parents also know all about your column now."

"Yeah, I had to tell them when I asked for their help—" He stopped abruptly, his eyes flicking down.

"Ask for their help?" Samantha echoed, furrowing her brows. "I thought it was Missy who told them what happened."

After a few moments of Timothy staring resolutely at a soy sauce stain on the table, Samantha leaned forward. "Timothy," she said in a voice that brooked no opposition. "What do you mean?"

Finally, he raised his eyes to her face. "After you left the gala, I immediately went to find Missy. I told her I would do anything if she could intervene and tell everyone that you were just someone working in PR who wanted to get a lay of the land, instead of, you know—"

"A fraud who got played by you," Samantha said flatly.

Timothy grimaced but to his credit, he didn't try to deny it. "As a rule, Missy never asks me who I'm writing about since she probably knows them and it would put her in a tricky spot. So she had no idea that Melody was you. And when I admitted you didn't know about the column, she totally went off on me. Gave me a huge lecture on journalism ethics, which I absolutely deserved. And at the end of it, she said she doesn't have the authority to send out the memo I had in mind to hundreds of Asia's most important people, and that I had to fix my own mess."

Samantha didn't dare blink as she looked at Timothy, hanging on to his every word while a horrible suspicion crept into her mind.

"I knew the only people who had more authority than her are my parents, so I went to them." He grimaced slightly. "I don't think I've ever seen them so mad before, especially my father. He shouted that he would have no face left if anyone found out a

Kingston was wasting his time on something so stupid and demanded to know why the hell I was trying to sabotage him by criticizing people he and my mother knew." Timothy raked a hand roughly through his hair. "But I told him I would return to KMG, throw myself wholeheartedly into the job, and never even think of leaving again if he agreed to step in. He finally relented, and I had his lawyers draw up the email for Missy to send out."

Samantha jerked forward in her seat. "But you hate working there!" she burst out, her heart twisting into knots. Timothy had done the thing he hated most for her.

As though he could hear her thoughts, Timothy shook his head. "That's why I didn't want you to know. I didn't want to make it a big deal or have you feel bad for me when this was the least I could do after what an asshole I was. Besides, you grew to love your PR job at Arrow even though it wasn't your first choice. Who knows—maybe that will be me with KMG someday."

There was a note of finality in Timothy's voice that told Samantha he would not be talked out of his decision, so she acquiesced. She watched as he tucked back into his kaya toast, finishing what was left in a few quick bites, before turning to the counter. "Madam Pang, your kaya is the best thing I've eaten in a long time!"

Samantha's jaw dropped as sixty-something-year-old Madam Pang giggled like a schoolgirl. "Thank you," the older woman trilled. "Come by more often!"

"If Sam will have me!" Timothy called back, but his eyes were fixed on Samantha's face.

Samantha swatted his hand. "Stop charming *my* kopitiam lady. You already have your overpriced Starbucks."

Grinning, Timothy shrugged. "Well, I want to know this part of your life better. One kopi and one kopitiam owner at a time."

Samantha looked down at her coffee cup to hide her pinking

cheeks. Wordlessly, she drizzled evaporated milk into her kopi and mixed it around. If she focused on making perfect whirlpools in her cup, she wouldn't have to meet Timothy's eyes. Did he mean that, or was it just part of the Timothy Kingston charm that he used indiscriminately on kopitiam ladies and unsuspecting ex-girlfriends alike?

For a few minutes, their table was silent except for the clink of Samantha's stirring spoon in her cup. Then Timothy suddenly said, "You know, I did ask my father if I could be put on Merlion Media's portfolio."

Samantha's hand stilled and she raised her head. "What did he say?"

"He said hell would freeze over before he did that, which honestly I'm not surprised by. He probably wants to keep me as far from S as possible given all the mess I created."

"Good," Samantha blurted, then caught herself. "I didn't mean 'good' as in 'I'm happy your dad said no'," she stammered, her face warming. "It's just . . . you know, I'm under Merlion, and if you're overseeing the portfolio, there might be a conflict of interest here if we . . ." Her voice trailed off as a smile flickered across Timothy's face.

"Stop," she said sternly.

His eyes widened innocently. "I didn't say anything."

"Whatever," Samantha said, trying to hide a smile. Even though Timothy had helped save her job, she still wasn't about to let him off the hook that easily—after all, he was the reason they had gotten into this mess to begin with. "So, if you aren't handling Merlion Media, what would you be doing at KMG?"

For the first time all conversation, a hint of mischief flickered across Timothy's face that made him seem much more like his usual self. "Turns out I won't just be working under my father, but also my mother as well."

"*You're* going to be taking care of KMG's philanthropy?"

Timothy raised a brow. "Thanks for the vote of confidence."

"You know that's not what I meant! I just . . . didn't think that's something you were super interested in."

"Sounds about right, because I am *not* part of the Kingston Foundation."

"You jerk!" Samantha flung her napkin at him. "You made me feel so bad."

Laughing, Timothy plucked the napkin off his torso and dropped it onto the table. "Sorry. You just always have the best reactions."

Samantha rolled her eyes but could feel her mouth twitching. "Seriously, what's your new job?"

"Even though joining the family business wasn't my first choice, I figured I could reclaim some agency and play down my nepotistic beginnings by launching my own project—kind of like what you did at Arrow with *Deluxe Eats*. So, I came up with an idea that combines my personal interests with KMG's strategic goals, discussed it with my mother, and together, we approached my father to pitch my plan for creating an art fund."

"What's an art fund?" Samantha asked, smiling slightly. Timothy probably didn't even realize that his mouth had quirked up on the word "together."

"An investment fund overseeing the acquisition and sale of artworks. I'll be a research analyst specializing in ancient Mediterranean art, so I get to combine my classics background and arts interest with the data and finance aspects that my father loves so much. My mother's also coming on board in an arts consultant role." His expression softened further. "As usual, she didn't show much emotion, but I think she's pretty thrilled to give up her position at the Kingston Foundation and return to the professional arts world."

There was a genuine gleam in Timothy's eyes as he spoke, the words pouring out of him as his voice ticked up. Something tender bloomed in Samantha's chest. Not only was this a way for him to bridge his family obligations and his own passions, but it could also be a chance for him to finally bond with his parents—or at least his mother.

"Tim, I think that role suits you. I know I said rather, um, nasty things about your column—"

He shrugged. "Rightfully so."

"But I can't deny that you achieved some pretty cool things with As Seen by Argus. In less than a year, it became Singapore's most-read column, and have you seen the thousands of angry comments left on S's social media after they announced it's no longer being printed? You have a keen instinct for what people want to see, a willingness to take risks, and not to mention, excellent writing skills. All important qualities for a hedge fund analyst to have."

"It means a lot to hear that from you," Timothy said quietly, his dark and intent eyes locked on hers. "Speaking of Facebook posts, I saw the one announcing your new column. Congratulations—I can't wait to read it when it's out."

"Thank you. Fiona and I just had a meeting yesterday to finalize my first article. That email you got Missy to send out went a long way toward rescuing my reputation. There were still a couple of people who were wary about me, but I told them that if I could convince people I was a socialite, it probably proved I know a thing or two about public relations and branding. And they totally bought it!"

"Right on!" Timothy held out his hand for a high five that Samantha slapped with relish. "You know, my mother and I are looking for ways to promote our new art fund. If only there was someone who could write about it . . ."

Samantha drained the last of her coffee and chuckled. "That's actually perfect. Arrow's thinking of having me take charge of a great variety of projects, so you can be my first client outside of food and beverages. We can discuss more once I'm done with the Alter Meatgo project."

"Is that soon?"

"The launch party's one week after my column debuts. Genie couldn't be happier with the timing."

There was a beat of silence, then Timothy asked, "Do you remember the promise I made at the *Deluxe Eats* party that I would attend every event you organize?"

Samantha's breath hitched. "Yeah, I remember," she managed to say over the lump that had swelled up in her throat.

"I meant it then and I still mean it now. You told me at the gala you didn't love me, but . . ." Timothy swallowed. "I knew what we had was real, even if it might not be love on your part."

Samantha shook her head. "It's true that I initially only cared about how our Fraud Squad scheme could help me achieve my dream, but—"

"But what?" Timothy prompted, his eyes scouring her face.

"But I ended up falling in love with you along the way," Samantha admitted. "I only said those words to hurt you because I felt so betrayed then. I know most people might think of you only in terms of your family background, but that was never the part of you I loved."

Timothy pushed his plate away and leaned forward. "Do you mean that?" he asked hoarsely, and for a moment, Samantha was cast back to the night of the gala when they had fought in the foyer and he had asked her those same exact words. But maybe, here was a chance to rewrite the script.

She looked back at him steadily. "I fell in love with Tim, not Timothy Kingston."

"Oh." Then, "*Oh.*" He hesitated, a kaleidoscope of emotions flashing across his face. Finally, he asked, "And do you think you could still love me?"

The naked fragility in his voice carved fresh nicks on Samantha's heart. "Tim . . ."

"I know I fucked up. And I hate myself every day for hurting you when all I ever wanted was to give you the best of everything. I swear to you, no more lies or deceit, just complete openness and honesty between us from now on. I love you, I'm not ready to give up what we had, and I'm hoping you'll agree to give us a second chance."

Samantha nudged away her cup and took a deep breath. "Tim, I love you."

The unadulterated joy that broke across Timothy's face nearly undid her resolve, but Samantha steeled herself. "But we can't be together, at least not now," she continued, her heart sinking as his smile froze. "There've been so many lies and so much hurt between us. We only got close in the first place because of our Fraud Squad ploy, and three whole months of scheming and deception can't be a healthy start for any relationship. Right now, I just want to take things slow and rediscover you—rediscover *us*—away from our past."

Timothy's eyes were large and intent as they roamed her face, as though looking for a punch line. But he must have seen something in her expression, something resolute and unyielding, for, in the end, he simply nodded, looking quietly resigned.

"I understand. You know how I feel about you, but I respect your decision."

"Thank you," Samantha said softly.

He attempted a smile. "Here's to being friends then. Maybe you can introduce me to some of your other neighborhood favorites, show me more of the famous *kampong* spirit."

"You're on. You brought me into your world, and now's my

turn to show you mine. Next time, we can go to this other kopi place I like. I bet you've never drunk coffee from plastic bags before."

"I can't say I have." His voice turned tentative. "So, there will be a next time . . . ?"

Samantha looked at Timothy, her eyes running over his hunched shoulders, earnest gaze, and the uncharacteristically shy smile revealing the apprehensive hope beneath. It felt both like she had known him forever and also like she was meeting him for the first time.

And how would she appear to him? Maybe slightly more glamorous, but hopefully also wiser and more settled than the starry-eyed woman he'd met all those months ago at Enzo. Perhaps, someday, they could carve out a place for themselves in each other's lives again—not as the Kingston heir or socialite Samantha Song, but just as Tim and Sam. Sam and Tim.

Samantha felt her lips curve up. "Yes," she told Timothy. "There will be."

ACKNOWLEDGMENTS

亲爱的爷爷奶奶，姥姥姥爷，爸爸妈妈，和弟弟：言语不足以表达我对你们一生给我的爱的感激之情。这本书，如我所做的一切，是为了你们。

Angela Kim: back when Alex was putting together the list of editors to submit my manuscript to, your name was the only one I mentioned when Alex asked for suggestions. There was no one else I would have trusted as much with my story, my characters, and my own dreams. You have proven over and over again to be not just the best editor for *The Fraud Squad*, but also an absolute rock throughout my foray into publishing. Thank you for making my debut experience the best it could be (and for introducing me to DeuxMoi!).

Alex Rice: hands down the most amazing agent in the world. You have been an unwavering pillar of support, and my biggest cheerleader and champion since Day One. I couldn't be happier that you're the one next to me on publishing's wild ride, nor more thankful for your astute instincts, your warmth, and your steadiness. This book might very well still be just a Word doc in my computer if not for you.

The biggest thank-you to everyone else at Berkley Publishing who gave so much of their time, effort, and passion to bring my story out into the world. My managing editor Christine Legon and production editor Alaina Christensen—this book was made possible by your hard work, enthusiasm, and vision. My art director

Vi-An Nguyen and artist Natalie Shaw, who created a cover more beautiful than anything I could have imagined and breathed life into my characters and settings. My copyeditor Angelina Krahn, who thoroughly amazed me with how big her brain is. My interior designer Ashley Tucker, who showed how the right styling can make black-and-white words leap off a page. My subsidiary rights director Tawanna Sullivan, who helps me find the perfect homes around the world for my book. My marketers Catherine Barra, Jessica Mangicaro, and Bridget O'Toole, and my publicists Dache' Rogers and Tina Joell—you all blow me away with your ideas and creativity and how you unfailingly dream big for me. I owe each and every one of you a debt of gratitude for translating my dream into a reality I can share with the world.

And I couldn't be more thankful for the rest of the team at the Creative Artists Agency who have worked so tirelessly to guide me through my publishing journey. Berni Barta, my extraordinary film/TV rep who always aims for the stars and inspires me to do the same, as well as her assistants Sydney Thun and Adi Mehr. Jamie Stockton and his assistant Bianca Petcu, who always went to bat for me on my contracts. Ali Ehrlich, Kate Childs, and Kate's assistant Khalil Roberts—the absolute best at what they do and whom I am so lucky to have in my corner.

To my dear friends, who have been so generous with your love, support, feedback, and advice; who believed in me even at times when I didn't believe in myself: Alex Felix, Alexandra Deianria, Angela Montoya, Annika Cosgrove, Benjamin Lubet, Birukti Tsige, Catherine Clarke, Chloe Bridgewater, Christina Greer, Christina Ooi, Courtney Kae, Elise Carlson, Erin Connor, Esme Symes-Smith, Eunice Kim, Famke Halma, Gabi Burton, Gabriella Buba, Hanna Kim, Hayley Walsh, Jamie Lee, Jennifer Elrod, Jessica Lepe, Jess Parra, Kalie Holford, Kayla Jasmin, Kiana Krystle, Laura Holtzclaw, Leanne Schwartz, Lilly Lu, Maddy Beresford,

ACKNOWLEDGMENTS

Matthew Lin, Melanie Schubert, Morgan Routh, Nadia Persaud, Natalie Budeša, Olivia Liu, Rhea Basu, Rosalie Lin, Rose Ferrao, Ryan Ramkelawan, Sabrina Lunavong, Samantha Van Dine, Sandeep Brar, Sandra Popescu, Sanyukta Thakare, Sara Hasham, Sara Kapadia, Sarah Underwood, Skyla Arndt, Stefany Ramirez, Sydney Langford, Taylor Grothe, Tyler Lawson, Vishaka Sriram, Wen-yi Lee, who read the awkward first draft and still cheered me on the whole way, and Yuchi Zhang. The best thing by far about writing is how it brought you all into my life. I'm very fortunate I get to do what I love alongside people who mean so much to me.

To all the book bloggers and book influencers on Twitter, Instagram, and TikTok who have cheered for my book: thank you from the bottom of my heart. Your support and enthusiasm mean the world to me, and I couldn't be more honored to work with you.

My fellow Berkletes—my debut journey wouldn't have been nearly as fun or as comforting without you. Seeing you all get so excited for me makes me that much more excited too. I'm still sometimes in disbelief that I now exchange memes with authors whom I've looked up to for so long. All of you are incredibly brilliant and kind, and I'm honored to call you my friends.

To Taj McCoy, Pitch Wars founder Brenda Drake, and the tireless group of volunteers who helped provide this platform and community for aspiring authors: thank you for giving me the push I needed to bring my book to the next level, and for introducing me to some of my closest friends.

To the teams at *Vogue Singapore*, *Harper's Bazaar Singapore*, and *Tatler Singapore*: thank you for taking me under your wing and trusting me to write for my favorite magazines. I value those opportunities and my time with you all dearly.

C, you were the first person to know about this book. Thank you for believing in me when I didn't even have ten thousand words. That helped me believe I could see it through to the end.

THE FRAUD SQUAD

Kyla Zhao

DISCUSSION QUESTIONS

1. How do you think each member of the Fraud Squad trio embodies the concept of "fraud" in their own way?

2. A central theme of the book is the double standards placed on men and women when it comes to career and relationships. How do you think this gender gap is similar or different at the various socioeconomic levels explored in the story? And how might those double standards play out similarly or differently in your culture?

3. Almost every character in the book exhibits some form of morally gray behavior. Do you think those behaviors by Samantha, Anya, Timothy, Lucia, and Samantha's mother, An Jie, are a result of their innate personalities or a response to their environments?

4. What do you make of Samantha's decision to not get back together with Timothy at the end of the book?

5. Taking that one step further, how do you think Samantha and Timothy's relationship might develop after the book's ending?

6. Do you think it is possible for two people from vastly different socioeconomic backgrounds to be equals in a relationship—be it a romantic relationship or friendship?

7. *The Fraud Squad* is set in Singapore (Southeast Asia). How do you think Samantha's pursuit of upward mobility might have unfolded similarly or differently if the story took place in your country? Would it have been easier or more difficult for her to infiltrate high society?

8. Do you think Tim's frustration with his parents' expectations of him are justified, or does he have a certain obligation to go along with the less appealing aspects of his status since he gets to reap the privileges?

9. Did you agree with Raina's take that Samantha has changed for the worse? If so, at what point do you think Samantha's shift in perspective and priorities crystallized?

10. Samantha, Anya, Timothy, and even Lucia all have complicated relationships with their parents. Did any parent-child relationship stand out to you, or did you relate to one more strongly?

11. There is a sparsity of Asian representation in Western media. For Asian readers, were there certain themes, characters, and/or scenes that you particularly related to? For non-Asian readers, what did you learn about Southeast Asian society and culture?

12. If you were Samantha, which society event in the story would you be most excited to experience? A few options are: the dinner with Tim's friends, the Christian Dada launch event, the Kingstons' dinner party, the *Elle* photo shoot, Daisy's engagement party, Anya's birthday party, the S Gala.

Author photo: Kyla Zhao

Kyla Zhao had her first women's magazine byline at the age of sixteen, writing about weddings for *Harper's Bazaar Singapore* before she even had her first kiss. Since then, she has also written for the Singapore editions of *Vogue* and *Tatler*. A native Singaporean, Kyla now works in Silicon Valley after graduating from Stanford University in 2021. She's still trying to understand why Californians adore hiking and Patagonia fleeces so much.

CONNECT ONLINE

KylaZhao.com

KylazingAround

Ready to find
your next great read?

Let us help.

Visit prh.com/nextread

Penguin
Random
House